Witch of Ware Woods

SONJA F. BLANCO

FIVE &
THREE
PRESS

For Lena ~
Thanks for the mints and so much more

*The mightiest oak in the forest is just a
little nut that held its ground.*

~ Unknown

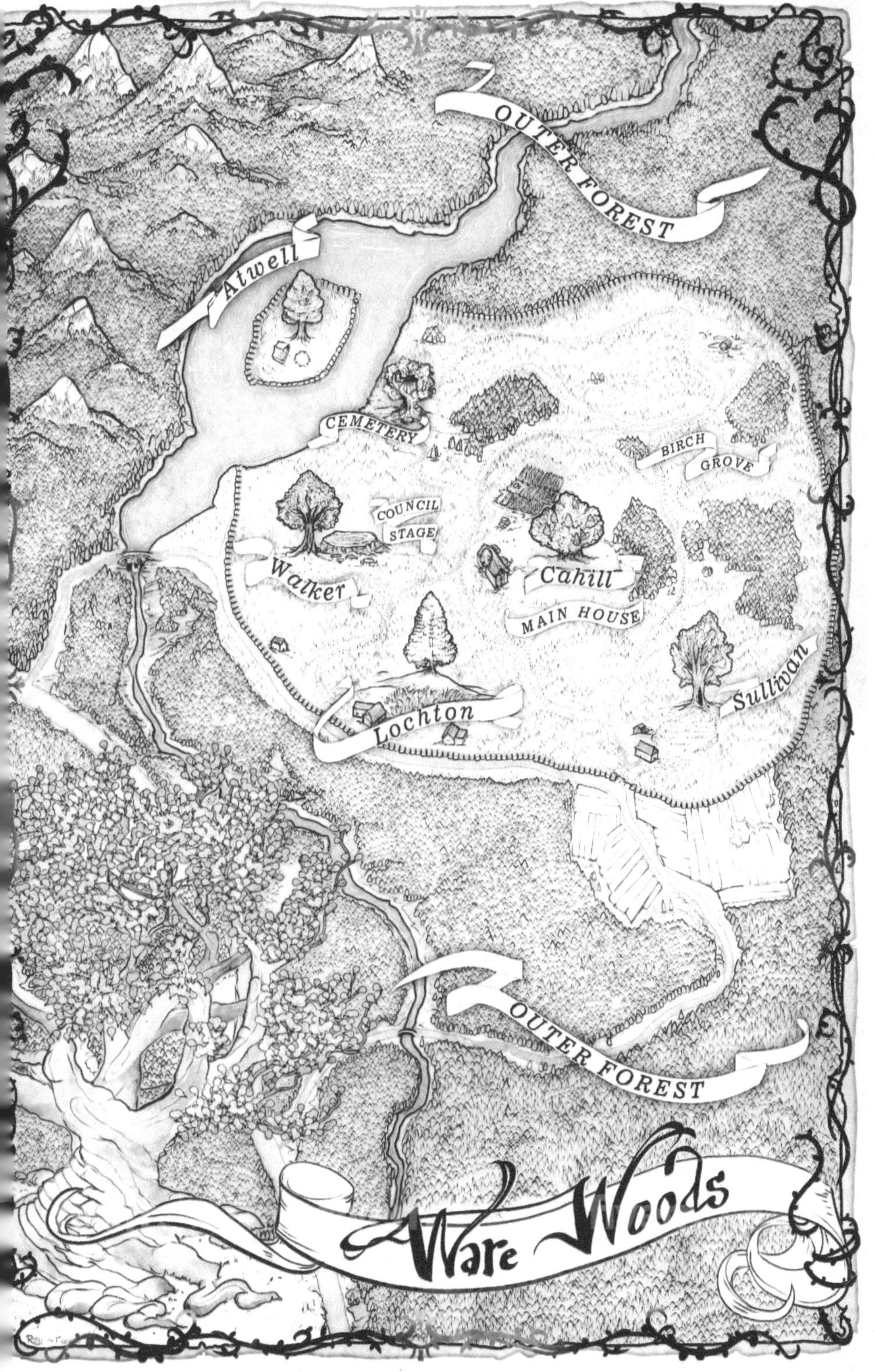

OUTER FOREST
Atwell
CEMETERY
BIRCH GROVE
COUNCIL STAGE
Walker
Cahill
MAIN HOUSE
Lochton
Sullivan
OUTER FOREST
Ware Woods

CHAPTER 1

UNDER THE SHELTER of a sprawling oak tree, Sara paused to consider the least dangerous choice before her: continue trudging the long route home and suffer the ominous thunderstorm pressing upon her, or take a shortcut through the crowded plaza. Both options had their own consequences, and both were potentially deadly.

She scowled at the dark sky only to be met by a rumble of thunder that rattled her chest and every leaf on the tree. Any semblance of a warm summer afternoon had vanished under roiling black clouds. With a soft curse, she tucked her chin and headed into the cobblestone plaza.

Cold raindrops bled from the clouds, forming an obstacle course of inky puddles. Keeping her head down, she hunched into her thin, hooded sweatshirt and clutched the cell phone in her front pocket. If she hadn't lost her driving privileges, she would have been warm and dry at home by now. And safe.

A burst of laughter cut into her brooding. She shivered and glanced up from the slick cobblestones to spy a cluster of college students headed in her direction.

Her gaze swept the collective group, and she inadvertently made eye contact with not one but many familiar faces.

Crap.

She swiveled her head, scanning the plaza and assessing escape options.

The group laughed again, this time with a wicked edge revealing their delight in spotting her alone. She gritted her teeth and forged ahead, refusing to give them the satisfaction of making her turn around, tail between her legs.

Sara quickened her pace, tilting her head to use her hoodie as a pathetic shield against their leering stares. This pack of local kids had tormented her throughout elementary and high school until she opted for homeschooling halfway into her sophomore year. Despite being considered the good kids from locally prominent families, they were as cruel and devious as they were vapid and immature. Sara avoided them, not because she feared them but because of what she feared she could do to them.

"Hello, murderer," the queen of the group, Isabell, sneered through the rain. "How bold of you to come out of hiding."

The group snickered as it deftly circled and herded Sara toward a service alley tucked between the plaza shops. Someone darted behind her and yanked her into the shadows. She stumbled, barely stopping herself from sprawling into a puddle that shimmered with oil. Even the drizzling rain couldn't conceal the alley's sour odor of rancid grease and vomit. With a growl, she whirled around, taking stock. There were six of them. A few carried backpacks and stainless-steel water bottles. Not the best of odds.

She straightened her shoulders and faced Isabell—the girl who had once been her friend. "Do you need something?" Sara spat. "Because if you wanted to piss me off, mission accomplished. Happy now?" While her voice was harsh, her knees felt ready to buckle.

"Happy? You ruined my family. How can you live with yourself? Pretending to be innocent when you know you aren't." Rain dripped down Isabell's red face as her hands clenched into fists.

Sara pulled back her hood and glanced again at the surrounding pack. Nothing she could say would get her out of this mess.

Isabell was right—she wasn't innocent. *I did you a favor, you bitch.* She grimaced at the red-faced girl.

"How many more people do you plan to kill?" Isabell took a step toward her.

"I don't *plan* to kill anyone."

"She doesn't plan—she just does it," sniggered a male voice to her right. From the corner of her eye, Sara glimpsed his arm swinging up in a wide arc, metal water bottle clutched in his hand.

Son of a—

The bottle slammed into the back of her head with a sickening crack. Blinded by pain, Sara doubled over and raised a hand, checking if her skull was still intact. Instead of a bloody dent, she palmed a softball-sized knot. She groaned, blinking back stars until she could see the puddle before her.

Laughter rang out.

White-hot anger sluiced through her veins, replacing her pain. "Get away from me," she rasped. It was a warning, but the tremor in her voice made it sound like a plea.

Isabell ignored her and leaned in. "I know you killed my uncle, and someday I'll prove it. Your piece-of-shit hippie parents can't protect you forever."

Sara fisted her hands, nails digging into her palms, and lifted her chin. The lights in the alley flickered as rage wracked her entire body. She narrowed her eyes at Isabell. "*What* did you call my parents?"

Isabell gasped a strangled cry, her face turning from red to bruised purple, terror shining in her wide eyes.

Sara's hands tingled with pent-up energy. Isabell gurgled, hands pulling at her shirt collar, while Sara held her stare. She was so focused on choking the life out of Isabell that she barely registered the sound of a door opening in the alley behind her.

"Holy shit," breathed the boy with the water bottle. He sprinted past Sara, grabbed Isabell's arm, and dragged her into the plaza. The door slammed, scattering the rest of the pack after them. Their retreating footsteps were drowned out as thunder rumbled through the alley.

Sara turned to face what waited behind her and felt the blood drain from her face, her anger melting into fear.

A hulking man with a neck as wide as his bald head stared at her. He glanced at the storm clouds and then started for her, a jagged black pendant bouncing against his white shirt with each powerful stride. The intensity of his gaze cut through the rain, chilling her bones.

Fear rooted her for a heart-pounding moment until the phone in her pocket vibrated, jolting her instinct to flee. She lunged for the plaza, grateful for the throng of college kids rushing through the rain on their way to the bars for an end-of-term celebration. Without hesitating, she slipped into the crowd and ran a full block before the pain in her head forced her to stop beside an elm, its thick canopy protecting her from the rain. Gulping down air, Sara glanced around for any sign of the pack and chuckled, giddy with adrenaline, at owing her escape to a burly bar bouncer.

She leaned against the tree and pulled out her phone. Only one person ever texted her.

Mom: *Are you on your way home?*

Sara sighed and merely replied: *Y.*

Her head throbbed. With a wince, she shoved off from the tree trunk and pulled her hood back up. The rain pounded harder as she rounded a corner and cut through a small park, passing a rose garden and a shiny memorial plaque to some long-dead college founder. After popping out of the park at a busy intersection, she waited for a car to pass and then crossed over to Green Brier Lane. She relaxed her shoulders and headed up the street, stepping over a familiar tree root that cleaved the sidewalk.

A few years ago, she and her parents had moved to a rental house on this lane, partly because it had an extra room for her mother's small floral business but mostly because her mother loved the trees that lined the street—giant, wondrous trees with trunk girths the size of doors. Their branches, like muscular arms, reached over the lane and entwined with one another to form a canopy tunnel. The tree in front of their house was so big its roots buckled the sidewalk, and its branches grazed the roof of their white-and-gray wooden porch. At nearly nineteen, Sara still enjoyed climbing the tree and settling into its open crux to draw in her sketchbook and peer down at unsuspecting neighbors.

The street had an intimate feel, which typically stopped outsiders from cutting through to avoid rush-hour or college-event traffic. Local neighbors drove slowly and waved at one another. A few still waved at Sara even though she never met their eye. She wasn't exactly a people person. At least that was what her mother said whenever Sara's behavior came across as rude.

People made Sara anxious. They often stared at her, the unwanted attention twisting her stomach and burning her face every time. Although her parents claimed she had a *natural beauty* and to expect stares, she knew it was her dark eyes that startled people—eyes so dark they appeared as piercing, black voids. At first glance, most people merely seemed curious. But after prolonged scrutiny, they became frightened, as if they saw true darkness—or perhaps, she feared, her own soul. It was unnerving, and from a young age, she found freedom in sunglasses, often wearing them no matter the weather or time of day. Some people took pity on her, assuming she had a vision impairment; others called her a vampire. Or, in the pack's case, a murderer. She only wanted to be invisible.

In a rush to complete her flower delivery before the college secretary left for the day, she had forgotten her sunglasses. Given the run-in with the pack, perhaps it had been a blessing. They had already taken countless pairs from her.

She scowled at the thought of them and tried to devise revenge tactics. But she couldn't focus when her head felt like it was being punched with every throbbing heartbeat and her bones ached from the cold rain.

Water squelched through her thin canvas shoes. Sara stopped trying to avoid puddles and looked up from the cracked sidewalk. A few houses down, her father's red SUV was parked in their driveway. She stopped in her tracks and checked the time on her phone—6:02 p.m.

Her father, Charles Harbour, was a renowned and respected metaphysics professor at the nearby University of Michigan. He was a favorite among students for his engaging lectures, youthful appearance, and charismatic smile. While he enjoyed teaching, it was his private research on groundbreaking theories that he was most passionate about, and which usually kept him at his office until midnight.

Sara frowned as to why he should be home so early when two things suddenly grabbed her attention: the first was the Anderson's golden retriever, Murphy, loose again and racing toward her across the lane, tongue lolling, wet tail wagging; the second was the angry whine of a car speeding toward him.

Terror sank needle-sharp claws into Sara. She loved that dog like he was her own.

Her chest tightened. Fear stole her voice and cemented her legs to the sidewalk. As she watched in horror, a wave of adrenaline surged through her, causing her skin to tingle and her hands to warm. She instinctively held out her palms, as though the futile gesture could stop Murphy and the car from colliding.

Frustration pushed her to her knees, but she refused to lower her hands, the rain sizzling against her now burning palms. She shut her eyes and silently screamed into the rain, thinking only of saving the dog.

But instead of screeching tires and a sickening thud, there was a beat of silence, and then the tinkling of metal tags. Murphy slammed into her, sending her backward—straight into a puddle.

Her eyes flew open, and she gave the dog a tight squeeze, gladly enduring his sloppy kisses. After patting his sides and finding no injuries, she hugged his neck and pulled herself up with a snorted laugh.

"Guess we're both lucky to live another day."

The dog nudged her, dancing about and licking her hands. She gently tugged his ears and then turned her attention to the car speeding down the lane. Her smile dropped.

Heat coursed through her and pulsed in her fingertips. She fixed a death stare at the car as anger flared inside her. The anger merged with the festering hatred she felt for Isabell and the pack and inflamed the monstrous rage she so desperately sought to push down every day. The monster inside her reared its head, threatening to split her skin, and bellowed to be released.

Sara faltered and lost control. The sensation of fire shot through her fingers as a bolt of white-hot power surged from her and slammed into the beige sedan. It lurched and swerved over the slippery pavement. The driver veered away from a tree, over-corrected, and smashed into a light post at the intersection. A dull crunch sounded through the rain as the car crumpled like an empty soda can.

Shit.

Just as fast as it had consumed her, the anger dissipated, leaving a hollow dread in its wake. Sara's heart thundered in time with the pounding rain, her gaze fixed upon the silent car. When the driver finally opened his door and stumbled onto the curb, she sighed in relief and promptly turned away to walk home, Murphy at her side.

CHAPTER 2

S SHE APPROACHED the small Greek revival house, Sara glanced up and saw her mother sitting on the porch swing—watching her every move.

Her mother, Eliza Harbour, had dark wavy hair, high cheekbones, and a sunny disposition that worked magic on whoever she met. She also had an affinity for plants and could turn cut flowers into vibrant works of art. Sara never believed anyone who said she resembled her mother. She knew her nature, just like her eyes, was far too dark to even remotely resemble her mother.

Sara stopped short and leaned into the dog, clutching his wet fur. She softened her expression, trying to hide her guilt, before meeting her mother's hazel eyes. Eliza's typical brightness was as clouded as the stormy sky above. By the disappointment reflected on her face, Sara knew she saw right through her mask of innocence. It was a look her mother rarely gave her, but it was always duly warranted. They stared at each other for a long moment, the rain pattering off the tree leaves and streaming down Sara's face.

Her mother rose from the swing. "Take Murphy home and get cleaned up for dinner. I'll leave a towel for you by the door." She looked down the street, where neighbors gathered around the smashed car. The driver sat on the curb, his head in his hands, while someone holding a phone seemed to ask him questions. Her mother turned away, wiping her hands on her florist apron, and went into the house, the screen door banging behind her.

Sara exhaled, spitting rain, and let her shoulders sag with a sudden tiredness that weighed on her. With a firm grip on Murphy's collar, she walked the dog across the driveway and to the adjacent home. She took the liberty, as she usually did, to open the Anderson's side gate and return Murphy to the backyard.

Slogging back toward her house, she dragged her feet and welcomed the rain, deeming it a penance for losing control. At the end of the street, a siren wailed, and white and red lights shimmered through the rain. She paused and squinted, tracking an emergency vehicle as it pulled up to the intersection. After noting the responder's casual demeanor as he exited the vehicle and approached the driver, Sara turned away and climbed the porch steps.

No rush to the hospital—he's fine. And so is Murphy.

As soon as she stepped onto the dry porch, she peeled off her wet sweatshirt and kicked off her shoes. The sweatshirt slapped onto the floor before she could catch it. On a sigh, she bent to pick it up and spotted something dark glistening inside the hood. Instinctively, she recoiled, but then checked herself with a gruff snort. Whatever it was, it lay lifeless. She squatted for a closer look and flicked the hood open, revealing a long lock of hair curled upon itself like a dead snake.

With a sharp inhale, she raised her hands to the nape of her neck, fingertips searching until she felt a harsh blank patch where the lock of hair had been. She gently tugged on the rest of her hair, relieved when no more gave way. Biting her lip, she patted the back of her head and then pressed her icy fingertips to her temples. Her headache and the knot at the back of her skull were both gone. *Maybe the blow to my head hadn't been so bad. Then why did my hair—*

She swallowed hard. The blow hadn't caused her to lose a chunk of hair—it had been her anger.

Shit.

Sara grabbed the pale-green towel her mother left on a nearby chair, quickly wiping her face before draping it over her shoulders. She plucked the hair from her sweatshirt and clenched it so tight, water dripped from it and splashed onto the light-gray floor. After yanking open the screen door, she ran up the narrow staircase to her bathroom, locked the door, and flushed the lock of hair. With her backside pressed against the sink, she angled a hand mirror to inspect her scalp. It wasn't as noticeable as she feared. In fact, with her hair down, no one would know. Unlike last time.

Instead of shedding a single lock, something terrible had once rendered her completely bald, as though her own scalp couldn't bear the secret she'd buried inside herself that day. She had been in second grade, and the shock and disappointment she caused her parents was impossible to forget, as was the relentless taunting at school. It took many cups of bitter tea administered by her mother, but her hair eventually grew back, though thicker and lighter than it had been.

Since then, she'd accepted her parents' overprotective rules—the spoken ones such as "*no more sleepovers*" and "*don't be out after dark*" and the unspoken ones of not getting too close, too friendly, with others.

And then there was the rule she'd made for herself. The rule she struggled with and failed at—to control her rage and not hurt anyone else.

To appear as a normal—albeit boring—teenage girl, she forced a smile when appropriate, kept to herself, helped her mother's small floral business, and occasionally assisted her father with his metaphysics research.

Sara padded to her bedroom, shucked off her wet clothes, and put on pajama pants and an old T-shirt from some physics convention her father once attended. Hearing the clatter of dishware, she hurried to the bathroom and hung up her wet clothes. After one last glance in the mirror, she fluffed her damp hair and, convinced they wouldn't notice, headed down the narrow stairs past family photos and to her fate.

As she approached the dining table, her parents stopped mid-sentence and turned their gaze to her. They each held a glass of ice water and wore an anxious expression. Sara felt more tired than hungry, but sat and served herself a bright, colorful salad that clashed with the tight atmosphere of the room. The ominous storm beat against the house, rain streaking down the windows.

She cleared her throat and met her father's eyes. "So . . . Dad, why are you home early?"

Her father regarded her for a moment before setting down his drink. "Thought I'd work from home tonight." He gestured toward the window when Sara shot him a puzzled look. "In case the storm gets worse. Plus, now I get to be home with my beautiful girls." He smiled, stretching out his hand, palm up, toward her mother.

She smiled and took hold of his hand. "It's always nice to have you home, dear."

Her parents were typically affectionate, and Sara had grown accustomed to their star-filled gazes, lingering touches, and whispered laughs. When she became a teenager, she realized most parents did not behave like hers. And the hungry stare of a boyfriend was not the same as the loving, electric look between her parents. Sara had recently hoped for that same electric look from one of her father's grad students, but the handsome boy broke off their fling, or whatever it was, and avoided her. It always hurt and was always inevitable. She seemed to repel not just boyfriends but friends in general, as if they also knew the unspoken rule to not get close to her.

Or perhaps because they looked into her cauldron-black eyes and saw a monster.

Sara hid her loneliness and staved off desperation by genuinely enjoying the company of her parents and their love, a love so obvious it seemed to energize the surrounding air.

She narrowed her eyes at them. They released their hands, but not before she noted the unusual tightness of their grip.

"Right," she said, still squinting at her parents, waiting for any hint of contrariety to their calm façades, or some sort of recognition as to what just happened on their sleepy little lane.

Her mother delicately buttered a piece of bread and straightened her shoulders. "I'm glad you made it home safely. The roads must be quite *slippery*." She arched her left eyebrow at Sara.

Charlie paused his chewing and studied the two of them. "Is that so?" His rhetorical question did not seem directed at road conditions. He had an uncanny knack for reading people. Once, when she was little, Sara called it his superpower. He had dismissed her notion and given her a dull lecture about emotional intelligence.

Beyond the sliding door, the storm pummeled the garden. Sara shifted in her seat and struggled to swallow a particularly tough piece of kale.

"Everything okay, Sara? You look . . . distracted." Her mother's tone was flat. When Sara turned to her, an unreadable expression covered her face.

Sara's mind reeled, but she relaxed her forehead and feigned a sense of calm. "Oh, I . . . I need to check the floral website for updates," she said. Her mother's website automatically updated at midnight, but since Sara handled the tech side of things, it seemed a plausible evasion. Clearly, her mother hadn't told her father about the car incident, which Sara preferred to forget rather than discuss.

Her mother raised an eyebrow again, waiting for more.

"And I'm tired. Must be the weather." Sara ended the discussion by stuffing her mouth with a forkful of salad. Truly tired and wanting to avoid her mother's unusual scrutiny, she rose from the table, put her bowl by the kitchen sink, and grabbed a piece of bread. "I'm turning in early. Thanks for dinner, Mom," she said over her shoulder as she headed upstairs, hoping she sounded casual.

"Goodnight, firecracker," her father called after her, a hint of amusement in his voice.

At the top of the stairs, she closed her bedroom door, letting the click echo through the house before sitting on the landing to eavesdrop. Nibbling on the bread, she stretched her neck and strained to hear their voices over the continual patter of rain.

"Charles, we can't ignore this anymore. I'm worried about—" For a moment, rain and wind obstructed Sara's hearing. "—and the safety of others."

Her father's deep voice carried up the stairway without issue. "I know, I am too. We just need to keep a close watch on her, don't let her get too emotional."

Sara straightened her back, popping the rest of the bread into her mouth. *Too emotional!*

"But that's it," her mother said. "We do keep a close eye on her, and things still happen. I've taught her some self-calming techniques, but it's a struggle for her. We can't regulate her emotions any more than she can."

Her father didn't respond. Sara held her breath and started to rise, afraid he was walking toward the stairs. When her mother spoke again, she sighed and settled back onto the landing.

"We've done everything we can. We pulled her from school when teachers grew concerned about her behaviors. We discouraged friendships. You know she hasn't had a friend since the sleepover incident." She paused. "Mother Mary, I didn't think her hair would ever grow back."

Pulling her knees up to her chest, Sara clucked softly at the mention of the sleepover from long ago. *Yeah, well, it's probably best I don't have any friends. They'll just want to crack my head open someday.*

Her mother continued, "She can't even go to college like normal kids. Getting an online degree and working for me is okay for now, but she's a smart, talented girl, and she can't do this forever." After a pause came a barely audible, "We can't do this forever."

Wind lashed the house, and Sara slid down a step to hear her mother continue. "I'm telling you, she's getting stronger. Remember Gary's chainsaw catching on fire?"

Sara stiffened. It was no surprise her parents knew she kept a secret, but they never discussed the dangerous powers lurking inside her. That was another unspoken rule. As if talking about it would give it more power. To name it out loud would define her—forever. Murderous monster.

It was Gary's own fault for trying to cut down a healthy tree at seven in the morning.

"She manipulated a car tonight. A *car*, Charles. And she didn't seem to care about the driver."

I didn't touch the car! The driver was speeding and lost control. Besides, he walked away. No harm done. And Murphy is fine, thank you. Sara frowned and rubbed the back of her neck, fingertips scraping over the circular sandpaper patch.

Her father spoke, but his words were drowned out by the stacking of dishes. The soft pounding of rain filled the stairway, and Sara thought the conversation was over until her mother said, "It's time to go back."

Sara's head jerked. *Back? Like, to our previous rental across town, the one with all the birds and little fountain in the backyard? The one with the nosy neighbors I told to go to hell?*

Shifting her cramped legs, Sara strained to hear her father's response. She expected him to question her mother's crazy idea and was surprised when he said, "You're right. I came home early because Ted called again. The blight is getting worse, and they all could use your help. He also said the Walkers and Sullivans want to put a break in the wall."

Her mother's gasp eclipsed the storm.

Thunder rattled through the house. By the time the noise

cleared, her father was speaking again. "—dreamed we returned. The same dream I had."

Sara tilted her head. Her parents regarded dreams as subconscious messages. Some were simple reflections of hopes and fears, but others were powerful premonitions to be heeded wisely. The tone of her father's voice implied this particular dream was the latter.

"And, of course"—her mother's tender words cut through a lull in the storm—"there's Ian."

She didn't need to see her parents to know they were embracing. Their words grew muffled, then stopped altogether.

Feeling dizzy and slightly sick, Sara gripped the stair lip and pressed her cheek against the cool beadboard wall. She had no idea who all these people were. They didn't have any close friends or family, and none of those names sounded like her father's coworkers. She was an only child, her mother was estranged from her parents, and her father's parents had died in a car accident long before she was born. Harbour family vacations consisted of camping in the woods, a tent for three—not visiting relatives or family friends. She bit her lip to keep from shouting down the stairs, demanding to know who the hell Ian and Ted were.

Her father's heavy footsteps paced in the kitchen. "There are no coincidences," he said, using his lecturing voice. "These are all signs to go back. But"—his tone changed—"I can't shake this uneasy feeling."

Her mom mumbled and then, more clearly, said, "Something does seem off, but a quick visit should be okay." Sara lost the conversation when someone turned on the kitchen faucet. After a few heartbeats, the rush of water and clink of dishware stopped. She strained to hear her mother's voice. "Maybe she was wrong. Maybe time has changed the prophecy."

Prophecy? No, she must have said "property." A property with walls—cared for by Ian and Ted?

"You're right. We'll go," said her dad. "They need help with the blight, and we owe it to Sara and Ian. If it doesn't work, we can leave again."

"How soon should we go?"

"I'm thinking in two weeks, at the end of the month. If that works for you?"

Her father's voice sounded closer, his last word followed by the zip of blinds being lowered for the night. Sara held her breath. He was in the living room, close to the stairwell. She turned and crawled up the steps and into her room, quietly latching the door before stretching out on her bed and staring up at the ceiling.

CHAPTER 3

SARA SWALLOWED THE nausea coating the back of her throat. A jumble of thoughts and emotions churned inside her, ratcheting her heart rate. With one hand on her chest, she focused on her breathing while staring at the bedroom's sloped ceiling. In and hold for three seconds, out and hold for three seconds—as if on a ventilator. Her mind flashed through memories, searching for anything related to the information she'd just heard. She found nothing but the start of another headache.

Perhaps the people her parents mentioned were distant relatives, estranged for some petty reason regarding walls and blight. Maybe they were part of a reclusive cult, hoarding food and useless junk. Or maybe—she smiled dreamily—they lived in a fortified castle, complete with warriors and a magnificent dragon.

She chewed her lip. Regardless, her parents must have a reason for keeping whatever this was from her. With no plans for the summer, as usual, it would at least be entertaining to consider this a game. Pretend she hadn't heard their conversation and let it unfold naturally. Realizing she had absolutely nothing to lose caused her headache and nausea to flare. Her mother's words echoed in time with her throbbing head: *"She can't do this forever."*

Do what? Keep up the façade of pretending to be a good, normal person? I live in a bubble, afraid to make a mistake and lose control, waiting for the inevitable, horrible moment my secret destroys me.

I'm not strong. I'm pathetically weak. My own emotions give me whiplash. I'm scared to death of what I can do—and at the same time, I want to kill anyone who pisses me off.

I'm not normal. I'm not anything remotely normal.

The sudden thrashing of wind and rain against the window seized Sara's attention, stopping her mind from unraveling. She jolted off the bed and peered out her window overlooking the lane. Through the rain and darkening sky, she could barely glimpse the intersection where the accident had occurred. The only sign of a collision was the bent lamppost, which surprisingly still worked.

Sara turned to her desk and nudged her computer's mouse. The screen lit up, displaying Taoist documents she was researching for her father. After clicking save and shutting everything down, she closed her pale-yellow curtains—the only color in her room—and gratefully sank onto her bed.

Running a hand over the familiar fluffy white comforter, she looked around at the white walls and minimal decor. She liked simplicity, as if compensating for a complex world. Her room was safe and comforting, a cocoon against the judgmental looks and cruel intentions of others. It was a sanctuary she often needed to quiet her mind.

The windows rattled again. Sara thought of Murphy and hoped the dog was safe from the storm. She had always wanted a dog of her own, but the rental homes never allowed pets. A dog would be nice to cuddle with during a storm like this, and a dog would always love her no matter what. She rubbed her bald patch and lay back on the bed, listening to the thudding rain.

A sharp blast tore through the night. Sara lurched forward, sitting in bed and gasping as if she had been drowning. Lightning flickered, and then everything fell dark. Panic clawed at her when she heard only silence—not a single drop of rain.

Wide-eyed and heart racing, she stared at her window. It glistened as if it were a mirror of solid onyx. Sara shivered at the void and, for a split second, wondered if that was what people saw in her eyes. Fathomless black, as hideous as it was bewitching.

Lightning pulsed again, illuminating a sinuous dark cloud directly outside the window. But instead of thunder, a deep, blaring tone rumbled. A warning. The sky darkened, and the window returned to a greasy void.

Sara struggled to breathe, the air in the room heavy and deathly still. She swore she had closed her curtains, but maybe her mother had come in and opened them. She stole a glance at her shut door. Her instincts screamed at her to open it and turn on the lights, but she couldn't move, her body pinned down by fear. An attempted yell produced nothing more than a hoarse gargle. Her throat burned with a tight rawness, as if she'd swallowed broken glass.

The room's temperature dropped to bitter cold, and goosebumps crawled across Sara's skin. Her shallow breaths puffed and hung in the air.

The sky lit up, this time revealing the cloud in a large skull-like shape. Transfixed, she watched it undulate and tighten upon itself until it became the gaunt face of a man wearing a smoky wisp of a top hat. His hollow, vacant eyes stared at her as his mouth stretched into a leering grin, taunting her before darkness reclaimed the sky.

Her eyes widened, desperately searching the black night for any movement. Sweat froze along the sides of her face. The ominous blare resounded, shaking her bones as an acrid, burning stench crept into the room and stung her sinuses. The sky lit up again. But instead of a haunting face, the black cloud had swelled into a writhing mass of tendrils.

One tendril unfurled and tapped the window, a gentle *ping* reverberating through the room. Another tendril caressed the glass.

Lightning flickered, and a thick coil of smoke reared back, poised to strike.

Silence fell upon the room. Everything turned black again. She held her breath, hoping whatever was outside her window had magically disappeared.

A bone-snapping crack pierced the stillness, followed by the high-pitched splintering of glass. Another flicker of light revealed dark smoke seeping through the fractured window.

Sara squeezed her eyes shut and imagined stopping this moment. If only she could slow time and summon her anger to release a monster far greater than the one before her. But fear gripped her with thick claws that seemed to puncture her lungs. She gasped for breath, completely and painfully helpless, the predatory smoky darkness coiling around her.

With a sudden crash, the bedroom door flew open, and her parents burst in, shouting her name and turning on the lights. The splintering screeched to a halt, and the cold darkness jerked, releasing its hold on her. It recoiled and dissipated through the fractured window.

Sara slumped against the pillows, her head like solid stone and her eyelids sealed shut. Someone grabbed her hands, the sudden warmth burning her icy skin. She wanted to tell them to stop, that it hurt, but it felt like she lay pinned at the bottom of a deep lake. The shouting echoed in all directions until it became a dull roar. A velvety black, soft and warm and full of starry promises, enveloped her. She relaxed into the embracing darkness, and it tenderly snuffed out all thought.

Sara woke to daylight warming her face and winced at the brightness. Her mind grasped at dreamy remnants of a dark-green forest with shimmering trees, but the images evaporated like smoke.

She slowly opened her eyes and took in her familiar bedroom.

The window by her desk was covered in a web of blue painter's tape, each piece tentatively holding together the cracked glass. Foggy with sleep, she strained to recall what had happened.

Her breath hitched at remembering icy terror. She shoved back the white comforter to flee the room, but her arms and legs flailed clumsily, and her body ached as if she had been pummeled by stones.

Slender hands pushed her down and rubbed her arms. "Calm down, you're safe." Sara yelped at the familiar voice.

Her mother sat on the edge of the bed staring at her, green eyes ablaze with golden light that shown through the taped window. "Good morning, sunshine," she said. Her tone was cheerful, but her smile didn't reach her eyes.

Although Eliza wore her usual clothes—a bright-colored tunic and leggings that reflected her favorite seasonal flowers—it was her hair that caught Sara's attention. Her mother's long hair typically flowed in soft, loose waves. Today, it was pulled back in a low pony-tail, which gave her an air of severity, most unlike her easygoing nature. Something was definitely wrong.

Sara opened her mouth but could only utter a raspy breath. Her throat burned, and her tongue felt fat and wooly.

"Drink this. It will make you feel better." Her mother handed her a blue glazed mug, the same mug Sara had given her last Mother's Day.

Sara cupped the heavy pottery with both hands, grateful for the warmth, and brought it to her face. A tentative sniff followed by a deep inhalation helped discern what ingredients her mother had used this time. Sara did not care for anise or dandelion, which the teas often included—her mother claimed they were good for digestion and hair growth. This tea was pleasantly fragrant, with a blend of citrus, mint, and some sort of berry. She took a sip and tasted honey and flowers, as if her mother had harvested a warm summer day and boiled it down into the perfect cup of tea. Sara gulped down half the mug, her mouth and throat instantly feeling better. Warmth flowed through her and settled in her bones, alleviating the last hold of an icy chill.

"What is this?" Sara marveled, tilting the mug to peer at the drink.

Her mother smiled and tucked a lock of Sara's hair behind her ear. "Liquid sunshine," she said, pulling her into a hug. Her fingers brushed against the bald spot, and she stiffened. "When did this happen?" In a higher pitch that belied her calm demeanor, she asked, "Is anything else wrong?" She yanked back the covers and examined Sara's skin, running her hands down her arms and legs like Sara was a little girl who had fallen off her bike.

"Mom, I'm alright . . . at least I think I am." Sara set the mug on her nightstand and pulled the covers back up. "What happened last night?"

Her mother settled onto the bed, hands in her lap, and eyed the fractured window.

"Lightning hit the house, it fried everything electrical. You . . ." She hesitated, her gaze fixed with a far-away look. "You must have passed out—"

"My computer!" Sara slid out of bed and stumbled to her desk, tapping on the keyboard and power button. "My phone!" She grabbed her phone, yanked off the charging cord, and desperately hit the blank screen. "*Seriously!* It's like I'm cursed."

"Calm down. I'm sure insurance will cover most of it. You're not the only one affected. My phone and computer are down too. Your father is checking in with the neighbors on what damages they have."

Ignoring her words, Sara repeatedly stabbed at the phone and computer until her mother stood and grabbed her by the shoulders. "Breathe, Sara! The world is not out to get you. Just breathe." She grabbed her hands, placed them on her chest, and modeled deep breaths for her.

Just as Sara's heartbeat had finally slowed to normal, the front door slammed. Footsteps thudded up the stairs, two at a time. Her father stepped into the room, bending his tall, wiry frame where the ceiling sloped. "Everything okay?" His brow furrowed into one uniform eyebrow as he studied Sara, hands tapping nervously at his sides.

"We're fine, Dad." She pulled away from her mother, smoothing her hair around her shoulders.

Charlie's eyes flicked to the fractured window as he pulled out Sara's desk chair and sat. He slouched and ran his hand through his hair, causing it to stick up. "Gary said they had no damage. I checked with a few other neighbors—they only had rain. No one saw lightning or heard thunder. Just us." He spoke slowly, his gaze fixed on her mom. Eliza and Charlie stared at each other for a long, quiet moment.

Sara shifted, uncomfortable with the sudden tension in the room. Her father blinked and turned to her, forcing a smile. "Let's take a vacation this week while we let the insurance folks straighten this out." He stood and ushered Eliza with him on his way out of the bedroom. "Pack up some clothes and necessities. I want to leave before noon."

"Where are we going?" Sara asked, stunned he wanted to leave so soon. Her family occasionally took day trips, but they hadn't been away for an entire week in over a year, and even then, her parents took months to carefully plan it.

Her dad paused at the top of the stairs. "Oh, I have a place in mind, but I haven't been there in a long time." With an odd twist of his lips, he added, "It'll be a surprise until we get there." He turned and followed Eliza, their footsteps echoing in the stairwell.

Sara barely caught her mother's murmured, "Quite the surprise."

"Are we camping?" Sara called after them, unsure what to pack.

"Not exactly," said her father, his voice fading down the stairway. "Something . . . better."

Sara snorted. She loved the peacefulness of camping in the woods. And after her run-in with the pack and last night's storm, she could use the calm, healing energy of a forest. "What could be better than camping?"

Certainly not walls and blight and people I don't know.

CHAPTER 4

Alone in her bedroom, Sara moved to the window and lightly traced the rough tape and fine cracks. She shivered at the cold, remembering the icy presence of the black cloud. She hoped she had imagined how it changed shape and tried to attack her, but the feeling of terror still lingered inside her chest despite her mother's tea. Shaking her head to stave off the memory, she turned away from the fractured glass and slid open her closet door.

Amid a pile of art supplies, a black duffel bag—yet another conference-swag item of her father's—lay on the floor. She propped it open and filled it with a mix of jeans, shorts, T-shirts, and an extra pair of tennis shoes. Next, she threw in her sketchbook and a small pouch of assorted pencils. On impulse, she grabbed a stuffed animal from the collection patiently gathering dust in the corner of her bedroom. It wasn't any old toy but the small white dog with blue eyes she'd favored during her bald period following the sleepover incident. Not knowing where she was going made her uneasy and, although she was too old for stuffed animals, she jammed her old friend into the bag. Careful not to catch his fur in the zipper, she closed the duffel and headed down the stairs.

At precisely twenty minutes before noon, Sara's punctual father pulled out of the drive. As their SUV splashed through puddles on the rutted asphalt, she glanced at the Anderson's gate. It remained closed. Assuring herself that Murphy was fine, she shifted in her seat and looked out the back window of the SUV. She stared at their little gray house, watching it shrink smaller and smaller, until it disappeared altogether when they rounded the corner. Not once did she shift her gaze to acknowledge the damaged lamppost.

For a vacation, the mood in the car was somber, the sunny sky a stark contrast to the apocalyptic feeling of leaving home without her phone—no internet, no earbuds, no music. Fortunately, her father's phone had been spared from the electrical surge. He forgot to charge his phone so often that Sara usually had to call his office at the college when she needed to get ahold of him. After plugging it into the car console, Eliza first called Charlie's department secretary to announce he was taking the week off, then canceled the flower arrangements scheduled for the week, apologizing profusely to a regular customer who was upset she wouldn't have a fresh bouquet for her ladies' luncheon on Thursday. Sara itched for the phone but had no one to contact, and screen time playing games or watching videos in the car usually resulted in a headache.

She kicked off her shoes and looked out the window. "You know I don't care for surprises," she pressed. "Mind telling me where we're going?" Wherever these people—Ted and Ian—lived, she hoped it was rural and not the city. Crowds and noise were not her idea of a relaxing vacation.

"Nowhere," was all her father replied. He chuckled when he said it, but his knuckles turned white as he gripped the steering wheel.

Sara grumbled about being kidnapped but gave her father a slight grin when he glanced in the rearview mirror. An adventure was a welcome change of pace to her boring life. It wasn't the unknown part of their destination or even meeting new people that really bothered her. What troubled her most was a nagging sense of trying to flee something impossible to run away from.

For hours, the world flashed by. She kept her cheek pressed against the window, failing miserably at stopping herself from recalling the dreadful black cloud and gaunt-faced man that she could have sworn was real. With a silent curse for not grabbing a book, she opened her bag and pulled out her sketchbook and favorite pencil. Biting her lip over the strange cloud attack and her parents' hidden motives, she considered sketching a rabbit with a waistcoat and watch; but instead, she drew a fat rabbit lazily chewing grass.

"Nice drawing, honey. You have a lot of talent." Her mother had turned and was leaning into the back of the SUV.

Sara rolled her eyes. "Thanks, but you say that because you're my mom." She turned the page, shifting the sketchbook out of her mother's view, and waited until she sighed and settled back into the front seat before lifting her pencil to sketch a few trees. Each tree depicted fractal branching patterns and roots that dug so deep they bled off the paper. She flipped to a blank page and absently doodled for a few minutes before her mother twisted around again, asking for a snack from the rear seat. Her hazel eyes widened at the open sketchbook and then flicked to Sara's face. "What's that?"

Sara shrugged. "Just some pendant I saw on a guy."

"When did you see this?" Her mother didn't hide the anxiety in her voice.

"Yesterday." Sara drew out her response and arched a brow, but instead of commenting further, her mother turned back to the front seat, snack forgotten.

When her father accelerated, noticeably picking up their pace, Sara loosed an irritated sigh. Feeling queasy, she tossed the sketchbook back into her bag and lay across the back seat. She heaved another sigh, this time not from boredom or exasperation but from a calculated plan to learn more. Still as death, she pretended to sleep, perfectly positioned to listen.

Despite her intentions, the hum of the car lulled her to sleep. She woke to her parents whispering about a forest and the strange names mentioned before. Whoever Ian was, he seemed to be an ill little boy.

"Ted is expecting us at around ten. He figures we'll be up all night once we see Ian. Says he hasn't told him anything but will leave it up to us . . . to tell them together." Her dad blew out a breath and shifted in the driver's seat, likely tired from driving all afternoon. Even with her eyes closed, Sara could sense him pushing up his glasses to rub the bridge of his nose and running a hand through his hair.

"I'm sure he'll have lots of questions for us," said her mother.

"They all will. I just have an odd feeling. Maybe it's because we've been gone for so long, but . . . I'm not sure."

Sara expected her mother to say something encouraging. Instead, she replied, "I don't know either. Something does seem . . . off." The pause before she said "*off*" was concerning, and when her mother stirred in the front seat, Sara, her face partially covered by a blanket, held her breath. "But we need help, and it sounds like they do too. Besides"—her voice hitched—"I've missed him terribly. All our family. And the forest." Her last words were full of longing.

"Me too, honey. Me too," said Charlie as the car slowed down. "Let's grab some dinner before it gets dark."

When the car came to a halt, Sara faked rubbing sleep from her eyes and then blinked at a small diner. Her parents opened their doors, and the scent of coffee and French fries made her stomach grumble. *This better be some forest. But first—food.* She pushed open her door and put on her best game face, determined to play out the charade without revealing her hand.

After a questionable dinner of greasy food and guarded conversation, Sara insisted on driving. She told her parents they looked tired, which was true, but she thought surely now, they would tell her where they were headed. She hadn't driven their SUV in almost two weeks, not since a college security officer caught her speeding through campus. The officer hadn't given her a ticket but had told her father, who promptly suggested she spend a few weeks doing flower deliveries on foot.

Charlie peered at her over the top of his glasses, a habit that made him look like a professor, despite his boyish face, and admitted he could use a little rest. Raising his eyebrows at Eliza, he handed the keys to Sara.

She grinned as she slid into the driver's seat and turned on the navigation system. "Where to, Dad?"

Settling heavily into the passenger's side, he reached over and punched in "Ware, Massachusetts." He gave a half smile at the red navigation pin floating in the middle of an eye-shaped lake.

"Like I said, 'No Ware.'" He laughed at her confused expression. "Listen, don't speed. And wake me when we get to the town of Greenwich. After that, I'll have to direct you. There's no address for where we're going." He buckled his seat belt, reclined the chair, and shut his eyes.

Sara turned and saw her mother already lying across the back seat.

"Thanks for driving, honey. I don't know why I'm so tired, but a short nap should help. Love you," Eliza mumbled through a yawn.

Alrighty, then. Sara hoped wherever they were headed had a hot shower and a quiet bedroom for her. She eased out of the diner parking lot and onto the main route, excited to be driving again. Not just driving—but being in control. Her parents still treated her like a child, and she constantly felt the need to prove herself, to show she could make good decisions . . . at least most of the time. They never talked about it, but she hoped to get a place and live on her own. Someday.

After driving over two hours, she flexed her fingers on the wheel.

Her parents were sound asleep when fat raindrops splashed the windshield. For once, she drove slowly—not wanting to wake her parents or hit any animals that might dart from the thick vegetation lining both sides of the road. She had passed a few victims of roadkill already, and visibility was limited to their headlights—no streetlights stood along the old route they were on. The rain fell heavier, smacking the hood of the SUV as she adjusted the wiper speed.

Her mother stirred from the back seat. "Where are we?" she asked, pushing herself up.

"We're close, Mom, about another hour, I think." Sara hit the high beams back on after a van passed in the opposite direction. It was the only car she had seen for miles. Wherever they were headed was definitely remote—probably couldn't get Wi-Fi or cell service even if she did have her phone.

Lightning lit the sky, and Sara's heart skipped a beat. The rain now hammered the little SUV, waking her father.

He pulled up his seat and checked the navigation. "The next town is just a few more miles. Then you can pull over and I'll drive the rest of the way," he shouted over the rain.

Even with the wipers on at max speed, a curtain of water covered the windshield. Sara's pulse quickened, and she adjusted her clammy hands on the steering wheel.

Lightning cracked and struck a tree so close to them, the impact was deafening. She floored the gas. The tree crashed behind them, branches scratching the rear of the car.

"That was a bit close," said Charlie with light amusement. His attempt to relieve the tension fell flat.

Gripping the steering wheel, Sara sped down the middle of the road, determined to outrun the storm and get to the next town as quickly as possible. The wipers whined against the rain, each swipe giving a moment of visibility and creating a strobing effect to the road rushing at them.

"Charles," said Eliza in a deathly serious tone. She pulled herself up between them, practically sitting on the console, and stared out the windshield.

Her father had his head between his knees, yanking on the car charger to pull up his phone. "I know. I'm gonna call Teddy. He can come get us in his truck."

The rain stopped, and Sara skidded to a halt.

Above their heads writhed an enormous cloud, its smoky darkness an impenetrable black against the indigo night sky. As if it had a heartbeat, the cloud pulsed, each beat thumping with a loud blaring noise. The cloud swelled larger, twisting and turning, tendrils uncurling and spreading from a core illuminated with lightning from within.

"Sweet Mary protect us," whispered Eliza, grabbing on to them both.

Ice crystals cracked across the windshield, and the car engine sputtered and died with the sudden drop in temperature. Sara's ragged breathing froze into ghostly gasps. Trembling uncontrollably, all she could do was stare at the living nightmare before her.

This cannot be happening!

Inky-black tendrils grabbed at the night, propelling the writhing mass closer while it continued its thunderous alarm. Like a giant squid about to swallow a ship, the smoky coils unfurled and lunged for the car.

Charlie dropped the phone and whipped his head to Sara. "Stop it! You—"

He was cut off when something slammed into the back of the car. They jolted forward, toward the gaping maw of the black cloud.

Later, Sara would remember seeing her mother fly headfirst through the windshield, her father's head smash into the dashboard, and his seat crumple into the front of the car. But a solid white wall would interrupt her thoughts, and then there would be nothing.

Not even a drop of rain.

CHAPTER 5

Time stood still—nonexistent. Her soul floated in dark oblivion until a white light cleaved the nothing and an invisible force tugged at her being. Pain ripped through her as she was shoved back into her battered body and mind.

Sara scrabbled at the fragments of memory flashing before her. The sharp pain faded and her senses slowly woke, but nothing made sense. Instead of a steering wheel, she clutched fistfuls of starched sheets. And instead of her mother's floral perfume, she smelled antiseptic. The patter of rain had been replaced by the muffled dull throb of her own heartbeat. She struggled to focus, but her head felt like it had been hit with a sledgehammer. Repeatedly. Surely, her ears were bleeding and leaking brain matter.

"Hello," called a disembodied voice. The word floated and dissolved, as if spoken underwater. Exhausted, Sara lay too tired to move a fraction of an inch or even flutter an eyelid . . . assuming she still had eyelids. A warm breeze drifted across what she hoped was her face and not a pulverized mass of flesh. The breeze smelled of cinnamon and laughed a beautiful music, tickling Sara's attention.

"Wake up, sleeping beauty," the breeze chuckled, its words echoing in Sara's head. "Come on. Open your eyes now," it coaxed.

A loud clap jolted Sara, and her eyelids snapped open. She

stared directly into a woman's chestnut-brown eyes. Eyes that were much too close to Sara.

The woman leaned back. Her smile disappeared for a moment, and she tilted her head uncertainly. Sara did not blink. Though hardly a wrinkle creased the woman's glowing, sepia complexion, the assuredness in her eyes suggested she was older than she appeared. "Well, aren't you something," the woman said. Her voice sounded muffled and distant.

Sara's eyes stung and welled with tears. She blinked, and the woman gave a deep, hearty laugh that, oddly enough, reminded Sara of roses and cherries. A warm sensation overcame her, as if the final scraps of her soul were pouring back into her body. Blood pumped in her fingertips and toes, and a rather unpleasant rawness wetted the side of her face. She blinked again and listened to her breath. *Inhale three counts, exhale three counts. Repeat.*

The woman stood patiently with a smug smile on her chapped lips. "What site are you from?" she asked, eyes wide with a golden glimmer.

Sara stared at her, freezing her face into the expression her teachers had called *"shark eyes"* whenever she had blanked out in class.

"Are you from Ware Woods?" the woman asked. "That's where I was headed when they dragged me here."

Something flickered deep inside Sara at the mention of Ware Woods. It seemed familiar, yet she couldn't remember why.

The woman shifted her weight. Her mischievous expression transformed into a pinched look of intense curiosity. With her hands low at her sides, she waved one back and forth like a one-sided handshake. Sara tracked the motion with her eyes but remained silent, her face a mask hiding her growing suspicion that this woman was crazy. And if so, why was she near her?

Cold skittered along Sara's bones as her mind skipped, recalling an uncomfortable moment waiting outside the principal's office.

It had been too easy to overhear the heated words between her parents and the principal.

"*She may have anger management issues, but she is not bipolar or psychotic!*" Outrage had replaced her mother's usual calm demeanor. "*And even if she was, she is not a threat to this school.*" Her parents had exited the office, her mother trembling with fury while her father snapped the door closed behind them. The harsh exchange had marked her last day of public school.

Sara rolled her eyes, shaking off the memory, and warily took in her surroundings. She lay in a hospital-like room filled with cold, heavy air. Definitely not the sanctuary of her bedroom. She had to get out of here—wherever *here* was. Screaming internally at the effort to move her stony body, she focused on the blood pulsing in her fingertips, and willed her hands and feet to jerk awake. Her foot twitched, and her legs labored to scissor back and forth, straining against the tight sheets. Focusing all her will, she drew up her hands and pushed back the sheets and knitted blanket that tucked her in like shrink wrap.

With a sucking noise, she opened her mouth and clicked her thick tongue. Drool cascaded down her chin. The woman chuckled. Ignoring her, Sara swiped her jaw and felt something sticky and rough—as if she had peanut butter on the side of her face. When she held her hand in front of her, ointment glistened on her fingertips. She wiped them on the crisp sheets and struggled to sit, the effort causing her head to throb. Reaching a trembling hand to the left side of her face, she felt her fingertips brush a bandage covering her ear and cheek. Gently, she traced her puffy lips and forehead, finding more sticky ointment. She tilted her head to feel the nape of her neck and frowned at a vaguely familiar bald patch of scalp.

Her frown deepened at the ID bracelet which caught on her thin pastel gown. Running her hands up and down her arms, she sighed in relief at finding no serious injuries other than a few nasty black-purple bruises. The annoying buzz in her ears lessened, only to be replaced by the woman's breathing. Sara shifted her shoulders to take in more of her surroundings, including all potential escapes.

The sterile room was clean but worn, the only décor being two generic flower prints in frames bolted to cream-colored walls. Near her bed sat a wooden end table and an upholstered chair which, given the sheen on the fabric, was probably not comfortable. Adjacent to Sara was a matching bed set complete with an identical mauve blanket. The room had two wooden doors, both of which were closed.

Sara tilted her good ear toward the doors—at the sound of voices approaching.

"Get down!" said the woman in a harsh whisper, pushing Sara back and tugging the sheet and blanket up to her chin. "Pretend you're still asleep," she urged. In one fluid motion, she grabbed a magazine from the end table and hopped onto her bed.

Sara's head throbbed. Unable to think straight, she simply reacted and closed her eyes. The magazine rustled as the woman flipped through pages too fast to be reading them.

One of the doors clicked open. A pair of female voices broke off their conversation and entered the room.

"Hello, Naomi. Thanks for taking on a new guest in your room," said a woman, her voice light but tinged with condescension.

The magazine stopped fluttering. "As if I have a choice," shot back Naomi. "When are you going to let me leave? Hmm? I've been here for months now and haven't once caused any trouble. I'm all better and perfectly fine."

"Naomi," the light voice bit out, "we've discussed this. You know we need to contact your family before we can release you."

"And I've told you, I haven't got any more family," said Naomi, her voice sharp and tight.

"Right," said the woman. "You think your entire family was murdered. But we haven't found evidence of this, and we need to go through proper procedure before we can release you. Just be patient with us. I know it's a long process."

Naomi grunted.

Two sets of footsteps approached Sara. Her bed jostled as the women leaned toward her. Their close presence made the hair on her neck prickle with irritation. The smell of coffee and musky perfume hit her nose. She lay still and focused on keeping her breathing deep and steady. It took all her concentrated effort not to recoil when a cool hand felt her forehead and then held her wrist so tight, a thumbnail cut into her skin.

"Seems fine. They must have given her too much sedative at the hospital, but she should wake up soon. Keep me posted." The woman with the light voice dropped Sara's hand and walked away, the door latching behind her.

The magazine ruffled and thudded against a firm surface. Naomi cleared her throat and spoke to the remaining woman. "I'm kinda tired and don't feel like going to group today. Can I stay here? I promise I'll let you know when she wakes up."

The other woman finally spoke, her voice deep and husky. "Fine. I'd rather take a break than babysit. Here's the water you wanted. And come get me in the staff lounge when she wakes." The woman's shoes squeaked as she bustled out, the door snicking shut after her. The room settled into a heavy stillness, save for the hum of fluorescent lights.

"You still awake? 'Cause you look pretty convincing," said Naomi with a throaty chuckle.

Sara sat up and put her hand against the bandage over her ear. "What happened to me? Where am I?" she rasped, her voice rough and thick with phlegm. She cleared her throat and eyed the cup on the end table. Without hesitation, Naomi handed the cup to Sara. The woman's kindness startled her. Most people avoided her, never mind shared anything with her. She paused before grasping the cup and taking a gulp. Cool water rolled down her throat.

"The doctor that just checked your pulse said you were in a car accident, not hurt too badly except for whatever happened to your ear. But you must have freaked out at the hospital because they sent you here, to the mental facility." Naomi took the now-empty cup and set it back on the end table.

Crazy or not, Sara was grateful for the water and information. Her throat felt better, but her head was still pounding. She tried to recall what had happened—it was hard to discern what was real and what was hopefully just a bad dream. She had been in the car with her parents. It was raining so hard she stopped the car. Darkness enveloped her, followed by a flash of white. Lights and voices came to help . . . but she refused to be held down.

She had to find her parents.

"My parents," she said, and looked around wildly while pulling back the sheets and swinging her legs over the edge of the bed. "I was with my parents. I need to find them—make sure they're okay. I need to leave here." She struggled to stand, but a piercing pain, fast and sharp like an ice pick, stabbed her head, forcing her to fall back onto the bed.

"Shh, calm down!" hissed Naomi, her eyes on the door. "If you get amped up, they'll sedate you again. You need to get better so we can get out of here. Whatever they give you, don't swallow it. Hide it really well in case they check, or spit it up when they leave. Trust me, I spent my first month as a vegetable from their crap. And don't talk too much or ask questions. Just be polite and do what they say." Naomi's rapid instructions came to an abrupt halt when a nurse entered the room.

Naomi flashed a saccharine-sweet smile. "I was just about to get you. She woke up and said she needed the bathroom."

Sara glanced at the nurse, a matronly woman who was twice her size and easily filled the doorway. She looked Sara up and down before leaning into the hallway and calling someone to the room. "She's up." Her husky voice was laced with annoyance. Holding the door open, she turned back to Sara. "The doctor is coming to see you."

A short woman wearing a conservative gray dress and a male orderly in blue scrubs entered the room. "I need to remove the bandage and check your wounds," said the doctor, her light voice instantly recognizable. She turned to the male orderly, who handed her a pair of gleaming scissors.

Sara's eyes fixed on the sharp instrument, and she fought to sit still when the doctor brought the scissors to her face. She winced as the bandage was cut and peeled away from her skin with a wet, sucking noise.

"Your stitches look good, and your eardrum should heal by itself within a few weeks," said the doctor. Sara raised her hand to her ear, which suddenly itched. The woman swatted her hand. "Don't touch the stitches."

Sara growled at her.

The woman cleared her throat and took a step back. "Do you know your name?"

"Sara. Sara Harbour," she said, coughing up phlegm and forcing herself to swallow instead of spitting at the doctor. Saying her last name sent her mind racing. She clenched her jaw, trying to focus on something she knew was important. She remembered a dark sky, her father asking her to stop, a white flash . . . and then nothing.

The doctor took another step toward the doorway, slipping behind the orderly and large nurse.

Sara leapt up and stepped toward the door. But her vision darkened, forcing her to stop and lean against the bed to keep from falling over. "Where are my parents? I want to see them right now. I want to go home."

"Easy now, you took a good bump to the head," said the large nurse, grabbing Sara's arms.

"How did I hit my head? What happened to me?" Panic swelled inside her. She straightened and tugged her arms, but the nurse strengthened her grip and held them down. She caught a glimpse of Naomi sitting on her bed with pursed lips, giving an almost imperceptible shake of her head.

"You were in a car accident. An airbag saved you but gave you a concussion, some facial lacerations, and ruptured your eardrum," stated the doctor from the doorway.

Sara tensed and narrowed her eyes. In a throaty growl, she asked again, "Where are my parents?" She jerked an arm away from the nurse, swaying slightly before regaining her balance. The nurse shifted to allow the male orderly closer. His heavily muscled arms were taut, daring Sara to make a move.

The doctor cleared her throat. "Your father is stable, but he's in a medically induced coma to manage the swelling in his brain."

Sara choked on a sob, and her knees buckled. The nurse squeezed her arms, holding her upright. Not her dad, her brilliant and strong dad. Her chest hot and tight, she gasped for air. "My mom?" she pleaded, tears stinging the wounds on her face.

"Your mother went through the windshield and broke her neck. By the time paramedics arrived, she had died." The doctor paused. "I'm sorry."

Sara roared, a sound so primal it did not seem human. The nurse loosened her grip and Sara lunged for the door, baring her teeth like a wild animal. She knocked the doctor into the hallway before the male orderly tackled her to the floor. Her hands burned, and she welcomed the pain with a snarl. But before she could turn on him and unleash her rage, he deftly stabbed her with a syringe, sending a deep ache into her left shoulder. She howled and sank her teeth into his forearm before her vision collapsed. The last thing she saw was Naomi's face, her eyes wide and a finger to her lips.

CHAPTER 6

SARA AWOKE IN a small room with a single gray metal door, its chipped edges revealing a mint green past. Lying on a cot, she watched a pool of drool spread through the paper sheets, creeping toward her good ear. The thin vinyl mattress crinkled and groaned as she pushed herself up and leaned against the wall. Her tongue tasted like dirty socks, and her head felt inflated and stuffed with cotton. She gingerly fingered the stitches poking out at the base of her ear.

A small window in the door let hazy light into the room. It was impossible to tell if it was night or day. Sitting up made the room spin and her head pulse. Sara groaned with nausea and fought the urge to vomit. Her skin slick with cold sweat, she shivered and pulled at her thin gown.

She wanted to get up, open the door, and be back in her own bedroom with her parents downstairs making breakfast. She shut her eyes and imagined herself sitting at the dining table, smelling her mother's cinnamon rolls and listening to her father whistle as he scrambled eggs. A sudden sharp pain from her ear erased the image.

She opened her eyes and took in the closet-sized room. Except for the cot, there was nothing—no table, no chair, not even a light switch. It wasn't so much a room as it was a rectangular cell with linoleum flooring so old that the tiles curled up where they met the beige walls.

Hot tears spilled down her face. "No, no, no," she moaned over and over again, rocking herself back and forth on the bed. This wasn't real, none of this was real. The black cloud, the accident . . . her parents.

She slammed her head against the wall and instantly regretted it. The splitting pain nearly crushed her back to unconsciousness.

The pain was real. All of this was horribly real. And if it was all real . . . perhaps she was in hell. Exactly where she always knew she belonged.

She slumped back onto the bed, not caring about the pain in her head, on her face, in her heart. She wanted to fall sleep forever, escape reality and dream of a life with a happier ending. Staring at the wall, she lay numb until the door clicked open and someone approached.

"I see you're awake, so don't pretend otherwise," said a husky female voice.

Large Nurse.

Sara ignored her.

"I don't want you pissing the bed, so I'm taking you to the bathroom. Sit up and have some water first," she ordered.

At the mention of piss and water, Sara's body clenched with opposing needs. The nurse pulled her upright, and Sara edged her legs over the side of the cot. She tore apart her dry lips and frowned at the rusty taste of blood.

Large Nurse held out a cup and Sara grabbed it, her tongue chasing the straw into her mouth to suck down cool water. Relieving herself became a necessity, and she welcomed the nurse's tight grip as she led her across the hall and into a tiled room with a toilet.

She didn't care that the toilet had no seat and the room had no door. In the corner was a shower head, and in the center of the floor gaped a slotted drain. Large Nurse stood in the doorway, giving Sara a false sense of privacy until the male orderly walked by and grinned at her.

An image of a leering black cloud flicked in her mind, and for a moment she imagined attacking the orderly and gouging out his eyes. But her anger faded, and she sank back into despair, not caring, numb to everything around her.

Sara allowed the nurse to shuffle her back to the tiny room, where she curled up on the cot and stared at the wall. She knew something terrible had happened and that she was not in a good place, but to open the door to reality would open the floodgates to a personal hell of grief and pain. And overwhelming guilt for not being able to stop the black cloud. It was easier to lose herself in the void of nothing, staring at nothing, thinking of nothing . . . being nothing.

Sara couldn't tell if hours passed or days before Large Nurse barged into the room and yelled at her to eat something. Her senses dull, Sara obediently put a piece of bread in her mouth. It tasted like cardboard. She took some water and choked it down along with pills the nurse gave her—two blue and one white. Grateful for the gift of oblivion, she sprawled across the cot, too numb to be bothered by the chill in the air or to notice how cold her hands had become.

The routine—bathroom, food, pills, nothing, repeat—happened so many times, it played like a loop in her mind.

Eventually, her stitches were removed, her hair grew matted, and her fingernails became ragged and dirty from scratching the walls in her sleep. Few people ever came to her door—Large Nurse, the doctor, a nurse with greasy blonde hair who smelled of stale smoke, and the muscled orderly who leered at her.

It could have been weeks or just days of staring at the wall, avoiding herself. She blinked, and an image of a tall pine tree projected into her drug-addled mind. The sight was so vivid she could smell the green needles and feel a breeze on her skin. A longing washed over her, and something deep inside her twitched, as if someone had nudged her desperate soul.

She blinked again when the nurse with greasy hair came to the door and announced she had a visitor. Probably another doctor to shine a light in her abysmal eyes and cringe, knowing they could do nothing but sedate her pain and guilt and anger. Curing or even taming the monstrous power inside her was beyond anyone's ability.

Sara remained staring at the wall, hungry and nauseous at the same time. The visitor stepped into the room and gasped, his deep tone distinctly male. From the corner of her eye, she watched him hesitate before approaching her bedside. His movement scented the air with fresh pine, the smell matching the tree that still shadowed her mind. She held her breath, holding on to the scent while remaining still.

He cleared his throat and said in a low voice, "Sara, I'm Ted." He paused. "Your dad's brother."

Sara blinked at the wall.

"I . . . want to take you home, but they say you need to get better, that you need to be able to walk out of here." He stressed the word "*walk*" as the nurse holding the door coughed and shouted down the hall. Ted leaned over her, his scent so strong she could see herself in the forest. "Please, Sara, this is important—you do not belong here. You need to come home to the forest as soon as possible," he whispered. One hand lightly touched her shoulder while his other hand placed something in front of her, breaking her trance with the dingy wall.

In a rush of squeaky shoes, the doctor and male orderly raced into the room. "What are you doing here? I told you no visitors until she gets better. Out, now, before she has an episode."

They grabbed Ted and physically escorted him from the room.

"You are overly medicating this girl," Ted said in an angry but even voice. "And this facility," he spat, "is appalling. I'll be back soon to take her home."

Sara listened to his footsteps as he walked away, quick and confident, until her door clicked shut and silence settled once more.

For the first time since the accident, she felt warmth. Heat radiated from where Ted had touched her shoulder. Her core warmed, thawing the heavy weight she hadn't realized was holding her down, and her hands tingled as if she had just come in from the cold.

She felt like she had been asleep for years, that the accident was a dream from long, long ago and had happened to someone else—not her. But Ted was real. She had an uncle. An uncle who cared about her.

She struggled to focus on the object he'd placed in front of her. It was white and the size of a small pillow. A pillow would be nice, she mused. Hell, socks would be nice. Surprised to have a clear thought, she concentrated on moving her hand. After a few agonizing minutes, sweat beading her brow, she jerked her hand upward, bringing the object to her face. It tickled her lips and felt familiar in her grip . . . something from her life before the accident.

Pushing her head back, she shook foggy double images from her vision and narrowed her gaze on a stuffed white dog with blue eyes. The same dog she packed so long ago.

Her heart skipped a beat, half expecting the dog to lick her face, to lick away the hot tears that now flowed from her.

A huge part of her was missing, and the rest of her wasn't sure it could live without the missing part. Her tears were interrupted when the nurse with greasy hair opened the door.

With shaking hands, Sara wiped her face and pushed the dog under a rumpled paper sheet. She groaned and shoved herself up against the wall.

The nurse set a tray of food at one end of the cot and handed her three pills and a cup of water. She grinned, revealing stained, rotten teeth. "Damn near lost my job but made me fifty bucks," she said, patting her pocket. "You can stay a vegetable, and I'll take my chances earning money for visiting rights."

Sara had put the pills on her tongue but paused when the nurse said "*vegetable*." Her senses bristled.

Greasy Nurse laughed. "In fact, there's someone else who will pay me for visiting rights," she whispered, the odor of stale coffee and decay escaping her lips. Her close-set eyes fell on Sara's thin gown, and she grinned again.

The hair on the back of Sara's neck prickled. She kept her gaze focused on a curling linoleum tile in the corner of the room while she gulped down the water, her pills carefully tucked inside her cheek.

As soon as Greasy Nurse left, Sara spat out the pills and ground them into a gummy paste between her fingers. With a grunt, she stumbled across the room and wiped the pulverized drugs under the floor tile. She had wallowed long enough—too long—in despair and fear of facing her new reality. Ted was right. She did not belong here. She needed to get better . . . and fast. Her father needed help, and the smoky dark *thing* that haunted her—that killed her mother—needed to be destroyed. Sara's mind raced with vengeance, but after a few more wobbly steps, her stomach churned and her head throbbed. Crashing onto the cot, she instantly fell asleep and dreamed of the black cloud and gaunt-faced man. But this time, instead of running from his image, she ran toward it.

CHAPTER 7

SARA WOKE TO a raging headache. Her stomach heaved, and she barely lurched over the side of the bed before vomiting on the floor. Large Nurse cracked open the door and swore at her, then made her clean it up. Sara's entire body shook so violently she slipped in her own mess, smearing herself in bile. The nurse shoved her into the bathroom without a door to strip down and shower. Exhausted and trembling, Sara sat on the floor to shower with her back to the open doorway, hoping the male orderly did not walk by. The water pounded her as she vomited again.

When she was finally done retching and washing, the nurse pushed her back to her room and made her change the paper sheets. For a moment, the stuffed dog was exposed. Large Nurse either didn't notice or ignored it before proceeding to swipe Sara's forehead with a thermometer and give her more medicine. Sara tucked the pills into her cheek again and took the cup, intentionally gulping the water.

As soon as the nurse left the room, Sara crushed the pills into a gap between the wall and a floor tile beneath her bed. Her wet hair soaked the back of her gown, this one pale blue with a pattern of white diamonds. Her hands trembled and her back ached. Sweating and shivering at the same time, she curled up in a fetal position on the bed with the dog tucked against her chest.

She drifted asleep and dreamed of a dense forest. At first, the leafy trees bowed in welcome, but then they shuddered, dropping their leaves and twisting into crippled forms that raked the sky. Blackened vines slithered across ashy ground and snaked around her legs, biting into her skin. Their thorny grip jerked as the entire forest shook with the thunderous approach of a beast crashing through tangled undergrowth. Shadows bled from the lifeless trees, wrapping her in darkness and licking her with razor-edged tongues. She screamed and thrashed against the vines, unable to see the beast as it lunged through the trees. Her chest exploded when it crashed into her and sank its claws into her flesh.

Sara's body twitched and jerked on the bed, her eyes snapping open to see the male orderly watching her from the window.

For days, Sara hid her medication in the cracks of the broken room and played along as the numb, obedient patient while silently detoxing. Though the tremors, restlessness, and nausea were annoying at best, the panic attacks and memories of the accident terrified her most.

And then there was the guilt.

The gaunt man in the black cloud wanted her. She should have been the one to crash through the windshield and die, not her mother. "*Stop it,*" had been her father's last words, as if he had known she was responsible for the darkness following them.

Having no more tears left, she focused on getting better, stronger. She wanted to see her father, help him get well . . . and beg for his forgiveness. And she wanted to meet Ted and visit his forest home. If necessary, she would even plead to stay with him, because going back to Green Brier Lane didn't seem possible. Not without her mother.

But what she wanted most was to kill the gaunt-faced man.

No longer in denial, she knew in the pit of her soul that the man controlling the black cloud was real—as real as she was—a living monster with murderous powers.

For coming after her and destroying her family, she would squeeze the life from him—slowly. The thought brought a grim smile to her face.

She narrowed her eyes, parsing out the two biggest challenges to her plan. First, she needed to get out of this mental hellhole and regain her strength—not impossible, but definitely blood, sweat, and tears worthy. Second—and this was the most concerning challenge—was she capable of being the bigger monster?

In her waking hours, Sara fought to avoid the emotions that threatened to overwhelm her and instead focused on controlling her breath to quiet her mind and think clearly.

During one of these meditative states, her thoughts flickered to Naomi. Either Naomi was truly crazy or surprisingly sane. Maybe it didn't matter. Sara felt a connection to her, perhaps because they were both trapped here against their will. After all, Naomi had said, "We *need to get out of here*," which made her as close to a friend as she'd had in a long time.

Short of fighting her way out and likely destroying herself in the process, Naomi and Ted were her best options for escape.

Sara sat on the cot, stroking the stuffed dog, and thought of Ted. Frowning, she wondered why her father had never mentioned him. Maybe he was ashamed his brother was a forest dweller. But that didn't seem right. She chewed her lip and twisted her mouth in thought.

Her father had told her on more than one occasion to always be respectful and open-minded because every person had unique abilities and knowledge—and sometimes secrets—that could be beneficial to the world. Hippie, indeed. She always thought this advice was a bit too sunshine-and-lollipops for her, but now she realized the truth of his words. In fact, she herself had a big secret—she was a monster on the inside and capable of terrible things. The obvious problem being that her secret was *not* beneficial.

The magnitude of her situation grated on her. She clutched the stuffed dog and absently rubbed a seam along its back. Her fingers lingered on a puckered section she didn't remember. The long white fur parted, and she found stitching on the outside of the seam, indicating a repair. Pulling on a thread caused the seam to unravel, and a small piece of paper popped out. Her breath hitched.

She stole a glance at the door before unfolding the paper. The looping cursive script, although neatly written, was difficult to decipher: *Wear it and tell no one.*

She stared at the scrap of paper, reading it again and again. The penmanship was unfamiliar, certainly not from her mother or father. Maybe Ted wrote it. *Wear what?*

Hoping the dog held the answer, Sara poked a finger inside the hole and wiggled it deep into the fluffy stuffing. Her nail tapped something hard and smooth, and her fingertip tingled in response. She ripped the hole wider and eagerly fished out the hidden object.

After picking off tufts of stuffing, Sara cupped a rounded object, somewhat flat and slightly larger than the size of a quarter. Although it resembled a polished stone, it felt light and airy. In her hunched-over shadow, the object appeared dark. She angled it to catch the hazy light of the room and gasped, nearly dropping it.

The stone glowed red with such intensity, it was as though fire lived inside. It flickered and pulsed in the room's unnatural light. To see it in sunlight would be a marvel.

"Wear it and tell no one." . . . How am I supposed to wear this? Sara clenched it in one hand, warmth seeping through her fingers and spreading up her arm. With her other hand, she propped the dog in her lap and dug into the stuffing, exploring every limb and cavity, but found nothing else.

She set aside the dog, opened her fist, and palmed the stone;

its smooth surface and solid presence were oddly calming. Pondering the note, she rhythmically rubbed the stone until she felt a slim twisting, as if a strand of hair had stuck to it. Though she saw nothing, she felt whisper-thin threads far too silky to be hair or fiber filling. Her vision seemingly deceived, Sara entrusted her fingers to gently tug the strands, which wrapped around the stone and stretched out like a leash.

Not a leash, her fingers decided, but an invisible chain. A necklace. *"Wear it."*

Using her sense of touch to guide her, Sara pulled and stretched the unseen strands until the stone appeared to hover in midair. She looped the necklace over her head. The stone slipped under her gown and settled low on her breastbone, resting tight against her skin. A warmth spread across her chest as the fiery stone pulsed in unison with her heartbeat. For the first time in a long while, Sara felt hope. Hope in knowing she had the strength to leave this place and hunt the gaunt-faced killer.

She picked up the note, contemplating how to hide this secret, when Large Nurse burst into the room. Sara shoved the paper into her mouth and slowly turned to face her.

"Dinner's early tonight," huffed the nurse, catching her breath. She stooped to the floor and set down an open box with a prepackaged sandwich and cup of applesauce. "Hurry up now, I ain't got all day. The other nurse hasn't come in yet, and I'm stuck doing meds before I can leave." She held the door open with one foot while she pulled out Sara's meds from her front pocket.

Choking down the paper note, Sara leaned over and peered at the food. A dry film coated the top of the applesauce.

"Damn, I forgot the water! Just take these with the applesauce." She tossed Sara a small paper cup of pills. "Brad!" she yelled into the hallway, and hustled off.

As soon as the door snicked shut, Sara grabbed the pills to crush and dispose of them before Large Nurse returned. But it was the orderly who suddenly barged into her room. He gripped a cup of water in one hand, his muscles flexing with tension, and held it up to her face. His arms were shaven and smooth, save for two pink, arched scars on his forearm.

Sara put her hand with the pills behind her back, but he saw her sudden movement and grabbed her wrist.

"What's this? Aw, now," he taunted. "I hear you're a good girl and will do *everything* I tell you." He licked his lips and leaned in.

He was much too close, his sour breath on her face. She wanted to punch him and run, but knew she couldn't get past him. Not yet, anyway.

"Take it," he ordered, thrusting the cup forward again and pushing her hand to her face.

Sara took the cup and placed the pills on her tongue. When she tucked them inside her cheek, he pried open her mouth and pushed them down her throat with his thick fingers. She dropped the cup, splashing water on his shoes, and gagged, choking on the pills now lodged in her throat.

Brad loomed over her. "You, are my golden ticket. Some creepy bastard says he'll give me *anything* if I pull some strings and release you to him. But before I do, you and I are gonna have some fun. Consider it payback for biting me." He sneered. "I'll let the drugs hit you before I come back." He left the room, shaking water from his shoes and squeaking along the way.

Sara bent over and heaved. But her stomach was too empty to spit up more than one partially dissolved pill.

Shit.

She lunged for the applesauce, gulping it down before devouring the sandwich. Food would lessen the sedatives—but eating so fast gave her a stomachache, which she tried to ignore while she paced the small room.

A yank on the doorknob confirmed it was locked as usual.

I am so screwed. No! Breathe. Think.

If Brad was talking about the gaunt-faced man, this could be her chance to get out of the mental facility and kill him. But to do that, she would be at Brad's mercy. And there was no way she would be his plaything and pawn.

She scanned the room, stopping her gaze on the paper food box. It could take days or weeks for Ted to come back. And she had no idea if Naomi was still here. Her only option was to fight her way out.

Sara grabbed the box and folded the thick paper into a pitiful dagger. A quick stab to the neck or eyes would show Brad her idea of fun and hopefully cause enough of a distraction for her to escape.

Of course, if the dagger didn't work, she had another option, but it would cost her dearly, and she preferred not to lose any more of herself. She ran a hand over her bald patch and then flexed her fingers and smirked. He would pay for sticking his hand in her mouth, for getting so close to her. For leering. The last person to look at her in such a way had suffered the consequences.

But then, so did she.

CHAPTER 8

SARA DANCED AROUND the puddle of water near her bed, bouncing on her bare feet like a boxer preparing to fight. She cracked her neck and paused beside the door.

Her whole body taut and listening, she heard the faint ringing of a bell. The sound faded, and then the unmistakable squeak of Brad's footsteps echoed in the hallway, growing louder and louder until they halted.

She pressed her back against the wall, hiding from the view of the window. The doorknob turned, then stopped. Her breathing tight and shallow, she shook her head to clear away the dizziness already descending on her from the medication. The paper dagger softened and warped under her sweaty grip as her hands burned with anticipation.

The door clicked open, and Brad stepped into the room.

Sara grabbed the knob and snapped the door back into him, prepared to do it again and again until he dropped to the floor, but he easily overpowered her and shoved the door into her face. Her nose popped and a wet warmth instantly flowed down her lips and chin, the metallic taste of blood seeping into her mouth.

Brad snarled, pushed the door wider, and entered the room.

With a deep-throated yell, she launched at him, aiming the

dagger at his eye. He ducked and grabbed her arm, forcing her off balance, and then threw her back.

She skidded in the water and fell onto the bed, smacking her head against the metal frame. Her vision clouded, and she dropped the crumpled weapon. Fighting to remain conscious, she gulped down air and listened.

She didn't have to see him to know where he was. Remaining limp on the bed, she waited until his heavy breathing and sweaty bulk were almost on top of her before she kicked out with both feet and caught him in the chest and neck.

He reared back and slipped in the puddle of water. A heavy crash shook the room, followed by a sickening thud as his head bounced off the linoleum floor.

Pushing herself up, she scanned the room. Brad lay on the floor, face up and motionless. She lunged for the door, her blurry vision making her scramble to find the knob, but it was locked.

Brad grunted, his key ring clicking on the floor.

Determined to free herself, Sara sprang to him and grabbed the metal keys attached to the waist of his light-blue scrubs.

His eyes opened, revealing large and unfocused pupils, while his arms swept the floor as if swimming in slow motion.

Locking her gaze on him, Sara pulled the ring free, ripping the loop on his pants, and backed up to the door. She narrowed her eyes at him, the keys hissing against the hot energy gathering in her hands.

Brad jerked with a guttural gasp and pawed at his neck, choking as foamy mucus gathered at the corners of his mouth.

She stared at him with a hard smile. He deserved to suffer, to choke until he died. Just like Isabell's uncle—the man who tried to touch her at that sleepover so long ago.

The man she murdered.

Sara cursed and tore her gaze from Brad. Though she wanted to kill him, she didn't want another death weighing on her soul.

Spitting blood, she turned her attention toward the door and tried one key after another. On her third try, something cold and clammy seized her ankle—Brad had crawled to her, his grip as weak as a wet noodle. She kicked free of him and turned the key.

Click. Sara sighed and opened the door.

After slipping into the vacant hallway, she pulled the door closed behind her until the lock slid into place. Glancing back through the window, she grinned at Brad vomiting on the floor. The only remorse she felt was for leaving the stuffed dog behind.

From her bathroom breaks, Sara knew a dead end lay to the left. She turned right and stared down the hall at a set of double doors, beyond which came the faint ding of a bell.

She clutched the keys with one hand and wiped her nose with the other, smearing blood along her face and forearm. The floor tilted violently, forcing her to walk with her legs spread apart like a drunken pirate.

She stumbled down the hall until she reached the double doors with wire mesh windows and a panic bar. *Please be unlocked. And don't lead to more orderlies.* Peering through the glass, she spied a familiar carpeted hallway lined with wooden doors. *Naomi.*

Sara pressed the panic bar, and it released. Another *click* to freedom.

Once in the carpeted hallway, the sound of the bell grew louder and was joined by the voices of two men. When the door closed behind her, the ringing stopped, and one of the men called out, "Hello? Hello!"

Sara panicked. The corridor to her right was another dead end. She sucked in a breath and rounded the corner to her left, toward the men, keys held out like a weapon. Before her was yet another long, carpeted hallway. At one end was a nursing station, the counter draped in red, white, and blue streamers. Two men stood beside the counter, staring at her.

"Sara!" shouted the shorter man, who had sandy blond hair and a faint goatee. The other man was younger, more boy than man, tall and lanky, with golden-brown skin and curly hair hanging almost to his eyes. He stared at her, wide-eyed and mouth agape. "Sara!" the shorter man shouted again, grabbing the boy's arm and rushing around the desk toward her.

She froze, partly because she knew she couldn't go back the way she came, but mostly because the man's voice sounded familiar. His shouting had stirred the hallway occupants, and door after door opened, curious faces peeking out. One door swung wide, and Naomi charged into the hallway. She almost collided with the men before joining them in a rush toward Sara.

The shorter one waved his arms and shouted, "It's me, Ted!" A plump nurse with a severe bob of gray hair skirted the desk station and yelled for security.

"We're leaving right now! Follow me," said the lanky boy to Sara, gesturing toward the end of the hallway. He wore white jeans and a gray T-shirt emblazoned with *Wicked Gamer* in red print. When he strode past her, he gave her a wary look, as if she were a feral animal.

Sara stared at him, skin tingling either from shock or the drugs.

"I'm coming with you," said Naomi. She grabbed Sara with one hand and with her other, waved a low one-sided handshake at Ted.

Eyes wide, Ted raised a hand and waved back. "Come on, then," he said with a quick snort of laughter. They ran after the lanky boy, down the hallway and through an emergency exit to a dark stairway with treads caked in dust. They thundered down the steps, Naomi keeping a firm grip on Sara to hold her steady. Behind them, Ted shouted to the boy—already an entire flight below them—"Ian, get the truck!"

Sara jerked her head, peering down through the stair rail at the mop of curly hair bounding down the last flight. She knew that name. But this wasn't a sick little boy. Ian appeared healthy and close to her own age.

She slipped on a stair, her head banging into the wall. Brad's keys fell out of her grasp and clattered to the landing below.

A loud crack echoed through the stairway as Ian threw open the ground-level door.

Sara winced, expecting to see daylight for the first time in weeks, but the door opened to darkness, like a portal to another world. She stumbled down the remaining stairs, partially carried by Naomi. Ted launched himself in front of them and held open the door while angry voices shouted after them from the top of the stairway.

Once outside, Sara raised her chin to the night sky and sucked in fresh air. By the time Naomi led her around a bush and over a curb, a red truck roared up, tires crunching and spitting loose gravel before coming to a sharp stop in front of them. Naomi yanked open a door, pushing Sara and herself into the back seat. Ted jumped in front, and the truck took off.

Ian flicked off the headlights as he tore out of the parking lot. After a glance over his shoulder at Sara and Naomi in the back seat, he pursed his lips and shot a concerned look at Ted.

Naomi laughed, a deep-throated chuckle, but stopped when they passed a streetlight and she caught sight of Sara's face. "Here now, let's take a look at you." She took Sara's head in her hands and turned her face back and forth. Still in shock, Sara didn't flinch at her touch. "Hmm, seems like your nose is busted, but don't worry, you're still plenty pretty." Naomi smiled and moved her hands to the back of Sara's head, her fingers feeling for lumps where she'd hit the wall.

Nauseous and dizzy, Sara leaned into her hands. Naomi gripped her hair to hold her head up, but one hand gave way as a clump of hair fell out, and Sara collapsed into her lap.

"What the Mother," breathed Naomi, the words grazing Sara's ears before floating away.

A loud *boom* jolted Sara awake. For a terrifying moment, she thought she was back in the stale isolation room. But then soothing voices filtered into her consciousness. Her head rested on something soft and warm. She remained still, eyes closed and mind reeling to place where she was. In a car—no—a truck, with her head on Naomi's lap.

Her initial panic subsiding, she listened to Naomi's husky voice. "—barely got out in time. I was on my way to your forest when Takers surprised me. I got away, but the police picked me up and brought me to the mental facility. It was a couple of months before Sara showed up." She paused before adding, "You sure she doesn't know anything? 'Cause when I saw her, I knew she was gifted. I tried to help, but they took her away. I haven't seen her for a few weeks. Until tonight."

Sara jerked. She had been in that hellhole for weeks? Her mom gone and her dad in the hospital . . . for *weeks*? Feeling Naomi's gaze, she decided it best to open her eyes. Eavesdropping only stirred up questions, and she already had too many churning in her mind. Besides, Naomi's talk of "*Takers*" and "*gifted*" sounded completely crazy.

Another *boom*, this time followed by a rapid crackling. She jerked again, eyes wide open.

Naomi helped her up and pointed out the window. "Fireworks," she said. Sara stared at the sky, unsure if she was dreaming or physically inside a stranger's truck, going somewhere she didn't know, under a sky filled with sparkling fireworks. She sat back and fumbled for the seatbelt. Dream or not, she needed the security.

"That's the nearby town celebrating July Fourth. The border to our forest is down the road, past these fields," said Ted. He turned to Sara, his kind, concerned expression similar to her father's.

"Where's my mom and dad?" she blurted, her words slurred by sedatives. Maybe the hospital had been wrong; maybe both her parents were fine. Maybe Ted and Ian were taking her to them right now.

Ian clicked on the headlights and readjusted his tight grip on the steering wheel.

Ted sighed, then said in a low voice, "I'm sorry, Sara, but Eliza . . . your mom died in the car accident. Your dad is still recovering at the hospital."

Sara's chest constricted, and her entire body grew cold. She blinked at Ted. Through the darkness, she knew he was telling the truth by the anguish on his face.

"We need to go back for my dad. We can't leave him in—" She broke off, her voice tight with panic at the thought of him suffering as she had.

Ted maintained his calm expression and held her gaze. "Your dad is not at the mental facility. He's in a medically induced coma at a nearby hospital. The doctors are doing everything they can to heal his internal injuries and get him well enough to be released to our care."

Sara clutched her seat to steady herself and keep from retching inside the truck. Either the sedative or the hit to her head, or likely both, were making her dizzy again.

"Hang in there, kiddo. We're almost home, and we'll get you cleaned up and feeling better soon," said Ted. "Then we can see about a visit to your dad."

He turned to Naomi. "You okay meeting with the others tonight? I'm afraid your story can't wait, given all that's going on around here."

She nodded in agreement, her mouth opening, when Ian interrupted.

"Takers ahead!" He slammed the brakes, swerving to avoid a van in the middle of the road. A monstrous-sized man wearing a stone pendant jumped from the stopped vehicle and rushed toward them.

Ian hit the gas, and the truck lurched from the road and into the field. The truck swayed back and forth upon impact, tossing them about the truck cabin. Sara hit the door before Naomi pulled her to her side. Ian floored the gas again, and they roared across the field, tall grass scraping against the doors.

"We need to make it to the wall," said Ian, his voice calm even as he jostled about, gripping the wheel. "I hope they're ready for this," he said with a glance at Ted.

Another *boom* sounded, this time directly overhead. Sara pushed away from Naomi and pressed her face against the cool window just as the sky flashed white and a crack of lightning hit the field ahead of them. In that moment, she glimpsed the gathering black cloud above, tendrils curling. Beckoning her.

Panic and guilt squeezed Sara. She put them all at risk. Now was not the time to face her mother's killer. Not when the drugs in her system smothered her rage with the sharp, bitter taste of helpless fear.

Ian swerved away from the lightning strike, catching a tire on a boulder. He floored the gas, but the engine whined in protest, wheels spinning and sinking the truck into soft soil.

"Run for the wall!" Ted yelled. He swung open his door and whipped his gaze toward the road. "They're coming!"

Naomi released Sara's seatbelt buckle and kicked open her door. They tumbled out the back, landing beside Ted, as Ian bolted to them.

"There're too many to fight. Just make it over the wall, and you'll be safe," said Ian, pointing at a low stone wall and house at the far end of the field.

The black cloud roiled overhead as hulking figures ran toward them, the grass trembling in their wake.

Sara froze, unsure what was more terrifying: the gaunt-faced man who controlled the black cloud or the things running straight toward her. Normal men couldn't move that fast—this was something else, some kind of beast capable of lunging through tall grass with preternatural speed.

"Come on!" Ian yelled, wide-eyed. He and Ted turned and sprinted for the wall.

Naomi pulled Sara's hand, and they took off together, thick blades of grass cutting into their legs and hands. Without shoes, they stumbled on rocks and clumps of mud. Their attackers getting closer, Sara dropped Naomi's hand to run faster. She was close enough to the wall to see people waiting on the other side but not close enough to outrun what sounded like an animal the size of a bison barreling toward her. It was nearly on top of her when a high-pitched whistle cut through the air. An arrow screamed past her and thunked into the beast, whose guttural roar ripped into the night.

Whipping her head around, she spotted Naomi in her pale gown near the safety of the wall. Ted and Ian were gone. Sara grunted with effort to force her stony legs to move. But they buckled, and she stumbled. Her chest burned as she gulped at the cool summer night.

Another rumble tore from the dark sky above. The air pressure dropped, pulling the black cloud and its gloomy coldness into the field. A sharp chill raked its icy talons across Sara's skin.

Another arrow screamed past, this one so close she saw the glint of its pointed head. She grabbed her thigh and thrust her heavy leg forward, determined to make it to the wall or die trying.

When she lunged again, her legs gave out completely. She toppled forward, smashing into a boulder, and collapsed onto the muddy ground.

Not. Like. This.

Pain radiated throughout her body. She glanced at her split knee and instantly regretted it. Gritting her teeth, she rolled onto her back and clutched her mud-covered hands to her chest. The snarling and panting of beasts grew closer while the black cloud pulsed overhead, as though laughing.

Tears ran down her face. She wanted her rage to consume her and destroy everything around her. But instead of fiery rage, fear held her in a death grip. She stared at the churning black mass, too terrified to even cry out as ice crystals cracked along her skin and her fingers stiffened with crippling cold.

All at once, the ground beneath her tilted, and the sky swirled. A sense of weightlessness washed over her. Fighting to remain conscious, she gasped against the crushing tightness in her lungs and felt the air about her tremble with a beast's approach.

A blur of white swept over her with a deadly snarl. All she could do was stare blankly while her hearing and vision faded to black. Just before unconsciousness fully claimed her, she felt herself being dragged.

Most likely, she thought, to hell.

CHAPTER 9

THE SCENT OF pine, so fresh it smelled like crushed nee-dles, roused her awareness. For a moment, she expected to hear a tent zipper and her mother's voice teasing her about sleeping in.

But something was wrong.

She couldn't move, couldn't joke with her mother in return. And her bones ached with a brutal chill far too cold for a cozy tent. To her horror, a pitiful whimper escaped her lips. Strong arms gently pulled her closer to a warm chest, and she noticed a hint of cinnamon mixed with the pine.

"Hang on, we're almost there," said a male voice, the tone calm and faintly familiar.

Struggling to place the voice and see who was holding her, she tried to open her eyes but found only darkness. Footsteps thun-dered in time with her heartbeat, painfully jostling her with each racing step. They clattered across a hard surface, and she whim-pered again.

"Bloody hell!" cursed a female voice as more footsteps stomped about.

The painful bouncing stopped, and Sara was laid onto some-thing soft. Two people immediately began tending to her wounds, clucking over her face and body. Warm hands clasped her icy fingers, driving out the cold, and the stabbing pain in her knee ceased.

"Can you fix her?" asked a separate male voice, anxious and also vaguely familiar.

"Of course we can," snapped a different female, the one who held her hands. The woman leaned over her, and the fresh scent of peppermint filled Sara's nose. "Mother Mary, how many were there?"

"At least a dozen," said the anxious male.

"Shit," hissed the peppermint woman.

"It was bad, Gran," said the pine-scented male. "A dark witch came."

Both women gasped. The warm hands shuddered. In a grave voice, she asked, "Was anyone else hurt?"

"Albert took a hit, but everyone else is fine." The anxious voice sighed.

The woman released Sara's hands and tenderly wiped her face with something warm and wet. Someone cocooned her with a soft blanket.

At the mention of a dark witch, images of the roiling black cloud flashed in Sara's mind. She fought to stay awake, to find the strength to open her eyes and ask all the questions pounding inside her. But she slipped in and out of consciousness, lulled by the murmur of conversation. She was just about to fall asleep when a thick snarl and loud footsteps cut through the calm.

"Well, that was a dramatic entrance," sneered a deep-throated voice.

"Thanks for being there," said the anxious male.

The deep voice huffed. "Didn't give me much choice, Ted." Silence. "Shit, Takers are one thing, but to have a dark witch at our door—Mother below!"

One of the women spoke, her voice close to Sara. "Is . . . is it still here?"

Heavy footsteps echoed as the angry male prowled the room, his deep voice trailing after him. "No. They all disappeared when she was dragged over the wall." More footsteps. "Matthew took Albert back to the island to recover. Sullivans are taking care of the bodies."

A husky female voice purred, "I got two with my crossbow."

The male stopped prowling and barked at her, "And you'll do better next time. Violet got three, including the one that hit Albert."

The female growled, but he dismissed her by continuing his rant. "Shit. We're damn lucky it wasn't worse." He paused. "This girl is causing us trouble already. You know how Kane and I feel about this."

Sara wanted to disappear, to sink into the soft surface she lay upon, pulling her guilt and shame with her like a shadowy cloak.

The woman sitting beside her sprang to her feet, placing herself between Sara and the angry male. "You do your job and patrol the wall. This girl," she said, "is my granddaughter—and she *deserves* to be here. Need I remind you we already had a few Takers and the blight *before* she came." Tense silence filled the air. "Perhaps she is the solution and not the problem."

The male waited a moment before responding, his voice sounding less gruff this time. "We'll see what happens at the Council meeting. They both need to be tested." He resumed his pacing. "And we have to be ready for another attack. Now would be a good time to put a break in the wall before they come back." His footsteps quickened and faded as he stalked off, putting an end to the discussion.

Grandmother? I don't have a grandmother.

Sara compelled her heavy eyelids to open a fraction, her vision blurry as she peered through her lashes. Near her head, a woman stood with her back to her. Relieved at not having a pair of eyes staring at her, Sara shifted her gaze across her chest. In the dim light of the room, she glimpsed lodge-style décor and stout furniture. Overhead extended a fluttering darkness, as if there was no proper ceiling. On the far side of the room, a man wearing jeans and a dark T-shirt, sleeves stretched taut over his biceps, strode through a massive archway and onto a moonlit deck. He broke into a run, his boots thundering on the wood planks, and leapt from the edge. In mid-air, he phased into a large gray wolf and vanished into the night.

Sara blamed her half-conscious mind for warping her sense of reality. But then a tall girl with flaming red hair followed, her bare feet silent on the deck until she launched and phased into a slim, russet wolf. Sara's eyes rolled back, and she passed out.

Silky darkness surrounded her. What she hoped was sweat dripped down the back of her neck. A rancid smell pinched her nose as she strained to hear anything. Silence. And then a deep-throated chuff blew across her face. She froze—every inch of her skin crawling with dread.

The darkness rumbled, reverberating through her chest before falling back into a heavy silence. Before her, a beast released another fetid breath, followed by the clacking of teeth. An icy wetness licked the full length of her arm, and the darkness rumbled again, as if laughing. It pissed her off enough to fight against her fear. She shook with sheer will to move her frozen body but stopped cold when a sudden flash of light revealed her surroundings. A massive bear reared up through billowing dark clouds, nose and lips pulled back from its open mouth, teeth as long as daggers about to sink into her neck—

Sara jolted and pitched upright, her eyes snapping open to the soft light of dawn. Gasping for air and slapping a hand to her neck, she scanned her surroundings. She was still in the lodge-style room. Through a multitude of gaping window and door openings, a light and airy breeze drifted across her cheek. Instead of structural beams, living trees grew through the floor and stretched into a cathedral ceiling of green leaves that stirred, as though the room opened to the sky. Before her, the wood floor flowed seamlessly through a vast archway and out onto the deck. To her right, a massive stone fireplace dominated one side of the room, its chimney extending through the vaulted ceiling of greenery. She kicked off the blanket and swung her feet onto the floor when someone to her left cleared their throat.

Wide-eyed, Sara stiffened and turned.

"It's alright. You're safe," said an older woman who sat in an adjacent oversized chair. Her voice was calm, and she smelled of peppermint. Surprise flitted across her face, but not the repulsion Sara's fathomless black eyes usually elicited. The woman's own eyes were steel blue and shone with a familiar cleverness as she held Sara's gaze. After a few heartbeats, she slid her gaze to Sara's neck. She smirked and nodded.

"I'm your grandmother. My name is Rosetta, but you can call me Gran." She picked up the quilting squares in her lap and placed them on an adjacent end table.

Sara grunted, her throat and mouth too dry to speak the questions bubbling inside her.

The woman plucked a coffee mug from the table and extended it to her. Sara took it and peered at the clear liquid inside. *Definitely not coffee and hopefully not poison.* A tentative sip rewarded her with a light, sweet flavor. Not juice, but something that tasted like a crisp spring day. Sara gulped it down, wiped her mouth with the back of her hand, and looked to find the woman, her grandmother, beaming at her.

"It's sap," she said, taking back the mug and setting it on the table.

Sara cleared her throat. "Grandmother? But . . . I don't understand . . . any of this." She craned her neck and spied a sizeable kitchen behind her, then peered around the woman's chair at another cluster of furniture. A slight gasp escaped her. Ted dozed in a recliner. Beside him, Ian slept sprawled out on a couch. Another male, mouth open and softly snoring, lay asleep on yet another couch.

A breeze swept over her skin and ruffled the leafy ceiling. Though there should have been a chill to the early morning air, the expansive room was surprisingly comfortable.

Sara shifted her attention to the archway and deck. Dawn light glimmered on multiple trees that grew through the wooden floor and shaded groups of patio tables and chairs. Beyond the inviting deck was a park-like common, backed by a thick forest.

Am I still dreaming? And if not—

She straightened and felt her nostrils flare. "Where's Naomi?"

"Sleeping upstairs." The woman lifted her chin toward a second-story balcony directly above them.

Sara let out a breath and looked down at her hands in her lap. Although her nails were ragged, dirt no longer caked them, and her wrists were free of ID bracelets. She frowned at the dirty hospital gown, then swept her hand over a bandage on her knee. Her frown deepened at the memory of falling—of paralyzing fear and brutal, icy darkness.

"Sorry you had to endure that hellhole of a . . ." The woman hesitated before spitting out, "Facility."

Sara tilted her head and curled her lip with a slight grin. For that comment alone, she decided she liked this woman. Her grandmother. Gran.

A morning birdsong floated into the main room while Gran continued in a softer voice. "Your dad, Charlie, is my son. We'll bring him home as soon as we can." She shifted in her seat, the chair groaning beneath her. "Your mother—"

"I know," interrupted Sara, not wanting to hear the words spoken aloud. She kept her gaze down, fingering the satin edge of the blue blanket.

"Eliza was very special to all of us. She was like a daughter to me even before she married Charlie."

Sara looked up at her grandmother, at the grief reflected in her eyes. "Why did they lie to me? Why am I here?" Her voice was a throaty whisper. She didn't want to wake the males sleeping nearby, and she wasn't entirely sure if she wanted honest answers.

Gran leaned forward in her chair, her expression changing from calm to a restrained fierceness. "Your parents made difficult decisions because they thought it was the only way to keep you safe—to keep *everyone* safe." She stole a glance at Ian, his arm shifting across his face. "But things have changed, haven't they?" She did not wait for an answer. "The safest place for you is here—in the woods." With a long sigh, she shook her head. "Gaa. Just keep an open mind and stay within the forest wall." She stood up, surprisingly quick for an older woman, putting an end to Sara's questions. "How about a hot shower and clean clothes before everyone wakes up?"

Afraid her voice would crack under a mess of emotions, Sara simply nodded, eager to be rid of the thin gown that exposed her. She pushed herself to the edge of the couch, expecting a hand up, but her grandmother was already by the stairs at the far side of the room.

Alrighty, then.

Through gritted teeth, she hauled herself up, anticipating pain from the bandaged knee she'd so gracefully smashed open the night before. She winced at pain that never came. Letting go of the couch, she tentatively stepped toward the stairway. Still no pain. She put more weight on her leg, bending her knee until the bandage crinkled. Nothing. She should have been covered in cuts and bruises from stumbling through the sharp grass. Her head should have been pounding from all the blows she'd suffered, her nose broken from her fight with Brad. But she felt fine—rested, even.

Distracted by her impossibly quick recovery, Sara jolted when Ian shifted on the couch. A shower and clean clothes became a priority. Crossing her arms over the front of the gown, she weaved through a maze of sturdy furniture. When she reached the wooden staircase, she stopped and gawked. Grandiose honey-brown steps cascaded before her. The fluid construction and perfect alignment of grain and knot patterns sang like fine artwork. Even the railing along the edge was a wonder. Instead of typical straight balusters, a web of branches supported a wide, graceful handrail that organically poured from the second-story balcony, flowed down the steps, and curled around a tall tree at the base of the stairs.

She touched the tree with her fingertips and glanced up the staircase. Eyeing her grandmother near the second level, she gripped the smooth rail and pulled herself up.

CHAPTER 10

AFTER A GLORIOUSLY long, hot shower, Sara found a comb and nail clippers waiting for her on the bathroom counter. She glanced at the locked door but decided she didn't care how they got there.

Wrapped in a fluffy white towel, she snipped her nails close to the quick before tugging knots from her hair. She paused to let her fingers inspect the back of her head. The consequence of attacking Brad had cropped up as a new bald spot—directly beside the patch marking her loss of control with the careless driver. She frowned and fervently resumed yanking out knots. By the time she was done, the condensation on the vanity mirror had completely evaporated.

Ignoring her pale reflection, she scooped up her filthy bandage and gown and shoved them into the bathroom's small trash can, pushing them all the way down. Her mouth twitched into a slight smile when they compacted with Naomi's gown, as if they both sought to bury the past.

The T-shirt and shorts Gran provided smelled of lavender and reminded Sara of her mother. Gran said they belonged to someone named Rebecca, who must have been a bit bigger than Sara because the shorts hung loosely on her waist. Her stomach growled. The need for food overcoming her wariness, she stepped out of the bathroom and into the second-story hallway. On her left was the balcony overlooking the main room. A gray blur of movement in the tree canopy ceiling snagged her attention. *Was that a squirrel?*

"Sara!" Naomi came up beside her and gave her a hug. Sara froze at the contact, and Naomi released her. "Are you okay?" Naomi's gaze lingered on the faint pink scar on Sara's knee.

"Crazy, isn't it?" said Sara, more to herself than Naomi, brushing her fingertips over the mark. She straightened, surprised to see another woman behind Naomi. This woman radiated confidence, her gray hair braided and arranged in a wreath around her head. She wore overalls dusted in flour and rested her hands on a wide set of hips.

She studied Sara up and down. "I see the poultice healed you up nicely." She sniffed and narrowed her eyes. "Hmm, seems Rosetta gave you something else too. Not surprising. Your grandmother does what she pleases." The woman shook her head and, before Sara could ask, stated, "She went to get some rest and will meet you later today."

The woman smiled, faint wrinkles feathering the outside corners of her hazel eyes. Her face shone in the morning light pouring through the open windows of the main room and onto the nearby balcony. "I'm Helen Cahill. My cousin, Larry, is your grandfather. So, forgive me if I consider you to be my granddaughter too." She leaned toward Sara and said in a lower voice, "Cahills are proud to be the largest family in this forest." She smiled broadly at Sara, then fixed her eyes on Naomi. "I trust you slept fine? Seems Rebecca's clothes fit you better than Sara."

Naomi grinned, patting her shorts. "It's nice to finally have clothes. Thank you for your hospitality."

Helen dismissed her formality with a wave of a hand. "Our pleasure. We rarely get outsiders, but when we do, we take care of them like our own. Our forest has plenty of accommodations, but you're welcome to stay here at the Main House if it suits you."

"Thank you," said Naomi, the apples of her cheeks swelling with her smile.

Behind Helen, the hallway stretched its rich wooden flooring, the polished surface glinting in the sunlight. The walls were adorned with quilts so expertly crafted, the space could have been an art gallery.

"Come along, I'll fix you both a nice big breakfast." Helen motioned toward the balcony and strode past them, the wide hallway easily accommodating her stout figure. Before heading down the stairs, she stopped and leaned her upper body over the railing, her gaze searching the area under the balcony.

"Morning, Helen," Ian's voice floated up from below.

"Ian, start up the oven, will ya. The girls are up, and I need to get going on making more biscuits."

Naomi chuckled and murmured, "Girl."

Sara glanced at her—Naomi appeared at least her mother's age, if not older.

As Helen lumbered down the staircase, Sara approached the balcony of entwined branches, some still green with leaves, and peered over. Directly below sat a kitchen island large enough to comfortably fit a dozen people. At one end, three people were perched on barstools: Ted, looking disheveled from a night in the recliner; a mountain of a man, wearing a T-shirt and overalls, his thick white hair aglow in the early sun as he sipped a coffee mug; and the male she'd heard snoring earlier, perhaps a few years older than Sara. The latter grabbed a mug from the island, his attention directed into the kitchen, and said, "Dude, relax. She'll be fine."

Sara stepped away from the edge, out of their view, and followed Helen and Naomi down the grand staircase. She made it halfway down before pausing to glance around the room. From her vantage point, and with the sun shining through the many windows and door openings, she beheld the vast floor plan in its entirety. With living trees functioning as structural beams, the architecture was more natural forest than fabricated building. Her jaw dropped at birds flitting in and out, their songs echoing through the room.

Helen descended the staircase and bustled over to the kitchen while Naomi stopped short at the base of the stairs and inhaled loudly. "Now *this* is a great room," she declared.

Near the middle of the room and partially under the second-story balcony, Ted turned to her from his seat at the kitchen island. His hair stuck up and his clothes were rumpled. "You're quite chipper for being up most of the night."

Sara reached the bottom of the staircase—keeping a firm hold on the loose elastic waist of her shorts—and arched a brow at Naomi.

Together they weaved through groups of couches, chairs, and tables. "This may not make any sense to you yet," Naomi said, "but I'm from another sacred forest. It was destroyed by Samson, the dark witch that attacked us last night." She sighed. "I was up half the night telling my story to their Council."

Sara frowned at her. Either Naomi should have stayed at the mental ward or Sara's entire world was about to turn upside down. *No. Naomi's delusional—probably trying to make sense of what happened. The gaunt-faced man controlling the black cloud and whatever those "Taker" things are is after me.*

Maybe he knows my secret.

She slowed her pace, a chill snaking up her spine. No one could know her secret. "You're right. I have no idea what you're talking about," she said in a flat tone with what she hoped was an innocent expression. Swallowing her guilt, she fought the urge to check her bald spot and instead smoothed her damp hair over her shoulders.

Naomi smirked and strode ahead to the kitchen island. Behind the counter, Ian greeted her with a coffee mug and a big smile, as if he had known Naomi all his life.

Sara wrinkled her nose, irritated by their ease. She still had no idea where the hell she was or who these people were. As if on cue, all three people sitting at the island slid off their chairs and turned to Sara. She sucked in a breath and flicked her gaze at Ted.

"Morning, Sara," he said, stifling a yawn. "Glad you're doing better." He nodded at her knee, and Sara shifted her weight to glance down at the faint pink scar.

She looked back at him but said nothing. Her cheeks heated with the unwanted attention.

The younger male to Ted's right wore jeans, a green T-shirt, cowboy boots, and a goofy grin. He wasn't tall and lanky like Ian but stocky with broad shoulders and a golden tan, like he worked outside all day. His sandy hair was tousled worse than Ted's.

The older man to Ted's left seemed a gentle giant, well over six feet tall—taller still with the heavy work boots he wore. He stood with his shoulders back, his head grazing the lower branch of an oak tree growing from one end of the kitchen island. He took a step toward Sara, arms extended, but paused when she stiffened.

Dropping his arms, he cleared his throat. "I'm Larry Cahill. Eliza's father." His tone sounded strained in a futile attempt to soften his booming voice. "Please call me Larry, everyone else does." He hooked his thumbs in the front straps of his overalls.

Sara lifted her chin, taking in his ruddy face lined by years of hard work. Her mother had been quite tall, taller than Sara's proud height of five feet, eight inches. She squinted and recognized him from an old photograph her mother hid in her nightstand.

"Everyone calls you *Uncle* Larry," said the one with the goofy smile, pointing at him with his coffee mug.

"She can call me whatever she wants, just not 'Grandpa.'" He stroked his white beard, his hands large enough to crush boulders, and winked at her. "I'm too young for that," he said. The goofy-grinned male howled with laughter, and from behind the kitchen island, Ian and Helen joined in. Uncle Larry jerked an elbow at him. "And this cocky bastard is Caleb Cahill, your cousin. Feel free to call him whatever you want. I promise you won't offend my delicate ears." His eyes twinkled, his whole face smiling.

"Caleb will be just fine," the male said. He put down his mug and squared his broad shoulders at Sara, sun glinting off golden flecks in his green eyes. "Well, this is awkward. Shaking your hand is too formal. I'd like to hug you, but I have the impression you might punch me, and there's the distinct possibility you may lose your shorts." He nodded at her hand, clutching the loose waistband of her borrowed clothes. "I have that effect on the ladies," he added with a wide smile, revealing a slight gap between his front teeth.

Ian snorted and choked on his coffee.

Caleb shot him an incredulous glance. "I get into town a lot more than you," he said, giving a smug nod.

Sara couldn't help the smile tugging at the corners of her mouth.

"You'll have to excuse Caleb. He has no filter," said Uncle Larry. He nudged Ted. "Ready to go?"

Ted gulped the rest of his coffee, slid the mug toward a wide farmhouse sink on the far side of the island, and rose from his barstool. He stepped around Sara and said, "We're off to get the truck out of the field. Ian will show you around today." Ted and Uncle Larry inclined their heads in farewell at the group and strode out the vast archway. Uncle Larry's boots thumped across the deck until they disappeared around the side of the lodge.

Naomi broke the silence. "This kitchen and building"—she waved a hand at the massive island, clusters of furniture, and living trees—"are amazing. How many of you are there?" She turned to Helen and began helping her place drinks on a tray.

"There are five main families. The Cahills are centrally located in the forest, so we usually gather here. We call it the Main House," said Helen, grabbing a pitcher of juice and a small bottle of green liquid from an industrial-style fridge. She placed the juice on the tray and handed the bottle to Ian. "Drink it before you have any more coffee," she said, like a doctor administering medicine.

"Helen is being modest. We gather wherever she cooks," said Ian. He popped the top and knocked back the green liquid in one swallow before placing the empty bottle in the sink. A fresh, pungent smell of cut grass and pine needles cut through the scent of baking biscuits.

Caleb sidled up to Sara and followed her gaze. "Ian and I used to take baths in that sink as babies," he drawled.

Ian shot him an indignant look. "Dude, she doesn't want to know that." He pushed his hair out of his eyes, glanced sheepishly at Sara, and came around the island.

Before Caleb could respond, Helen ordered him to grab the drink tray and insisted everyone head out to the deck. She waved them all off before turning to the oven and promising to bring along hot biscuits.

Sara trailed Ian and Caleb toward the deck but stopped just inside the threshold. Sunlight illuminated a tree that framed the open archway, beads of amber sap glistening along the trunk. Inhaling the fresh pine scent, she cupped her hands to catch the warm light, as if she could drink it. She hadn't felt sunlight in a long time. *Too long,* she thought with a grimace.

She chewed her lip, fighting the urge to pinch herself. *What else have I been missing for far too long?* This Main House and forest, the family she didn't know she had, were real and somehow familiar. Maybe her whole life up to this moment had been a dream—the anger and sadness, feeling different and alone . . . the accident, which changed everything. Maybe now she was waking up to what was real. Maybe now was how it always should have been.

Sara snapped out of her spiraling thoughts when Naomi stood beside her and took a loud, deliberate breath. Naomi held out her hands, palms up. "Sunshine and fresh air, how I missed you." Her husky voice rang out into the yard, scattering a few birds into the dense forest that lined the clearing.

Tilting her shoulders away from Naomi, Sara rolled her eyes

and then swept her gaze across the grass. Between the yard and the forest edge were clusters of buildings and homes; the open grassy area flowed between them like a common green. At the end of the expansive yard stood a large barn and what appeared to be a greenhouse of sorts with tree branches and greenery spilling out of its open doors and windows. Chickens scratched and pecked along one side of the barn, and distantly, a horse neighed. Off the other side of the barn grew gardens bursting with summer fruits and vegetables. Behind them, fields of hay and alfalfa rippled in a slight breeze. Similar to the grassy common, the fields and gardens were tightly hugged by thick forest growth.

Though the carved-out farmland was impressive, it was the common green that stole Sara's breath. In the center of the green stood an enormous tree. Its trunk was larger than a car and its towering height dwarfed the pines, birches, and maples that lined the clearing.

"Your forest is beautiful," breathed Naomi as Caleb set the tray of drinks on one of the deck's many tables. He stood in the shade of a tree growing through its center.

"Welcome to Ware Woods," said Caleb with a flourish of his hand.

Ware Woods.

Sara froze at the memory of her father's lighthearted chuckle and playful words—"*No Ware.*"

"You wanna sit outside?" asked Ian, approaching Sara carefully, as if she were a wild animal. His hands lightly tapped his legs before gesturing to the deck's assortment of tables and at least a dozen extra chairs.

Sara sensed apprehension and a touch of fear in his expression. Everything else about him suggested a vaguely familiar, easygoing nature.

She nodded, holding on to her shorts and stepping across the threshold. Choosing a chair near the edge of the deck, away from

Caleb and Naomi, she sank into the deep seat and crossed her ankles. The chairs were unlike any Sara had ever seen. They were all made from the same golden wood and had a smooth finish—the kind only achieved after hours of sanding and polishing by hand. Each piece of furniture was a unique design of intricately woven branches and roots, as if it had grown into becoming a chair. She ran her hands over the edge of the seat and traced the connected branches that formed the chair arms. The wood vibrated under her touch.

Ian handed her a glass of water, which she immediately drank after murmuring a soft, "Thanks."

He hauled over a chair and sat beside her. "I'm sorry about your mom."

She lowered the glass to her lap but didn't respond, preferring to stare at the tree in the center of the common instead.

"She was kinda my mom, too. Before she left, I mean."

Sara clenched her jaw at his awkward attempt to console her. He couldn't possibly have known her, never mind knowing her well enough to say such an absurdity.

He shifted his gaze and stared at the tree with her. After a prolonged silence, he cleared his throat and continued. "So . . . Uncle Larry is your grandfather—from your mom's side. Gran is from your dad's side. Ted is your uncle, and Caleb is technically your second cousin." He paused, his foot tapping the floor. "And I'm . . . your brother."

Sara turned her head and stared at him, her heart pounding. In a scratchy voice, she said, "That's impossible. I'm an only child."

He huffed a nervous laugh. "That's what I thought too. We have different mothers, but we share the same father—Charles Lochton."

"My last name is Harbour, not Lochton," said Sara, sounding more defensive than she intended. She set her empty glass on the deck beside her chair and scrutinized him, catching him running a hand through his floppy hair. The gesture stirred something in her. She flicked her gaze to a familiar cleft in his chin.

Could it be?

"I guess Harbour is the name Charlie and Eliza chose when they left Ware Woods," said Ian, blowing out a breath and scanning the common. "I wish Ted were here to explain. I only know what he told me a few weeks ago . . . after the accident. I didn't know anything before then. He said Charlie and Eliza wanted to tell us everything together."

Together. That was what her father said in the car. "*To tell them together.*" He meant her and Ian.

A flush of warmth spread over her, like she had been doused by a bucket full of adrenaline, hope, and longing. All her life she had known something wasn't right—and she'd always yearned for an explanation.

A jumble of puzzle pieces swirled inside her mind, smashing wildly in their haste to click together. This forest, this family, was the missing piece. The piece that possibly completed her.

She dug her fingernails into the chair. The murderous secret buried deep in her soul twisted and turned—a reminder that she was different and a danger to everyone around her.

Could I ever be complete? To be accepted and belong here, or anywhere, with what lurks inside me?

Do I even deserve such a thing?

CHAPTER 11

IAN'S REVELATION AND the very existence of Ware Woods—of a family and place of belonging—slammed into her.

A peculiar itch crept across her face, freezing her expression. Eyes open but unseeing, she retreated into herself, numb with shock. She no longer felt the chair under her or heard Ian beside her. Instead of sitting on the wooden deck, her mind projected her to stand before a giant oak tree. Slanted rays of sunlight streamed through its thick canopy and sparkled in the misty air. Long grass swished against her legs as she stared at the gnarled trunk. The tree called to her with a deep, resonant beat, a drum keeping time for the entire forest. Its canopy shook in her presence, causing dappled sunlight to dance around them. She reached for the tree, but the image shimmered and faded.

"Sara, can you hear me? Are you okay?"

A voice that sounded like her dad's tugged at her attention. She shook off the vision and regained her sight. Ian knelt before her chair, holding her shoulders and staring into her face. He was so close she could smell cinnamon and pine on him—the same scent that had pulled her away from certain death on the dark field and carried her to safety. Tears welled and threatened to spill down her cheeks.

"You're my brother," she said, a statement rather than a question.

Ian nodded.

And then—because he'd saved her, because she had to feel him to be sure this was real, because she'd lost her mother and felt she'd lost herself—she dropped her guard and leaned into him, gently wrapping her arms around his stiff shoulders. His hands loosely patted her sides when she tightened her embrace. She breathed in his fresh scent, her face pressed against his collarbone, and held him until his shoulders relaxed and he wrapped his arms around her, holding her just as tightly.

She wanted to hold him until childhood memories of what should have been came flooding back—of them laughing, playing, fighting, riding bikes, going to school together. Graduations and perfect photographs of a smiling family of four. She hoped for all of that so fiercely, it almost seemed real. Her nose started to run, and she huffed a laugh, shamelessly rubbing it on his shirt as she released her grip.

Ian fell back onto the deck, his face a wide smile. Not a trace of apprehension or fear remained.

"I have a brother," she sighed, and dared to rumple his curly hair.

"Now that's more like it," said Caleb from where he and Naomi had been watching from the center of the deck. He strode over, easily hauled Ian up and pushed him out of the way before grabbing Sara's wrist and pulling her out of the chair.

Shocked at his sudden movement, she could manage nothing more than to hold on to her shorts as he swung her around, roaring with laughter. He set her down with surprising gentleness and took a step back—just out of arm's length.

Instead of punching him, Sara surprised herself by laughing.

Helen stepped onto the deck, one hand balancing a plate full of buttered biscuits and the other holding a bowl of plump strawberries.

Caleb whipped around, a grin lighting up his eager face, and took the food. He set it next to the drinks on the large table and plopped into the closest seat.

"Okay now, let me get another good look at you," said Helen, wiping her hands on her overalls and eyeing Sara.

Sara straightened and faced her, relieved at the friendly glint in her gaze.

"Your knee is all better, yeah?"

"Yes," breathed Sara, bending her leg to show the faint scar on her knee. "How did you do that?"

"Pfft," said Helen, her hand waving off the question. "It was nothing. Don't worry, I'll teach you in due time. You too, Naomi." She glanced at Naomi, who nodded as she sat beside Caleb.

Helen turned back to Sara. "Well, you certainly have Eliza's slight build and wavy hair." She squinted. "Not sure where the dark eyes come from." Helen glanced from Ian to Sara. "But you both have your father's straight nose." She pulled her into a hug. Sara instinctively stiffened but then relaxed. "We knew you'd be back someday. We just wished your parents hadn't been stubborn and waited so long."

Sara leaned back from the embrace, away from Helen's matronly bosom and overall buckles, which pressed uncomfortably into her chest. "Oh, almost forgot!" Helen tugged a spoon and jam jar out of her front pocket and plunked them on the table. Sitting heavily beside Caleb, she gestured to Ian and Sara. "Sit and eat," she ordered.

"You don't have to tell me twice," said Caleb, grabbing a biscuit and splitting it open. He popped open the jar and heaped a spoonful of dark-purple jam into his biscuit. When he took a bite, jam oozed over the sides like a jelly doughnut.

Sara hiked up the waist of her shorts before sitting and grabbing a biscuit. She silently cursed to herself when butter dripped off her hand and left a greasy stain on the wood table.

"Don't worry about it," said Helen without glancing up.

"And let's get you some better-fitting clothes today. I believe Ted brought home everything from the accident. I'm sure you packed some clothes." And then, as if reading Sara's mind, added, "And shoes too."

Helen passed a glass of juice to Naomi. "You should see Becca today for more clothes and shoes as well."

"Becca's my mom," mumbled Caleb with a full mouth. "She's probably at home serving up breakfast to the littles before going to the gardens." He wiped jam from his chin and grabbed another biscuit.

"Manners, Caleb," Helen chastised, swatting his shoulder. "I know you were born in the barn, but we insist on proper etiquette in these woods. We're not savages, as some may think." She threw a wink at Sara.

After polishing off a second helping, Naomi glanced under the table and announced shoes were a priority.

"Of course," said Caleb. "Let's catch my mom before she leaves." He grabbed a fistful of berries before escorting Naomi toward a house near the barn. Similar to the Main House, the home was two stories with a stone chimney. Trees grew through the porch, their trunks functioning as support beams on the first level, while canopy branches formed balconies on the level above. An intricate branching trim along the roofline reminded Sara of icing on a gingerbread house.

Helen wiped her brow with a cloth napkin and stood. "Just leave all this when you're done." She gestured to the plate of food and drinks. As she headed back to the kitchen, she called over her shoulder. "Ian, after you help Sara with her clothes, don't forget to meet Gran at the lake."

Finding herself alone with her brother, Sara turned to him and glanced at his straight nose. *Indeed.* She huffed a laugh and flicked her gaze around the clearing. "Do you live in one of these houses too?" She wanted to ask him so many questions at once, to know all about him—and to avoid facing whatever Ted had brought back from the accident.

Her life was split now, defined by *before the accident* and *after the accident*. Seeing anything from before would mean it had all been tragically real. Her childhood, which now seemed like a lie, her anger and loneliness, her mother dead, and her father injured, lying alone in a hospital.

It would be easier to start over with no memories, with no consequences. She felt the two bald patches at the base of her scalp and knew she was not so lucky. She could never escape herself and the things she had done.

She shook off her gloom to find Ian narrowing his eyes at her, his forehead puckered between the brows as if he glimpsed the shit storm in her head. She cleared her throat and lowered her hand to her lap.

"Are you still hurt?" he asked, leaning over and looking at the back of her head.

She pulled her hair over her shoulders and tried to shift away from him, but she was too slow.

"What happened to your hair?" A bit of distress edged his tone. He tilted his head, studying her.

Sara flushed with panic. She wanted him to think she was the perfect sister, not a hideous one with secrets and dangerous faults. "I'm fine—it's n-nothing," she stuttered.

Ian angled his head more, eyebrows climbing.

She sighed. "It's happened before, but my hair grew back. I'm sure it'll grow back again." She forced a smile.

"This has happened before? And it grew back?" Definite distress marked his features.

He seemed overly concerned about her hair. Either he really was a caring brother, or somehow he knew why it fell out. And if he knew that, then he would know her secret too.

She swallowed hard. "Yeah. The color is lighter for some odd reason, but it grew back just fine."

"And it did that all by itself?" He stared at her so intently she thought he was reading her soul.

Sara dropped her gaze away from his golden eyes. "Well, my mom made me drink a bitter tea. She said it would help." She cleared her throat. "There's no tea now, but I can feel it growing back. It kinda hurts a little, like pins and needles sometimes."

"Huh," Ian grunted. Tapping his fingers on his chair, he glanced into the Main House at Helen bustling about the kitchen. "Strange. I'll have to ask Helen about the tea. Eliza was gifted when it came to potions. In fact, she's the one who figured out how to save me."

"Potions?" Sara never thought of her mother's teas and herbal concoctions as potions, but she supposed people who spoke of dark witches would prefer potion to tea. "Wait . . . save you?" She wondered from what, and she thought of her rage, of the monster inside her. If they were brother and sister, maybe Ian had a monster too. One her mother had cured with a potion.

Ian's laugh stopped her racing thoughts. "You have a lot to learn. Come on, let's start with getting your clothes, and I'll try to answer all your questions." He took her hands, squeezing her fingers while pulling her up from the chair.

Her shorts slid low around her hips, and she withdrew a hand to grab the waist. "Okay," she said, doubt lacing her agreement since he clearly ignored the question she had just asked. Instead of pressing him, she jerked her chin at the cluster of homes skirting the clearing. "So . . . do you live here?"

"Nah, this is all Cahill. They're the largest family in the forest and the only family to live near the middle. Most of us live on the perimeter." Ian jumped off the deck and walked toward the enormous tree in the center of the clearing.

"Most of you?" she said, taking the deck stairs and trying to keep up. "You mean the other four families?"

"Well, yeah—kinda."

"*Kinda*? Help me out here. Why do five families live in a secluded forest? Are you all hiding from something?"

"Kinda." He chuckled when she glared at him. "This forest—Ware Woods—is a sacred site, and we protect it. To help us, the forest gifts us special powers. For example, the Cahills are earth witches. Some Cahills, like Helen and Eliza, are great with potions. Caleb works magic with wood—he enjoys making furniture. The deck chairs? He did those. Others excel in the garden, which is good because we grow a lot of our own food. We try to be self-sufficient."

Sara stopped, her bare heels digging into the soft grass. At first, she thought he was joking, but he gave no sly smile, no burst of laughter. Ian's nonchalance indicated he told the truth with the same calm he might use to describe taking out the trash on Tuesdays.

Her mind spun. What he said seemed preposterous, and yet . . . after witnessing the cold, dark power of the gaunt-faced man, people who seemed to shift into wolves, and the healing magic of Helen's poultice, she knew it to be true. Perhaps she had always known magic to be real. As real as the monstrous rage she fought to control.

Sara held her breath, afraid and excited to tumble down a rabbit hole she might never come back from. "So . . . what are you?" she breathed.

"I'm a Lochton, same as you," he teased, flashing a lopsided grin over his shoulder.

She wanted to punch him, but he was too far ahead of her. She settled for a scowl. "No, I mean, what's your special . . . gift?" She hustled to keep up with his long strides.

Ian slowed his pace. "I'm empathic. I can read people. Their emotions, intentions, what they're thinking."

He turned to her. *"And I'm telepathic,"* his voice sounded in her head.

She stumbled and shot him a horrified look.

He hunched his shoulders and added, "But I don't intentionally read minds. That's rude. Most Lochtons are gifted with some form of mental skill." He stopped talking when they stepped into the shade of the tree.

"Seriously?" Sara halted, her hands gripping her shorts as her mind skipped about like a mouse with a head made of cheese. "What's my—*our* dad's gift?"

He shrugged. "I don't know for sure."

"What's Ted's?"

Ian rolled his shoulders and massaged his neck. "Ted can read minds too, kinetically move objects, and"—he shrugged—"a few other things."

Sara knew he was holding back details, but she couldn't stop from asking her next question. "What about me? Do I have a gift?"

He stared directly into her eyes, startling her with his sudden intensity. "I don't know. Do you?"

She jerked back and averted her eyes from him, a dark thought making her skin break out in goosebumps. Her secret wasn't a gift; it was a terror she struggled to control. It was quite the opposite of a gift. Maybe it was punishment for *not* being where she belonged—in Ware Woods. Maybe now she could be fixed by some magical potion.

"Stop," said Ian. "Whatever it is you're doing, just stop. It's making my brain hurt."

Sara grimaced. "Don't read my mind."

He looked hurt at the accusation. "I'm not. You just have a lot of uncontrolled energy. Besides, there's nothing to think about. Our magic gifts don't work outside the forest wall, so you wouldn't have had any."

She cocked both hands on her hips. "If magic doesn't exist outside the wall, how did those *things* attack us last night?"

"Let me clarify," he said. "Our magic—good magic—stays inside the wall. Dark magic exists outside. Takers occasionally—"

The blood drained from her face. She looked away from Ian, her eyes wide with a sudden and terrible realization. An affirmation of her worst fear. *Dark magic.*

Ian broke off. "You okay?"

"Um, maybe." *Maybe not.* She couldn't breathe.

"Sorry. Am I going too fast?"

She shook her head, finally sucking in a ragged breath. "No, no. It's fine. You're fine."

He tilted his head again, obviously not believing anything about her was fine, but continued where he'd left off. "Anyway, they sometimes bother us. They're just 'normals' poisoned by black magic to serve a dark witch. Think of them as henchmen. Strong and dangerous, but usually too drugged on poison to be much of a threat. But a dark witch is someone we definitely don't want to tangle with. Ware Woods has rarely been bothered by one. Naomi thinks the witch from last night is following her, says his name is Samson."

Sara pursed her lips. He was wrong. Samson wasn't after Naomi. Sara knew he was hunting her.

Ian shifted beside her. "You're overthinking again."

"Right," she said, keeping her tone even to hide the terror clawing at her insides. She swallowed, pushing down her panic, and forced a smile at him.

He narrowed his eyes ever so slightly but then relaxed his face. "Don't worry," he said. "I'll help you with the whole overthinking bit. It'll save me from future headaches." He kept his eyes on her, grinning as he walked backward toward the massive tree trunk. "My turn to ask a question."

Determined not to make a mess of her situation, Sara locked her fear deep inside and trailed behind him, curious why he seemed to be luring her closer to the tree. She squinted at the dense canopy, failing to identify the species of what was possibly the largest tree she had ever seen.

He held out his hand. "Do you trust me?"

She froze. Except for her parents, she had never trusted anyone. And considering how her parents had lied to her about this secret forest and family, trusting them may have been a mistake. Trusting someone meant opening yourself to disappointment and rejection; it meant being vulnerable and dependent—two things Sara could not stand to be.

Ian wiggled his fingers. "You're doing it again," he said.

"Give me a minute," she countered with another scowl. To his credit, he waited patiently. Ian had been good to her, rescuing her from the mental facility and from Samson. And here she stood, not knowing exactly who she was or even how to trust herself. The only choice she had was to take his hand. "Fine," she sighed.

As soon as she touched him, Ian stepped back, and they were both pulled into the trunk by an unseen force. Her eyes grew wide as thick, shaggy bark wrapped around them so tightly, she wasn't certain if they were next to the tree or inside the tree, standing or floating. All she saw was static gray. She could feel Ian's hand, but she couldn't see him. A whooshing noise, like amplified blood flowing through veins, filled her ears. The sound so loud it was disorienting. A breeze, cold and warm all at once, brushed against her legs and tugged at her hair and shirt.

And then it ended, and they were under a different tree, in a different clearing, at the top of a small hill.

CHAPTER 12

SARA WOBBLED AND widened her stance, her toes digging into plush moss as she swept her gaze across the view. At the bottom of the hill, a path wound through clusters of bushes and a patch of tall grass before stopping at two houses. A large, square garden, oddly fallow for summer, lay between the two-story homes. The nearly identical buildings were simply constructed with dormer windows, a porch off the back, and what appeared to be detached garages. The house nearest to them was painted slate blue with white trim, while the other house was completely dark brown. From the viewpoint of the hill, Sara glimpsed green front yards bordered by a low wall and faded gray road.

Sara turned to the tree behind them, tugging Ian with her. "Sorry," she apologized, releasing her sweaty death grip on his hand. "What just happened? Did we time travel or something?" She tilted her head back and gaped at the perfectly straight trunk of a towering pine tree. An old ax marking in the shape of an arrow scarred the tree halfway up its trunk. Observing the tree's densely clustered needles, she recognized it as a white pine. Her mother would be proud.

Ian glanced toward the brown house before turning back to her. "The time is exactly the same. We just traveled from one part of the forest to another."

"Do all the trees do that?" She stepped closer to the pine, searching for a hidden outline of a doorway or, if she could see through it, back to the Cahill clearing. Stretching out her hand, she felt the air pull at her fingertips and heard the static hum of electricity.

Ian tugged her back by the shoulder. "If you get too close, you'll be sucked in. Which is probably not a good idea if you don't know where you want to go." He kept a firm grip on her until she took another step away from the tree. "Ware Woods has five soul trees. They connect to one another kinda like portals, but you need to visualize where you want to go. It's called looping," he explained. "Each family lives near one of the soul trees. This"—he gestured to the tree—"is the Lochton pine. The Cahill tree is a chestnut." He pushed his hair out of his eyes and gazed at the thick forest beyond. "Supposedly, there is another soul tree in the forest. Legend says it's a doorway to somewhere else, but we've never found it."

The back of Sara's neck tingled, and she whipped around just in time to see something run up the hill and launch itself at Ian, knocking him over. She gasped, fearing it was another attacker from the night before. Her eyes darted around for a large stick—anything she could use as a weapon. But there were only moss and pine needles within her reach, and without shoes she had no hope of outrunning it.

Her heart raced. Maybe she could grab Ian and pull them back through the tree to safety at the Cahills. Hearing him struggle, she turned around and froze—he was laughing and hugging the animal.

"Bailey girl! Did you miss me?" He laughed again, letting an excited yellow lab lick his entire face before holding her back. "Bailey, this is Sara." He stood and steered the dog in Sara's direction; he appeared to tense up as Bailey cautiously sniffed the air.

Sara, heart still beating rapidly, glanced at Ian and knew this was a test of sorts. Most animals were naturally drawn to her unless she was in a foul mood and raging uncontrollably—in which case, no animal or person dared approach her. Instead, they fled.

Despite taking a slow, deep breath to calm herself, her mind lurched into a torturous shuffling of thoughts: *I always wanted to have a dog of my own; Ian has one, but I don't. If Mom and Dad hadn't left the forest, I could've had a dog, or two or three. If they hadn't left, Mom would still be alive. I wonder how Murphy is now that I'm not there to protect him; I just wanted to teach the driver a lesson—*

Her thoughts came to an abrupt halt when Bailey knocked her down onto a carpet of moss and licked her face. Laughing, she put her hands up to stave off the kisses. "Okay, okay, calm down," she said with a chuckle. The dog obediently sat, tail wagging hard enough to move her entire body. Sara stood and ruffled the loose fur around the dog's shoulders. "Good girl."

Bailey barked, as if in agreement, and ran circles around Sara and Ian.

"I guess she likes me," said Sara, watching the dog take another victory lap around them before racing halfway down the hill and back again.

"I'll say," said Ian, his eyes wide. "She only acts that crazy for me, and sometimes when Helen gives her cheese." He laughed and gave Sara a nudge. "Relax, by the way. You're safe here. Nothing bad can cross the stone wall protecting Ware Woods."

"Wish you'd told me sooner." She punched him in the arm. Once again, Bailey ran halfway down the hill, stopped, and turned around to bark at them. "Looks like she wants us to follow her."

"She wants to take you home." Ian smiled, rubbing his arm where she'd punched him, and pointed at the brown house.

"Home?" The word echoed in her head and stabbed at her heart.

Her mother was gone and her father still lay recovering in a hospital. She could never return home to the little gray-and-white house on Green Brier Lane. Not to all those memories. Yet she wasn't sure if she should stay in this forest. She liked everyone—

her newfound family—and felt a sense of belonging. But it scared her. She was already getting attached and, with that connection, knew something was off. It was irritating, like a mosquito bite on a perfect summer day. Something in this forest wasn't right. And maybe, just maybe, *she* was the thing that was off. What if she was *not* supposed to be here?

"Yeah, home. Stop overthinking." He gestured for her to follow him down the hill.

Bailey ran to Sara, head-butting her legs until she ran after Ian. By the time Sara caught up to him, she could not stop running, her legs still weak from being confined in isolation. Ian grabbed her before she ran into a thick bush. "Thanks," she gasped, backing away from him. She waved her hand at the dozens of bushes, each one covered with green leaves and clusters of waxy, light green and purple berries. "Are these blueberry bushes?"

"Yeah," said Ian, petting Bailey at his side. "They should be ready soon. Braxton always lets us know when they're ripe. He's been stopping by almost every day lately to check on them."

Sara lightly squeezed a firm berry between her fingers. "Who's Braxton?"

"A bear." He turned and strode for the path snaking between the bushes, heading toward the brown house.

"Oh." A shiver ran through her as she recalled her nightmare. "Of course he is." It would be just her luck to finally feel a sense of belonging, only to be slaughtered by a bear. She paused, scanning for any sign of Braxton. Spotting nothing suspicious, her gaze settled on the slate blue house barely visible above the bushes. Its peaked dormers looked like sad eyes, which seemed at odds with the lush surroundings and sweet scent of ripening blueberries. She plucked a berry, rolling it between her fingers as she followed Ian along the path, carefully picking her way to avoid rocks and sticks. Bailey stopped running around bushes and scaring birds to trot patiently beside her.

"So, what was it like living on the outside?" Ian asked, failing to conceal a hint of wistfulness.

Sara flung the berry and frowned at the question that seemed to imply he was a prisoner of Ware Woods. Maybe he meant to ask what it was like to live with a mom and dad. "Well," she stalled, struggling to find the right words, "fine, I guess. Except for all the stupid and cruel people. You certainly haven't missed anything."

Ian snorted.

"You can leave the forest, right? I know you and Ted came to get me, but can everyone here leave anytime they want?" Sara's tone revealed a bit of panic. After all, her parents had left for a reason, and she still didn't know what that reason was.

"We can leave, but without our powers, we need to be careful," said Ian. He opened his mouth again but snapped it shut and continued walking along the path.

He didn't have to elaborate. She knew they were vulnerable without powers, and perhaps hunted by the things that attacked last night. She chewed on this as the path ended at a tall patch of grass.

A faint wind stirred the air, causing the grass to ripple. The thick blades stood taller than Ian, who Sara figured was just over six feet tall. As he approached, the grass parted like a curtain and he stepped into the opening. Bailey gave a high, excited bark and went after him, the grass closing in after her wagging tail.

Sara hesitated, remembering the stinging cuts she received the last time she went through grass. But when she approached, it pulled back and let her enter unscathed to follow a narrow path through the mounding clumps. It was calm inside the sea of grass— the only sound a hushed rustle of leaves, their spiked tops waving against the pale sky.

"Watch your step on the way out." Ian's voice cut through the mesmerizing greenery.

Sara glanced down just in time to see a wood plank partially sunk into a muddy ditch. The board yielded with a slight dip and dull thunk as she stepped across it and onto a grassy yard.

She wiped her feet on the lawn, ridding herself of the dirt and leaves she'd picked up along the path, while Bailey shot past, chasing a chipmunk. Near her towered a tree with bright green leaves and a blue swing hanging from one of its branches. Across the yard, a patio wound between the back porch and detached garage. On the far side of the garage, an extended overhang protected a stacked pile of wood, the logs nearly the same rich brown as the building.

Sighing at the softness beneath her feet, Sara followed Ian toward the back porch, where a whirligig rhythmically clicked in the breeze. As they approached the house, she gazed down the empty driveway at the low stone wall that hedged the front yard. Instead of stopping at the drive, the wall gracefully dipped below it like thread stitched into fabric. Beyond the border, weeds grew through the cracked surface of the road.

Ian stopped and turned to her. "This is our house."

She couldn't help but flinch when he said "*our.*" It rubbed in the salty fact that she currently had no home. And there remained the distinct possibility he wouldn't be so welcoming if he knew what she had done—what she was capable of.

IAN GESTURED TO the brown house before dropping his hands to tap his sides. He stopped when Sara glanced at his nervous habit. On the rare occasion that her father—*their* father—was nervous, he had the same tic.

"After Charlie and Eliza left, Ted and Gran moved in to raise me. They used to live next door in the blue house." He nodded toward the empty garden and house beyond it. "After I finished school a few years ago, Gran moved in with the Cahills. Said she wanted to be closer to her BFF, Helen, but I think she wanted to give me and Ted some space."

"School? So, you do leave?"

"Only for the local high school. To be socialized." A shy grin turned up the corners of his mouth. "Most of our education is homeschooled."

Sara frowned at the mention of high school. The dull clicking of the whirligig filled the silence as Ian watched her. "Wait. How old are you?" she asked.

"Twenty."

She sucked in a breath. "We're barely two years apart in age. Why—how could Mom and Dad leave you?" Her voice cracked, a hot mix of sadness and anger bubbling up inside, her emotional roller coaster of a day threatening tears. Lots of them.

"I know," said Ian, sighing. "But they had their reasons." His gaze wandered down the driveway, and he shifted his weight. "My biological mother was Winona. She came from another sacred site. I don't remember her. I was still a baby when she and I were attacked outside the wall. She died, and I almost did too. But Eliza created a special medicine and saved me. Then she moved in with Charlie to help raise me and take care of us." He glanced at Sara and shook his head at her surprised expression. "Uncle Larry says it wasn't strange at all. Eliza and Charlie had always been close. She is the only mother I remember." Ian stared at his feet while he spoke, his voice so soft Sara could barely hear him. "He said she loved me as if I were her own."

"She did," whispered Sara, recalling the tenderness in her mother's voice when she had mentioned his name.

She stepped in front of him to catch his eye. "So, I'm guessing my parents fell in love." Sara huffed a breath—she didn't know her parents as well as she thought she did. "But why did they leave?"

Ian turned away, refusing to meet her gaze. "They left because— because they thought it was the best thing to do. And they couldn't take me because my medicine comes from the Lochton pine."

Sara froze, understanding why he'd asked her about "*living on the outside*." He could never leave the forest, at least not for long. But maybe none of them could leave for long, not with dark witches like Samson out there.

Ian cleared his throat and started for the back porch. "After they get the truck, Ted and Uncle Larry plan to visit the hospital and check in on Charlie. Hopefully, he can be released soon," he said, clearly changing the subject.

Sara followed him up the back steps, her hand skimming the black metal railing, and hesitated. Overwhelming guilt washed over her. She'd let the accident happen by not stopping Samson. Her father's last words echoed in her head: "*Stop it!*" Would he even want to see her?

Ian tugged open the screen door and looked back at her, his face pinched in a painful expression. "I'm sure Charlie will be okay," he said in a reassuring voice.

Sara shivered in the sunlight, wishing she could shake off the guilt. "Yeah, I'm sure he'll be fine." Then she added, "Don't you lock your doors around here?" as the screen door banged shut behind them. *Two can play at changing the subject.*

Ian walked across the enclosed porch—which, judging by all the coats and shoes, seemed more of a mud room—and into a small blue-tiled kitchen. "We never lock doors around here. No one ever visits, except the occasional outsider from another sacred forest. When our grandfather was here, he wanted the paper delivered, but none of the town kids dared get this close to Ware Woods. Ted and I have tried to order pizza, but they claim we're not in the delivery area. Even getting utilities installed was a challenge." He shrugged and leaned against the counter.

A soft clattering rang across the floor, followed by Bailey crunching on dry dog food. Sara stepped past an impressive coat rack to join Ian. A diner-style table with matching blue pleather chairs partially blocked the entry into the spotless kitchen. Sunlight filtered through thin curtains, spilling across the floor. The stove appeared brand new, and the shiny countertops were bare except for an old-fashioned toaster and an elaborate coffee machine, complete with a frother.

"Why wouldn't anyone want to visit? Looks like you could serve some serious coffee." Sara stepped closer to inspect the curious machine.

"Ted made that." Ian patted the top of the coffee maker. "It can pretty much make anything. Do you want an espresso or something?"

"No thanks." Sara turned away from the machine. What she wanted was more information. "Back at the Cahills, you said I have a lot to learn. So, tell me—why doesn't anyone want to visit?" She needed to know what she had gotten herself into. She crossed her arms and waited, expecting Ian's answer to burst her bubble by telling her the forest was, in fact, one of the seven layers of hell, and she was exactly where she was meant to be.

"Right." Ian pointed to the ceiling and then nervously shook out his hands. "Okay, I'll start at the beginning." He nodded at her, seemingly more for his approval than hers. "Long ago, some people noticed how special this forest land is, its energy and abundance. They were the Cahill, Atwell, Walker, and Sullivan families who lived in this area. A few"—he hesitated, studying her face—"powerful women also lived here."

Sara's unchanged expression seemed to irritate him. He cleared his throat and resumed his story, one foot softly tapping the tile floor. "The families and the women lived in mutual respect, but the townspeople feared the women and tried to make them leave. Their fear spread to the surrounding villages. After many failed attempts to drive the women away, the people decided to flood them out by damming the river." Ian frowned and shook his head. "Their plan drove a lot of innocent people out of their homes. They *justified* their decision by claiming the growing parish needed a reservoir for drinking water."

Bailey finished eating and shook herself, ears flapping loudly. The dog trotted into the adjacent living room and flopped on the Berber carpet. Ian followed her and sat on a small sofa while Sara pulled up an upholstered stool and faced him, waiting for him to continue.

"Even with the threat of flooding, the families refused to leave. They knew this land was special, so they banded together with the women to protect it from being destroyed. But they were greatly outnumbered when gangs of angry, foolish men invaded the forest. They set fires and cut down trees, including an ancient soul tree. And the river—it surged, wiping out part of the forest. Two Atwell children drowned, and one of the Cahills died trying to put out a fire." Ian looked at Bailey sitting beside him and stroked her ears. "They say the townspeople and villagers were laughing." His jaw clenched. The ticking of a grandfather clock filled the room.

"But then . . . something happened, and the flooding stopped. Rain put out the fires, and the stone wall border appeared as if it grew out of the ground. The townspeople and villagers were scared and ran. They said the land was cursed and then turned their backs on the destruction they caused." Ian glanced at Sara, his eyes glistening with emotion.

"One of the powerful women died. Her name was Mary. They say the trees wept real tears that day." He shifted on the sofa. "No one knows exactly how it happened, but when the families and the forest grieved for one another, their energies became entwined. A powerful magic bound them and blessed the families with special gifts. Gifts to help them continue to protect the land and themselves from future dangers."

"A symbiotic relationship," whispered Sara, her knuckles white from gripping the stool's edge.

"Right," said Ian. "Over the years, we learned to master our gifts, keeping them secret while coexisting with locals. They leave us alone, and we pretty much stick to ourselves. We take care of the lake and help them with regional wildlife and conservation. Local people respect our work, but they are leery of us and absolutely terrified of the forest. They think it's haunted and cursed."

Sara dragged her gaze to the window behind him. Through the thin curtains, she could see the grassy front yard and the stone wall.

Ian rubbed his face and then settled his gaze on the floor near Sara's bare feet. "You still need your clothes. Come on, Ted put everything in his room." He unfolded himself from the sofa and motioned for her to follow him.

Furniture cramped the small living room, forcing them to navigate between an oversized recliner and a floor-to-ceiling bookcase. As she and Ian squeezed by, Bailey pushed beside them, bumping into the lower shelves. The bookcase creaked and jerked forward, the many books packing the shelves sliding toward them.

Ian grabbed the closest shelf. But it was no use—the bookcase was too heavy. Dozens of books fell forward, two bouncing off Bailey before thumping to the floor. Her high-pitched yelp caused Ian to shudder, his hold slipping.

Sara's instinct to protect flared white hot. Her hands tingled and burned as she reflexively reached out, shutting her eyes against the crashing chaos. The noise instantly stopped, and a silence hung in the room; even the grandfather clock ceased to tick.

"Sara, look!" Ian's shout broke the quiet.

His urgent tone made her wince. She did not want to see whatever she had done. An image of Bailey crushed by books, followed by one of Ian pinned under the case, flashed in her mind.

Ian gently touched her shoulder.

She opened her eyes—most of the bookcase's belongings were suspended in mid-air. Bailey gave a soft bark, her fur brushing Sara's legs as she trotted to the far side of the room and barked again from a safe distance.

"Did you know you could do this?" said Ian, his golden eyes fixed intensely on her.

She turned away, and his hand fell from her shoulder. Out of habit, she touched the back of her neck and lightly traced her bald spots to see if they had grown larger. The tilted bookcase came alive with a high-pitched splintering crack, like breaking ice.

"Sara, stop it," shouted Ian, grabbing a large tome with a gilded cover from the air. She went rigid with panic—remembering the expression on her father's face when he said those very words. The case groaned again, and a massive hardcover book bounced close to her bare feet.

Ian's voice sounded in her head. *Just push it back.* His calm tone soothed her fear.

She closed her eyes and tried to relax. Her hands tingling, she reached out and imagined a bright light pushing back the case and aligning the books onto the shelves.

"Look," said Ian in her mind.

She opened her eyes, stunned to see the case upright, everything back in its place, save for one paperback on the floor and the gilded book Ian still held in his hand. Her legs too weak to stand, Sara crumpled to the floor and reached for the paperback. Her hands trembled from both the effort and guilt of tapping into her monster.

"Hey," he said, getting down on a knee and taking the book from her. "That was amazing." His eyes were wide, his face a big goofy grin. Sara glimpsed what he must have looked like as a little boy. "We rarely have such controlled powers until we drink the Council tree sap."

She exhaled the breath she had been holding, relieved Ian didn't fear or hate her. Clearly, he hadn't considered what else she was capable of. At least not yet.

"Kinetic powers are the Sullivans' specialty." Ian's smile turned to a slight frown. "But you're Lochton and Cahill." Brow furrowed, he placed the books back on the shelving. "No matter, just glad we didn't get squished." He shrugged it off and stood, extending a hand to Sara. "You good, Bailey girl?" He grinned at the dog, who had rolled over to scratch her back on the carpet, all four paws in the air, tongue lolling from her open mouth.

Sara stood on her own, avoiding Ian's hand so he wouldn't feel the tingling heat that lingered on her palm, and tried to copy his nonchalant demeanor.

"Right, then," he said, dropping his hand and turning into a narrow hallway. "Here are the bags we recovered. I think we got everything." He ushered her across the hall and into a bedroom. "Take as much time as you need to go through everything and change," he said, starting to close the door.

"No! Leave it open," she said, lunging for the door. She could practically smell the stale antiseptic of the dismal mental facility.

Surprise and then understanding flitted across his face. "Of course." He swung the door wide open. "I'll be upstairs getting cleaned up myself. Spent all night on a couch with Caleb snoring next to me." He laughed and walked off. "Holler if you need anything," he called over his shoulder.

CHAPTER 14

Sara leaned against the first proper bed she had seen in weeks and ran a hand across the quilted cover, her fingertips grazing the intricately stitched pieces. Though crowded with furniture, Ted's room was bright and welcoming, with four open windows facing the back and side yards. Thin white curtains, matching those in the living room, framed the windows and ruffled slightly in a gentle breeze. On the far side of the room stood a dresser and an end table. In a corner, by the windows, was a large desk covered with neatly stacked papers.

Centered behind the workspace hung a framed photo of Ted running behind a boy on a bicycle, a wide smile plastered on his face. Sara approached the desk and peered at the photo. The boy was Ian, and he was laughing, his floppy hair blown back by the speed of the bicycle. She pressed a finger to the image, which was nearly identical to the photo her father had in his home office on Green Brier Lane. But in that picture, it was her rather than Ian smiling.

Sara ached to see her father, to ask him all the questions twisting in her head, to let him explain, to hug him tight. But his last words still echoed in her heart. Even if he could forgive her for not stopping the accident, Sara could never forgive herself.

She stepped back and bumped into a bench at the base of the bed.

Two black duffel bags, unzipped and slightly open, sat on the end of the bench, waiting for her. Beside them rested her mother's brightly colored floral bag, the padded handles crossed on top like folded arms.

She sucked in a breath, parted the handles, and unzipped the bag. Her mother's lavender perfume drifted up, kissing the surrounding air. Her lower lip trembled as her throat tightened and tears dripped onto her mother's belongings. Pulling a purple flannel shirt from the bag, she clutched it in both hands and pressed it to her face. The last time she saw this shirt, her mother was alive, smiling in the morning sun while she picked herbs from the garden and waved her mug of tea at Sara.

"Oh, Mom," Sara moaned. "I'm so sorry." She perched on the edge of the bed, one hand on her mother's bag and the other wiping her tears away with the soft flannel.

Dragging the shirt down her face, she stopped mid-sob when movement in the backyard caught her eye.

What appeared to be a white ghost emerged from the tall grass and moved toward the back porch. Blinking back tears, she focused on the image. It wasn't an apparition but a real girl, quite slender with long blonde hair and wearing a pale sundress. Though she was the size of a child, she calmly carried herself with mature confidence.

Sara stiffened, hoping the girl hadn't heard her crying through the open windows. Now was not the time to open the basement of self-pity. She put her mother's shirt aside, took a deep breath, and pulled back the flaps of one of the black duffels.

It was her father's bag. The sight and smell of his belongings instantly made her homesick.

A pleasant, "Hello," at the back door interrupted her thoughts of home. Sara paused, considering closing the bedroom door when footsteps clamored down a flight of stairs. Muffled conversation between Ian and the girl drifted from the kitchen.

Sara sighed and moved on to the next bag, the one she'd hastily packed before her entire world changed. She grabbed a pair of cut-off denim shorts, an old science museum T-shirt, underclothes, a ball of socks, and her canvas shoes. Hiding behind the bed and away from the view of the open windows, she let the oversized clothing fall off and slipped on her own comfortable clothes.

A chair scraped in the kitchen, and Ian's voice carried down the hall. Despite his hushed voice, she heard him mention her name and something about a path. Ears burning, she shoved the oversized clothes next to her duffel bag and made a mental note to return them to Caleb's mother. The thought squeezed her chest, and she ran a hand over her mother's floral bag. She zipped it closed and crossed the straps, leaving it exactly how she had found it. Grabbing the flannel shirt, she sniffed it once more before tying it around her waist. Curious to meet the girl and eager to interrupt their conversation about her, she took one last look at her mother's bag and left the room.

Bailey greeted her in the small hallway, her excited whine making Ian stop mid-sentence. As Sara entered the kitchen, he turned in his seat to face her.

"Nice shirt," he said with a nod.

She wasn't sure if he was referring to her faded green tee, which referenced the element dysprosium, or the flannel shirt around her waist. Before she could comment, the girl stood from her seat at the table. She was barely taller than Ian sitting down. Instead of approaching Sara, she stayed at the dining table and put a hand on his shoulder.

He smiled at her. "Sara, this is Lily Atwell. Her family lives at the lake."

The girl, whose skin matched the paleness of her hair, shone with a confidence suggesting she wasn't as young and frail as she appeared. She wore a yellow linen dress and had large gray eyes. Her pink, heart-shaped lips spread into a kind smile. "Hello, Sara. It's nice to meet you."

"Hi," said Sara, giving a short wave before dropping her eyes and sticking her hands in her pockets. She always felt uncomfortable meeting new people, never mind magical people. She hoped Ian hadn't told Lily about the bookcase. An explanation would likely tip them off that she was different, and not necessarily in a good way.

Lily dismissed the awkward introduction. "Ready to see the forest?" Her light and airy voice reminded Sara of an angel. Instead of waiting for a reply, she walked across the porch, a bounce in her step, and banged open the screen door.

Sara strode past the dining table while arching a brow at Ian. He grinned and tossed her an apple from the fruit bowl on the table before grabbing one for himself.

"Lily doesn't like apples," he said, holding open the screen door for Sara and Bailey. He let the door bounce shut as he jumped down the stairs after them.

Sara frowned and considered throwing her apple at his head for possibly reading her mind.

"Come on," he said with a playful nudge. "Even if that question wasn't on the tip of your tongue, I didn't want you to think I was a jerk for not offering her one."

She nudged him back, hard enough to make him stumble. Ahead of them, Lily burst out with a hearty laugh. Sara rubbed the apple on the front of her shirt and took a bite, juice dribbling down her chin. Not only did the apple taste good, it kept her mouth full enough to evade answering any questions about herself.

"We'll loop from the pine to the Council tree and then take a path to the lake," said Lily, leading the way.

Ian devoured his apple and chucked the core aside before they even left the backyard. He wore cargo shorts and another gray T-shirt, this one with an image of polyhedral dice. Gaining Lily's side, he started a light banter, the two moving with a rhythm like good friends—or even brother and sister, Sara thought with a twinge of jealousy.

She squinted at them. Or perhaps . . . there was something more.

Once they reached the pine, Ian turned to Bailey, then simply stared at her until she barked and took off back to the house. When Sara raised her eyebrows at him, he said, "I told her to go home. Come on." He grinned and held out his hand, wiggling his fingers at her.

She shot him a lighthearted frown and clasped his hand as they followed Lily. Sara closed her eyes, hoping she wouldn't get dizzy this time, and let Ian lead her into the static hum of the tree. Her heart raced and her skin prickled as a gentle wind pulled her in different directions. She held tight to Ian's hand and listened to what sounded like a crashing wave. After a few thunderous heartbeats, the roaring faded to silence, and Sara opened her eyes.

"I'm sure I'll get used to that someday," she said, dropping Ian's hand and rubbing her arms.

Lily turned to Sara with a smile. "You will. Once you visit all the soul trees, all you have to do is visualize where you want to go and *whoosh,* you're there."

Sara looked up as sparrows chirped, flitting among the branches overhead. Though this tree was shorter than the Lochton pine and Cahill chestnut, it had a multitude of low-hanging branches that were as thick as its trunk. Beside the tree stretched an enormous flat stump, creating a stage before a large clearing filled with wooden tables, chairs, and benches. A pair of squirrels chased each other among the furniture, stopping now and again to scratch in the soil.

She approached the stump and ran her fingertips over the furrowed edge. Hundreds of concentric rings undulated across the weathered top of the stage. "Is this the tree the villagers cut down?" she said with a glance at Ian. He nodded, jumping on top and striding to a shaded spot on the far side. She tilted her head at the tree they'd just emerged from. Its wide green leaves splayed open like a hand. "Maple?"

Memories of family camping trips whirled through her mind. Her parents patiently teaching her how to identify trees, distinguish wildlife signs and tracks, and recognize which plants were beneficial and which were poisonous. During one such trip, Sara woke to find her mother softly crying under a full moon. Her mother had wiped her tears and smiled, saying she wept for the beauty of nature. But now, Sara realized, her mother had wept for this forest—her home.

"Sugar maple," said Ian, pulling Sara back from her memories. "The Council meeting will be here in two days. You can meet most everyone then."

Sara imagined all the tables and chairs filled with people, people she didn't know, people who would stare at her. People who might know she was a monster. She shook her head and shivered in the warm air.

"Don't worry," said Lily, her light, soothing voice drifting to her. "Everyone's excited to meet you."

Sara glanced at the back of the stump stage, where Lily stood beside Ian in the shade. She thought of the man who had shifted into a wolf. He hadn't been excited about her—he had been angry. Not caring to think about meeting new people who possibly hated her, she resumed tracing the stump's furrowed rings and imagined how the ground must have shaken when the tree fell.

A curious breeze shifted her hair and rustled the leaves of the maple, stopping the overhead birds mid-song. Lily and Ian darted to the edge of the stage near Sara, their attention focused on the rear of the seating area.

Sara turned and followed their gaze, but saw nothing. What sounded like a gust of wind caused the bushes behind the seating to tremble. Ian shifted on the stage, his tension almost tangible in the quiet air. Sara held her breath, waiting.

She blinked, and a young man emerged from the forest's edge. He flashed a grin at her.

At the sight of him, her heart skipped a beat and her cheeks burned. Despite the warm summer day, he wore dark pants with a matching vest over a royal blue button-down shirt. Even from afar, she could see the richness of the fabrics and the tailored fit, complementing his lean waist and broad shoulders. His dark hair was styled with precision, as was his tightly groomed stubble of a beard. He held something at his side, but Sara couldn't look away from his eyes. Eyes as blue as his shirt. So brilliant they appeared to be shimmering with blue flames when the dappled sunlight touched his face.

She tilted her shoulders to ask Lily who he was but stopped short when he rushed in a blur of movement and stopped directly in front of her. The air stirred around him, smelling faintly of ash and musk, with a coy hint of honey. His height was similar to Ian's and his smile was confident. Too confident.

"You must be Sara. I'm Thomas." He spoke slowly, deliberately, his smooth voice deeper than she'd expected.

She stared, barely breathing and unable to respond, trying to process his striking appearance and how quickly he had moved.

In one swift motion, he leaned forward and took her hand, the calluses on his fingers scraping her palm. His touch sent an electric pulse up her arm, and she fought the urge to gasp. Shocked by his boldness, she merely gaped as he lifted her hand to his lips and whispered a kiss, her skin tingling at the contact. She could have sworn he hesitated before releasing her hand. He gave a slight bow, a smirk tugging at the corners of his mouth. She wanted to punch him for touching her, but she had the distinct feeling he might easily grab her fist and send another electric shock through her. She tried to scowl and failed.

"The pleasure is mine," said Thomas. He stepped back and

held out a petite bouquet of blue and yellow wildflowers tied with long, green grass.

"Um, thank you," she stammered, not sure if this was a gesture of condolence or something else entirely. She studied the hand holding the flowers. Though his nails were neatly manicured, faint scars traced his knuckles. She took the bouquet, carefully avoiding his hand and the possibility of another electric shock.

He blinked lazily and raised his gaze over her shoulder. "Lily, Ian." He nodded.

"Thomas," they said in curt unison.

He fixed a sly smile at Ian, eyes glimmering.

Ian breathed a curse.

Thomas's smile spread into a wicked grin. He casually shifted one foot behind him and turned his attention back to Sara.

"Forgive me for interrupting, but I wanted to be sure you were alright." He stole a glance at her bare knee. "That was quite an exciting arrival last night."

Sara stood entranced by his flashy smile, his eyes, the vest and blue silk shirt stretched tight against his muscular shoulders. *Damn him.*

"Thank you, Thomas, for your concern," said Lily, breaking Sara's trance. "Sara is fine now."

"Yes, I can see," said Thomas, his lips curving upward.

She wanted to say something, anything, but her heart was pounding and her mind racing.

"Well then, I'll see you tomorrow night," he said, but instead of leaving, he eyed the thick canopy overhead. "Apparently I'm not the only one who couldn't wait. Appears Trouble is following you." He stole another glance at Sara and then rushed from the clearing, his movement so fast he seemed to disappear. A trembling of leaves and faint ashy scent lingered in his wake.

Sara released her breath and then jumped when a raven squawked overhead. It swooped down and perched on the arched back of a nearby Adirondack chair.

"Hello, Trouble," Lily said to the raven before tipping back her head and sweetly calling, "And hello, Moira."

A red squirrel, chattering angrily, ran down the maple trunk and streaked across the ground before stopping at the chair. It was still chattering as it stomped its tiny foot and instantly changed into a beautiful girl with flaming-red hair.

Sara stumbled back, scraping her legs against the stage. It was the same redheaded girl she'd seen leap off the Cahills' deck and turn into a wolf. The girl casually settled into the chair with the air of a bored queen, disgust on her face. The raven squawked again and hopped onto the girl's shoulder.

Ian jumped from the stage, landing beside Sara. "That was Thomas Sullivan who left so expeditiously—always the charmer. And this is Moira Walker, who certainly was not spying on us." His voice held a touch of irritation.

Sara's stomach clenched. This girl had *shape-shifted* directly in front of her and was now glaring at the bouquet in her hands. Though appearing similar in age to Sara, she wore a tight, revealing top and cutoffs so short, white pockets peeked out. An inordinate amount of makeup tinged her face. Sara straightened her shoulders and steeled herself.

The raven fixed its shiny black eyes on Sara and cocked its head. "Hi," she said, more to the raven, which bobbed its head at the greeting, than to the surly girl.

Moira turned her amber eyes to Sara; without blinking or breaking her stare, she said, "It's no coincidence that you show up right when dark magic attacks us." Her husky voice was laced with venom. The raven bobbed its head again and hopped back to the chair. Moira stood and turned her attention to Ian and Lily. "I was on my way to help Helen with the blight, something you should be doing instead of sightseeing with the inbred." She shot another withering glare at Sara before phasing into a ferret-type animal and vanishing into the woods behind the stump stage. The raven continued to scrutinize Sara until Ian waved it away. Squawking with laughter, the bird took flight after Moira and disappeared.

Sara set the flowers on the stage and balled her hands into fists. Narrowing her eyes at the dense forest, she whispered, "Nice to meet you too." She never thought she could punch an animal, but there was always a first time for everything. *Inbred? What the hell?*

"Now, *she*," said Ian with a hint of mockery, "is the most vicious animal in the woods."

Lily gracefully leapt from the stage, landing beside them. "Moira can't help her alpha instincts. She can be rude and a bit intense, but she does have some good qualities."

Ian snorted. "Really? Such as?"

"Well, she's our best shape-shifter, she has a wicked volleyball serve, and—" Lily paused in thought. "Oh! And she gave me a necklace once." She smiled at Ian.

He rolled his eyes. "As I recall, the necklace was made with poisonous seeds that gave you a rash."

"You still remember?" Lily gently touched her neck.

"Of course I do," he said, laughing. "Your neck was bright red until Helen fixed it."

Lily smiled and lightly dipped her head.

"Okay," said Sara, interrupting their reverie, "so she hates everyone, not just me?"

"Moira doesn't hate you," said Lily. "She just loves to intimidate. Best to keep your distance for a while."

Sara's heart raced from meeting Moira and Thomas—her emotions a conflicting mixture of anger and a peculiar thrill. Ware Woods was a lot to take in. Her chest tightened, and she struggled to breathe, feeling as though she were drowning on dry land.

She stepped away from the shade and turned her face to the sun. Closing her eyes, she inhaled, held it for three counts, and exhaled, imagining pushing everything away with her breath. She thought of her mother's hand on her chest, warming her heart and grounding her.

After taking another deep breath, she opened her eyes to find Ian staring at her. She cleared her throat. "So . . . is this Council tree also the Sullivans' soul tree?"

"No," said Ian. "This maple is the Walker tree. The Sullivans have a white ash on the east side of the forest." He held his intent gaze on her while gesturing to the right of the stage.

Sara rubbed the back of her hand, recalling the soft jolt of electricity from Thomas's touch. "What exactly did the forest gift to the Walkers and the Sullivans?"

"The Walkers are shape-shifters and the Sullivans have kinetic powers." Ian paused. "Both families are natural-born fighters. Thomas, for example, can't say no to a challenge." Not a trace of a smile showed on his face.

Sara tilted her head at him, puzzled why he felt the need to tell her this.

He narrowed his eyes and added, "I'm telling you this because he sees *you* as a challenge. Be careful with him."

She blinked, not sure if this was an actual warning or an older brother's protectiveness.

"Come on, let's head to the lake. Gran is expecting us soon." He turned and strode to a path beyond the stage clearing—a path Sara could have sworn hadn't been there moments before. She hurried to keep up with him, glancing back at Lily, who gathered the bouquet and followed.

CHAPTER 15

As soon as they left the Council tree clearing and stepped into the forest, a cool reverence wrapped around Sara. Tree canopies blocked most of the bright sun, allowing hazy rays of light to filter through to the thickly padded forest floor. The air was heavy with the scent of life and decay.

A phoebe's two-note song echoed through the stillness. Bird wings fluttered, and squirrels chattered overhead while far in the distance, a woodpecker knocked about for a quick meal. Patches of plush moss clung to the base of trees along the path. The dark-green growth contrasted with a swath of light-green ferns, their fuzzy heads curled tight at the tip of their long, elegant stems.

Ian strode ahead of Sara, while Lily trailed behind. They walked single file along the narrow path, which curved through the sea of fiddleheads. Grateful for the lack of conversation, Sara held out her palms, skimming the ferns.

Eventually, the trees thinned, allowing a glimpse of sun reflecting off water in the distance. Grass replaced the ferns as the path opened to a wide clearing beside a lake of midnight blue water, its sparkling surface like a starry sky.

In the center of the lake rose a circular stone wall whose flat top appeared to be three to four feet above the waterline. Large tree canopies crested over the wall, their varied heights indicating the wall protected an island that lay below the lake's surface.

Sara stared at the glassy lake and peculiar walled island. "How beautiful. I wasn't expecting . . ." She trailed off, realizing she was alone at the lake's edge.

Ian and Lily had walked off through the open clearing of cropped grass and toward a low fenced area, which backed up to the dense forest. Green and golden grasses weaved in and around the fence, almost obscuring it. Behind it stood a tree, completely void of leaves and seemingly dead. From its thick, twisted trunk, scraggly branches stretched out like skeletal fingers reaching for the sky.

Sara stumbled, as if tugged toward the tree by an invisible cord. Shaking off the feeling, she tightened the flannel shirt at her waist and strode toward Ian and Lily. Her legs burned when she quickened her pace up the slightly inclined clearing, eager to see what lay behind the fence. Midway between the lake edge and fenced area, Sara spotted an opening in the intricately designed wrought iron and stopped in her tracks at what lay beyond. Her eyes widened at the unmistakable sight of headstones.

While a few stones seemed new, with deeply etched and legible names, most of the stones were weathered and covered in lichen, their names faded with age.

Sara smiled at the sight. She found cemeteries to be calming and peaceful, their quiet solitude a comforting embrace. The perfect place to be alone without feeling alone.

Soft grasses and wildflowers grew throughout the cemetery and waved in the slight breeze. A monarch butterfly flit among white Queen Anne's lace, daisy-like fleabane, and blue forget-me-nots. The insect fluttered to the base of the cemetery tree just as Ian and Lily appeared from behind the massive trunk.

Another soft tug pulled Sara toward the cemetery and curious tree. But before she could reach the fence, Gran bustled through a cluster of birch trees along the clearing's edge and approached her. "Perfect timing," she said, breathing heavily and swinging a bag at her side. She smiled at Sara, wrinkles gathering at the outside corners of her eyes. "It's good to see you up and about." An awkward moment ensued as Sara stiffened. "Gaa. I'm not the hugging type either," said Gran, waving her hand and dismissing the tension while Lily and Ian joined them. "Before you go there"—she nodded at the cemetery—"come with me to visit Albert." She fixed all three with a determined glare and started down the sloped clearing toward a weathered dock and an old rowboat.

"Lesson one, always do what Gran says," said Ian, watching the woman amble away before dashing after her.

Sara gazed at the cemetery, preferring its solitude over visiting a stranger.

"Come on," said Lily, her cheerful voice reflecting her warm smile. "Albert is on the island with my family." She gestured to the fortified wall in the middle of the lake and waited for Sara to fall in step with her to the dock.

Although the boat easily accommodated the four of them, no motor was visible—nor even oars. Contemplating whether she should state the obvious, Sara nearly slid off her seat when the boat rocked and floated away from the dock. Wide-eyed, she cocked her head, listening for the sound of a small electric engine, but heard nothing besides the gentle lapping of water against the boat.

Ian and Lily sat next to each other, knees almost touching, while Gran, clutching the bag in her lap, sat beside Sara. None of them appeared surprised.

Clearly, the boat's mysterious movement was normal to them. Instead of asking what surely sounded silly, she leaned over the side to better inspect how it was moving through the water. Perhaps a rope below the surface pulled the boat toward the island.

Sara peered into the water and shook her head in disbelief. Not only was there no rope, but fish that normally didn't swim together—bass, pike, and bluegill—undulated alongside the boat.

Lily tilted her head back and laughed. "They like you, Sara," she said, and put her hand in the water, petting the fish that pooled about her.

Sara gripped the weathered side of the boat and leaned farther over the rail. Swarms of fish, and even a few turtles, were now swimming alongside them. They splashed her, and this time it was Ian who laughed.

"Well, sister, looks like you may have a touch of Atwell magic," he said.

"What magic?" Sara asked, whipping her head round to him and Lily, who still had her hand in the water.

Ian leaned forward, forearms braced on his thighs. "Atwells have a natural affinity for water and air elements." He closed his eyes and squinted, as if deep in thought.

Gran patted Sara's knee, startling her. "He's checking if anyone is in the preserve," she said, gesturing to the thickly forested shoreline. "The Ware Woods boundary extends into the lake and includes the island, but the far shore is the outer woods. We own it as a private preserve. It's a buffer between Ware Woods and the normal world. But occasionally, people wander in."

"What happens if someone is in the preserve?" asked Sara, straining to see the distant shore.

Gran grunted. "Then we kindly but forcefully escort them out."

"And what if someone crosses the wall into Ware Woods?" Sara raised an eyebrow.

"They can't do that unless we welcome them, or they're lured by Dorcas." Gran tightened her grip on her bag.

Sara narrowed her eyes, about to ask who Dorcas was when Lily interrupted. "Dorcas eats them," she said, her sweet tone and placid features a direct contrast to her deadly comment. "It hasn't happened in a long time. Local legends of people disappearing in these woods help keep them out. They call it the 'Be-Ware Woods.'" She wiggled her fingers and laughed, her giggles reminding Sara of delicate bells.

Sara jerked back at Lily's casual attitude and the threat of some man-eating animal named Dorcas.

Lily stopped laughing. "Don't worry. Dorcas doesn't like the taste of gifted—" Her sentence was interrupted when Ian snapped his eyes open and nodded at her.

"Go ahead. No one's here," he said.

She clasped the side of the boat and leapt over the edge.

Sara gasped, expecting her to plunge into the lake. But Lily stood upright atop the water, a big grin on her pale face as she walked on the lake's surface. Sara fell back, Ian catching her before she sprawled onto the floor of the boat.

Lily laughed and ran, her steps lightly spraying water. Her yellow dress fluttered and snapped around her legs as she sprinted to a small dock jutting out from the island wall.

Sara scrabbled to the side of the boat and touched the water's surface, half-expecting to feel something solid lying beneath it. A trout jumped out, sides shimmering with a rainbow of colors, and splashed water directly into her open mouth. She reared back, spitting and wiping her face.

Gran chuckled. "Even the fish know you're special."

Sara shot a glare at the water. "I'm not special. The fish are just mocking me."

"We're all special," said Gran.

Sara fought the urge to roll her eyes at the grandmotherly tone.

"Even those without strong magic still have natural talents and gifts, like me and my sister, Alice. We have vague memories of using magic when we were children, but it disappeared when our mother died. That would be your great-grandmother Ann," she said as the boat gently pulled up to the dock and a beaming Lily.

Sara's heart clenched at the mention of death and disappearing magic. She faced Gran, and was relieved when, instead of elaborating, she shifted her attention to the island. Gran stood, the boat holding steady, and stepped onto the weathered landing, her bag tight against her chest.

Ian stepped out next. "Lucky for us, Gran can't throw fireballs, but she is an exceptional quilter. The only one in the forest who can quilt with spider thread." He gave a broad smile.

Spider thread. Sara put a hand over the stone hidden beneath her shirt. Ian eyed her, but she ignored him and followed Gran and Lily to a stone stairway at the end of the dock. The staircase flowed down into the walled island, where the ground lay below the surface of the water.

Lily descended the stairs first and turned to look up at Sara. "When the valley was flooded, my ancestors stood their ground to protect the soul tree on this knoll. The wall was created from the surrounding earth to hold back the water and protect the tree." She patted the stones.

Sara placed both hands on the wall and gasped. It swelled in and out, as if breathing. She gazed over the island's impossibly large forest; the vast area inside the wall seemed much bigger than the island appeared to be from the outside. The massive tree near the center of the island, its green leaves shimmering in a slight breeze, stretched its crown above the lake's surface.

"Alice," said Gran. She quickened her pace down the stairway to where a woman with long, white hair appeared at the base of the wall. "Don't you worry about Albert. I have a new batch of salve and a *special* ingredient that should do the trick." She patted her bag with one hand and reached back with the other. "Sara, come meet my sister, Alice." Gran nodded at Sara and gestured for her to hurry up.

Stunned by Alice's beauty, Sara stumbled down the last step. Age had done little to diminish her high cheekbones, smooth skin, and snowy white hair, which grew past her waist. But it was her fiery amber eyes that caught Sara's breath. Alice's gaze seemed to peer into her soul. Sara glanced away.

"I'm sorry about the accident," said Alice. Her voice had a soothing tone with a lilt similar to Helen's. A lilt Gran curiously did not have. "Your mother was a powerful earth witch and very loved. Your father will be home soon. I can feel it," said Alice.

"Thanks," said Sara softly, twisting a foot in the silty dirt. "It's nice to meet you."

"We'll have plenty of time for tea and conversation later. Right now, we need to tend to Albert," said Gran. She grabbed Alice's hand and marched toward a path leading off into the island's forest. As the two older women bustled ahead, Ian and Lily joined Sara in trailing behind them.

"When Ann died," said Ian, "the Atwell family took in Alice and Gran and raised them. Gran was a wild thing and couldn't stay out here for long. But Alice prefers the island. Rarely leaves." He shoved his hands into his pockets and eyed Lily, who tracked a blue jay flying above them. "Albert and Alice are . . . close. When they were young, Alice had crossed the wall, and a Taker found her. Albert is a Walker and had been patrolling the wall when he saw it happen. He shifted into a wolf and leapt over the wall to save her."

Sara frowned. "I thought good magic only exists inside the wall. How could he do that?"

"Right." Ian kicked a pinecone off the path. "If a shifter phases and crosses the wall, they become stuck in animal form. Albert knew this." Ian shrugged. "He and Alice have been inseparable ever since."

Sara bit her lip—he knowingly sacrificed himself. "They love each other," she breathed.

"Yes," said Lily, her voice light as a breeze. "But don't feel bad for them. With Albert in wolf form, they could finally be together."

"Finally? What do you mean?" said Sara, furrowing her brow. "Wait, is he still a wolf?"

"Yes," said Ian curtly. He cleared his throat rather loudly and picked up his pace, mouth pressed into a thin line. They both ignored Sara's other question. Instead of pushing them, Sara scanned the undergrowth for any signs of a wolf until the path abruptly ended.

Before them sat a rambling ranch-style home made from the same stones as the island wall. In front of the house spread a large, circular courtyard of smooth pebbles, its focal point a pond-like water feature with a gurgling center.

Lily skipped up the wide stone steps of the porch and through open double doors of thick carved wood. The doors were painted a weathered whitewash that matched the window frames and gave the house a light and inviting appearance.

Sara crossed the porch and stepped into a large foyer with a cathedral ceiling. "Albert is in the back room," said Lily as she veered to the right and started down a long, wide hallway. Her tiny feet were silent on the stone floor.

Trailing Lily, Sara cringed at the sound of her own timid, hollow footsteps until Ian's confident steps joined hers in echoing down the hall.

CHAPTER 16

AFTER PASSING MULTIPLE closed doors, they entered a large family room, brightly lit from a row of windows along the back wall. At one side of the room stood a stone fireplace flanked by floor-to-ceiling shelving with hundreds of leather-bound books. A large support beam made of carved, whitewashed wood rose through the center of the room. Clusters of light-gray couches and matching tables decorated the open space around it. The soft gurgle from the courtyard pond and a songbird's cheerful melody floated in from the open windows. Although the room was full of sunlight, a heaviness emanated from a small group of people huddled near the back.

A slim man with blond hair and a trim beard parted from the group and greeted them near the center of the room. "Ian, it's good to see you."

Ian gave a courteous nod. "Orsen, this is my sister, Sara." He gestured to Sara while Lily joined the man's side. "Sara, this is Orsen Atwell, Lily's father."

Sara wasn't sure if a formal or informal greeting was expected of her. She straightened, wiped her sweaty palm on the flannel shirt around her waist, and extended her hand. "It's a pleasure to meet you. You have a wonderful home—er, island."

Orsen glanced at her outstretched hand and hesitated. Lily

cleared her throat, and he smiled and took Sara's hand in both of his. "I'm glad you're here, Sara. Welcome home." His gray eyes seemed sincere and his touch gentle. "I just wish it were under better circumstances. I am sorry for your loss." He released her hand and averted his gaze to a vase of flowers on a nearby table.

"Thank you," Sara whispered. She shuddered, shaking off the grief that clung to her, and eyed the people behind him.

Alice and Gran knelt on the floor, tending to something—or someone—between them while a cluster of adults hovered nearby. Peering between the adults were three children, their wide eyes fixed on Sara.

Lily approached them and ruffled the hair of a towheaded boy closest to her. "It's not polite to stare," she said.

The boy laughed, squinting his gray-blue eyes, and tried to pull away from her.

Lily rumpled his hair again before releasing him and turning to Sara. "These are my siblings: James, Johnny, and Ophelia."

"Pleased to meet you," said Sara with a playful bow. The children were smartly dressed and seemingly well behaved.

Ophelia, about six years old, giggled, but then clamped a hand over her mouth when James elbowed her. The boy shot Sara a concerned expression and said, "Can you help him?" He stepped back as Gran, still kneeling on the floor, shifted to the side.

Sara jerked at the sight of a large silver wolf sprawled across a blue tick mattress. His head hung over the side, resting in Alice's lap. She stroked the fur along his nose while whispering to him.

Albert's eyes shifted without focus while he panted, foam gathering along the sides of his pale tongue. He convulsed and curled back his lips, revealing sharp white canines.

Sara looked from his mouth, down his massive, heaving chest and to his hindquarters, where Gran pressed a white towel.

"Sara, come help me," said Gran, motioning her over to continue pressing on the towel. "My old bones can't kneel on the floor any longer." She stood slowly, resting her hands on her knees before sitting heavily in a nearby armchair.

All eyes on her, Sara swallowed and quietly approached the wolf. She loved animals but being close to an injured predator caused her to tremble, the urge to flee nearly overpowering. Kneeling before him, she turned to Gran and asked, "Are you sure I'm not hurting him?" She lightly held the towel to the wound on the wolf's hindquarter, her hands visibly shaking. When her grandmother didn't answer, Sara glanced up, searching for assurance from the pale faces around her.

A woman with kind eyes and cascading waves of blonde hair gave her a tight smile and nodded.

Sara pulled her legs under her to sit on the floor, careful not to disturb the wolf's claws. A thick, black substance oozed from under the towel. She pressed harder, her head close to the wolf's body. His shallow breathing barely stirred the white fur on his belly.

She had never been this close to a wolf before. Unable to help herself, she took one hand away from the towel to graze his soft fur. The moment she touched him, her spine locked and her eyes snapped shut, a memory grabbing hold of her senses.

She was no longer at the Atwells but lying in tall grass, pain pulsing through every nerve. Terror squeezed the air from her lungs as voices urging her to run echoed and faded. She wanted to let the darkness swallow her, but the instinct to live forced her to breathe. It was then that Albert leapt from the wall and lunged over her to fight off a Taker, while Ian appeared at her side, scooping her up and carrying her to safety . . .

The vision ended, but Sara kept her eyes closed, not bearing to face Alice. Albert had saved her life last night, but he'd paid the price with a wound apparently infected by dark magic. His selfless act was about to cost him everything.

Eyes shut, she focused her thoughts on Albert, as if her gratitude could somehow relieve his suffering. She held her position, arms and hands eventually falling asleep with a warm tingle. Ignoring the soft murmurs around her, she remained pressing on the towel.

Albert trembled and fell still, his rapid breathing now slow. Afraid he was taking his last breaths, Sara sat back, letting her hands fall, head hanging over her lap. This was her fault. Surely this counted as murder.

Someone patted her shoulder, and she jolted at the contact.

"Well done, Sara," said Gran, her voice breaking the stillness of the room.

Sara opened her eyes. Albert lay peacefully sleeping, his face relaxed with a curved lupine smile. The towel fell away, revealing a rosy pink scar along his upper leg, the black substance no longer present.

Alice reached over and touched Sara's knee. "Thank you," she whispered.

Sara shook her head, her eyes wide with disbelief. "It wasn't me. Gran made the salve—" Her raspy voice broke off as Ophelia crashed into her with a hug, and they both tumbled to the floor.

"I knew you could do it," said James, joining their hug on the floor.

Sara stiffened at the attention but then huffed a polite laugh at their sweet faces. She gently pushed away from them and stood.

"Your great-grandmother was a healer, and it seems you are too," said Orsen with a nod of approval. "Ah, where are my manners. This is my wife, Elizabeth." He smiled and held out a hand to the stunning woman with long blonde hair. "And this is Elizabeth's mother, Claire, and her uncle, Ben." He gestured toward the two people near Albert. They both stood with their shoulders back, hands clasped before them in a formal manner.

Sara stifled a gasp. It wasn't their formality that struck her as odd but how young they appeared. They could be Elizabeth's siblings—not a generation older. Though they both nodded politely, their expressions remained severe.

A stern cough from the other side of the room cut through the introductions, grabbing everyone's attention.

Elizabeth stepped forward and gently touched Sara's arm. "We save the best for last," she said. Barely a trace of wrinkles crossed her fair complexion as she smiled and led Sara to an armchair by the fireplace. "This is my great-uncle, Kingsley Atwell."

The old man, dressed in fine slacks and a crisp button-down shirt, had an air of aristocracy. Even while sitting, he had impeccable posture. His full head of hair gleamed snow white, and his gray-blue eyes, slightly clouded with age, fixed Sara with an intense gaze.

"Kingsley, this is Sara," said Elizabeth, releasing Sara's arm and stepping back.

Avoiding his stare, Sara looked at the hands lying still in his lap—weathered hands with thick calluses on his fingertips that conflicted with his stately appearance. "Pleased to meet you," she said in a voice she hoped sounded both formal and kind.

"There's a prophecy about you," he said, his voice scratchy but strong, with an accent reminiscent of Alice's. "You must be careful. We must all be careful, or we could lose the whole forest." He glanced around, projecting the last part to everyone in the room. He leaned forward, eyes directed toward Albert, before swiveling back to Sara.

She stood, dumbfounded, her face burning as Gran crossed the room toward her. Before Gran reached her, Kingsley whispered ominously, "You're being watched." His voice was so low, Sara knew no one else could hear him.

"That's quite enough," Gran warned.

Sara raised a brow at her cranky demeanor, unsure if Gran was admonishing her for standing like an idiot or Kingsley for behaving strangely.

Gran turned with a nod to Alice and waved at the rest of the Atwells. "Albert should be fine now. Ian, Lily, will you leave with

Sara and me?" Gran phrased it as a question, but it was stated like an order. She bustled out of the room without waiting for a response.

Once outside, Sara heaved a breath and hurried after her grandmother along a new path leading away from the courtyard.

"You did well back there," said Gran, her steely eyes twinkling with an emotion Sara couldn't place. "Don't mind Kingsley. There are so many myths and legends around here, he's too old to keep them straight."

Sara rubbed her arms. "Gran, I didn't do anything to Albert. It was your salve—or maybe he was getting better on his own, and I just happened to be there." She shoved her hands into her pockets. "It was my fault he was injured—"

"It was *not* your fault," Gran interrupted. "Don't you believe for one second you are to blame for *any* of this."

The harshness of her tone caused Sara to clamp her mouth shut and swallow her burning questions about the prophecy. She followed her grandmother in silence down the path and along a fenced-in garden filled with tidy rows of ripening vegetables and herbs. The fresh scent reminded her of her mother's raised flower beds. Behind the garden stood a small gray barn with chickens and goats milling about. One goat, a young black-and-white mix, sprang over to Sara and bleated until she pulled her hands out of her pockets and rubbed its neck. It nuzzled her before giving her a soft head-butt and jumping away to chase a chicken.

Sara glanced at the late afternoon sky and decided to test her grandmother's cantankerous attitude with a simple question. "Does this path lead to the dock?" She looked back at Ian and Lily who trailed far behind, caught up in their own conversation.

"Of course it does—we're on an island." Gran pulled a red-and-white star-shaped mint from her pocket and popped it in her mouth. "I came this way to show you the Atwell soul tree. It's quite a magnificent black gum. We were fortunate to save it from the flooding. Isn't she a beauty?" Gran exhaled as they arrived at a massive tree on a grass- and moss-covered knoll.

The tree perched atop the hill like a monarch on a throne. Although the knoll's elevation lay below the lake's waterline, the tree stretched itself high as if peering out at the surrounding water.

"In the fall, these leaves turn bright yellow and red. It looks like it's on fire," said Gran, waving a hand in the air.

The trunk was smaller than the other soul trees, but it possessed a sense of power, easily supporting multiple branches that extended parallel to the ground. A triangular-shaped crown of glossy summer-green leaves shimmered in a breeze. Something about its regal posture reminded her of Kingsley Atwell. She frowned, thinking of his warning that the entire forest was in danger and she was somehow involved. Or maybe even responsible.

Gran glanced at her. "Don't you worry, now. That old prophecy is hogwash. I never thought your parents should have left the forest with you. But they did what they thought was right. The prophecy came from Makwa." She spat out the name, grimacing in disgust. "Just because she can't tell a lie doesn't mean she's to be trusted. It's no secret Alice and I have never liked her. There's something not right with that witch."

For a moment, Gran had a faraway look in her eyes. She shook her head and focused her steel blue gaze on Sara. "Stay away from her, and don't believe anything she ever tells you." Her words were both an angry statement and concerned plea.

"Am I . . . in danger?" Sara choked, holding back her real question, the one she already knew the answer to—*Am I a danger?*

"We all are. With a dark witch at our door . . . You just stay inside the wall while Council handles this."

Visions of Samson's leering face flashed in Sara's mind, and the stone hiding beneath her shirt pulsed. She placed a hand on her chest. "Did you give me—"

"Gaa!" Gran threw up her hands and continued in a hushed

voice: "Do not speak of that to *anyone*. Or the dark witch at our door will be the least of our worries. Do I make myself clear?"

Sara yanked her hand down and gaped at her. "Crystal."

"Good." She whipped around—surprisingly quick for someone who was just complaining about her old bones. "It's about time you two caught up with us," she called to Ian and Lily at the bottom of the knoll. Her tone had changed from solemn to playful. "I need to get back to my quilting. But first, I'll tell Helen about Albert's improvement. You know she's good to spread the word like wildfire. And I want you both to take Sara to the cemetery and keep her company."

"Of course," said Ian. "We'll take the boat back."

As Gran climbed the grassy knoll, Ian hollered, "Tell Helen to expect us for dinner." He patted his lean stomach and grinned.

Gran waved back in acknowledgement and disappeared into the tree trunk.

"Are you always thinking about food?" chided Lily.

His fingers drummed his sides. "Well, not always. That would be Caleb."

Lily laughed, heading to a path opposite the knoll. "Come on, Sara, we're almost around the island. The dock is just a bit farther."

Flustered by Gran's warning and distracted by her guilt for endangering the forest, Sara remained quiet for the rest of their walk. Not until they were in the boat, gliding back to the forest mainland, did she turn to Ian. "Thanks for saving me last night," she said in a low voice.

His face pinched with an expression she couldn't read. "You don't need to thank me. We're family." His last word echoed over the water.

She glanced at his narrow shoulders. "Did you carry me *all* the way to the Main House?"

Ian snorted. "Gifted are stronger than we look . . . at least inside the forest wall. We also heal faster and live longer."

This time it was Sara who snorted. *You gotta be kidding me.* "Do you fart unicorns too?"

Lily exploded with laughter, and the boat responded by vigorously rocking back and forth. Ian shook his head, chuckling, while Sara dug her fingernails into the wooden bench to keep from sliding over the rail.

CHAPTER 17

Wʜᴇɴ ᴛʜᴇ ʙᴏᴀᴛ finally calmed to a gentle sway, Sara relaxed her grip on the bench and flicked her gaze from the upcoming dock to Ian and Lily. "Why did Gran ask you to take me to the cemetery?"

Ian's smile disappeared. He tapped his fingers on the boat rail and stared out over the water, squinting at the reflection of the setting sun.

"To visit Eliza," said Lily. "We laid her to rest a few weeks ago, right after the accident. It was a beautiful ceremony. More like a colorful party . . ."

Sara stiffened but managed a polite nod at the reverence in Lily's voice.

As soon as they pulled up to the dock, she jumped from the boat and ran to find her mother's headstone in the long-jagged shadow of the cemetery tree. The petite bouquet from Thomas rested beside the stone.

This can't be real. Sara fell to her knees and placed both her hands on the stone. Trembling, she ran her fingertips along the etched vines and flowers surrounding her mother's name. Her throat tightened, and tears spilled down her cheeks. Unable to hold back her grief, she let herself go—screaming and crying until her sides hurt, until every last memory and future hope with her mother spilled from her and leaked into the ground. When she was too exhausted to shed another tear, a hand touched her shoulder.

"Leave me alone," she rasped before collapsing face down onto the grave. She burrowed her hands into the soft earth and surrendered to sleep.

A dream of hazy faces and childhood memories brushed her consciousness. Though she couldn't see her mother, she felt her presence—a tender mix of love and happiness and hope. Her breathy voice whispered a saying she had often told Sara: *"Believe in yourself. You are destined to do great things."* Sara tried to grab on to the voice, only to wake and find herself lying alone in the cemetery. Overhead, the twisted branches of the cemetery tree reached up toward the night sky and appeared to be holding the moon.

As she hauled herself up to sit against the gravestone, her hand brushed a soft blanket. It was the familiar two-toned blue blanket from the Cahills. Beside it was a pillow and a basket with a thermos and small potpie—still warm.

Sara opened the thermos and gratefully gulped down cool water, soothing her raw throat before choking down most of the pie. Comforted by the food and her mother's words, she untied the flannel shirt from her waist, put it on, and burrowed under the blanket.

Quieting her breath, she lay atop the grave, serenaded by the chirping of crickets, when a deep, soulful note floated through the night. She pulled back the blanket and heard it again—the haunting, deep chord of a cello floating across the surface of the lake. Without pause, the single, open string note poured into a soothing prelude. The music echoed upon itself, building and blending its multiple layers into a sublime concert. Any remaining tension in her body melted, and she fell into a deep and restful sleep.

The scent of dewy grass and lake water filled Sara's nose, gently pulling her awake. Her eyes were still clouded with sleep as she looked up at the cemetery tree. Its outer branches seemed green against the pale morning sky.

Sara blinked and focused, trying to discern if a mass of insects had alighted on the tree. Spreading her hands into the wet grass, she pushed herself into a sitting position. Her sudden movement caused something brown and furry to dart behind the food basket near her feet.

Instantly awake, she held her breath and nudged the basket aside with her foot, and then let out a soft chuckle at the rabbit staring back at her. Strands of grass disappeared below its twitching nose. Keeping an eye on Sara, the rabbit stretched forward and sniffed the basket. Confirming that nothing to its liking hid in the basket's depths, it jerked, kicking its legs and twisting in the air to land beside Sara.

She yelped and studied the rabbit warily as it relaxed against her and closed its eyes. After a few deep breaths, she dared to gently touch it. The fur, more gray than brown, was silky soft behind its delicate ears. A fluffy white tuft stuck out from its rounded hindquarters.

With her hand resting on the rabbit, she tilted her head back and squinted at the tree. It wasn't insects but tight green buds sprouting from the branches.

"Making friends, I see," said a voice from the thick pine trees pressing in behind the cemetery's iron fence. She swung her head to see Caleb and Ian emerge from the pine boughs. They stepped over the low fence and wove through the stones toward her. The rabbit shook its ears and hopped to a nearby cluster of grass, selectively chewing clover from a safe distance.

Sara stood to greet them and gingerly touched her face. Finding her cheeks still swollen from crying, she tucked her chin and busied herself with folding the blanket.

"You okay?" asked Ian, drawing closer until she looked up at him. "You fell asleep out here and it seemed you wanted to be alone. Lily brought you a few things before she went home last night." He nodded at the toppled basket.

"I'm fine," said Sara, too quickly to be convincing. "I like the cemetery, and it was nice to spend the night with her." Leaning against the gravestone, she swept a hand over her mother's deeply etched name before bending down to pick up the pillow and basket. "That was thoughtful of Lily," she mumbled. She chewed her lip, unsure if she felt relieved at receiving such kindness or irritated at needing help.

The rabbit shook its ears again, and Sara straightened to gaze at the lake. "I heard the most beautiful music drifting across the water . . ." She let herself trail off instead of speaking the rest of her thought—*like it intended to lull me to sleep.*

"Ah, that would have been Kingsley playing cello," Ian said.

"In the middle of the night?"

"He's so old, he does whatever he wants, whenever he wants. Even eats dessert before dinner . . . *and* after." Ian chuckled but then stopped short, his eyes fixed on Caleb.

She ignored his distraction, too focused on trying to reconcile a kindly cello-playing Kingsley with the ornery old man who whispered what seemed to be a threat about her being watched.

"Would you look at that," Caleb exclaimed, startling Sara as he stared wide-eyed at the cemetery tree. "It's budding! I knew this oak tree was still alive. The heartwood always had a faint flicker." He put his hands on the trunk, leaned in, and pressed his ear against the gnarled bark. "I can definitely hear it now." His grin stretched from ear to ear. "Come listen." He waved her over. Sara hesitated, her mind desperately trying to keep up with Ware Woods.

"I'll take these," said Ian. He took her belongings before glancing at the branches overhead. "Caleb, how is this possible?" Ian frowned at the noticeably larger tree.

"Dude, stop worrying all the time. This is a good thing," said Caleb. His callused hand gently patted the trunk next to his face. "Listen here," he said to Sara.

She leaned against the tree, acutely aware of how close her face was to his. She held her breath and listened, averting her gaze from his sparkling green eyes. Expecting to hear the swishing hum of the soul trees, she was surprised to hear utter stillness—and then a faint thump like a pinecone falling onto the forest floor. The sound was so faint, she thought she imagined it. Putting both hands on the trunk, she pressed in closer, this time hearing and feeling a slight thud reverberate through the bark. Eyes wide, she pulled back. "Is this a soul tree?"

"Yes," said Caleb at the same time Ian said, "Not exactly."

"Okay, so which is it?" said Sara, turning to Ian and ignoring Caleb's put-out expression.

Ian adjusted the pillow and blanket under his arm. "This is Mary's tree. Supposedly it marks the spot where she died. I don't think anyone has ever seen it bud or grow. In fact, many thought it was dead and wanted to take it down, but Gran and Alice refused to let anyone touch it." He eyed the tree. "This is strange. It's always looked the same, never even losing a branch in the heaviest of storms." He pursed his lips and turned to Caleb. "We need to tell the families."

"Right, and we will." Caleb gave the trunk one more loving pat before pushing off. "We can talk about it at the Council meeting tomorrow night. But first, I have a special project to work on." He glanced up at the tree, rubbed his hands together, and cracked his knuckles.

"Caleb . . ."

"Dude, don't worry." He slapped Ian on the shoulder and winked at Sara. "You know me—I prefer asking for forgiveness over permission. Besides, this is gonna be great!"

"Don't do anything crazy, or you'll have Gran to answer to."

"Yeah, yeah." Caleb waved him away. "Gran loves me," he added with a smug smile, his eyes twinkling in the morning sun.

"What are you planning, Caleb?" asked Sara in a low voice, squaring to face him directly. Perhaps it was self-righteous of her to question him, seeing as she hadn't lived in the forest her whole life. She hadn't even known this tree until yesterday, but she felt a connection to it. As if somehow they needed each other.

Despite his broad chest and stocky frame, Caleb took a step back from her stance. "Just a little . . . enhancement is all," he said, his tone serious instead of playful. "You can check it out tonight. But for now, I'd really appreciate it if you two would take my spot and help Helen with the blight potions today."

Ian shrugged and muttered, "Yeah, yeah." He left the pillow and blanket with Caleb and strode toward the back of the cemetery.

Sara hesitated again until Caleb shooed her away. "See you later," she called warily over her shoulder, and ran to catch up with Ian.

Upon reaching the Cahill's Main House, Ian turned to Sara and nodded at the grand staircase. "Ted dropped off your bag upstairs. Go ahead and shower while I fix us some breakfast."

She glanced at the dirt under her nails. "You'll make me breakfast? Who knew having a brother was so convenient?" She grinned and prodded him with her elbow before dashing upstairs.

After a breakfast of biscuits and eggs, Ian and Sara met Helen at a vast open workspace in the barn. For the rest of the day, they helped her grind, liquefy, and mix potions of various natural ingredients, from ambered pine resin and fermented cider to peppermint oil and soap weed. Each complex concoction was then sealed in a glass jar and labeled in accordance with Helen's detailed notes.

Sara was grateful Ian kept the conversation light and on such things as weather, the barn animals, and seasonal crops. He and

Helen never asked her any pointed questions, and she didn't share any personal details, mostly because she felt her life had been so pathetically boring. Especially compared to living in a forest that bestowed magical gifts.

After a quick lunch, Sara asked Helen about the blight. She deflected Sara's question, only acknowledging the blight as a general nuisance before retreating to the far side of the workroom, where she pored over her detailed notes.

Sara frowned, her gaze sweeping the dozens of potions along the back wall. She set aside a mortar of crushed chokeberries and black walnuts and approached Ian while he rearranged a stack of boxes.

He stopped his shuffling and gave her an open-faced grin. "You've been quiet for too long. Go ahead and ask whatever questions are burning your tail."

She stole a quick glance at Helen before asking, "How's our dad?"

"No change, otherwise I would have told you. But you already knew that. So, what's your real question?"

Touché. Sara leaned toward him and lowered her voice. "How do you kill a dark witch?"

He held her gaze as he flicked his wrist, the sudden movement shifting his watch and corded bracelet. "*You* don't."

She flared her nostrils. "Don't tell me what I can and can't do."

"Mother, help me." He sighed. "You're as strong-willed and stubborn as Gran." He dodged her punch and resumed organizing boxes. "It's almost impossible to kill a dark witch. Don't worry about it. Council will figure out what we should do."

"Speaking of this Council, why did Lily tell me 'not to worry' about the meeting? That implies I *should* be worried."

"Help me stack these boxes, and I'll tell you." He grinned again and tossed a small box of labels at her.

Rolling her eyes, she caught it, plunked it down, and reached for another box.

"We have a Council meeting every full moon to discuss issues such as harvesting, building improvements, forest wall security, relations with the adjacent townspeople, and any newcomers to the forest," Ian explained.

Helen thunked an empty jar on her notes and rose from her workbench. "We rarely get newcomers," she said, crossing the workroom. "Ware Woods is a quiet, sacred site. The only newcomers we get are usually pulled by the Mother and Father to find a significant other. It's what keeps our bloodlines clean."

Sara barely heard her explanation before Ian dropped a box of lids, the round metal seals ringing against the stone floor. They stooped to chase and pick up the pieces when the workroom door rolled back with a loud rumble.

Uncle Larry strode into the room, followed by another man who wore muddy jeans and a T-shirt that hugged his round belly. They smelled like the day, sweat and sunbaked grass, and wore the same concerned expression.

"Sara," boomed Uncle Larry, his voice echoing in the workroom. "This is Eddie, Helen's husband." He turned to the man and clapped him on the back. "Eddie, this is Eliza's daughter . . . my granddaughter."

The man stole a glance at Helen before contemplating Sara and nodding. "Sara," was all he said, his voice like gravel.

Sara dropped metal seals into a box, the pieces clanging against one another. "Nice to meet you . . . Eddie," she said, awkwardness hanging in the air.

Eddie removed his faded ball cap, revealing short gray hair, and greeted Helen with a kiss to her cheek.

Alrighty, then. Sara turned away to watch her grandfather stride across the room.

He approached the counter on the back wall, picked up one of the glass jars, shook it, and set it back down. While the potion contents swirled and sparkled, he leaned over the counter and pinned a map to the wall behind it.

The map, which had many folds and wrinkles, was a faded satellite image of a dense forest. A blue ribbon of a river started from the north and swelled into a large, eye-shaped lake; in the lake's center was an island and a large tree outlined in thick green marker. The forested land to the east of the water had four more outlined trees. The same green marker indicating the five soul trees also outlined the Ware Woods boundary. With her gaze, Sara traced the boundary line, which encompassed most of the eastern forest and extended into the lake to include the island. Outside the thick green line, angry red marks dotted the forest.

Sara stared at the map and rubbed at the sudden prickling on the back of her neck. Helen had lied. The blight was more than a nuisance; it was an obvious threat.

Uncle Larry jabbed a finger at the red marks and inclined his head toward Helen. "Found more again today. This blight doesn't discriminate—it's attacking all tree varieties, from deciduous to evergreen. We've never seen anything like this."

Eddie wiped sweat from his forehead before putting his cap back on and nodding in agreement. "It's unnatural. Your treatments aren't even slowing it down." His eyes shifted from Helen to the rows of sparkling jars.

Stepping closer to inspect the map, Sara noticed a small X near the lake's edge. "What's this?" She stood on tiptoe and stretched to lightly tap the mark.

Uncle Larry cleared his throat. "That's the cemetery. Before the villagers flooded the land, old family burials were moved here. Mary selected this location." He absently scratched his beard, considering something. "Ayuh, she died there protecting it too."

Helen set down a potion jar, this one bright green with shimmering flecks of mica. "That's enough for today. We'll discuss the blight at tomorrow's Council meeting." She turned away from the map and forced a smile at Ian and Sara. "You two better get cleaned up and head off to your party." She patted Sara on the arm before following Eddie and Uncle Larry out the back door.

"What party?" Sara blurted. They had been together all day, and Ian had said nothing about a party. *All day*. She reeled on him. "In case you haven't noticed, I don't appreciate surprises, and I'm not exactly a party girl."

"Relax, it's no big deal," he said, pushing back his hair. "Some of us get together to just hang out, eat, play games. We call it our 'nearly-full-moon party.' Been doing it since we were little kids."

"Sounds lame."

"Do you have *any* control over that mouth of yours?" His tone was serious, but a smirk pulled at his lips. As if satisfied with her surprised speechlessness, he started for the open barn door. "Lily and Caleb will be there. And did I mention there's food?" he called over his shoulder.

Sara frowned, her gaze lingering on the map, at the ominous red marks creeping toward the thick green outline of the forest wall. Her stomach growled, breaking her brooding, and she sprinted from the workroom to catch up with him.

CHAPTER 18

Aﬞﬞ FTER USING ONE of the barn's outdoor hose spigots to
wash off potion ingredients, Sara followed Ian to the Main
House kitchen where he introduced her to Caleb's mother,
Rebecca. The woman seemed young enough to be Caleb's sister
and looked just like him, round-faced with sparkling green eyes
and a dusting of freckles across the bridge of her nose. Rebecca
waved off Sara's thank-you for the borrowed clothes and squeezed
her in a tight hug before sending them off with four large bags of
food for the party.

As if sensing Sara's anxiety, Ian distracted her by pointing out
the Cahill buildings and farmland. They passed free-roaming chickens, goats, and horses by the barn and strode by vegetable plots,
hay, and alfalfa fields until they reached a wide clearing with a long
wooden picnic table, slightly grayed with age. Beside the clearing
was a football-field sized plot of overgrown grass, rippling in the
early evening breeze.

Ian set the bags of food on the table, angled his long legs over
the bench, and sat with his back to the grass. Startling a few grasshoppers, Sara rounded to the other side of the table and sat facing
him. She leaned back to glance at the sky, grabbing the table to
steady herself, when a sharp pain stabbed her thumb.

She jerked her hand back and cursed at a long splinter partially imbedded under her nail. Turning aside to keep blood from dripping onto her shorts, she gritted her teeth and pulled it out. Grateful that Ian appeared preoccupied with the bags of food, she flicked away the splinter and bit down on her thumb, swallowing the bitter taste of her blood.

"Aww, did the table bite you, or do you still suck your thumb?" Moira's husky voice taunted, the grass parting as she glided from the field like a snake.

Sara pulled her thumb out and winced at both the wet sucking noise it made and the pain under her nail. She glared at Moira, wanting to spit in her face or at least hurl a nasty insult about her heavy makeup and nearly see-through top. But before she could do either, Ian spoke up.

"You okay, Sara?" His expression begged her not to engage with Moira.

She shot a death stare at the redheaded girl. "I'm fine," she said through clenched teeth while pressing out a drop of blood on her shorts. *Alpha bitch.*

As Moira slinked up to Ian, he narrowed his eyes at her. "You could be nice," he said.

"Where's the fun in that?" she purred.

Ian frowned at her. He seemed about to say something when Lily and Thomas emerged from the woods and approached the table.

Lily looked from Ian to Moira. "What's going on?" She set down a cake with fluffy white frosting and sat beside Sara.

"Just some friendly banter to get to know Sara," Moira said, her voice dripping with saccharine. She shook back her flaming hair and flashed a sharp smile.

Thomas drew up behind Moira and put his hands on her shoulders. Instead of the fine clothes he'd worn the last time Sara saw him, he was now clad in a simple black tee and shorts.

Her heart skipped a beat.

With a narrowed eye on Sara, Moira leaned into him, a lazy grin on her face.

Sara contemplated lunging across the table and attacking Moira when Thomas said, "If you're wanting *friendly* banter, here comes your brother." He squeezed her shoulders and pointed his chin at the trees beside them, where a red fox appeared.

It sauntered toward them and phased into a tall young man. Sara blinked, gripping the worn bench. He sported a gray sleeveless shirt and blue athletic shorts; lean muscle corded his arms and legs. His stride was confident and graceful, the setting sun illuminating his amber eyes and mop of red wavy hair. He looked strikingly similar to Moira.

He scanned the table and pinned his attention on Sara. "I'm Matthew," he said with a smooth smile, flicking back his hair. He slid onto the bench beside Lily. "And yes, we're twins. Moira loves me as much as she hates me." He wagged a finger at Moira, who gave him a disgusted sigh.

Sara smiled in greeting at Matthew and then stole a glance at Thomas. Her smile disappeared when he sat beside Moira and winced, a hand pressed to his side.

"You good, bro?" asked Matthew, one eyebrow cocked while he sniffed the bags of food in front of them.

"Never better," said Thomas, catching Sara's eye. She glanced away, but not before noticing his sly grin.

"The chicken is in *this* bag, idiot," said Moira, dumping the contents of one of the brown paper bags. She opened several containers of fried chicken, which Thomas and the twins kept at their end of the table, while Ian laid out a feast of salads, breads, and pastas on the other end. Still passing out food, Ian paused and looked up at Caleb approaching from the barn, arms full of clinking bottles.

"Beers on me!" he shouted, handing out bottles to everyone.

Sara accepted the one Caleb thrust at her but turned to Lily and whispered, "I don't drink."

Lily simply popped the top off the bottle in Sara's hand and said matter-of-factly, "Neither do we. Magic and alcohol are not a good mix."

"It's birch beer," said Caleb, taking a seat beside Ian and helping himself to potato salad. "Kinda like root beer but way better."

She grasped the bottle, thankful for the icy coolness on her sore thumb, and took a tentative sip. It was sweet and crisp, light and full of fresh flavor, with a slight minty aftertaste. "Much better than root beer," she agreed, licking her upper lip.

"Once the blueberries are ready, you can help me make blueberry birch beer," offered Caleb, before stuffing his mouth with food.

Moira snickered from her end of the table.

Sara was keenly aware of everyone watching her. "That'd be great. Thanks, Caleb." Not liking everyone's attention, she cleared her throat and picked at her food, trying to think of something to say that didn't convey how stupid and insecure she felt. *Now would be a good time to be gifted the power of invisibility.*

The buzz of grasshoppers grew louder in the awkward silence. She swept her gaze across the gently swaying grass and froze at a small, unmoving portion. With her eyes fixed on the still area, she whispered, "There's something in the grass."

Thomas calmly stood and turned toward the field. "Violet, you can come out now. You do realize we knew you were there the whole time." He put his thumbs in his pockets, his posture rigid, and waited.

Sara's heart skipped again at the sight of his T-shirt stretched taut across his back.

A girl, not much younger than Sara, wearing all black and a scowl on her face, materialized from the grass. Her eyes were a darker shade of blue than Thomas's. "Come on, can't I join the game tonight? I'm almost seventeen." Crossing her arms, she gave Thomas a fierce look.

"You'll be seventeen next month, and *then* you can join in the game. That's the rule, and you know it," he said. Violet didn't move, and neither did he; their intense eyes locked on each other. "I'm sure Father isn't pleased you're late for dinner," he said, slowly enunciating every syllable.

At the mention of their father, Violet sneered and broke her gaze. As she turned to leave, Lily jumped from the table and handed her a generous piece of cake. "I'll make another cake for you next month," she promised.

Violet mumbled a thank-you, took a bite, and slipped into the trees, her long black hair obscuring her presence in the darkening wood. Thomas watched the forest for a few heartbeats before sitting back down.

Eyeing the cut cake, Ian and Caleb simultaneously reached across the table and helped themselves to huge portions. "Seems our trip has been postponed indefinitely." Caleb sighed and licked frosting from his fingers. "Too many Takers and . . . all." He flinched mid-sentence when Ian kicked him under the table.

Moira groaned and dropped a naked chicken bone onto her plate.

"We can have a party at the lake," offered Lily, handing out cake to the others. "It's not the same as the beach, but we can play volleyball and have a big bonfire," she said with a halfhearted smile.

"Sounds good to me," said Ian, filling the lull in conversation. "We can go to the beach another time."

Sara kept her eyes on her plate, her stomach churning with insecurity. She had never been to the beach with friends and doubted anyone here would include her in any gatherings once they realized how different she was from them. Not gifted, but cursed with an uncontrollable, deadly monster. She may have up righted the bookcase, but she just as easily could have crushed it to dust.

"Enough, let's get going," declared Moira, pushing away from the table. "I'm it tonight." Her gaze swept them before settling on Sara, like a predator homing in on its prey.

"Ah, Hells. This will be a quick game," cursed Caleb, throwing down his napkin and getting up from the table with the rest of them.

"No, it won't," said Matthew and Thomas in unison.

"Wait—what are we playing?" asked Sara, figuring she was less of an idiot to ask than to try playing a game she knew nothing about. The evening was now thick with dusk, the moon peeking through the trees behind them as they all huddled beside the table.

Ian stood close to Sara, as if protecting her from Moira . . . or Thomas. "It's basically tag," he said. "You need to make it through the grass and the woods behind it until you reach the largest tree in the birch grove." While he explained this, the rest of them stretched and scanned the grass like generals assessing a field for battle. Fireflies blinked in the evening air.

Sara shifted her stance, feeling underprepared in her thin canvas shoes and cutoff shorts. She eyed the grass and hoped it wasn't razor sharp. She enjoyed running, the wind in her hair, the slight release from the fear and rage that haunted her. But she hadn't run in weeks, not since before the accident.

Thomas started toward Sara but was intercepted by Lily, who swooped in and took her hand, giving it a squeeze. "I'll take Sara with me," she said.

A flicker of disappointment flashed across Thomas's face. Matthew slapped him on the shoulder and chuckled.

"Come on, we got this," growled Matthew in a low voice, a glint in his eye as he winked at his sister.

"You wish," Moira spat at him.

"Okay then, same rules as always. And *play fair*," said Ian, glaring at Moira, Thomas, and Matthew. Moira grinned, tossed her hair, and phased into a fisher cat before disappearing into the thick grass.

"Mother below! She's supposed to give us a head start," said Caleb. He ran after her, the grass instantly parting for him and then swishing shut behind like a heavy curtain. Before the grass stopped swaying, Matthew phased into a fox and leapt into the green wall, followed by Thomas, who glanced back at Sara, his blue eyes and slight smile the last thing she saw before he vanished.

Dusk slipped into night, and the grass fell silent. Even the peeper frogs she'd heard earlier seemed to hold their breath.

Ian eyed Lily, nodded once, and disappeared into the field.

"Come on," said Lily as she pulled Sara into the grass behind Ian. "Be quiet and don't let go of my hand," she whispered. The smile on her face did not match the concern in her watery-gray eyes, which glimmered in the early moonlight. Keeping a firm grip on Sara with one hand, Lily extended her other hand and effortlessly parted the tall grass into a green tunnel. A cool breeze smelling faintly of lake water blew back their hair as they raced ahead.

Sara tried her best not to stumble on clusters of grass roots and fall into the thick blades, which looked lethal in the moonlight. A nearby rustling caused Lily to pivot and change course, running in a wide arc to their right. Sara tripped, but Lily tightened her grip, and the lake-scented breeze pushed her back from falling. Glancing at the sky, she spotted the tips of pine trees through the wispy top of their tunnel.

A guttural cry ripped through the night, causing Sara to falter. She recognized the voice as Caleb's, and the hairs on her arms stood up. She tried to pull Lily back to help him, but Lily ran faster.

"He's fine." Her hoarse whisper came on a gasp as they burst from the field and ran, ducking under the lowest boughs of the pine trees.

Sara strained to hear a laugh or even a curse from Caleb, but all she heard was the thundering of her feet on the thick forest floor.

Another distant yell cut through the forest, this time coming from in front of them. Sara's jaw dropped in disbelief at Moira's speed in quickly tagging out two people that far apart. She held tight to Lily's hand as they stuck close to the protection of the larger trees and headed for a small clearing.

Panting, Sara willed her legs to keep moving and hoped the birch tree was close. She glanced up from the forest floor and over Lily's shoulder. Beyond the clearing shone the birch grove, each white trunk glowing like an ephemeral spirit in the moonlight. The striking image stole her breath, and she stumbled again. At the base of the birch trees hung a hazy mist, seeping from the grove and creeping toward them.

Captivated by the mystical scene, Sara didn't notice the dark shadow fluttering above them until Lily drew back and shoved her aside. Blonde hair flaring, Lily whirled and pulled the mist around her like a cloak. But before she could vanish into the haze, a fisher cat slammed into her back with surprising force, launching her into the air. A gust of wind caught her fall and set her down onto a patch of ice that burst across the forest floor. The ice crackled and stretched before Lily like a royal carpet. She skated with effortless grace and laughed as the fisher cat lost its footing and slid off into the bushes with a yowl.

She turned to Sara and pointed toward the birches. "Run to the tree!"

Sara hesitated, completely in awe of Lily's power. Another fluttering shadow swooped toward her, and a firm hand clamped onto her forearm, pulling her into the mist of the birch grove. She gasped, her mind flush with thoughts of the hospital orderly, Brad.

"It's me," said Ian. She noted his fresh pine-and-cinnamon scent and sighed in relief.

"Go on, Trouble," he snarled, and waved off the raven flapping around them. Trouble let out a loud squawk just as the fisher cat leapt at them from behind. Ian swiftly turned, protecting Sara in his arms, with the cat tagging him instead of her before it disappeared back into the hazy grove.

"I'm out now too," said Ian with a disgusted glare at Moira's raven, which guttered a laugh. "She ran off to stop Matt and Thomas, so now's your chance. Make a run for the big tree. Straight ahead—you can't miss it." He gestured urgently.

With Ian's confidence bolstering her, she broke into a run through the grove. The mist cleared, and she saw her opening to a magnificent birch with multiple trunks and a crown of shimmering leaves.

Blood pumping and excitement spreading across her face, she reached out to touch the trunk, only to be struck from the side by a fisher cat with lightning speed.

CHAPTER 19

SEARING PAIN TORE along her upper thigh. Sara curled into herself, protecting her leg, as she hurtled forward from the force of the tag, slammed into the birch, and crumpled at the base of its trunk. With a defeated groan, she turned her head, scraping a cheek against the rough bark. To her left, an invisible force flung the fisher cat away from her. Its bloodcurdling scream sent shivers down Sara's spine.

Thomas knelt beside her, his rigid posture appearing uncomfortable. He was so close she could feel heat radiating from him.

"Are you okay?" he asked, extending a hand.

She hated that question—it meant everyone thought she was broken. "I can take care of myself," she said through gritted teeth. Ignoring his hand, she struggled to stand on her own, a deep scratch on her leg throbbing with pain. Moira crept along the edge of the tree's shadow, flicking her tail. Sara glared at the fisher cat and flexed her fingers, hands tingling.

Shit. Keep it together. I cannot lose it over a stupid game.

She was tired of being weak and not fitting in. Tired of being pummeled by a cursed life. She didn't care about the scratch on her leg or losing a stupid game . . . or even a crazy prophecy.

What she cared about was getting her father out of the hospital and killing the dark witch.

Shit. Save this anger for the one who truly deserves it.

Leaning against the tree, she fought to slow her rapid heart-beat—to keep her anger at bay.

Thomas clenched his jaw and stood, letting his hand fall into a fist at his side. "Go away, Moira, before I hurt you," he growled in a low whisper. A breeze ruffled the shadows, and moonlight flickered across his inner forearm, revealing the raised welt of a symbol branded into his skin.

Sara stiffened at seeing the familiar sign.

"Moira!" shouted Ian, as he and Lily ran to the birch tree.

The anger in his voice shocked Sara. The fisher cat looked wildly from Thomas to Ian before hissing and vanishing into the night.

Matthew dropped from the tree, soundlessly landing on his feet. "I'll go after her," he said with a sigh. He phased back into a fox and disappeared, his red tail flashing behind him.

Jogging up just in time to see Matthew leave, Caleb held his side and gasped for breath. "What . . . happened?"

Distracted by Caleb's disheveled appearance, Sara didn't notice Thomas sliding closer to her until he was right beside her.

"Your face is bleeding," Thomas said, frowning at the gash on her cheek. His hand brushed aside her hair.

Sara jerked back and felt her ears burn. Turning into the shadows, she gingerly touched her cheek. "It's just a scratch. I'm fine." She squared her shoulders and faced the group.

"I should have known she would do this," said Ian. His voice had calmed, but his hands were clenched.

Lily spoke up. "We all know Moira cheats, but she's never hurt anyone. That's a strict rule we've never broken."

Sara may have lost the game, but she couldn't stand the thought of being a victim. "It's my fault," she blurted. "I tripped and fell into the tree."

They all focused on her as moonlight twinkled through the birch leaves. Besides a pair of owls hooting back and forth, no other sound broke the humid night air.

"I'm clumsy and out of shape," she said in a lighthearted tone, looking pointedly at Caleb, who was still puffing.

Caleb took his hands off his knees and stood up to his full height, a wicked grin spreading across his face. "Are you suggesting I'm out of shape?" A deep chuckle broke his mock aggression, like he knew she needed a laugh. "I'm just big boned. It's hard to run when you're Hercules." He flexed and grunted.

Thomas snorted, and Sara laughed out loud for the first time in weeks. She glanced around and caught Ian and Lily staring at each other.

Lily gave an almost imperceptible nod before saying, "It's getting late. Thomas, will you help me pick up the table while Ian and Caleb get Sara settled for the night?"

Thomas cocked an eyebrow and smirked at Ian before sliding his gaze to Lily. "Of course." He nodded politely, his voice silky smooth. Ian bristled and remained tense until Thomas and Lily headed back to the grassy field, taking the mist with them.

Ian shifted his weight and broke the quiet. "You're always welcome at our house and—"

Caleb interrupted and completed his sentence, "—and at the Main House, but I put something together today that you might like. Ya know . . . for whenever you just need a place of your own." Caleb cracked his knuckles nervously.

Sara stared at him. "You made something. For me?"

A breeze shimmered the leaves overhead and moonlight fell on them, illuminating the scratch on her leg.

Ian frowned. "Maybe Helen should take a look at you tonight. You can check out Caleb's creation tomorrow."

"No," she said with a quick shake of her head. "I'm fine. Really." She turned to hide herself from the gaze of the moon and tucked her still-swollen thumb into her shorts pocket. Recalling Caleb's exquisitely crafted table and chairs at the Main House, she secretly hoped he'd fashioned such a chair for her. Her face flushed with excitement, and adrenaline eased her hurts. "So where is this creation of yours?"

"Down by the lake," said Caleb, angling his head to the left. "We can take a shortcut." He pointed to a path that suddenly formed, trees and understory bending out of the way, as though the forest was yawning. Sara stepped toward the curious path. A rustle of leaves and creak of branches sounded as it stretched, winding among the trees. She ran ahead, trying to catch the forest's mysterious movements.

"After everything, you still wanna race?" Caleb chuckled, jogging alongside her. "You won't get too far without me," he said, holding out his hands, the trees bowing out of their way.

Running in the dappled moonlight, the forest alive and moving about her, Sara lifted her chin and smiled at the starry sky. An overwhelming sense of wonder filled her, and for just a moment she let herself think . . . perhaps she did belong here.

When the path abruptly ended at the back of the cemetery, she stopped short, Caleb and Ian nearly crashing into her.

"That was quite the shortcut," she said, wheeling around in disbelief. Fireflies blinked among the gravestones.

Her attention immediately went to her mother's headstone, which seemed oddly darkened by shadows instead of illuminated by the moon. Looking up, she gasped at a multilevel treehouse sitting perfectly in the open palm of the oak tree. The building was so well placed that it was difficult to tell what was tree and what was building, both entwined as one.

Ian stepped over the cemetery fence and let out a low whistle. "Wow, Caleb, this is amazing."

Caleb strode to the curved stairway that cascaded down the trunk. "Yeah, well, still needs furniture and window glass. If you want them." His voice was humble, almost apologetic. "If you like it, anyway," he said to Sara.

"I love it," she breathed, tilting her head back to take it all in.

"But . . . how did you do this? In one day?" She expected to see lumber, tools, sawdust, but saw nothing. The cemetery was exactly as it had been that morning, not a nail left behind or flower out of place—just the treehouse seamlessly constructed into the natural shape of the tree.

She stared in awe at the curved stairway, which had no handrail and no obvious support connecting the stairs to the tree. The spiral staircase seemed to have grown into place, flowing down and around the trunk.

Keeping one hand on the tree, she ascended the steps. At the top was a large main room with a wrap-around deck. She crouched and touched a knot in the deck flooring, the wood impossibly sleek beneath her fingers. The outside of the treehouse blended into the gnarled gray trunk, while the interior woodwork was a smooth golden-brown, rich with grain, as if she'd stepped inside the tree itself.

Sara inhaled deeply, surprised to smell a weathered, oaky musk rather than fresh-cut wood. All the woodwork, even the thick and undulating floor planks, had graceful, rounded edges, not a cut visible. Indeed, the entire house appeared to have grown into place, carefully coaxed and caressed into a living wooden wonder.

She stepped into the main room and studied the ceiling, which was ribbed with twigs that flexed and sprouted tiny green leaves. Moonlight shone through multiple window openings and doorways and, near the trunk, a steep, narrow staircase led to another level above.

Sara felt Caleb watching her from the center of the main room. She turned to him, eyes wide. "How . . ."

When he only grinned, Ian spoke. "Caleb is a gifted earth witch. Trees are his specialty." He placed one hand on the tree trunk by the steep stairway. "This is your best work yet. How did you awaken the tree? It seemed dead all this time."

"She spoke to me this morning," said Caleb, running his hand along a beam overhead that was more a living branch than honed construction. "The tree, I mean," he added in response to Sara's confused expression. "She led the way. I'm not sure I did much. I don't think anyone could do anything to this tree if she didn't will it." He strode toward Ian, his footsteps thudding across the wooden floor, and put both hands on the trunk. "I've never felt any tree like this before. Not even the soul trees have the same energy as this one."

Caleb extended an arm to the staircase and turned to Sara. "Check it out, there's your bedroom and then a turret and upper deck on top."

"This is for *me*?" She stared all around her. Like the Atwell island, the treehouse felt much larger on the inside than its outward appearance suggested.

"Yeah. There's just a bed for now, but we'll help you furnish it. Maybe even add a little furnace for the winter months. If you want," Caleb added, cracking a thumb.

"Oh, Caleb, thank you." She stretched on tiptoe to hug him, careful not to press her bloody scratch onto his shorts. He returned the hug with a crushing tightness before she pulled away and wiped a tear from the corner of her eye.

"Okay, then," he said, cracking his knuckles and averting his eyes from her tears. "Get a good night's sleep, and we'll see you for breakfast at the Main House."

Ian hesitated before following Caleb down the spiral stairs. He fixed Sara with a protective older brother look. "You sure you're okay?"

"Stop asking me that. I'm fine. Just tired," she assured him.

"The forest paths can be a bit tricky, so Lily or I will swing by in the morning to walk with you. If you need anything, just call me."

"Call you?" she said, perplexed. Her cell phone had died long ago at Green Brier Lane. Besides, she had seen no type of phone, cell or landline, anywhere in Ware Woods.

Ian tapped his temple as he descended from view. *"With your mind,"* said his voice in her head.

CHAPTER 20

S ARA SPUN AROUND the main room, a breeze blowing back her hair and whispering through the leaves. The many window openings and doorways created the feeling of being on a tree branch rather than being inside a house. Excited to see the next level, she ran up the little staircase, hands grabbing the steep stairs like a ladder.

Though smaller than the main room, the second level was plenty spacious. Before her sprawled a large four-poster bed, each post a slender trunk growing through the floor and continuing into the twig-lined ceiling. To her surprise and relief, the bed had already been made with crisp sheets and the familiar blue blanket and pillow. On top sat her black duffel bag, its contents the sum of her current worldly possessions.

Turning away from the bag, she stepped to one of the large window openings. Perched on the sill closest to her was a thermos and a bottle of birch beer. She grabbed the bottle, popped the cap with the front of her shirt, and peered out at the moon shining on the lake.

Physically exhausted, she wanted to fall into bed, but her mind whirred with a jumble of racing thoughts: the red-stained map, slamming into the birch tree, running along the moonlit path, the treehouse, missing her mom, wanting her dad to answer all her questions, and—of course—figuring out how she fit into Ware Woods.

Distracted by her worries, she nearly dropped her beer at the sudden presence of yellow primrose blossoms on the window ledge. She touched the flowers to determine if she was awake or dreaming. The butter-soft petals dusted her fingertip with pollen and released a delicate sweet scent. Clasping the sill, she leaned out and froze at the sight of a figure standing near the rear of the cemetery.

Her heart skipped a beat, longing to see her mother's spirit. But it was Thomas who stepped out from the shadows, his confident white smile shining in the moonlight.

Sara glanced at the flowers and then back at him. "Did you just . . . send these?" she asked, incredulous.

"Yes, I whished them. Like this." He rose from the ground and levitated toward the lower level of the house. Grinning at her, he sketched a tight bow in the air, one arm flourished as he slightly dipped at the waist. "May I come in?"

Sara gripped the glass bottle so tightly she thought it would shatter, and stammered, "Oh—of course." Still clutching the beer, she skidded down the steep stairs to see Thomas glide forward and land on the lower deck. "Can you do that all the time?" She stepped toward him slowly, afraid he might fly away.

"Yes. And I can do more than whishing." He grinned again, this time with a bold slyness, and the bottle slipped from her fingers and flew into his hand. He took a long drink and then held out the bottle to her.

Sara wasn't sure what bothered her more—the fact that he brazenly drank from her bottle or the way he looked at her while he did it. She grabbed the beer, straightened her shoulders, and stared into his eyes, taking an equally long drink before handing it back to him.

Thomas cocked an eyebrow and huffed a laugh. With a slight

tilt of his head, he accepted the beer from her and strolled into the main room.

"Your cousin has outdone himself," he stated, his tone full of genuine admiration. He completed a slow turn, keenly observing every structural detail. "I could force the wood together, but it would never look like this." He took the last sip of beer and whished the empty bottle to a window ledge. His movement was so controlled that the bottle settled without so much as a clink.

Sara leaned back and narrowed her eyes at him. "Is that why you're here? To check it out?"

Thomas turned to face her and faltered for a moment. "Um, yeah." He rubbed the back of his head, the filtered moonlight casting shadows on his face.

"Okay . . ." she drawled, still squinting and not entirely sure of his motive. "Let's check out the turret. I haven't seen it yet, but I'm sure the view is amazing." She motioned for him to take the stairs in front of her and then silently cursed herself for suggesting a view to someone who could apparently levitate and fly at will. Despite Ian's warning, his presence intrigued her, and she didn't want him to leave.

He backed away from the steep stairs, a hand lightly pressed to his side. "Sure, I'll meet you there." He strode onto the deck, stepped off the edge, and rose out of view.

Watching him step into the night sky caused her breath to hitch—nothing below to catch him. She clambered up the stairs to the bedroom loft and then climbed a ladder of entwined branches into the round turret, whose peaked ceiling was a magnificent sculpture of swirling twigs. Surrounding the circular room was a wall of window openings and a wide doorway facing the lake. Golden-brown flooring flowed from the room and out the doorway to form a small deck tucked into the tree's upper canopy. Similar to the lower level, the deck had no railing whatsoever.

Sara sucked in a breath at the sight of Thomas sitting with his back to her, legs dangling over the edge. Keeping a tight grip on the doorway, she crept onto the deck and sat against the curved turret wall.

The treehouse creaked, and he stole a glance over his shoulder. "Don't worry, I won't let you fall." He sounded sincere, like he'd known her his whole life. As if she mattered to him.

She hugged her knees, careful not to touch the scratch on her thigh. She wasn't entirely sure his gift could save her if she pitched over the edge.

A soft wind murmured through the leaves, somewhat easing her tension. She didn't make a move to join his precarious location, and he soon pushed away from the edge, kinetically sliding across the deck to sit beside her against the wall. In his movement, she caught another glimpse of the brand on his forearm. The mark was a unique combination of the infinity and yin-yang symbols—an oblique figure eight with an open circle inside one loop and a solid circle in the other. A tattoo of the same sigil was inked into her father's back, right below his neck.

She chewed her lip, debating if she should ask Thomas about it. But really, all she wanted to do was touch it—to trace the loops and magically take away the pain it surely once caused him.

"Why did you lie about tripping and falling?" His words lingered in the still air, his expression curious in the pale light.

She turned away, avoiding his blue eyes. "I don't want anyone's pity. I'm stronger than people think."

Thomas huffed again, followed by a wince. "I never said you're weak. On the contrary, you seem quite . . . fierce." He watched her for a long moment before joining her in gazing at the lake.

She resumed chewing her lip. Maybe Ian was right. Maybe Thomas did see her as a challenge.

Maybe she didn't care.

She tried to focus on the stillness of the night, the slight breeze in the cool air, the occasional shadowy flicker of bats on the hunt. Anything to distract her from the heat radiating from his body.

Minutes passed. Although he said nothing, the soft hush of his shallow breaths confirmed what she already knew.

Alrighty, then. If you won't state the obvious, I will.

"What's wrong, Thomas?" she asked, her heart skipping a beat at saying his name out loud.

"Nothing, just enjoying the view." Keeping his shoulders pressed against the wall, he turned his head to her. Amusement replaced his curiosity.

Her heart skipped another beat as he stared into her eyes without flinching in the slightest.

His words seemed genuine, but Sara knew otherwise. Her father once told her she was a bullshit detector; she could instinctively recognize a lie and someone's true nature. It was both a gift and a curse, and it was the reason she knew she could trust Ian and Lily, but not exactly Moira. It was also the reason she knew Thomas was hiding something.

She squinted at his stiff posture. "Cut the crap. I think everyone tonight could tell you're hurt." She nodded to his side and bitterly added, "Did Moira do that, too?"

Thomas chuckled and pressed his side. "Don't let her fool you. Moira's bark is worse than her bite. This"—he winced, gently patting his side—"is a lesson from my father."

"He hit you?" Sara nearly grabbed his arm from a sudden burst of anger and instinct to protect him—to right a wrong.

He pulled back a fraction, eyes wide, before turning to gaze at the night sky. "Gifted heal much quicker than the average person. I'll be fine in a few days." He clenched his teeth, causing a muscle to twitch along his jaw. "Did Ian tell you my family, the Sullivans, are sentries of Ware Woods?"

"Ian mentioned each family has gifts that help the forest. But how does that relate to anyone hitting you, never mind your own father?" She shifted to sit facing him, no longer caring how close to the edge she was. A warmth tickled her bare knee when it skimmed his thigh. He flicked his gaze at their connection and took a sharp breath.

"You don't like it when someone is concerned about you, but you're quick to be concerned about others." Thomas shook his head, a smile tugging at the corner of his mouth. He kept his shoulders back, glanced at how close to the edge she sat, and inclined his head toward her. "My father takes our role seriously and trains us hard. He doesn't intentionally hurt us but . . . injuries are expected."

Sara could easily read anger and pain in his face. She felt it in her heart, as if she were a part of him. Startled by the pull of his emotions, she closed her eyes and exhaled to ground herself, but the yearning to ease his hurt tugged at her soul.

Without thinking, she reached out to him but was struck by a jolt of energy and a wave of unfettered *awareness*—as if she were him. She felt what he felt. He had a broken rib, one that had been broken before, and an excruciating headache, which plagued him from years of multiple concussions. She gasped at the sharp pains—his pains—that now coursed through her. Grabbing hold of him, she imagined a warm light washing over them and taking away the pain. She pulled him closer until the last ache dissolved, and they both relaxed.

Not wanting to let go of him, she tightened her grip, and a series of memories flooded her consciousness. The memories were not her own but belonged to Thomas, as a young boy. At first, they were happy memories, but then something changed. They grew darker, punched with sadness and pain.

"STOP!"

The flush of power snapped, breaking its hold on Sara. She opened her eyes to find their hands clasped together, their touch pulsing and tingling with energy. Despite her shock and guilt at seeing his memories, she lifted her chin and met his stare.

For a heart-pounding moment, they locked eyes and shared panted breaths.

Sara pulled her hands away. "I'm sorry. I didn't mean to—" She stopped, not knowing exactly what she had done or what to say next. He leaned in to tuck a lock of hair behind her ear, then ran his thumb across her cheek, his touch sending a shiver up her spine. "Your scrape is gone." His voice was barely a whisper. His callused hand ran down her arm, making the small of her back prickle. Dropping his hand, he lightly touched her thigh. "And your leg is healed."

She followed his gaze to her leg. The scratch was gone, her skin flushing with warmth where he touched her. She raised her hand to the nape of her sweaty neck, pushing her fingers along her scalp, and eased at finding no new bald patches or loose hair.

Thomas pressed his side, fingers tapping his ribs, before reaching up and rubbing the back of his head. "My pain is gone. Even the headache." He sounded relieved, but his brows were drawn. In a blink, his expression changed, and he grinned at her. "You're a healer. That's your gift."

Sara pulled back, turning away from his gaze and shaking her head. "Oh no. I'm far from it." Her eyes stung with the shame of horrible things she had done, the terrible, angry thoughts that sometimes popped into her head. She was the opposite of a healer.

Feeling his penetrating stare, her mind raced for a plausible explanation. "If I was, I would have healed myself earlier, right? It must be the house and the tree . . . or the cemetery." She gestured around them, desperate to divert his attention. "There's an energy here. I know you feel it too."

Thomas was quiet for a long moment. "Yes," was all he said, his voice deep and resonant in the still air.

Sara scooted to sit beside him against the wall, their shoulders shifting to touch like two magnets drawn together. She leaned back to rest her head, which suddenly felt very heavy, and shut her eyes.

She didn't know how much time had passed. It could have been minutes or hours, but she woke to find herself alone in the four-poster bed. Though still fully clothed, she lay tucked into the blue blanket while her shoes rested neatly on the floor. The yellow primrose on the window ledge was the last thing she saw before drifting back to sleep.

CHAPTER 21

Sara was running through the forest again, but this time, she wasn't laughing. Choking on thick smoke, she sprinted toward a fire that crackled and spewed embers, igniting the surrounding forest. An apocalyptic orange glow filled the sky.

She raced through the birch grove and past the fields, straight to the source—the Cahill chestnut tree. But before she could reach the common, flames and smoke dissolved into a snowy mist. The thick, cloudy haze blinded her, soothing her ash-filled throat and burning eyes. Skidding to a halt, she felt herself float up from the ground and into the mist.

"*Sara*," said a breathy, faraway voice. "*Sara*," it called, closer and clearer this time. Clear enough for Sara to know it was her mother's voice.

Dew caressed her face as the mist swirled into diaphanous flowers, loose petals fluttering around her. "*I am with you always. And now you are where you were always meant to be.*" The floral mist caressed her skin and rippled away, receding like the tide, taking her mother's voice with it.

Sara reached out to grasp the wispy petals, desperate to hold on to her mother.

"*Know you are being watched. Believe and trust in yourself,*" her mother's voice echoed.

The mist vanished, and Sara found herself in the four-poster bed, the soft light of dawn touching her face. A wren landed on the blanket and tilted its head at her before flying out the window opening to perch on a tree branch thick with new leaves. Behind the bird, movement on the lake caught her eye—Lily drifting in on the boat.

Shaking off the vivid dream, Sara slid out of bed and changed into clean clothes from the duffel bag on the floor. Every time she unzipped her bag, the sight and smell of her belongings reminded her of life before the accident. But the familiar scent of lavender laundry detergent was fading, replaced almost entirely now by the rich oak musk of the treehouse.

She grabbed the thermos from the sill and gratefully took a long, cool drink, drowning the remnants of her fiery dream.

Lily announced her arrival with a friendly breeze that blew up the stairs and rustled the treehouse leaves. "Good morning," she called out cheerfully and entered the main room.

"Hey, Lily," said Sara, descending the small staircase and pulling her hair back into a low ponytail to hide the bald patches. "Thanks for coming to get me. Otherwise, I'd probably get lost finding my own way. The paths seem to shift and change direction at will."

"Ah, yes. They do have a habit of doing that, but you'll get the hang of it soon enough. The trick is simply to *know* where you want to go." She smiled and glanced around the treehouse. "It's quite nice, isn't it?" she said matter-of-factly, peering out at the lake and running a hand over a smooth window ledge, her elbow close to the empty beer bottle.

Sara eyed the bottle, breath hitching at the memory of clasping hands with Thomas, and wondered if Lily was referring to the treehouse, the lake, or the entire sacred forest.

Sara cleared her throat. "Yes, quite." She agreed. "I know I just got here, but it seems like I've been here a long time. It's strange. As if a part of me has been here all along." Her gaze swept the forest.

Lily turned away from the water, her pale face and liquid gray eyes smiling at Sara. "I'm glad you're here. All the Atwells are. We never thought your folks should have taken you away. Remember that tonight at the Council meeting." She pivoted and descended the staircase, pausing at the bottom for Sara to catch up.

"Okay." Sara drew out the word. *What the hell does that mean?* She hesitated on the stairs, distracted by the sight of her mother's grave, last night's dream echoing in her heart. More wildflowers grew around her stone. The rabbit lay among them, its back legs spread out and its eyes half closed as it dozed in the shade of the treehouse.

After meeting Ian for breakfast, they spent the rest of the morning helping Helen with more experimental remedies for the blight. In the afternoon, they all returned to the Main House to prepare food for the Council meeting.

Sara wiped her forehead with the back of her hand, taking a break from prepping fruits and vegetables fresh from the garden. "Is this typical for every Council meeting?" She pointed with her paring knife to multiple simmering pots and platters of food large enough to feed a small army.

"Yes, 'tis," said Caleb's mother, Rebecca. "Cahills provide the food and Atwells bring dessert." She took crusty loaves of bread out of the oven, slid in more dough, and wiped her hands on an apron patterned with poppy-red flowers. "Every full moon, we meet to celebrate milestones and discuss important topics. This has always been the way for us," she said before heading back to the pantry.

Sara eyed the other Cahills bustling about the kitchen and wondered what particular gifts they possessed. They were friendly and joked around as they worked, but their aggressive kneading and loud, snapping knife cuts put a hint of tension in the air. She hoped it was the dark witch and not her presence keeping everyone on edge.

She finished slicing her last cucumber when Helen came in from the garden with more produce. Stifling a groan, she turned away from the cutting board to find Ian laughing at her.

"Come on," he said, handing her a square basket large enough to hold a week's worth of laundry. Sara peeked inside, seeing an assortment of linens, plates, and flatware. "Lily already left to get desserts. You and I can set tables at the Council tree." He nodded at Helen on their way out to the grassy common.

"See you later," said Helen, her face pinched with unease as she lifted her chin at them.

Sara bit her lip and silently followed Ian. When they approached the massive chestnut tree, he nudged her and gave a reassuring smile over the two baskets in his arms. "Remember, just know you want to go to the Council tree and that's where you'll be." He stepped and disappeared into the trunk.

Sara stared at the tree and gripped her basket, the woven handles cutting into her sweaty palms. Plates and flatware rattled, and she hoped not to lose any contents—or her lunch. She closed her eyes and stepped forward, trusting she would walk through the chestnut and pop out of the Council tree instead of smacking her face into the shaggy bark.

The familiar static energy of the soul tree pulled her in. Soft breezes danced over her skin, and the rhythmic pulse of living energy vibrated through her. When it stopped, she stepped forward again and found herself under the broad green leaves of the sugar maple, the Council stage to her left.

By the time Ian and Sara laid out dozens of place settings, the Cahills arrived and arranged food on a long table beside the stump stage. Next came Orsen and Elizabeth, followed by Lily and Gran, carrying trays of desserts. Lily set down her trays, waved at Sara, and then hurried to the rear of the clearing to help Ian.

Sara finished setting her last table and approached the sweets, the scent of cakes and pies making her mouth water.

"Make sure you try Alice's strawberry-rhubarb crumble. Next month will be my famous blueberry pie," said Gran with a nod.

"Where is Alice?" asked Sara, searching for familiar faces to ease an unsettling feeling, her shoulders tight with tension. She ran her fingers along the back of her neck and exhaled to the count of three.

Gran turned from the dessert display. "Alice is tending to Albert, who is healing nicely, thanks to you. Besides, she doesn't leave the island much. She's not keen on Makwa and Dorcas."

Sara shook her head, denying the credit. It had been the salve, not her, that healed Albert. Her eyes followed Gran's as they swept the clearing, people trickling in from all directions. "Who *are* Makwa and Dorcas?" The names felt strange on her tongue, like they were forbidden words. "What family are they from? Or . . . are they animals?" *Man-eating animals.*

"Gaa!" Gran bristled and waved her hand. "Never mind them. They are best ignored."

Taking Sara's hand, Gran escorted her to a table near the stage. "Now, dear . . ." She sat beside Sara and fixed her with a serious expression. "I'm sure the meeting will address the blight and any other issues first, and then you and Naomi will have your turn on the stage. I'll be here for you the whole time," she said, patting her hand.

Sara felt the blood drain from her face. "What do you mean . . . *our turn?*"

A thin smile stretched Gran's lips. "It's just a formality, really. Naomi has decided to join Ware Woods and, as such, is expected to pledge herself and drink the sap of the soul tree. You're Ware Woods family, but given your . . . situation, Council wants you to pledge yourself too." Gran snorted. "Don't roll your eyes. It's not a big deal. At the age of seventeen, every child does the same. While some children may exhibit magic at an early age, when the sap is drunk and they pledge themselves to the forest, their magic becomes stronger. It is a rite of passage."

Sara stared at the stage, her cheeks burning and her breathing shallow.

"So . . . I drink the sap and then I should have magic?"

The mere thought of standing before people terrified her,

knowing they would judge her—or worse, see through her to the awful things she had done and was capable of. But she was also excited at the opportunity to be gifted magic—good magic—and to no longer be the outsider in Ware Woods.

She bit her lip. Perhaps the sap could replace her murderous monster with something . . . less destructive, or maybe even beneficial.

Turning to Gran, she dropped her start of a smile and let out an irritated sigh. Gran had twisted in her seat and was talking with Elizabeth at an adjacent table.

Sara scanned the gathering crowd and spotted the twins, Moira and Matthew, sitting with their family toward the back of the clearing. At another rear table, Thomas—dressed in a light-blue button-down shirt—sat with Violet and a boy about ten years of age. As if he knew she was watching him, Thomas shifted his gaze directly at her, his blue eyes bright in the setting sun and his smile as sly as ever. He continued to stare at her while he unbuttoned his cuffs and rolled up his sleeves.

A slender woman in a dark-green dress stood at a chair beside him. Sara presumed her to be Thomas's mother, which meant the man standing behind him was his father. With a bold arrogance, he tracked Thomas's gaze to Sara, disapproval showing in his stern face. The judgment pissed her off, and she pursed her lips to keep from baring her teeth. Thomas instantly dropped his smile and shifted, busying himself with pulling out a chair for his mother.

Mr. Sullivan narrowed his eyes in open hostility, causing Sara to suck in a breath and turn away. Though she didn't know him, she already despised him. Tucking her chin, she yanked out her ponytail, letting her hair fall in a curtain around her face. She watched him from the corner of her eye as he placed a chair, angled toward her, and sat with his hands on his knees.

He seemed a formidable man—the stiff posture of a soldier,

not a hair out of place, and impeccably dressed, with a thick ring on his right hand.

Sara knew that ring. She had seen it in Thomas's memories and felt it hit his face as if it were her own.

Mr. Sullivan beckoned to Thomas, who leaned in, listening for a moment. When he sat back, Thomas's face was rigid, his jaw clenched. He stared at the ground and folded his arms across his chest.

"Hey." Ian's voice sounded in Sara's head, startling her. He brushed against her chair and stood blocking her view of the Sullivans, a reproving look on his face. "I thought I'd grab you both some food," he said, setting a full plate in front of her and handing another to Gran.

Sara grabbed his arm, pulling him into the chair beside her.

"Why didn't you tell me I'd have to get up there tonight?" she said, stabbing a hand toward the stage.

"Would it have changed anything?" He plucked a roll from her plate and took a bite.

Incensed by his calmness, she glared at him. "I don't know. Maybe I could have been better prepared . . . or at least dressed nicer." She grimaced at her faded tee.

Ian shifted in his chair, drawing her attention back to his face. "Don't worry about the Sullivans."

Sara flicked a glance over Ian's shoulder, toward the rear of the clearing, and leaned into him. "Are you reading my mind?" she accused him.

He clicked his tongue, eyes wide. "No, never. But you project your thoughts like a lighthouse. You should learn to be more closed." He wagged a finger at her and took another bite of roll.

She wanted to smash the roll into his face. "Well, shit, Ian, maybe if you taught me. Did the thought ever occur to you?"

Before he could respond, Naomi approached their table, hands full of food and drink.

"Naomi," said Ian, jumping from his chair. "I insist you join us." He smiled and pulled out the seat beside him. "I'll be right back with my own plate."

Sara glared at him as he went back to the food tables.

"A sibling fight already," Naomi said with a chuckle. She sat and took a long drink from her birch beer.

"Since when did you two get so chummy?" said Sara, her tone sounding more irritated than she intended.

Naomi choked on her drink.

"Naomi is Ian's aunt," said Gran, finally turning away from the Atwell table.

Sara's head jerked back in surprise.

Naomi laughed, nearly spilling her beer. "We figured it out when I saw his charm bracelet. It's the same protective charm I gave my older sister, Winona, when she left our site. It's no coincidence I found you and came to Ware Woods. Ian is all the family I have left."

Sara's jaw dropped. She faltered, unsure if she should be happy or sad for Naomi, when Ted approached the table and laid his hands on the back of Ian's empty chair. "Naomi, since protocol prohibits you from speaking until after you have pledged yourself to our forest, Larry and Kane will mention your experience." He kept his voice low while scanning the crowded tables.

"Thank you, Ted," said Naomi. "I want to help in any way I can."

He nodded at her and then focused on Sara, his concerned expression so much like her father's that her heart ached. "Relax," he assured her. "You have nothing to be worried about. You have many supporters here tonight." His smile disappeared when he noticed Thomas's father rising from his table. "Excuse me, we're about to start the meeting," Ted said, stepping aside to meet Mr. Sullivan and Orsen Atwell at the left of the stage.

CHAPTER 22

SARA PICKED AT the food in front of her while Naomi and Gran chatted. Ted's implication that not everyone approved of her presence mirrored Lily's comment in the treehouse, stirring Sara's suspicion that maybe she didn't belong in Ware Woods. The image of a hornet's nest flashed in her mind. *Am I about to step into a nightmare? Or cause one?* She chewed on her lip at her impossible situation—having finally discovered the big missing piece of herself only to fear it didn't want her or she didn't deserve it. Or both.

She wished their table wasn't so close to the stage. Sara had the distinct impression everyone was staring at her. When Ian returned to the table, she tried to hide in his slim shadow.

"Now," he said, laying out two plates of food for himself, "I can eat and enjoy the show." He grinned at her before stuffing his mouth.

"If I don't literally die tonight, I may have to kill you tomorrow." She held a faint smile, enjoying the sibling banter while burying a growing panic that she *could* very well die tonight. If they discovered her murderous power, would they banish her or kill her for what lurked beneath her skin? She needed to hide the darkness inside her, push it down deep enough to be imperceptible

174

to all the magical eyes on her. Then maybe—*maybe*—she could survive this rite.

A hush fell over the crowd. People stopped eating and talking and turned their attention to the large stump. Ted stepped onto the stage, faced the assembly, and waved his hand low at his side. Everyone responded by raising a hand above their head and waving back. In perfect unison, as if their words were as common as a noonday greeting, as familiar as breathing, the families recited a blessing:

"Mother below and Father above,
I give my true self unto your love;
To feel the earth and touch the sky,
I choose to live before I die;
For I am you and you are me,
We are the light, so mote it be."

Orsen and Mr. Sullivan joined Ted on the Council stage while he welcomed the families and launched right into the agenda.

"First topic," said Ted, "is the blight. Larry will provide the update on this growing threat." He stepped back into the shadows with Orsen and Mr. Sullivan.

Uncle Larry ascended a small set of stairs to the right of the stage and strode to the center. "As many of you know, the blight is rapidly spreading. We have never seen the likes of this and, so far, our efforts to stop it have been unsuccessful. This blight is not typical and is affecting all varieties of trees. Because of our observations and Naomi's experience, we know this blight is dark magic."

The families gasped—the whole clearing stilled, not even a blade of grass swaying.

Uncle Larry merely nodded and continued. "We are confident the blight cannot cross our wall, but we need to stop the spread before it destroys the outer forest. Anyone without an outside role is expected to assist."

As Uncle Larry listed tasks needing help, Sara leaned toward Ian and whispered, "What does he mean, outside role?"

Ian merely shoved a forkful of food into his mouth. *"Some of us have jobs outside of the forest."*

Sara nearly fell off her chair from hearing his voice in her mind.

"It helps bring in money and keep respectful relations with the neighboring towns." He gave a slight jerk of his head to the tables behind them. *"The Walkers have the best veterinarian practice in the county, and the Sullivans are powerful attorneys."*

Sara eyed Mr. Sullivan's fine clothes and shiny black shoes. Her mind raced with the memory of overhearing her parents discuss family donations. At the time, she had assumed it was for charity.

Her gaze swept across Orsen and Uncle Larry before flitting back to Ian. "What about the other families?"

He raised a glass of water to his mouth. *"The Atwells take care of our finances and the lake, and the Cahills handle all the crops and livestock."* He took a sip and, before she could ask, answered her next question. *"Lochtons typically handle communications and negotiations."* He shrugged. *"We're the glue that holds everything together, although someone else would enjoy that role as well."* Ian lifted his chin toward the stage.

With her eyes, Sara followed his line of sight to Mr. Sullivan. He stood motionless, his arms crossed and expression unreadable as he watched Uncle Larry continue his long list of tasks. A deep grumble escaped her, and Ian jabbed his elbow into her side. "What was that—" She cut herself off when Ian put his finger to his lips, nodding his head at the stage.

"Stop growling. Or did you want to attract attention to yourself?" He raised a brow at her and grinned.

Naomi leaned forward, peering around Ian, and shot a questioning look at her.

Sara scowled at both of them before turning her attention back to the stage.

Ted stepped forward as Uncle Larry left to return to his table. "Our second topic concerns forest wildlife. Bill Walker, please provide your update." Ted stepped back once more, and a man wearing jeans and a shirt stretched tight around his enormous biceps strode past the tables and leapt onto the stage. He had a dominant yet graceful manner, reminding Sara of an apex predator.

"The animals are uneasy," he said, his deep voice easily projecting across the clearing. "They sense a danger and are looking to us for aid. Early this morning, a herd of deer was attacked and a fawn taken. They didn't see the attacker but say it smelled like smoke and moved unnaturally."

Bill paced the stage and flexed his hands, muscles undulating along his arms. Sara recognized his voice and heavy footsteps as the man who paced the Main House her first night in the forest—the man she saw phase into a wolf. She slouched in her chair, wanting to disappear under the table.

"The herd seeks sanctuary within the walls, just as other animals will do if there are more attacks. We must eliminate this threat to protect all wildlife both inside *and* outside the wall." He stopped pacing near the edge of the stage and let Mr. Sullivan take the center.

Thomas's father stood before the crowd, moonlight glinting off the metal clip of a knife at the waist of his tailored pants.

"Our patrol has witnessed a significant increase in Takers. And now we have a dark witch at our door," said Mr. Sullivan. Another hush fell over the families. He glared pointedly at Sara, causing her heart to hammer, and then shifted his gaze to Naomi. "Naomi says this witch attacked her site and used similar tactics to kill surrounding wildlife and trees, then broke their barrier and massacred her people. He uses the name Samson, and we must assume he is here to do the same to us."

Sara jolted in her seat. A sharp pain like a red-hot poker pressed into her spine, right between her shoulder blades. Clenching her jaw to keep from yelping, she looked behind her, past Thomas—who tried to catch her eye—to a movement at the tree line, where two figures emerged from the shadows of the woods. Wisps of darkness clung to them like funeral shrouds as they descended into oversized chairs under a young pine tree. The tree swayed in a soft breeze, and moonlight briefly illuminated the two figures. Sara gasped, which she hid by feigning a cough. She turned away and took a sip of water, willing her hand to remain steady.

Ian shook his head, the expression on his face warning her not to turn back to the two figures. Gran visibly stiffened in her seat and kept a focused stare on Mr. Sullivan, who nodded approvingly at the late arrivals before continuing his speech.

"While no outside force can break our wall, we cannot sit idle, hiding in our *enclosure*. Without a typical Magus, the Sullivans and Walkers strongly advise we take the offensive by removing a portion of the wall to allow us to magically hunt and eliminate our attackers." Thomas's father enunciated each word, as though issuing a proclamation.

An instant uproar came from the families. The Cahills and Atwells rose from their chairs and shouted at the stage. The Lochton table simply froze in disbelief.

Even without knowing the full ramifications, Sara knew the idea of breaking the forest wall had to be ludicrous from the utter fury radiating from Gran and the fear that flicked across Ian's usually calm face.

Mr. Sullivan raised his voice, projecting above the discourse. "Consider the *signs*," he roared, and glared at the table in front of him.

Sara sunk lower in her chair and hunched her shoulders to shrink from his gaze, not entirely certain if he was looking at her or Naomi.

Bastard.

He turned back to the crowd and raised his arms, gesturing to the surrounding forest. Bill came to stand by his side, arms folded across his powerful chest. Mr. Sullivan continued. "It is our *duty* to protect the forest, and to do this we must strengthen our gifts and extend our protective service outside the wall and no longer be *victims* to dark magic." Applause from the Walker and Sullivan tables was met by shouts of dissent from the other families.

Sara gaped in disbelief and selfishly hoped the turmoil would effectively end the meeting, sparing her from taking the stage tonight. Her hope was dashed when Orsen came forward to the front of the stage, both palms raised to quiet the crowd.

"Hear, hear!" called Orsen. A gust of wind blasted the tables, knocking over bottles and tossing napkins until the arguing subsided. "What Kane is suggesting has never before been attempted or warranted." He paused. "Perhaps now is the time—" Kane and Bill smiled at Orsen's acknowledgement but then dropped their grins as he continued. "Or not. This is quite a serious matter and must be further discussed. Civilly." Orsen scanned every table. "Heads of families will meet to weigh the pros and cons before anything is decided."

Sara pushed her plate away, the sight of the uneaten food making her queasy. She rubbed the back of her neck and fidgeted in her seat as all five families whispered harshly.

Leaping from the stage with preternatural ease, Bill landed silently among the crowd and resumed a seat at his table, a slight snarl on his face. Kane swept a cool gaze across the gathering before joining Ted in the shadows at the back of the stage.

"Our next agenda item tonight," Orsen continued, "is the welcome and pledge of two new . . . outsiders." The families quieted again, tabling their heated discussions, and focused on the Lochton table. "Ted, I believe you're making the first introduction," said Orsen, exchanging places with him on the stage.

Sara wiped her clammy hands on the front of her shirt. But instead of addressing her, Ted gestured to Naomi. "I present Naomi Johnson, younger sister of Winona Johnson, aunt of Ian Lochton, from the former Hills sacred site." Orsen handed her an ornate cup when she took center stage and faced everyone.

"Thank you, Ware Woods, for accepting me. As you know, my site has been destroyed by dark magic. The same dark magic now plaguing your outer forest." Her eyes glinted, and she grimaced.

Anxious murmurs drifted among the tables.

With a shake of her shoulders, she eased her expression and continued over the rustling. "The Mother and Father guided me here. I was meant to find Ian—to come to Ware Woods and use my gifts and experience to help protect this forest as my own. And to defeat this dark magic." She held the cup up for all to see. "I pledge myself to Ware Woods, to protect it and its people, to protect the balance of nature, to celebrate the natural magic inherent within us all, and within every part of this land from animals, trees, and earth. To use my gifts for good. And for light to always triumph over dark." She took a long drink and then held the cup up high. The crowd applauded.

Orsen took the cup and refilled it from a tap in the Council tree. Kane stepped forward, his expression severe. His authoritarian voice cut through the clearing: "What gifts have you to protect this forest and its people?"

Naomi faced him and lifted her chin. "I come to you as a shielder and a spell breaker—the best from my site."

Kane moved his arms in a tight arc and put his hands together, firing a dark-blue ball of energy at her. Calmly standing her ground, Naomi simply stared at him, the blue light crackling and dissipating around her as though she were inside a protective bubble. The families roared their approval. Kane waved a hand, brusquely dismissing her to leave the stage.

She returned to her seat beside Ian, sitting heavily with a restrained grunt. Her tight smile matched the discomfort in her eyes, and beads of sweat dotted her brow.

Gut twisting and head pounding, Sara pressed a hand to the side of her face and massaged her temple. *Shit. I am going to die.* If her father was here, surely he would be amused by the reverse witch trial she found herself in. Any time she had exhibited what could be construed as extraordinary power, it was based on anger, completely uncontrollable and dark in nature. If she ever displayed such atrocities in this forest, they would know her murderous secret.

Sara thought of her mother and the words she'd whispered to her in her dream. She was certainly being watched by everyone, their expectant stares boring into her taut shoulders.

The maple tree swayed when Ted strode to the front of the stage and gestured to the Lochton table. "I present Sara Lochton, daughter of Eliza Cahill and Charles Lochton, granddaughter of Rosetta Lochton."

Gran nodded at Ted when he said her name.

Sara slowly stepped onto the stage, as though approaching her own pyre, and accepted the cup from Orsen. The metal cup, engraved with an intricate vining pattern, cooled her sweaty hands. Terrified to be standing before a crowd and completely clueless, Sara simply stared at her feet and clutched the cup with both hands to keep from dropping it.

Ted cleared his throat. "Sara, do you pledge yourself to Ware Woods to protect it and its people? To use your gifts for good and to help light triumph over dark?"

She froze. While protecting the forest was instinctual, the latter part of the pledge made her hesitate. Her fear of the monster dwelling inside her was so palpable she could taste its bitterness on her tongue. She wanted to be good but wasn't sure she could make this promise.

Not one leaf rustled in the heavy silence that settled throughout the clearing. Her mind reeled with images of Brad attacking her in the ward, of her defending herself against the pack, of the expressions on her parents' faces when Samson descended upon their car.

"Stop overthinking and just say YES!" Ian shouted in her head.

Sara jerked back, tightening her grip on the cup, and looked up at Ted. "Yes," she said in a ragged whisper.

Ted visibly relaxed his shoulders and gestured for her to drink.

She raised the cup and peered inside. The clear sap shimmered and smelled faintly of syrup. She recognized it as the same sap Gran gave her on her first night in the forest. She furrowed her brow and glanced at her grandmother, who had a cunning twinkle in her eyes.

Sara took a careful sip, the sweet sap melting on her tongue like newly fallen snow. Savoring the taste, she drank the full cup and felt it settle into her chest and around her heart.

The stone around her neck suddenly warmed against her skin. Sara failed to conceal a slight gasp but refrained from putting a hand to her chest.

She studied the faces of the families, her gaze first falling on the empty seat where Thomas had been sitting. A breeze shook the trees near the back of the clearing, drawing her eyes to the two figures sitting in back. Sara gasped again. One figure was an old hag, her spine so contorted it must have been agony to sit in the chair. Her sallow skin was pocked with age, and her greasy bald head was streaked with scraggly wisps of gray hair. Eyes clouded with blindness shone in the full moon like glowing voids. She couldn't possibly see Sara, and yet she was staring directly at her.

The other figure grinned, black lips pulling back to reveal large yellow teeth.

Their stares gripped Sara and stole her breath. While the hag was small and crippled, the second figure was massive. The large girth of a matronly woman in a shapeless beige dress and apron reminiscent of the late seventeenth century spilled over the sides of the chair. Leathered hands, as big as baseball mitts, rested on the arms of the chair, thick nails curling into the wood. Everything about the figure was disturbing, but none more so than the face. Although the monstrous body seemed human, the being had the face and head of a bear.

The stone at Sara's chest pulsed and burned, demanding her attention and breaking her gaze from the bear-headed figure. She shook her head to find the crowd staring at her.

Naomi half stood, sniffing the air, perhaps scenting her fear.

"You alright, Sara?" asked Ted. He held out his arms, looking ready to catch her if she fell.

She nodded weakly.

Ted straightened and faced the crowd. "Many of us had put hope in Eliza and Charlie returning to the forest—*their home.*" He emphasized the last words and peered toward the back tables. "We are pleased to have Sara home at last and expect Charlie to return soon."

Disagreement rumbled from the back of the crowd, and Kane cleared his throat loudly from his place on the stage.

Ted turned to her. "Sara, do you have any gifts you would like to share with us?"

CHAPTER 23

Here was the moment she dreaded.

While the sap tasted transformative, Sara felt no change, no tingling magic to impress the crowd and rescue her from this slow death by embarrassment. And if embarrassment didn't kill her, she had no doubt Thomas's father—Kane—would gladly finish her off.

Too afraid to tap into her monster and likely lose control, she pursed her lips and held her breath. Beneath her shirt, the red stone smoldered hotter. Every inch of her skin flushed with her burning blood. Although her insides threatened to combust, she stood frozen with fear, imploring Ted with her eyes to let her leave the stage.

Kane stepped forward, grabbed the cup from her hand, and shoved it at Ted. "You're a Lochton—can you read my mind?" His question had the bite of an interrogation. He stared down at her, a muscle twitching along the side of his jaw.

Even if she could read his mind, Sara had no desire to speak what he thought and make his contempt for her obvious to everyone.

Kane frowned and walked a slow circle around her, a shark playing with its meal. "No. Well, you're also a Cahill. Can you make this grow?" He twisted his hand, kinetically uprooting a seedling and levitating it before them.

Sara blanched, knowing she could not do this. Her unfocused mind ran like a terrified rabbit. All she wanted was to get away from him and every set of eyes on her. Sweat trickled down her sides. She desperately wanted to pull at the stone that burned into her chest, branding her.

Kane flung the seedling to the Cahill table, where it landed with a weak thud. "Hmm, there's talk that you healed Albert Walker. Perhaps you can heal me too?" In one quick motion, he pulled the knife from his side and sliced his palm, the cut so deep a thin stream of blood flowed onto the stage.

Sara closed her eyes, body swaying while she fought not to retch and pass out. The only thought in her head was an odd, rumbly voice repeating: *"You do not belong here."*

Someone moved to stand beside her.

"Enough," said Ted, a firm edge to his tone.

"Is it?" Kane's voice boomed across the Council clearing. "There are many of us here tonight who do not think she should be here. The prophecy says she brings death to our forest."

At this, the families stood and argued again.

Sara gasped, feeling like she'd been punched in the stomach. Her soul ignited with guilt when the monster inside her roared in response—at both the accusation and the possibility. She snapped her eyes open to see Ian and Gran lunging for the stage. A strong breeze shook the maple tree. Its leaves quaked and cast a momentary shadow, hiding Sara from the spotlight of the full moon. The deep, rumbly voice in her head shouted: *"RUN!"*

She pivoted on instinct. Her thundering heartbeat threatened to split her burning skin as she slid from the stage and disappeared into the open arms of the woods. She flung herself down a path that parted for her just as quickly as it closed in her wake. For once, her footsteps fell silently. Trees, boulders, and startled animals blurred in her periphery, her vision unable to keep up with her reckless flight.

The farther she fled from the Council, the more the stone at her chest cooled. Her sides heaving, she gulped humid air thick with the taste of forest floor decay and green summer growth, and finally slowed her steps.

Fear and shame changed to anger. *How dare he!* To humiliate and accuse her after she had lost so much. Her hands tingled, and her eyes, once blurred with tears, clouded with rage. Blinded, she crashed straight into the Ware Woods boundary.

Not a pebble dislodged from the dry-stacked wall when she bounced back, her left hip and knee screaming from the impact. She let loose a filthy string of curses, rubbing her hip while eyeing the waist-high wall. The interlocking lichen-covered stones vibrated, as if the wall lived and breathed. After spitting another choice four-letter word, she gripped the cool stones and hauled herself up. There, at the threshold of Ware Woods and the outer forest, she limped along the top of the wall, guilt and fear joining her rage.

What if the prophecy is true? Should I leave?

She didn't want to hurt anyone. But Ware Woods tugged at her, and she couldn't bear the thought of leaving. *Besides, where would I go?*

Distracted by a whirlwind of thoughts, she did not see the hulking figure that materialized from the shadows until it grabbed her ankles. In one swift motion she was flung into the outer forest, her head slamming against a rotted tree stump.

The Taker blocked out the moon as he loomed over her. Though he wore jeans and a studded belt, his chest was bare and slick with sweat. A jagged stone pendant swung from his thick neck. He was very muscular, even more so than Bill Walker, but his pale complexion and blue-black, stained hands cast an unhealthy aura about him.

She narrowed her eyes at him, recognition creeping into her mind. It was the man from the alley. But this was no bar bouncer. He rippled with dark magic, death glinting in his eyes—as though he craved the very darkness that consumed him.

"Well, aren't you something?" he rasped, eyeing her hungrily from her feet to her face. "Samson will be quite pleased I finally got you. But maybe I'll have you for myself." He pulled a dagger from a sheath at his side but then stopped, coughing violently. He doubled over and spat greasy black phlegm. The moss-covered forest floor twitched, recoiling.

Sara shoved her back against the stump and yielded—not to him, but to unleashing the tight hold on herself. Monstrous fury instantly consumed her. She turned to him without a trace of fear . . . and laughed.

The laugh seemed to surprise him. He stopped coughing and faced her.

"You shouldn't have done that." She smiled and merely stared at him until his murderous expression changed to one of sheer terror. He dropped the knife, his face turning a choked purple, and desperately clawed at his throat. Saliva foamed along his mouth, and black-red blood leaked from his nose.

Sara stood and took a step forward, hot energy coursing through her. Her hands burning and crackling, she gathered her anger and focused it on the Taker. "Go to hell!" The words came from her mouth, but she didn't recognize the voice as her own. She roared and pushed all her rage, humiliation, and grief at him.

He convulsed as first his clothes and then his skin ripped from his body. Sara let the remaining bloody form shudder for a moment before igniting it with white-hot flames.

Unable to suppress her anger, she felt energy pour out of her like a tidal wave, snapping trees and plowing through the understory until she collapsed onto her knees, gasping for air. The explosive release left her shaking with exhaustion and in desolate fear of her secret being exposed.

Shit. Maybe no one will know it was me.

And then she swore someone called her name.

"Sara!" The voice came from Ware Woods. She tried to quiet her breathing and failed.

Seriously? You have got to be kidding me.

Before she could even lift her head, Thomas grabbed her, swept her into his arms, and carried her back over the wall. Putting her gently on her feet, he kept a firm grip on her arm and with his free hand pushed back her hair. "Are you okay? What happened . . ." He trailed off, staring at a lock of hair that fell into his hand.

The shock and fear in his eyes startled her. She flicked a glance over the wall and touched the back of her head. The entire lower half was now bare. "I . . . I hit my head," she stammered and then froze, not at the sight of the Taker's body but at Thomas's judgmental expression.

His fingers closed tightly around the lock of hair. "No," he breathed, eyes darting to the decimated swath of land and charred remains of the Taker smoldering on the other side of the stone wall. "You totally lost control."

"He was going to *kill* me. I acted in self-defense—"

"I have no doubt he intended to kill you." His blue eyes bored into hers, his hand hot where he still gripped her upper arm. "But this was . . . excessive." He grimaced at the fallen trees and wrinkled his nose at the scent of burnt flesh in the air. Releasing her, he took a step back.

"Did you not catch a glimpse of Dorcas tonight?" He dropped the hair at her feet.

Sara recalled the crippled hag with the greasy bald head—*man-eater*—and felt sick, her sinuses burning with the stench of the dead body.

"You must learn to control yourself." His tone softened. "But how did you do this outside the forest wall? None of us have gifts outside the wall . . ." He frowned, one hand resting on his pants pocket, eyeing what was left of the Taker.

She straightened her shoulders, preparing to defend herself and doubtlessly bend the truth. "Apparently your father has the power to invoke that much anger in me."

He turned to her, eyes wide.

"Oh, right," she continued, chin raised. "You conveniently missed seeing him humiliate me in front of everyone."

Fury flashed across his face. He clenched his jaw and turned away. "Damn him! I knew he was up to something. I didn't want to leave." His expression turned sheepish. "But he ordered me . . ." He trailed off and began pacing.

"Ordered you to do what, exactly?" Eager to change the subject from her devastating temper, she glanced at the Taker and then tilted her head at Thomas.

He stopped walking. "I must be crazy," he muttered to himself while scanning the forest in the direction of the Council tree. He turned and regarded her, his eyes shimmering. "You can't tell anyone, or he *will* kill me. Swear to me you won't say anything."

A slight electric shock raced through her bones. She saw the fear in his eyes, and she felt it in her heart too. "I promise. I'd never do anything to hurt you," she said, and meant it—the promise etched deep on her heart, on her very soul.

"My father intends to break the forest wall with or without Council consent. In fact, he's already tried, but he's not powerful enough—yet. He went to Makwa and asked for her help to strengthen his gifts." He resumed pacing while keeping a watchful eye on the forest.

A shiver raked down her spine. "The bear witch," she whispered, recalling the black grin and thick claws, the fiery stare upon her back.

"No good can come from her. She's been here since the beginning, and we *know* she can't be trusted. But my father has quite the ego and thinks he can use her to get what he wants. She said the potion to strengthen his powers required an element from outside the forest, and I was sent as the errand boy."

He opened his hand to reveal a glass vial whose oily contents glistened in the light of the moon before he slid it back into his pocket. He sighed and re-rolled the loose sleeves of his shirt, the muscles in his forearms rippling. "The Taker was the one who delivered it to the wall. Kinda complicates things, don't you think?"

He stepped toward her and looked up from his cuffs. For a moment she saw a scared boy, but the image vanished, replaced by the hard, angular set of his jaw, the faint shadow of stubble on his face.

"Yeah," she breathed. He stood so close she could smell musk and ash, see his pulse visible at the open collar of his shirt. "Thomas, he can't have this. He'll—"

"I know," he interrupted, and placed his hands on her arms. A zing of electricity tingled along her skin before he released her and averted his eyes.

"I have a plan. But first"—he used the toe of his shoe to bury the lock of hair into the forest floor and then turned back toward the Council tree—"we need to explain this."

The undergrowth parted, and Ted, Kane, and Uncle Larry strode toward them.

Kane sniffed the air. "What the Mother is this?" He gestured angrily with a bandaged hand, first at Sara and then at the body and destruction outside the wall.

Ted rushed to Sara's side. "What happened?"

Kane glared at Sara and then fixed his eyes on Thomas. The intensity of his stare could have cut glass.

Sara sucked in a breath. She had seen that look before in Thomas's memory. "It was my fault," she blurted. "I . . . I stepped outside the wall, and he attacked me." She gestured to the gory remains of the Taker.

Uncle Larry stood at the wall, thumbs tucked into his overalls. Wearing a curious expression, his gaze traveled from Sara to the body and then to the broken trees in the outer forest.

"You," said Kane, wheeling to face Sara. "*You* did this? And outside the wall?" He raised his face to the moon and barked a laugh. "You"—he jabbed a finger in her direction—"are a liability. Gifted, but no self-control." He scowled at her, his contempt visible as dark-blue flames crackled in his palms.

Thomas stiffened, fists clenched at his sides. "She did us a favor."

"Did us a favor, did she?" Kane snorted. "She ripped up the forest. Not to mention, Takers will seek vengeance for this. It is as Makwa says—she brings death to Ware Woods."

Uncle Larry swelled to his full size, towering over Kane. "Makwa is not always right." His tone was deadly calm. "The blight and increased harassment from Takers started before Sara arrived. It is *why* Eliza and Charlie were coming home."

When her grandfather said Eliza's name, Kane turned away and shoved his hands in his pockets.

"Sara is my granddaughter and part of Ware Woods. She belongs here regardless of Makwa's *opinion*." Uncle Larry sniffed, grimacing at the stench in the air. "Sara just needs training to control her gifts."

She could have hugged Uncle Larry.

Kane whipped around and waved a hand at the devastation outside the forest wall. "Perhaps this means something you don't want to admit," he seethed.

"Perhaps they were both too close to the wall." Uncle Larry's rumbling voice threatened like thunder.

"Fine," spat Kane. "But *I* oversee the training." Not waiting for objections, he continued, "Violet will train her during the day, and I will *test* her in the evening."

Sara flinched when he stressed the word "*test*."

Ted shrewdly observed Kane. "Ian, Lily, and Caleb will also assist, provided it does not interfere with their work to stop the blight."

Kane remained silent.

"Well then, it's settled. Best be getting back. It's wicked late," said Uncle Larry, placing a hand on Sara's shoulder.

"You need any help with the body?" asked Ted, his brow raised at Kane.

"No," said Kane sharply. "Thomas will do it." He stood beside Thomas, his arms folded across his chest, and watched them leave.

As she walked off with Ted and Uncle Larry, Sara glanced back to see Kane glaring at her, his body blocking her view of Thomas.

CHAPTER 24

S ARA TOSSED AND turned in the four-poster bed, pajamas damp with sweat—not from the balmy summer night but from fiery nightmares of burning trees and charred bodies. In her dream, silky black smoke curled around her, its tendrils crushing her before engulfing her in utter darkness.

She jolted awake to moonlight spilling across the bed. Kicking back rumpled sheets, she touched the stone at her chest until her breathing quieted and heartbeat settled. A gentle breeze carrying with it the scent of oak and pine drifted into the room. The treehouse groaned and shivered, the gentle sway of its leaves eventually lulling her back to sleep.

The next time she woke, the trill of a cardinal calling the approaching dawn floated in through the window openings and doors. She shucked off her pajamas and changed into dry clothes, then slunk down the stairs and across the main room. There, she sat on the lower deck in the haze of the rising sun. Eyes partly open, she inhaled and exhaled, halting her meditation when she spied movement near the rear of the cemetery.

Her heart skipped a beat, in hopes it was Thomas, but she was equally relieved to see Gran carrying a basket of food.

"I figured you'd be up," she called out, ascending the wraparound stairs, her steel blue eyes studying Sara. "Help yourself."

Gran set the basket down and took a seat beside her on the top step. "Ted told me what happened after you fled the meeting."

Sara winced at her words as she pulled a thermos from the basket.

"Gaa. Don't feel bad about that. Kane was hard on you. Too hard. The bastard. You had every right to defend yourself against the Taker."

Sara choked on her water, eyes wide at Gran. "I'm glad you feel that way because Kane certainly didn't." She shrugged a shoulder to wipe her mouth. "What exactly is the prophecy he mentioned?" She kept her face a frozen mask of calm while her mind ran around shouting, *It's true! It's true! I am capable of horrible things . . . like death.*

Gran tsked, shaking her head, and hesitated a few nerve-racking moments before finally speaking. "When you were just a seed in your mother's womb, Makwa preyed on your parents' situation by saying a child conceived between the families would bring death to the forest, leading them to believe they had to take you away. It was a ruse to manipulate us for her own cruel enjoyment. Despite what some think, her prophecy is hogwash. And you certainly didn't need to hear it. Especially after all you've gone through." Gran shook her head, changing her expression from fierce to tender. "Your parents had a rare and powerful connection. Only good can come from such love." She patted Sara's leg, squeezing to emphasize her last statement.

"Now," said Gran, her lips curving into a shrewd smile. "I always knew you had gifts, but you need to learn how to control them before they control you. You know what I'm saying, yeah?"

Sara's mind spun. *Maybe the prophecy isn't true. If I can just learn to control my monster . . .* Brow furrowed, she gave a slow nod and considered just how much her grandmother might know. She swallowed hard, forcing down a bite of cinnamon roll. "How do I do that?"

"I'm sure Kane and Violet will have some interesting methods. Just do what they say and trust yourself. Magic comes from within—a combination of your mind, heart, and soul. It takes focus and trust to harness magical energy. So my mother told me and Alice, anyway." Gran stood and headed down the stairs.

Sara grabbed another roll and followed.

At the base of the stairs, Gran turned right and circled the cemetery tree, which grew larger every day. She stopped at an old headstone planted so close to the tree that a root had grown around it in a loose embrace. "This is where she lies—your great-grandmother Ann." Gran reached into a pocket, retrieving a handkerchief, and wiped her nose. "Allergies," she said before looking up at a stirring near the back of the cemetery.

Popping out of the pines and striding toward them was Violet. Similar to the Council meeting and nearly-full-moon party, she was dressed all in black again, with a matching black tactical bag slung over her shoulder. Her expression seemed bored, but her pace was quick, causing her long raven hair to flare behind her.

"Ah, here comes Violet. She's a good girl, more like her mother than her father. All the same, take this just in case." Gran popped a star mint in her mouth and handed Sara a folded knife.

"This knife isn't very reassuring." Sara flicked it open, closed it, and clipped it to her shorts. "Is this a forest thing? Do all grandparents hand these out like candy?"

Gran's steel blue eyes twinkled. "See you at supper," she called over her shoulder, leaving Sara to her fate.

Violet wasted no time in pushing Sara's physical capabilities. Most of the day they ran through the forest, around the soul trees, beside the protective stone wall, and along the lake. She allowed occasional water breaks and a quick lunch of sandwiches and trail mix, which she pulled from the tactical bag. But instead of rest, every break involved a lesson in knife throwing.

Violet eyed Sara like a coach assessing a new player. "Did you do any training in the outside world?"

Sara grabbed a water bottle from the tactical bag and contemplated the question. Her parents had no weapons—at least that she knew of—and she didn't think any of their frequent day-long hikes in the woods met Violet's definition of training. Sara helped with garden and yard work, and she occasionally ran for the sheer joy of it.

She gulped the cool water and remembered a failed attempt at training. After the sleepover incident, her parents enrolled her in a mixed martial arts studio—to bolster her confidence and calm her nerves, they'd said. But the class fueled her aggression despite her sensei's best efforts to encourage discipline and respect. He said she scared the other students and needed to work on calming her mind to balance her aggression. After a few months, her sensei told her parents not to bring her back to his studio.

Sara turned to Violet. "Unless you consider hiking and climbing trees as training, then no. My *outside* life was pretty dull." She chucked the bottle back in the bag and broke into a jog, preferring to run rather than discuss her lack of skills and her life before the accident.

By late afternoon, her legs were trembling with exhaustion. Violet stopped running, picked a fallen log as their target, and handed a knife to Sara. Every time Sara tried to focus on the log, her vision blurred and the knife wobbled off course. All day, her aim had been terrible, most throws skidding along the forest floor until Violet stopped them and whished them back.

"You're not trying," Violet chastised. At sixteen, she had the mature focus and discipline of a seasoned soldier, always aware of her surroundings and confident in her capabilities.

"I *am* trying," Sara said through clenched teeth. The log seemed to shimmer in the hot, humid air. She squinted and threw again, more forcefully; this time, the knife landed with a satisfying thunk but in a large pine to her far left. "Why are we just running and throwing? Shouldn't I be figuring out my gifts and learning how to control them?" The idea of seeing Kane in a few hours twisted in her gut.

Violet whished the knife back and carefully plucked the black blade from the air. "Ian said you have some kinetic abilities. Go ahead then. Try to explode that log. It's all rotted out, should be easy." She gestured to a partially decomposed log about fifteen feet in front of them.

Sara hesitated.

Violet raised her brow and gestured again.

Heaving a sigh, Sara stared at the log, with no idea even where to begin until she remembered Gran's words. "*Focus—mind, heart, and soul.*" She inhaled to the count of three and focused, as if trying to shoot a laser beam from between her eyes. Sweat dripped down the sides of her face, and a deerfly buzzed around her head. Nothing—not even a slight tingle in her hands.

Violet laughed.

Sara clenched her jaw and fisted her hands. She did *not* like to be laughed at. When Violet laughed again at her failed attempt, Sara let her anger slip and burn from her fingertips. She pushed out toward the log and watched it explode as if detonated by a bomb. Rotten wood splattered the forest floor, and a fine dust clouded the air. She felt drained but thoroughly pleased with herself—until she turned and saw Violet's furrowed brow and curled lip.

"Well, that was sloppy," chided Violet. "Your focus is way off." She waved her knife at her.

Sara groaned. She couldn't do anything right. "Why is this so *hard?*"

Violet rolled her eyes. "Because magic requires a sound mind and body. You need to be strong physically and mentally to properly focus. And only when you are focused can you be your best possible self. And *then*, when you know what you are capable of, you strive to be better." She pointed the tip of the knife at her own temple and then released her hand, levitating the blade, the knife both innocent and deadly as it hovered between them. Without even looking at her target, Violet flicked her hand and the knife shot through the air, cutting through a stump and out the other side to lodge into a dead tree.

Sweat trickled down the back of Sara's knee, and she regarded Violet a bit more seriously. *If Violet can do that, what is Kane capable of? What is Thomas capable of?*

Sara jerked her chin. "How'd you get so good? You haven't even drunk the sap yet . . . have you?" She wiped her brow, stalling for more rest in case Violet resumed their running.

Violet cocked an eyebrow at Sara while the knife came levitating back. She grabbed it from the air. "I've trained my whole life. You don't need sap to be gifted, but it can strengthen your magic. It only works once when you pledge yourself."

Sara glanced at Violet's toned arms and how easily she wielded the knife. She recalled the glint of an arrow whistling past her when she lay helpless in the field. *"Violet got three, including the one that hit Albert."* The girl before her was already positively lethal.

Violet gave her a hard stare, no trace of a smile on her lips. "Sullivans take their role as sentinels very seriously. I've already lost two brothers, and I won't lose Thomas or Connor." She pulled a rag from her back pocket and began lovingly cleaning the knife.

Sara's legs buckled, and she leaned into the tree beside her to keep from falling over. *Two siblings.* Thomas's memories flooded back to her—his sadness and pain. She studied Violet and knew that, like herself, Violet did not want pity or questions. Silence hung between them until a faint rustling grew louder and Caleb emerged from the forest undergrowth.

"Hello, Caleb," said Violet dryly without looking up from her blade. "You're louder than a foraging bear. I could hear you over a mile out."

Caleb smirked. "Well, good. I didn't want to surprise you and become part of target practice." He eyed the knives she was now packing away. "Helen's serving an early dinner. I thought you two would appreciate that."

Sara let out a sigh of relief.

As the three of them headed to the Main House, Caleb turned to Sara with his gap-toothed grin. "Ya know why her nickname is Vi, don't ya?"

Sara almost stopped short, her mouth agape at him. Obviously because her name was Violet and obviously because he was an idiot to tease a natural-born predator. "You do realize she's carrying a bag of knives and could gut you as soon as look at you?" She stole a glance at Violet, finding a hint of a sly smile on her lips.

Caleb plucked a piece of grass and bit the end, savoring his moment. "Because it's short for *violence*." He grinned ear to ear before Violet shoved him into the forest floor with a mere flick of her hand. He would have eaten dirt had he not reached out with his own power, a pine bough catching his fall, as he roared with laughter.

CHAPTER 25

After a quick dinner, Violet and Sara stepped into the chestnut tree and looped to the Sullivans' soul tree, a majestic white ash nearly a hundred feet tall with knobby dark-gray bark. Though Sara had marveled at the tree's appearance during her running, experiencing it from within was breathtaking. A sense of eternal strength and protection radiated from its core, tingling her skin as they looped and exited from a hollowed-out portion at the base of the trunk.

Sara stumbled forward, tripping over a root, and faced an old pasture of neatly cut grass. Earlier in the day, she hadn't dared raise her gaze from the uneven ground and risk falling on her face. But now, she paused and took in the view. Where the pasture met the forest, wood and straw targets of various sizes and shapes lined the edge. A few targets had been reduced to mounds of splintered wood or scattered straw, shredded by angry weapons. To the left of the pasture sat a small barn, weathered but sturdy-looking, with a long stack of firewood resting beneath an extended roofline.

Sara turned to gaze behind her at a two-story house painted steel gray with black trim, the tones matching the slate tile roof. The home was impeccably maintained, as was the detached two-story garage, set back far enough that it seemed like its own little house. Similar to the Lochton place, the Sullivans' also fronted the derelict road, the protective forest wall firmly standing between the front yard and the old pavement. On the far side of the road spread a large, familiar field. Sara swallowed. It was the same one she had tried to run across, nearly dying.

Violet laid her black bag of throwing knives on the ground and faced the garage. Kane stepped from the building, slamming the side door behind him. He glided across the lawn between the garage and soul tree, his unpleasant smile making Sara shift her weight.

Glancing at the setting sun, he jeered, "Done so soon, are we?"

Sara followed Violet's lead and did not answer.

"I haven't got all evening. Let's see what you can do," he said, gesturing impatiently. Clearly, he had just returned from work—he wore black pants and a starched button-down shirt, the color similar to the blue-gray of the house. His cuff links glinted in the sunset.

Kane glanced at the bag of knives, and Sara's stomach twisted, a sudden sense of lightheadedness washing over her.

"No knives. I have something else in mind," he said.

She shuddered, unsure if she should be relieved or not.

He shook his hands to straighten his sleeves and whished a large piece of firewood over the pasture, suspending it in midair. "Blow it up," he said, as if asking her to tie her shoe.

Resisting the urge to scowl at him, she wiped her hands on her shirt and focused on the wood. It appeared firmer than the rotted log she had exploded earlier, and it was much farther away. She narrowed her eyes at the log, but the more she concentrated, the blurrier it became. Gritting her teeth, she wildly pushed out nervous energy until she heard a crack.

The wood splintered and fell to the ground.

Her moment of triumph was fleeting as Kane regarded her with a disturbing thoughtfulness. He floated two more pieces of wood over the field and gestured to Violet. "Levitate between them." Then he turned back to Sara. His steely gaze made her skin crawl with dread. "Now, blow up the wood." He put his thumbs in his pockets and straightened his shoulders, muscles straining against the shirt.

Sara stared at him in disbelief, her chest tight and her stomach begging to heave up dinner. A cluster of birds wisely took flight from the pasture as she shook her hands, desperate to shake off the panic attack threatening to consume her. She faced Violet, who hung in the air, staring straight ahead, her lips pressed into a thin line. Sara trembled, terrified at the possibility of ripping into Violet like she had the Taker.

Bile crept up the back of her throat. With a deep groan, she sank to her knees in the muddy grass. "I can't . . . I can't do it," she rasped.

Kane huffed in disgust and flicked a hand. Sara heard the wood explode and felt Violet land beside her with a sickening thud. "You have no control, and you put this entire forest in danger. I can *smell* the fear on you," he said.

Keeping her gaze on the grass before her, Sara clenched her jaw. A fluttering of wings sounded overhead, followed by the cackling cry of a raven. She held her breath as Kane paced around her.

He slowed his steps. "You have five days to cut and stack three cords of wood"—he paused—"for *each* family."

Sara shifted her gaze to the four-foot by eight-foot cord stacked by the barn and knew what he demanded was nearly impossible. She had once helped her dad cut down and chop up a dead tree. It had taken them half a day and left her palms laced with blisters.

Kane continued, "No tools. Just magic. An *absurdly* trivial task, but at least this will put you to use while others contend with the blight. Start at the Walkers and finish here." He jerked his head at the little barn.

Refusing to meet Sara's eyes, Violet took a few stiff steps and bent to pick up her bag. Minor cuts from the splintered wood bled on her face, arms, and legs.

"Violet," Kane barked at her, "continue watching her during

the day, but do not lift a finger to help her." He strode off toward the house without looking back.

Violet gripped the black canvas bag, held up her chin, and roughly brushed past Sara to follow him inside.

Not even blinking fireflies and the rising moon could lift Sara's mood as she dragged her feet back to the cemetery. Emotionally and physically numb, she cleaned up in the cool lake water before sluggishly heading to the treehouse. After changing into an old shirt and cotton shorts, she made a mental note to take a laundry trip to the Cahills soon. She sat on the edge of the bed and closed her eyes, running a hand along the base of her scalp. It was still rough and showed no signs of growth. She could barely conceal it in a low ponytail. The thought of someday looking like the hideous witch, Dorcas, made her chest ache.

She sighed and padded to her window to say good night to her mother's grave when a figure standing in the shadows of the cemetery caught her eye. She stilled as Thomas stepped into the moonlight. Blood shone on his face, and he held one arm tight to his side. As she locked eyes with him, her jaw fell slack and a small gasp escaped her.

"Can I come up?" he asked politely, his voice sounding garbled.

"Of course, you idiot! Can you make it through the window?" She leaned over the sill to give him a hand.

"Don't lean out so far," he pleaded, gliding up toward her. "I may not be able to catch you at the moment." He swung his legs over the sill and landed softly in the bedroom, one arm folded tight across his chest. He scanned the room, eyes flicking over her bed and duffel bag. "I'm glad Caleb didn't put in windows, but some more furniture would be nice." He tried to smile, and winced.

"Seriously?" She felt both irritated and relieved that he could crack a joke. "What the hell happened to you?" She squinted at him, guessing the unfamiliar angle of his nose meant it was broken.

"I think you know my father was none too pleased today. Not to mention his *slight* disappointment when I lied and told him you melted the Taker before I could get the delivery last night." He lifted his free hand to prod the bridge of his nose. "He thinks I crawled off to the Cahills, but I was hoping you would help me. The way you healed my rib and stopped my headache is far better than Helen's remedies." He tilted his head up, momentarily halting the blood that threatened to drip from his nose.

"Can you sit?" she asked, eyeing the arm he held protectively across his chest.

"I think so, but I don't want to bleed all over your bed."

Without hesitating, she took two long strides to the other window ledge and grabbed her T-shirt, still wet from the lake. Nearly tripping in her haste, she returned to his side and handed it to him. "Use this. Your busted nose shouldn't be able to smell it anyway."

His eyes opened wide, blue flames flickering in his gaze. "It's fine. Thank you," he said, and pressed it to his face. He closed his eyes and groaned while lowering himself onto the edge of the bed.

Sara shook her hands, trying in vain to replace her nervous energy with the confidence to actually heal him. "I don't know what to do. I . . . I can't control it." She wanted to help him, and more than she wanted to admit to herself, she just wanted to touch him. The electric pull she felt for him seemed tangible, like an invisible cord connected them.

Thomas remained rigid with pain, his eyes closed. "Just try," he said, his voice muffled by the shirt.

The treehouse swayed and the floorboards rippled, nudging Sara into stepping forward. She huffed at the floor, drew in a breath, and stepped to stand between his knees. Shaking out her hands one more time, she glanced down to be sure his eyes were closed and then leaned toward him. Her fingertips grazed his temples, and a warm prickling sensation flushed through her entire body.

His eyes snapped open. He stared at her, his breathing shallow and rapid beneath the wet shirt. "Can you fix my collarbone? I think it's broken."

She pulled her hands back and held his gaze. There was not a trace of fear in his eyes, just trust and . . . pain. Seeing the hurt from his physical injuries was easy, but there was a far deeper pain he suffered. A pain she recognized and felt as a gaping wound ripped into her soul by the claws of grief. The agony of losing someone you love.

With a forced blink, she tore her gaze from his and focused on his broad chest. His left shoulder sloped unnaturally, the break clearly visible through his cotton shirt.

She wanted to feel angry about what Kane had done to him, what he'd done to her and Violet today, but she couldn't summon the hate. Instead, she felt confused. A soft lightness fluttered inside her chest, making her breathing uneven and sending her heart racing.

Ian's warning be damned. She felt drawn to Thomas, ached to hold him, but was terrified she would scare him away. Or worse, hurt him.

Closing her eyes, she reached out and gently touched his shoulder. He sucked in a ragged breath and froze. She felt his heat and smelled the tang of his blood mixed with musk and ash. The stone at her chest pulsed, and a warmth swelled inside her, spreading through her and into him. She tightened her grip on him and a part of her heart ignited, causing the warm energy to surge and embrace them both. The room filled with a crackling sound, like static electricity, and the sharp snap of bones resetting and mending into place.

Sara gasped and opened her eyes, watching as Thomas sighed and leaned forward to rest his head against her chest.

"Much better," he said, his voice no longer garbled but strong and steady. He reached out and put a hand on her hip, softly holding her to him.

She shuddered as a flush of heat flowed from his hand and sent tingles up her spine.

Keenly aware of how close they were, she forced herself to take a step back. He pulled his hand away and lifted his head, blue eyes fixed on her. Avoiding his intense gaze, she took the wet shirt from his hand and carefully wiped the blood from his face. A muscle twitched along his clean-shaven jaw, and his chest heaved with deep breaths that nearly shook the bed.

When she wiped away the last streak of blood from his cheek, he grabbed her wrist, the calluses on his fingertips pressing into her inner arm. Keeping his gaze on her, he whished the shirt to the windowsill and gently kissed her palm. A jolt of electricity shot up her arm and through her so quickly she didn't have time to gasp. "Thank you," he said, his voice raw.

She snatched her hand away, unsure of herself and of the thoughts racing in her head. "Are you okay?" She tried to sound normal, uncertain of what had just happened between them and whether he had felt the same thing.

"Yeah," he said, tapping his nose and then his collarbone. He grinned while stretching his arms overhead and flexing his muscles. "Good as new. Better, actually. But"—he dropped his smile—"you look tired."

"What a terrible way of saying thank you," she said with a yawn. Exhaustion crashing into her, she sat on the bed beside him. "Kick off your shoes and move over."

"So pushy." He chuckled, his eyes flickering. "Just for a bit. If my father catches me here, he might kill us both." With a short laugh, he kicked off his shoes and shifted over, but Sara knew he wasn't joking this time. Stretching out with his hands behind his head, he made it easy for her to lie beside him—too easy, their bodies fitting together perfectly. He kept his gaze on the ceiling above them as the treehouse gently swayed and rustled its leaves.

It was strangely comforting to be this close to Thomas. Sara felt she could tell him anything.

I must be crazy.

She stared up at the shimmering green ceiling and sighed. "I don't know what I'm doing. I'm trying, but I can't seem to focus and control my magic."

He brought his arm around her, his movement painstakingly slow, like he didn't want to startle her or stop her if she shifted away.

She didn't move.

His gentle embrace was warm and soothing. "You don't seem to have a problem with me," he whispered into her hair.

Her entire body tingled. Trying to appear nonchalant, she forced herself to relax and deflect his statement. "Maybe it's more you than me. I'm a terrible mess on my own. I . . . I'm scared of what I might be able to do." She whispered the last part of her confession, frowning at the moon through the window opening. "I hate to admit it, but your dad's right. I am a liability."

His thumb stroked her shoulder, his touch so comforting she fully relaxed. "I don't believe that, and neither should you. Trust in yourself. Your magic . . . I've never seen anything like it." He exhaled, putting his other hand on his chest.

Trust. Believe. Her mother's words echoed in her heart.

Thomas shifted closer to her, shaking the bed and causing the treehouse to creak and groan. "Don't worry about whatever task he has you doing. Just focus on trusting yourself. Magic takes mental and physical strength, but you also need to believe in it with your heart and soul."

Lightheaded, his touch lulling her to sleep, Sara closed her eyes. "Fine. But something needs to be done about your father. I can't believe the others tolerate this and let him treat you this way," she said softly, too tired to muster a bite to her words. She savored his warmth, the sides of their bodies now pressed together.

His chest swelled beside her as he inhaled a deep breath and slowly let it out. "It's complicated. But I have a plan."

"Hmm," she mumbled as sleep closed in around her.

"Do you trust me?" The seriousness of his tone pulled her back.

"Of course," she whispered, and meant it. She could have sworn he kissed the top of her head, or maybe she dreamed it because she wanted him to. She hoped the entire night hadn't been a dream, that this was real . . . that maybe he felt the same pull toward her.

CHAPTER 26

WHEN SHE WOKE to the soft light of morning, Thomas was gone, and a cluster of honeysuckle blossoms adorned the windowsill. She turned into the pillow, savoring the faint scent he left behind. It smelled like the embers of a warm fire.

After running most of the forest with Violet the day before, Sara easily found her way to the Main House for a quick breakfast, looped from the Cahills' chestnut tree to the Council tree, and then sauntered to the Walkers' home.

Stepping out from under the forest canopy, she viewed an oversized yard and beyond it a sprawling, green-paneled house. Similar to the Sullivan and Lochton homes, the Walker house sat close to the forest wall and old road.

She swept her gaze across the yard, spotting Violet between a low-slung barn and a pond large enough to use for hockey in the winter. As Sara walked across the clearing, Violet glanced at the sun and cursed.

"It's about time," she yelled. She sat perched on a boulder, inspecting arrows, a full quiver and bow at her feet. Her deep blue eyes were rimmed with purple-black bruising, her expression seething with contempt. Scabs marked her face, arms, and legs.

Sara gasped at the injuries.

Violet grabbed an arrow, its pointed head razor sharp, and jabbed it toward Sara. "You're not the only one being tested, so I'd appreciate it if you got your shit together," she snarled.

"I . . ." Sara stammered and stopped. Violet didn't need excuses. Sara hated taking direction, especially from someone younger, but she knew Violet spoke the truth. "You're right. I'll do better," she admitted.

Violet rolled her eyes and waved the arrow toward the dense woods behind them. "Start with gathering all the trees."

Sara hesitated and winced when Violet groaned and looked at her like she was the village idiot. Violet gestured again to the woods, her thick braid falling over her shoulder. "All the tagged trees. Lucky for you the Cahills already marked the forest for thinning this past spring," she said, an irritated edge to her voice.

Sara's stomach twisted at being responsible for Violet's wounds. Taking her chances with the arrow and Violet's hot temper, she stepped closer to the boulder. "Can I help you first?" She wanted to prove to Violet as much as to herself that she could heal her.

"Thomas said you were a healer." She clenched her jaw but dropped the arrow and sat still on the boulder. "Just don't blow me up," she muttered.

Sara shut her eyes and placed her hands on Violet's shoulders. Summoning the energy running in her veins, she let her heart lead the way to ease Violet's pain. Sara smiled at the familiar warmth filling her and extending through her touch.

When the energy subsided, she released Violet and opened her eyes to see the bruising and cuts completely gone. Violet's fierce eyes softened, and she touched the smooth skin on her arms and legs. "Thanks," she mumbled, and bent over to pick up the arrow.

Rubbing her temple to relieve the headache now throbbing behind her eyes, Sara tromped off to the edge of the wood. She eyed a tree marked with a white fabric tie and considered how she could chop it down with no tools. Her mind skipped to her life before the accident, when her only challenges were noisy neighbors. *Where's Gary and his chainsaw when you need him?*

Sara heaved a sigh. "Shit." She did not know how to focus, let alone cut the dead tree into pieces to be stacked. With another curse, she blindly shot out her power. The tree exploded, the sound echoing through the forest and launching a flock of birds into the sky. After surveying the damage, she picked out sizable chunks of wood and started a stack between the barn and shallow pond.

She rolled her neck and arched her back. Her approach was messy and tedious, but at least she could do something on her own. This went on all day, the only changes being a quick break for lunch (beef jerky this time) and the occasional sighting of a beaver with a bandaged tail in the pond. Violet kept her distance from Sara, babysitting from afar while she shot arrows into a hay bale she whished from the barn.

Wiping sweat from her brow, Sara grimaced at the late afternoon sun. She barely had one cord stacked.

Violet lowered her bow and let out a sharp whistle toward Sara. "He's coming," she warned, and pointed in the direction of the Council tree.

The undergrowth shuddered and parted as Kane emerged from the woods. He levitated toward Sara with surprising speed and frowned at the splintered wood. "I'd really like to believe the prophecy isn't true, but you fail to show this to me. All I see is proof you do not belong here. You"—he lunged, almost touching her chest with his finger—"are a disappointment." He spat the last word at her, letting her feel it on her face.

Sara shook with the effort of holding back from killing him. Her hate swelled up inside her, hands curling into fists and jaw clenching with a bitter metallic taste on her tongue. All that power swirling inside her, thundering in her veins and straining for release . . .

With a groan, her hold slipped a fraction. A wave of energy

surged from her and slammed into Kane, throwing him back twenty yards into the clearing before he caught himself and landed with one hand on the ground.

He rose, nostrils flaring as he stared her down. With a low growl, he threw out his hands, sending her flying into the pond.

She choked and struggled for breath, but his force kept pushing her into the murky water. Too panicked to summon her powers, she flailed and clawed at the mud. While her lungs burned for air, her mind whirled to a hard lesson she'd learned from the pack at school. The quickest way to stop a bully was to do the opposite of what they wanted.

Instead of fighting, she went limp. Kane's punishing force stopped.

Sara whipped her head out of the water, desperately swiping mud from her face, and gasped for air.

"I'm not wasting my time on you anymore, and neither is Violet. *You have four days to complete your task.*" Kane glided to her, hovering over the pond before delivering his next words. "If you fail, I'll personally throw you out to Samson and the Takers you cursed upon us." He snapped his fierce gaze away from her and rushed back in the direction of the Council tree.

Violet stared at Sara, eyes wide with shock, before turning away and silently trailing his wake.

CHAPTER 27

Sara wiped muck from her face and flicked her hands, scattering globs into the murky water. Curling her toes to keep from losing her shoes, she schlepped out of the pond and collapsed at the edge. Dirt gritted between her teeth and clung to her eyelashes. She leaned over, spitting until mud no longer coated the inside of her mouth.

Hitting Kane had felt good. Too good. Cursing herself, she glanced at the gouge he left in the pasture. She shivered to think what could have happened if she'd truly lost control and released the horrific power that flayed the Taker and destroyed a portion of the outer forest. Then she would surely be kicked out of Ware Woods . . . or worse. She hated Kane, but a part of her was scared he was right—she was a disappointment and a danger.

Scraping mud from her legs, she chewed a gritty lip and considered her situation. The thought of leaving the forest was unbearable. She wanted this to work, to have a family and a place to belong. She needed to control herself as much as she needed to kill Samson. Her two desires were seemingly at odds with one another. Control the monster or release it?

She hauled herself up with a wet squelch and headed straight to the lake, the forest parting with a mercifully quick shortcut.

After unclipping Gran's knife and washing out her shoes, Sara plunged into the lake and sighed in relief when the mud slid from her skin. She swam farther from shore and glanced around before removing her clothes. Nearly losing her shorts a few times, she washed out the mud and redressed underwater. Treading in place, she paused to enjoy the still lake before skimming a hand across the back of her head. Surprisingly, no new bald spots had appeared, but her hair was caked in dirt. What she really needed was a shower, but she moaned at the thought of trudging to the Main House. The lake would have to do for now.

She dove under and shook the mud from her hair. Popping back up, she grabbed a breath and yelped at spotting Caleb and Ian by the water's edge, a large flat box and steel bucket near their feet.

"Relax, we just got here," came Ian's voice in her head, his outright laughter carrying across the water.

"Woohoo!" hollered Caleb, kicking off his shoes and running into the water fully clothed. He got in as far as his knees and then launched himself, belly-flopping more than diving, into the water with a loud splash. Sara chuckled and watched Ian carefully remove his shirt and lay it on top of his shoes before running in to join them.

Caleb surfaced near her side, sputtering and splashing. He wiped his face and eyed her. "How the Hells did you get mud in your ear?"

With a grin, she pulled on her filthy ear and watched Ian approach. His wet curly hair stretched down his face as he swam up beside them.

He shook his head, spraying them both before opening his eyes. His grin dropped. "What happened to you today?"

Sara tilted her head and washed out her ear. "I pushed back at Kane."

Caleb whooped and pushed a wave of water at her. Ian merely frowned.

"I didn't mean to, it just happened . . ."

He arched a brow, tilting his head to gaze pointedly at her bald swath.

She shook back her hair and put a hand over the rough section along the back of her neck. Clearing her throat, she jerked her chin and asked, "What did you two do all day?"

Lacking buoyancy, Caleb gave up floating on his back and used his hands to squirt water at her. "I was playing in mud today too. Helen discovered covering the blight wounds with a muddy potion helps to slow the spread. Doesn't cure it, but seems to stop it."

"That's good news," she said, and pushed a wave back at him. She turned away from his retaliatory splashing and flicked water at her brother. "What about you?"

Ian ducked her spray and rolled onto his back. "I met with Naomi and learned more about Samson. It seemed he was after you, but she thinks he wants to get into Ware Woods and take our magic like he did to her sacred site." His tone remained calm, as if fighting dark witches were part of his regular routine. "We're figuring out how to get rid of him. Walkers and Sullivans still want to take the offensive, but the rest of us aren't convinced it's a good idea, let alone possible to break the wall. And even if it were, our gifts shouldn't extend to the outside." Ian floated easily, staring at the early evening sky. "Plus, there's my gaming empire, and I've been helping Ted negotiate with the hospital so we can bring Charlie home."

Sara snorted at the thought of Ian as a tech wizard. While she wanted to know all about her brother, it was their father who currently concerned her. She opened her mouth to ask Ian for more information when Caleb grabbed his foot and pulled him under. Caleb's gap-toothed grin lasted half a second before Ian yanked him and he too disappeared below the surface.

They tussled for a moment, churning the lake water before Ian popped up. Caleb followed and whipped his head, intentionally spraying Sara. "I'm starving. Let's eat," he said. Kicking and splashing, as if trying to make as much noise as possible, he swam back to shore.

Ian followed, his strokes controlled and quiet.

Sara bobbed under water a few more times, washing the rest of the mud from her clothes and hair before leaving the lake to join them under an oak tree by the water's edge.

Squeezing water from the front of her shirt, she watched in awe as Caleb effortlessly fashioned a picnic table, its apparent source the thick surface roots of the oak. With a quick touch to confirm its solid presence, she huffed a laugh and slid onto the bench.

Caleb took the flat box from Ian and sat down on the opposite side of the table, his wet shorts slapping against the wooden seat. "My aunt Jennie makes the best pizza," he said, flipping open the box and taking a slice, cheese stretching between his piece and the rest of the pie. The scent of fresh basil and garlic made Sara's mouth water.

Ian handed out birch beers and sat beside her, his hair already drying into tight curls. "When you didn't show up for dinner, we figured we'd bring it to you," he said, offering her a slice before taking one himself.

"Thanks, this is amazing," she said, her mouth full of garden-fresh flavors and homemade cheese. She smiled, grateful to have a pleasant end to a crappy day.

Her moment of contentment shattered when she remembered the impossible task ahead of her.

Ian shot her a look, like he felt her sudden mood swing. He paused before grabbing another slice. "We came to help you. Tell us what's going on."

Do all boys eat this fast? Sara eyed the few remaining slices and grabbed another before they ate it all. "I have four days to cut three cords of wood for each family. I have no idea what I'm doing. All I can do is explode things and make a mess. Seems to be my specialty." She grimaced, then twisted in her seat toward

Ian. "Kane says he'll kick me out of the forest if I don't complete the task. He can't do that, can he?" She hoped he didn't have that power over the families, but she didn't want to underestimate him either. Especially if more people rallied behind him and believed she was responsible for the current attacks. Which—if Samson was after her—maybe she was.

"No," said Ian immediately. "He can't, but I'm sure he'll come up with some other form of torment."

"Great," said Sara, voice dripping with sarcasm. She didn't know what was worse: being kicked out of the forest or a harrowing punishment from Kane.

Ian pushed away a half-eaten slice, reached into the bucket of beers, and pulled out a small bottle of green liquid. Keeping his eyes on the cemetery and treehouse, he pushed off the stopper with his thumb and downed the liquid in one swallow.

Curious about the strong pine scent and faint glow from the remaining medicine, Sara tilted her head quizzically. "What does that do exactly?"

He put the empty bottle in a side pocket of his cargo shorts and tapped his fingers on the table before glancing back to the cemetery, toward Winona's headstone. "When my mother and I were attacked, a shard of ice penetrated my heart. I don't remember it, but I went into a deep sleep. Gran says I would have died if not for the protective charm Winona gave me." Ian flicked his wrist, rotating his bracelet. "Eliza's potion saved me by regulating my heartbeat, but the effects aren't permanent. I have to take it every day just to be . . . normal."

Sara's stomach clenched at his wistful tone. "Has anyone tried to fully heal you?" She eyed him, wondering if she had the control and skill to heal a wound caused by magic—to heal a heart.

"Dorcas tried. She said the witch that cast the spell must die before the ice shard will melt. Only then could she *maybe* heal the wound in my heart."

Sara choked. "Dorcas, the man-eater?"

"She is very skilled and sometimes helpful. Gran says Charlie begged her repeatedly. But even she couldn't fix this." He gave a defeated shrug, and the usual gleam in his eyes guttered.

Sara's own heart twinged at imagining his suffering, both physical and emotional. "Normal's overrated," she said, losing her appetite and putting down her pizza. "I mean—I'm not normal, and Caleb definitely isn't either." She grinned as Caleb unabashedly finished their leftovers and let out a loud belch.

"She speaks the truth, bro." He took a swig of beer and belched again, causing Ian and Sara to laugh. "Nobody in Ware Woods is normal," he added with a wink. "Speaking of which . . ." He stood and plucked a small acorn from the tree. When he held it out to Sara, the nut's hard green surface shone in the last light of the setting sun. "Try to make this grow."

She shook her head. "Oh no, I can't do anything like that."

Caleb angled his shoulders and pointed behind him. "You see how much the cemetery tree has grown? It wasn't me. Now, just believe . . . and try." He held out the acorn.

Startled, Sara leaned back, remembering the dream with her mother's voice. She took the acorn and rubbed it with her thumb and forefinger. "What do I do?" Desperate for direction, she searched Caleb's eyes and waited.

He picked another acorn and held it between them, cupped in his palm. "Feel its energy and help it grow," he said, squinting at the seed. The acorn sprouted and grew in his hand, green shoots and roots twining and curling larger and larger. He stepped away from the table, circling and pulling his arms with graceful precision until the growth became a living Adirondack chair.

Sara snorted and stared at her little nut. She tried but couldn't focus on the acorn, her mind slipping and shifting as if a storm swirled inside her head. After a few minutes of jaw-clenching effort, the acorn cracked, and a tender green radicle peeked out. "Am I supposed to feel this exhausted?" She sighed at the minimal results and rolled her shoulders.

"Don't force it," said Caleb. "You can't force it to do your will. Use your heart to ask it."

Sara closed her eyes and thought of the acorn as a small child. She imagined extending the warm energy inside her and asking it to play. The seedling exploded with growth, uncontrollably twining up her arm. She yelped and jumped back from the table, holding out her hands, unsure what to do next.

"That's good!" whooped Caleb. "Now see if you can make a chair." He gestured to the Adirondack next to him as Ian sprang from the table and joined them.

Feeling like she was juggling a snake, she used both hands to grow the writhing seedling and set it on the ground, hoping for a semblance of a chair. When it stopped stretching and wrapping around itself, the seedling was indeed a chair, thick and ill-shaped with a distinct lean to the left, but still a chair. She rubbed her temples, attempting to soothe the headache that gripped her skull and burned behind her eyes.

"It's definitely one of a kind," teased Caleb with a wide grin. "But I'd say this is rather good for your first time. Do the same thing tomorrow. Don't force the wood to explode, but use its energy and ask it to split evenly."

She ran her fingers over the furrowed and twisted surface of the chair. "Why would it want to do that? Isn't that like . . . killing it?"

"No," said Caleb, eyes wide. He placed his hands gently on the back of the chair. "It's the life cycle of the forest. There is no death, only regeneration."

Sara saw the sincerity in his green eyes and followed his gaze toward the wildflowers almost obscuring her mother's headstone.

Ian, who had wandered to his pile of clothes, pulled on his dry shirt and tugged on his shoes while calling over his shoulder to her. "Go to the Atwells tomorrow. Lily will help you." He approached her as Caleb ambled off to retrieve his own shoes by the edge of the lake. "Don't worry, we'll help you complete this task and get Kane off your back." Ian hesitated, tapping a hand on his side.

"What is it?" Sara folded her arms. She didn't need to be a mind reader to know he was hiding something. "What aren't you telling me?"

He looked around nervously and leaned in. "Okay, don't take this the wrong way, but you still need to work on keeping your energy and"—he waved a hand in a circle over his chest—"*emotions* more to yourself."

Her eyes widened, mortified he might know about her feelings for Thomas—or worse yet, the secret she kept.

"Instead of unconsciously projecting your thoughts, hold them close like a second skin . . . or a tight flower bud." His raised brow disappeared under his curly hair. He grinned for a moment but then frowned, his gaze shifting from teasing to serious. "Be careful with Thomas," he said in a low voice.

Sara shot a quick glance at Caleb, who had stopped to skip a rock along the lakeshore. "Why? Because of the unspoken rule that the families shouldn't *comingle*?" She had suspected this was the reason.

He narrowed his eyes and studied her curiously. "Sometimes we can't help who the Mother and Father choose." He turned away, tapping his thigh. "It's just . . . Thomas has an *edge* that can be . . . let's say, challenging."

She stared at him, confused by his conflicting remarks. He seemed to imply that it *was* acceptable for the families to mix but at the same time to be careful with Thomas. Big brother indeed. If he only knew, it was Thomas who should be warned of *her*.

Ian's mouth curved into a wry smile. "Don't worry, your secret is safe with me."

She gasped, but the grin on his face confirmed he meant her feelings for Thomas. Her other secret, the murderous one buried deep in her soul, would never elicit a smile.

"What secret?" Caleb arched a brow as he hopped to the table, adjusting a shoe.

"Nothing," said Sara and Ian in unison.

Caleb snorted a laugh. "Right. Well, it's a small forest and no one can keep a secret for long."

Sara bristled at the comment, hoping it wasn't true.

He grabbed the box from the table. "You can keep the beer, but I gotta get this box back to Jennie or she won't make another pizza." He slapped Ian on the back and walked off toward the woods.

Ian grinned again at her before turning and dashing off after Caleb.

Scowling, she playfully turned up her middle finger at her brother's back, and his laughter filled her head. She grabbed her wet shoes, clipped the knife to her shorts, and headed for the treehouse.

Treading softly up the spiral staircase, she halted at the sound of footsteps on the main level above.

"I thought they'd never leave," floated Thomas's voice.

"Seriously?" she yelled up at him, her blood beginning to boil. "Don't tell me you're hurt again. I had another crappy day with your father, and he better not take it out on you." She released a breath to shake her lightheadedness and the headache that still gripped her.

Cresting the top of the stairs, her heart skipped when she saw him beaming at her from the center of the main room. Dressed all in black, including a tight vest over his T-shirt, he seemed taller, somehow bigger. She stopped short, scanning his chiseled face for any pain or sign he may have overheard her conversation with Ian.

"Do I need to be hurt to have an excuse to see you?" He didn't wait for an answer. "Vi told me what happened, so I came to congratulate you." Thomas flashed a wicked smile. He shoved his thumbs into his pockets, studying her up and down, and remained in the middle of the room like he was waiting for her to come to him.

"He nearly drowned me in mud, but his expression was worth it." She grinned in spite of herself and dropped her shoes on the deck with a wet thwack before stepping into the room. Still wet, hair dripping down her back and reeking of lake water, she purposely stayed at the threshold, resisting the magnetic pull into the room.

Through the dusk and shadows playing inside the treehouse, his eyes shone with blue flames. "I intend to see that same look for myself someday." He shifted, his heavy boots ringing throughout the empty room. "Well, now that I know you're fine and as beautiful as ever, I have to go." The words easily rolled off his tongue. With a smirk, he sketched a bow and headed for the rear doorway, his steps blatantly slow.

She wrinkled her nose at both his comment and the smell emanating from her. Both "*fine*" and "*beautiful*" were questionable at best. But seeing him walk away tugged at her. She took a few steps after him. "What do you mean, you 'have to go'?" She didn't hide the edge of panic in her voice at the thought of Kane making him leave the forest.

He whipped around and levitated to her, as though a magnetic pull did indeed snap them together. His sudden movement filled the surrounding air with his scent of woodsy musk and ash. "There's been an increase in Taker sightings. Matt and I are patrolling the wall tonight." His voice purred with delight, seemingly pleased with her concern. He stood so close she could see his neck pulse with a steady heartbeat.

She shoved her hands into her back pockets to keep from reaching out to trace his collarbone, heart fluttering while heat tinged her cheeks and burned her ears. Whatever this was, it was happening too fast. Her feelings for him were so strong that her knees threatened to buckle. Afraid to meet his gaze, she lowered her eyes and nearly gasped when she saw the many knives strapped to his chest.

She swallowed hard, remembering Ian's warning. "You look . . . dangerous tonight."

"I'm always dangerous," he said, his voice now rumbling with amusement. He leaned in, hovering for just a moment as his breath tickled her neck, and then rushed out the door opening like a gust of wind and disappeared into the night.

CHAPTER 28

DESPITE HAVING SEEN Thomas armed to the teeth, Sara slept soundly. She woke content and relieved to have a day at the Atwell island, no Violet to babysit her and no testing by Kane. After getting dressed, she sat on the main deck, about to meditate, when a raven, glinting blue-black in the dawn light, landed beside her with a harsh squawk.

"Your skills are shit," cried a voice as harsh as the bird's call. Sara peered over the deck and easily identified Moira by her flaming hair. She stood among the gravestones, hands on her hips, glaring at her. "Fine mess of *wood* you left at my place. Obviously, you have no idea what you're doing." She flicked her hair and flashed a sharp grin. "You know you don't belong here, and in a few days everyone else will know it too."

Sara fisted her hands and struggled to not spew the snarky comments burning her tongue. She needed to stay focused on her task to appease Kane and then kill Samson, not get tangled with Moira. Unclenching her fists, she merely steadied her gaze and remained silent.

Moira glanced at the bloody T-shirt still draped over an upper windowsill and sniffed the breeze. "Has Thomas been here?" She squinted disapprovingly, her predator's instinct focused on the slightest tell. Sara held her breath, but it was too late. Moira stamped her foot and growled. "Stay away from him. He's like a brother to me, and I'll kill you if you touch him."

She stared at Moira, biting her tongue hard enough to draw blood while imagining pulling in her feelings until they formed a tight bud inside her chest.

Moira shifted her fierce expression into a smug smile. "Good luck finishing your *task* while the whole forest is watching you," she snarled. Her sudden change in mood startled Sara, the back of her neck prickling at the memory of Kingsley Atwell's warning.

Moira phased into a fisher cat and disappeared into the woods behind the cemetery, Trouble taking to the sky after her.

Sara stood on the deck, nostrils flaring at the last sight of Moira. After a few deep breaths, she slipped on her shoes, and thudded down the stairs.

With the treehouse shaking in her wake, she sprinted through the cemetery gate and across the clearing for the dock. At the sight of the little boat, her mouth twisted to the side. *How hard can it be?*

The boat rocked gently in greeting when Sara slid into it and took a seat in the middle. Nothing happened. She scooted to the edge and peered into the water. A school of bluegills stared back, their unblinking eyes fixed on her while they darted around the boat. "How 'bout a little help?" Nothing. "Do you need a magic word or something?" She sighed and sat back, one hand idly rubbing the stubbly expanse at the back of her head while regarding the island—the mere smudge of a dock waiting for her in the distance. At the thought of the weathered dock and island wall, the boat glided forward, water calmly lapping its sides.

She peered into the glassy surface, still searching for an explanation—perhaps the fish did indeed push the boat. The surface rippled and then calmed, revealing a murky village at the bottom of the lake. Her eyes widened. Gripping the rail of the boat and hooking her feet under the seat, she leaned over far enough to put the tip of her nose in the water. Sara gasped at the dreamy scene of multiple houses, tree-lined roads, and even a church. But her wonder faded, replaced by a gut-wrenching awareness at remembering the villagers whose hate and fear grew so great that they sacrificed their own homes to flood the valley. She shook her head when a school of fish swam into view, causing the vision to shimmer and fade as the boat approached the island dock.

With a grateful pat to the boat, she disembarked and began descending the stairs into the protected island. Halfway down the steps, she glanced at the silty path below and nearly pitched headfirst down the stairs when a giant silver wolf emerged from the bushes. She grabbed the stone wall to steady herself. The wolf pulled back its lips and stretched out before her, head down in what seemed like a bow.

"Oh, Albert, I think you gave her a fright," said Alice, coming with Lily around a bend in the path. Lily smiled and held up a ginormous muffin for Sara. "Ian told us you would be coming."

"Of course he did." Sara snorted a laugh.

Similar to the forest mainland, the island's expansive forest held a trove of tagged trees, some dead, some crowded and needing to be thinned. Employing Caleb's lesson, she easily split the wood and, with help from Alice and Lily, stacked three cords under the overhang of a stone barn before noon.

After celebrating with a restful lunch by the courtyard fountain, Alice and Albert retired to the ranch house while Sara and Lily remained in the garden.

Sara leaned back in her chair, enjoying the cool breeze and hazy sky that held off the hot afternoon sun. "The weather is so pleasant here on the island."

"Thanks," said Lily. "It's quite easy, actually." She looked up at the gauzy clouds and then grinned at Sara. "You should try."

"What are you talking about?" Sara raised an eyebrow as she set down her lemonade, ice clinking against the glass.

Lily held her palms up to the sky. "It's an Atwell trait to call wind and water, including the weather, but you seem to have this power too. You used it when calling the elements to bring the boat to the island this morning." She smoothed back her long blonde hair and closed her eyes for a moment. The clouds instantly cleared and the breeze ceased.

Sara held up her hand to block the harsh afternoon sun.

"Okay, close your eyes and call back the clouds and breeze," said Lily, her tone confident and convincing.

Sara closed her eyes, but her concentration swirled and splashed about her mind, slipping from her grasp. She groaned in frustration at the sun burning her face and the headache squeezing her skull.

"Hmm," said Lily, laying a hand on top of Sara's, her touch light and cool. "Elements can't be called like a dog. You need to listen with your heart and then, when you hear them, gently pull them in around you."

Eyes still closed, Sara exhaled and released the tight bud she had formed earlier in the morning. She imagined it as a flower, blooming and reaching out, searching for rain. Cool moisture licked the edges of the flower, and a slight breeze caressed the petals. Sensing a shadow on her face, she opened her eyes to see clouds overhead.

"Now feel for the breeze," Lily encouraged.

Sara listened to the humming stillness of the courtyard and imagined wind blowing through the nearby trees. The humming grew louder until it became a swishing of leaves, and a soft gust blew across her face. Exhausted, she slumped back in her chair.

Concern etched Lily's face as she helped Sara back to the dock. "Maybe you just overdid it your first time."

Sara climbed into the boat and stretched out on the middle bench. "I'll be fine. Just need a little rest." She yawned while Lily used her power to push off the boat. Sara looked back at her, at the familiar smile on her pale face. "Thanks, Lily, for . . . everything."

Lily waved a delicate hand. "No need to thank me, silly. We're forest family." Her last word echoed over the water, and the gentle rocking of the boat quickly lulled Sara to sleep.

The sound of lapping water and the soft scrape of sand against the boat roused her. She woke to find the boat docked at the lake's edge. A glance at the cloudy sky proved useless in determining the time.

With a soft groan, she wiped a spot of drool from the corner of her mouth and squinted at the clouds. Perhaps Lily sent them to keep her cool. She bit her lip, remembering Lily's words. The kind, pale girl was more than a friend to her—she was *"family."* Sara stepped out of the boat and smiled despite the dull headache that still nagged her.

By the stillness in the air and the slight grumble from her stomach, she trusted it was late enough in the day for dinner at the Main House. She rounded a tall juniper and twin dogwood trees, then followed a new path into a stand of pines and toward the Cahills. When a soft breeze brushed her cheek, she grinned and redirected it to clear pinecones from the trail.

Ignoring the slight ache at the back of her skull, she took off in a run—excited to show Ian and Caleb what she could do and eager to get updates on her father and the blight. She also wondered if there had been any new threats from Takers or Samson—threats she intended to stop once she finished Kane's task.

Sara sucked in a breath and hurdled over a fallen tree that was much too big to move with her feeble powers. Landing with a gracefulness that surprised her, she quickened her pace—thoughts of dinner and a hot shower urging her on. Just as she was about to burst into the Cahill clearing, Samson's ominous blare tore through the forest, shaking trees and scattering birds. She tripped and crashed into the grass beside the path, narrowly missing a lichen-crusted boulder.

"Shit."

She rolled over and sprang up as an eerie silence fell on the forest. She cocked her head, listening. When the blare sounded again, she changed course and ran due east.

Directly toward the dark witch.

It was madness to think she could face him, but she couldn't resist. *I'll strangle him with my bare hands if I have to.*

To hell with Kane's task.

For her mom and dad, for Naomi and her people, she had to kill Samson.

CHAPTER 29

UTTER CHAOS SURROUNDED Sara. Flocks of birds darkened the sky, tree canopies shook with scores of furred mammals, and a herd of deer, eyes rolling, crashed past her in their desperation to flee Samson. A slim tree snapped and fell toward her. She pivoted just in time, its branches scraping her arm, and then pivoted again to avoid a bear lunging through the undergrowth. Her nightmare flashed in her mind as the bear hurtled past and disappeared into the heart of Ware Woods.

Again, the blare resounded and shook the earth. She scrambled up an incline, crested the top, and halted. A shroud of curling black smoke unfurled from the shadows and dove for her. She slipped, pitching forward into a tree trunk while her gaze remained fixed on the malevolent smoke. It slammed into the forest's protective wall and spread up an invisible barrier. Samson's ominous blare of frustration rattled her chest and rooted her to the ground.

Her ears rang and her vision clouded with the sheer pressure of the deafening noise. Swaying with dizziness, she closed her eyes and slumped against the tree beside her when something clamped onto her arms. No—not something. *Someone* gripped her tightly and shook her. The familiar scent of ash and musk filled her nose, and she pried open her eyes to see Thomas shouting her name. He was right in front of her yet sounded so far away.

He shook her again. Head snapping back and forth, Sara kept her eyes open until her vision cleared. She groaned and stared at the inky black presence pulsing and coiling with tension just outside the forest wall. Again, it gathered upon itself and lunged toward her, only to splay against the protective barrier, spreading smoke up toward the sky and casting a dark shadow on her and Thomas. A thunderous rumble rocked the trees as the dark cloud pulled back to the forest floor, contracting into a tall, gaunt-faced man—the man who haunted her dreams.

Samson.

He sneered at her before disappearing in a crackling shower of black and red sparks. Embers and smoke filled the immediate outer forest. When the air finally cleared, her dizziness had faded, and her hearing had returned.

"*Sara!*" Thomas's eyes bored into her, the heat from his hands making her skin slick with sweat.

Too close. He was much too close.

She held her breath, sweat running down her chest and clinging to the stone beneath her shirt. She had to break whatever this connection was between them. Not for her sake, but for his.

"How—what are you doing here?" She tried to step back, to free her arms from his grasp, but he tightened his hold.

"I'm running patrol! What the Hells are *you* doing here? He would have killed you if you'd stumbled closer to the wall." Anger and panic radiated from him as his fingers dug into her arms.

Her own anger flared in response to his. "Would he? Don't underestimate me. I came to kill him and now he's gone." She jerked her head toward the wall, at the last wisp of smoke in the outer forest.

"Are you *crazy?*"

"Most people seem to think so." Her palms burned and tears pricked the backs of her eyelids. She blinked furiously, inhaling to the count of three.

His expression eased. "Listen, I get it. You want revenge, but you can't go attacking a dark witch on your own."

"Like hell I can't." She tried again to break from his touch and failed. "Your fingers are burning me," she gritted out.

Thomas's eyes widened. He quickly loosened his grip, releasing her, and she stepped back—toward the wall. Panic flashed across his face, and his arms tensed, ready to grab her again. "Don't leave . . . please," he said, voice softly cracking.

Her anger melted at the tone of his voice, the subtle shift in his stance to close the slight gap between them. She froze, barely breathing—too selfish to turn away but too afraid to meet his gaze.

Leaning toward her, he said, "I'd kill him for you if I could." He heaved a sigh and raked his hands through his hair. "Mother, I'd do anything for you. I'm . . . *drawn* to you." His voice was heavy, thick with a longing that matched the ache inside her.

Her heart raced, swooning at the hunger in his words. But the flutter inside her suddenly twisted, and she stumbled back another step, overcome with guilt. It was too dangerous for anyone to be close to her—to the murderous power she strained to control. She wished Ian had been right about Thomas seeing her as an acquisition; it would make it so much easier to push him away. But she knew his feelings were genuine, felt it deep in her heart.

With her gaze focused on the forest floor, she trembled to find the strength she needed to sever their connection. "I'm just a challenge to you and . . . I'm not what you think I am," she said, struggling to keep her voice even.

He stiffened, like she had struck him. "What's that supposed to mean?" His tone had turned low and serious. He raised a hand as if to push back her hair but then let his arm fall and took a ragged breath. "I'd be lying if I said you weren't a challenge." He huffed. "But I mean that in the best possible way. I've never felt this *feeling*—Mother, it goes beyond a feeling. It's like I *know* you—us. Not me, not you, but *us*. I know you feel it too . . . every time we touch." He whispered his last word, and it hung in the air between them.

Her breath hitched, and her soul moaned at the aching pull between them—as if their hearts were already bound together. But she had to let him go. It was the only way to keep him safe from the monster inside her.

At last, she raised her gaze and faltered at the look in his crushing blue eyes. She blinked and shook her head to the side. "I . . . we can't do this," she uttered, her voice barely a whisper.

"I don't believe that," he said with a sudden fierceness, and she heard the fighter in him. Indeed, challenge accepted. She knew he would fight for her, for the possibility of them.

He said, "If this is about that unspoken rule, the whole forbidden coupling of the families, it's terribly outdated. I think your parents proved that. It's just an old idea to keep the bloodlines clean." His tone softened. "You're Lochton and Cahill but not Sullivan. You may be passionately excessive," he drawled with a grin, "but you're definitely not a two-headed monster."

Thomas dropped the grin and fixed his gaze on her hand. Not a breath escaped them as he slowly reached out and hesitated, waiting for her to make a move.

Though she stared at his hand, Sara imagined herself standing on the edge of a familiar precipice. But instead of the usual horrors skulking in the depths below her, a golden light shone. She drew a shaky breath, counted to three, and plunged off the edge. Trusting he would catch and hold on to her, no matter what truly lay before them, she slipped her fingers into his callused palm.

Flashes of blue and white energy snapped between them, and a fiery charge erupted through her heart and soul. Her back arched, and she gasped. Sparks danced around their joined hands, and her skin tingled with the same warmth that now heated her core. Wide-eyed, she met his flaming gaze and knew he felt it too.

Before she could catch her breath, a kinetic force pulled them together until all she could feel was Thomas, his embrace crushing her to his chest as her arms wrapped around his waist. The air crackled with electricity, and a flush of power ran through Sara so fiercely, her legs gave out. Thomas swept an arm under her knees and held her to him as they sank to the forest floor. He gently set her in his lap, bracing her with his arms and legs while her cheek remained pressed against his shoulder. Pine needles stirred around them, filling the air with their rich scent.

Keeping one arm around his waist, she placed her other hand on his chest. At her touch, a pulse of energy zipped through her. Thomas's breath hitched.

She nuzzled her head between his neck and shoulder, savoring the feel of him—the firmness of his muscles and the warmth of his embrace. She thought her skin would burst into flames at being so close to him. But it was the fire and tenderness inside him that truly undid her, igniting her heart—and her guilt. She had to tell him her secret—to warn him, to let him make a choice if this was what he wanted.

Sara shifted her head and looked before them, past the forest wall, to where Samson had been. Thomas stilled, and even the trees stopped their gentle swaying. She swallowed, hoping to push down her fear.

Fear of exposing herself—of losing him.

Tears welled in her eyes, and her throat threatened to swell shut. "I may not look like a monster, but I feel like one," she rasped. A tear slid down her cheek, and before she could brush it off, Thomas dipped his head and lightly kissed it away. She shuddered, aching from his gentleness. "I've harmed people. I've killed. And I know I have the power to do it again." She turned to the blue fire smoldering in his eyes. "I don't want to hurt you," she whispered, so close to him, she could feel his breath on her cheeks.

"Sara." Thomas sighed, his eyes glistening in the last of the evening light. Cradling the back of her neck, he brushed his thumb across her rough patch and wound his fingers into her hair.

She leaned her head against his shoulder and sobbed. To finally share her secret was like unshackling herself from a beast at the bottom of the ocean—a freedom so impossible she never thought it would ever happen.

"You could never be a monster," he murmured, his lips brushing her forehead. He was silent a long moment, waiting for her tears to subside. "Everyone has this fear. Especially those of us from sacred sites. Our power is both a gift and a curse. Just because you are capable of great and terrible things doesn't make you a monster. It's a choice to control your power instead of letting the power control you. Believe me, I struggle with this almost every day, but I try to do the right thing." He rested his chin on the top of her head, his face angled toward the outer forest. "Eliminating dark magic is what we do. It's our purpose, and the fact that you feel remorse tells me everything I already know about you." He paused. "Besides, if your heart wasn't pure, the sap would have killed you." He said this softly, like he was telling a secret.

"What?" Sara straightened and wiped her face with the back of her hand.

He shrugged. "It's just a precaution."

"You mean to tell me my *own grandmother* tried to kill me on my first day here?" Her voice was tight with both the realization that Gran was truly devious and the utter shock that she was still alive. *How am I possibly pure of heart?*

Thomas chuckled. "Gran is about as fierce as they come. Must be where you get it from." His lips grazed her ear before he leaned back and rubbed the nape of her neck again. "I don't care about this, or if you sprout horns—I *know* the good inside you. I *feel* it." He slid his hand from the back of her neck to the tender hollow at her throat, sending a shiver up her spine. His hand was close to her heart. Close to the stone.

She gasped and grabbed his hand, interlacing her fingers with his. Thomas grinned devilishly and tightened his grip, his thumb rubbing the back of her hand, each stroke sending ripples of energy up her arm.

Damn him. Using every shred of her willpower, she avoided his gaze and settled back into him, their chests rising and falling together.

He gave a short laugh, the soft rumble shaking them both. "You should know I'm definitely no saint either. Mother knows all the *wicked* things I've done," he purred, letting his words tickle her neck. She instantly stopped caring about his possible wickedness when his stubble scraped against her cheek and he hesitated. But instead of claiming a kiss, he simply held her tighter. From his rapid heartbeat, she knew he put his own want aside to give her the assurance she needed most.

She smiled, safely tucking her head under his chin. If they kissed right now, she wouldn't be able to stop herself from wanting more, and she had the distinct feeling Thomas felt the same.

He relaxed a breath, and when he spoke again, his tone was noticeably deeper and solemn. "I tell you I'm wicked, and you're still here." He squeezed her hand and paused. "And you know what a delight my father is. Sometimes I think I could actually kill him."

Sara snorted. "That makes two of us." She shifted and looked at his hand in hers. Her gaze traveled to his forearm and the branded symbol, which was now right in front of her eyes. She pulled her hand away from his waist and cautiously extended a finger, barely grazing his skin when he tensed.

"*Shit.*" He jolted off the forest floor, pulling her up with him. "He's coming." Thomas whipped around, protectively stepping in front of her as Kane burst through the bushes, followed by a giant gray wolf.

"What happened? Where is it?" demanded Kane, scanning the outside forest. He hovered over the forest detritus as though trying to avoid soiling his leather shoes.

The wolf sniffed the air and phased into Bill Walker. He cracked his neck and rocked back on his heels. His eyes narrowed on Sara and Thomas, his lips curling in amusement.

Sara swore she heard Thomas let slip a low growl.

She stepped around him and cleared her throat. "I heard the noise and came running. It . . . Samson tried to attack me, but the wall stopped him."

Kane flared his nostrils at her. "And where is it now? Why did it leave *without you*?" He pointed at her to stress his last two words. She scowled at him, fighting the urge to bite his finger.

Thomas folded his arms across his chest, muscles rippling with tension, and ground his boots into the soft earth. "It left when it saw me," he snarled.

"You?" said Kane. "What were you doing here?"

"Come on," Thomas said, an edge to his tone. "You know I left the office early to run patrol." He nodded at the crossbow and case of bolts behind him.

Kane straightened his shoulders and fixed a cool stare at Thomas, taking in his stance and the mussed carpet of pine needles, before turning his gaze to Sara. "You have no reason to be here. Three more days to complete your task, or I serve you up to Samson. And then, this forest can have some peace."

Before Thomas could lunge at him, before Sara could say anything, Kane flicked a hand, his power grabbing Thomas and forcefully dragging him behind as he rushed off into the forest.

As soon as they disappeared and the rustling of leaves faded, Bill smiled a toothy, lupine grin at Sara. He turned his back to her, effortlessly phasing into a wolf, and vanished.

Alone now in the quiet woods, Sara strained to hear anything over the thundering of her own heartbeat. Every part of her burned with longing, a fierce combination of want and need.

She cursed into the stillness, causing a slight breeze to kick up the surrounding needles. It wasn't the hurricane she wanted to unleash, but it would have to do.

Instead of continuing to the Cahills for dinner, she ran to the cemetery, grabbed the last two birch beers from the table by the lake, and headed to the turret. She sat on the upper deck, carelessly dangling her legs over the edge while she drank her dinner. Grimacing at the warm beer, she stared at the calm lake and considered her options.

She had three days left to complete her task, to get Kane off her back and then go after Samson. If she could somehow kill Samson, then Kane would have to leave her and Thomas alone. And if Thomas was right—if she had a choice in controlling her monster—then nothing could stop her.

CHAPTER 30

A T THE FIRST light of dawn, Sara jumped out of bed and scrambled about the treehouse, checking every windowsill and deck. But she found not a single bloom or sign of Thomas. The uneasy feeling in her stomach turned into a hungry grumble, reminding her she needed to take care of herself first. The only way to help Thomas and get Kane off their backs was to complete her task.

Hungry and eager to complete the Cahill wood cords, she jogged to the Main House, taking a forest path still wet with early morning dew.

Vaulting up the deck stairs and bursting into the house, she nearly tripped over herself to find Gran alone in the kitchen. "Morning, Gran. Where is everyone?" Sara sidled up to the island counter and picked up a strawberry hand pie, pausing before taking a bite. "I heard about the sap. How 'bout you warn me the next time I drink or eat something potentially fatal?" She arched a brow, squinted cautiously at the pie, and then bit into the sweet pastry.

Gran's eyes twinkled. "You would have done the same if you were in my shoes."

Sara merely shrugged; her mouth full.

Gran set down her tea mug and turned on the gas stove, heating a skillet. "Everyone ate and left already. Today's the last day to treat blighted trees outside the wall. After today, Sullivans and Walkers want everyone to stay inside." She looked up from cracking eggs. "Too many Takers in the outside woods, and Samson's attacks on the wall have been relentless. I've never seen anything like this."

Sara jerked back, recalling Samson's darkness slamming into the wall. Her mind skipped to Thomas and his tender embrace . . . his acceptance. A tingle of energy coursed through her at the memory of his touch.

Gran narrowed her eyes at Sara. "Don't worry about the dark magic. We're a crafty lot, and we'll get rid of them soon enough—without breaking the wall. Council denied that ridiculous idea. Besides, Ian and Naomi seem close to figuring out what Samson wants." She smiled, setting a plate of bacon and eggs before Sara. "And you'll be happy to know your father is coming home today."

"Seriously?" she shouted through a mouthful of strawberry pie. "Can I go with you to get him?" She had to see him, and beg for forgiveness.

Gran shook her head and set the skillet in the farmhouse sink. "Gaa, it's too dangerous for us to leave. Ted and Kane will bring him home."

"Kane?" Sara stopped chewing. The thought of Kane doing something nice struck her as odd.

Gran came around and sat on the stool beside her. "You should know that Charlie is still healing and may not be awake yet." She patted her arm. "The hospital did their best, and now it's our turn to help him. But we just don't know . . ." She trailed off, staring into the bottom of her mug before pushing it aside and straightening her back. "Focus on completing your task for Kane first, and then you can be there for your father. Understood?" Gran fixed her with a firm stare.

Sara plastered what she hoped was an innocent expression on her face. "Of course," she said before inhaling the rest of her breakfast. Indeed, she intended to appease Kane first. It was the going-after-Samson-to-avenge-her-parents part that no one needed to know about.

Gran stood and pushed in her stool with one hand while grabbing Sara's plate in the other. "Good. Now skedaddle. I'll wash up."

She kissed Gran's cheek and thanked her before heading out the back door in search of tagged trees.

Most of the marked trees around the Cahill compound were small gray birch, which meant she had to split twice as many to get enough wood. The slim round pieces rolled and tumbled into piles instead of stacking into neat cords.

She stood at the edge of the forest beside the barn and cursed. It was late afternoon, and the cords still needed to be stacked. Squinting at the piles of wood, she pulled up her shirt to wipe the sweat running down her face and stopped at a noise drifting through the forest. She yanked the shirt down and tilted her head.

All day, she had been expecting to hear the loud blare of another attack by Samson. But so far, only a tense quietness filled the air.

The sound now floating toward the Cahill compound seemed mechanical and urgent, not ominous. As she whirled around, trying to place the source of the noise, Caleb came through the barn and jogged over, his footsteps thudding across the packed earth.

"Hey, your dad's here," he called out. He stopped before her and gaped at the jumbled mess of wood. "Go on, I'll stack this." He waved off her thanks while gathering up the wood, easily carrying thrice the amount she could hold.

Sara sprinted toward the Main House, careening down the slope by the side of the barn and entering the common green just in time to see Ted's red truck bump along a path leading in from the Sullivans'. The truck stopped to meet Uncle Larry, who stood waiting along the path, his thumbs hooked into his overall straps.

Kane, wearing his standard button-down business attire, leapt from the passenger side of the truck, spoke with Uncle Larry, and flew, more than glided, back toward the Sullivan house.

Using a blanket for a stretcher, Ted and Uncle Larry carried her dad into the house. By the time she ran across the common and thumped over the deck, they were already settling him in an upstairs guest room.

"Dad?" she called out, bounding up the stairs. She stopped in the doorway of the room, panting and holding the frame for support. Gran adjusted her dad on the bed, tucking him in under a thin blanket. Ted and Uncle Larry clapped Sara on the shoulder when they brushed past her, their faces grim, and headed downstairs.

She stared at the person in the bed. She hadn't seen her father in weeks, hadn't been prepared to see him as anything other than the charismatic young professor and adoring father she knew him to be. His sunken eyes were closed, his cheeks gaunt, and a terrible stillness about him stole her breath. Gran wiped his face with a damp cloth and, without looking up, answered Sara's unspoken question.

"He's alive. Breathing fine on his own but still in a deep sleep. There's no more swelling of the brain and his internal organs have healed but . . . his spine is broken." Gran sat heavily in a chair and patted the side of the bed. She scanned Sara, her eyes desperate. "Sara, honey, sit. If all you do is sit with him, that will be enough."

Sara gently lowered herself onto the edge of the bed and took her father's hand. It felt light and papery, lifeless, as if this version of him were papier-mâché, a false replica of her real dad. She put her other hand on his chest, finding his heartbeat barely detectable.

Closing her eyes, she took a deep, shaky breath and searched for the warm glow within herself. Physically exhausted and emotionally wrecked, she struggled to catch a slight flicker buried deep inside. She coaxed it and pleaded with it to grow, to reach through her and pour into her father—to heal him. The effort nearly broke her, but when the light finally flowed from her hands, it sputtered and dissipated as soon as it touched her father. He was too withdrawn, and her light was too weak to heal him.

Hot tears ran down her cheeks and dripped onto the blanket. Pulling his hand to her face, she took another ragged breath and squeezed her eyes shut. "I'm sorry I lost Mom," she choked in a tight voice. "I can't lose you too."

Exhausted, she curled up beside him and fell asleep. Throughout the night, she drifted in and out of consciousness but never moved from her vigil. Gran came and went, constantly checking on them. At one point, Sara woke and sensed Ian watching from the armchair. He stayed until morning, quietly leaving when the first rays of sunlight brightened the room. Judging by the sun that now shone in her face, she must have dozed off after he left.

She shifted on the little bed, her stomach growling, when she heard a faint clinking of bottles. The door opened and Gran entered the room, holding a basket.

"Good, you're up," she said, approaching the bed. "Go down to the kitchen and get some food while I care for your father."

Sara rubbed her eyes, kissed her dad's waxen cheek, and then rolled over and off the bed. Stretching cramped muscles, she glanced at the basket of potion bottles in the chair beside her, and nearly stumbled when her grandmother surprised her with a hug.

"Get going. I'll take care of him." She turned to her basket, dabbing her eyes with a handkerchief.

With a tight grip on the railing, Sara descended the stairs and shuffled to the kitchen counter. The main room buzzed with multiple generations of Cahills milling about, eating breakfast, and discussing the blight and work chores for the day. Helen put a plate of food and a tall glass of water in front of her. Sara's gaze flicked over the food, but she made no move to eat. She felt hollow inside, numb and detached from everything around her.

"Hey," said Caleb, pulling a chair up beside her. "If you're not going to eat that, I will." He waved a hand in front of her blank stare. "Come on"—he bumped her with his shoulder—"you need to eat."

Slowly, she tilted her head to him, his infectious grin getting her to crack a tiny smile. She picked up a fork and took a bite, her dry mouth causing her to choke on the tasteless food.

"Here." He slid the water and a cup of coffee at her. She drained both before muttering a thanks to him. "He'll be fine now that he's finally home. He'll get plenty of care while you finish your task. No worries." Caleb flashed a reassuring smile, then turned in his seat and scanned the trees on the opposite side of the common.

She groaned. "You think I still need to do my *task*?"

"Why don't you ask the man himself?"

Sara twisted around as Caleb used his coffee mug to point at Kane coming through the trees and gliding into the main room.

Kane landed with a hollow thud on the wooden floor and regarded Sara with disgust. "Shouldn't you be stacking wood?"

Caleb choked on his coffee.

"Seriously?" Sara shot back. She slid off the chair and faced him, back straight and chin up. "My dad just got back, and our walls are being attacked. I'm ready to fight, but instead you have me doing chores!"

Kane's fists shook at his sides. "You'll be ready when I say you are. Right now, you do what I tell you!" The kitchen and main room fell silent. No one, not even Caleb, made a move to speak up for her.

She ground her teeth to stop from spewing curses, shaking with the effort to hold back her monster from destroying him, from choking the life out of him. Her vision wavered with rage and tears. Kane cleared his throat and coughed—as though her hands were indeed around his neck. She felt herself slipping—

"*Choice.*" That's what Thomas had said. She had a choice in controlling her monster or letting it control her.

She whipped away from Kane, stormed out of the lodge, and ran into the pines.

Instead of heading straight to the Lochton house to begin another set of wood piles, she veered her course into the thick woods, hoping a long walk would clear her head.

CHAPTER 31

AFTER A SOLID spell of brooding, Sara found herself in a remote area, far from the family homes and the route she ran with Violet. The undergrowth was thick with brambles that grabbed at her instead of parting into a path. Unable to continue forcing her way forward, Sara paused and glanced up at the unfamiliar trees, their shapes painfully twisted, when something slithered across her foot.

Choking back her scream, she whirled around to flee. But the brambles had closed in, making it impossible to tell which direction she had come from.

Silence blanketed the woods. Not a bird or insect could be heard. And instead of the typical leaf-strewn forest floor smelling of organic humus, her shoes sank into marshy soil that released a rotten odor.

The stone concealed beneath her shirt warmed and pulsed when she tried to push back the thorny brambles, at first with her foot and then her mind. Impervious to her efforts, the brambles grew in closer.

In her head, she screamed for Ian.

No response. Either he was too far away for her feeble powers, or she had somehow stumbled into a magical dead zone.

Her breath grew shallow and rapid. She grabbed a thick

vine, cutting her hand on thorns that looked like serrated knives, and tried again to will the brambles aside. The vine shuddered and creaked.

Her sigh of relief ended in a yelp at the sight of Dorcas.

Sara fell backward into the vines and stuck to them, a fly in a spider web. She stared at the man-eating witch. Dorcas's dress was torn and filthy—more rags than clothing—and her outstretched hands were grotesque. On each hand, six fingers, partially crippled by swollen joints, undulated abhorrently. The open sores on her skin and scalp glistened in the sun, and her cloudy, hypnotic eyes seemed to look right through Sara. She put a fat, twisted finger to her lips and exhaled.

Sara gagged on the putrid breath but didn't dare turn away from the witch. Dorcas tapped the side of her greasy head and pointed at Sara. The unexpected gesture startled her, and she stopped struggling against the vines.

"Listen, child," called a voice as sweet and alluring as honey inside Sara's mind. Dorcas tapped her head again, her eyes glowing. *"The bear witch has cursed you. Break her spell to release your magic and protect Ware Woods."*

A warning tingled at the back of Sara's neck. She tried to rub her bald swath, but the vine tightened its grip. "Wh—what are you talking about?" The panic and disbelief in her voice hung in the dank air.

Dorcas swayed her head from side to side, a snake before striking. *"I have been here since the beginning. I see everything."* She grinned, revealing bloody gums and a few rotten teeth. Her sweet, melodic voice contrasted sharply with her ghastly appearance, making Sara ill. *"We have been waiting for you."*

"Who's 'we'? Why are you telling me this?" Sara swallowed, fighting to calm her stomach and not vomit on herself.

"I am paying a debt for my salvation. In reverse and in advance." Dorcas lifted her face directly to the sun. *"Seek the spell breaker you*

brought with you. Hurry, before it is too late." She crept back and vanished, swallowed by the reptilian vines.

As soon as the witch disappeared, the brambles heaved Sara forward, their thorns releasing her with a wet sucking sound. Blood ran down her arms and legs as the vines pulled back, providing a narrow path through their thorny teeth.

Sara seized her chance. Clutching the red stone through her shirt, she fled the swampy thicket, running until she reached the comforting shade of the closest soul tree—the Lochton pine. She raised her hands above her head and gasped for air, her mind racing. Though she hadn't been able to perform a lick of magic, she still trusted her gut to detect a true lie. Dorcas had not been bullshitting.

Naomi said she was a spell breaker—*"the best from my site"*—and Naomi had come with her to Ware Woods. If Naomi and Ian were still working together, Sara's best bet to find her was at the Lochton house. She raced down the hill and wove through the blueberry bushes, completely ignoring an enormous bear gorging himself on ripe berries. The tall grass parted, and she shot through, leapt over the muddy ditch, and landed on the soft lawn.

"Ian!" she called out in her mind, sprinting across the backyard toward the patio door.

"I'm in the basement. Take the bulkhead," his voice sounded in her head, along with an image of the open cellar doors. She rounded the house and stumbled down the cellar stairs, startling Naomi, who stood analyzing a wall-mounted map. At the far end of the room, Ian sat before an extensive computer system. He swiveled around and winced at her bloody appearance as she skidded to a halt, staring at the basement's office-like appearance.

"What happened to you? Did a blackberry bush piss you off?" Naomi cocked an eyebrow, the corners of her mouth pulled back in a smile.

Ian scooted his chair toward Sara, his jaw slack and eyes wide. Disregarding the both of them, Sara slowly spun, panning the room. Intense curiosity momentarily replaced her urgency to break the spell.

To her right was a couch flanked by end tables and decorative lamps, while to her left—toward Ian—loomed a floor-to-ceiling technical system with multiple flat-screens and blinking equipment. Maps of various sizes and locations, some with green and black marks, others with pins and Post-it Notes, nearly covered the white walls. In the center of the room sat a full-size table and chairs, a formal meeting space. Stacks of books, papers, and more maps lay scattered across its surface.

Bailey woke from under the table, shook off her nap, and trotted over to her.

"What's all this?" Sara panted, catching her breath as she waved her arms around the room.

"My office," said Ian, drawing out the words, his eyes still wide. When she returned his shocked expression, he snorted a soft chuckle. "I wasn't kidding about running a gaming empire. But at the moment, this is Samson-research headquarters. We know he has plenty of Takers working for him and that he's responsible for the blight. But we still can't figure out *why* he's specifically targeting Ware Woods. Unlike Naomi's site, our wall is impenetrable, and even if he got in, it'd be suicide to go against our Magus."

He leaned back in his chair and gestured with both hands at her. "So what's all *this*?" He quirked an eyebrow. "What happened to you?"

Sara had forgotten about her bloody arms and legs, adrenaline suppressing her pain. "I . . . had a run-in with Dorcas."

Ian opened his mouth, but Sara interrupted him by blurting out, "What's a Magus? Kane mentioned it at the Council meeting."

Ian's eyes flashed. "With Dorcas?"

"Magus first." Sara widened her stance and shoved her tangled hair from her face.

Naomi edged out of the room.

A faint whine escaped Bailey, followed by a tense silence. Ian narrowed his eyes at Sara. "Gaa," he muttered before shaking his head and pushing himself out of his seat. His curly hair nearly grazed a low beam in the ceiling as he strode toward a large wall-mounted map of North America, the same map Naomi had been studying. Multiple green- and black-circled areas marked its surface. "A Magus is the most powerfully gifted person from a sacred site." He pointed to one of the green-circled areas. "Each sacred site has one Magus—be it a High Witch, Elder Vampire, or Alpha Shifter—who represents their site in the Global Council. Only a Magus has power outside of their sacred site." He kept a wary eye on the blood dripping down her legs.

Sara approached the map and swept a hand across it, over dozens of green circles, before stopping at Ware Woods. She tapped their location once before Ian answered the questions she impatiently projected into his mind.

"Ware Woods is unique for a few reasons. One, our Magus—Makwa—cannot leave our site; two, our wall is completely impenetrable; and three, our site is not homogenous but includes a mix of witches, shifters, and vampires. For these reasons, our site is usually ignored by good and bad magic alike." He shrugged. "Basically, we keep to ourselves."

Of all the inconceivable facts she just heard, she had difficulty believing one. "There are *vampires* in Ware Woods?"

"Just two. And believe me when I tell you to leave them alone. They *dislike* being bothered."

She frowned at him.

Naomi returned with a damp towel, holding it out to her. Sara ignored it, her attention once again focused on the map.

"And the black circles?" Her fingertip traced small and large black rings scattered across the map, their number appearing equal to the green circles.

Ian flicked the hair out of his eyes. "Those are concentrations of dark magic," he said. "Unlike white magic, which is bound to protect sacred sites, dark magic roams freely in the outside world. There are a few loners, but most dark magic clusters together."

Sara dropped her hand, finally taking the towel from Naomi. She swiped at the blood on her arms and legs. "Well, that hardly seems fair," she said. "To have white magic bound within sacred sites while dark magic gets to wander about."

Naomi grunted in agreement, no doubt thinking of her slain people, while Ian shook his head.

"Except for rare instances like Samson attacking the Hills site," he said, "it's actually a fairly balanced system. Dark magic is volatile and tends to kill itself, either by fighting for power, self-imploding, or slipping up and being taken out."

Sara narrowed her eyes at him, waiting for further explanation.

He folded his arms across his chest and continued in a low voice, enunciating every word. "If you use magic in the presence of a normal person, you are met with a swift, merciless death. By being bound to sacred sites, white magic is protected from such . . . mistakes."

"So much death," whispered Sara. "And fear of attack. You say it's rare, but we have Takers and Samson at our wall trying to get in. How is it good to be bound to a sacred site? And why does it seem like everyone is trying to kill us?" She wiped more blood from her legs and thought she might be sick had it not been for Bailey lying calmly at her side.

Ian shifted his weight. "Bound or not, it's an honor to protect Ware Woods. The living energy and natural balance of this forest is a vortex of power connecting the Mother below and Father above. The forest embodies their magic. Not only do we maintain and protect this land, but as gifted, we are an integral part of its power." He loosed a soft sigh. "By using magic for good, to help and protect, the energy is infinite. But to use magic for dark or personal gain, there would never be enough. Dark magic seeks our power to fill their void, but it never lasts."

Sara glanced at her cuts and the bloody rag in her hands, a chill dragging up her spine at recalling Dorcas's warning. "Why is it suicide to go against Makwa?" she asked, her voice a scratchy whisper.

Ian's golden-brown eyes bored into her. "Because she is a *very* old, powerful witch."

Her mouth went dry. "Dorcas said Makwa has cursed me." She looked from Ian to Naomi. "Can you help me?"

"Mother below!" cried Ian, hands pushing back his hair so tightly, his eyes squinted. He huffed a deep breath and dropped his hands, letting them slap his thighs before pacing around the table.

Naomi narrowed her eyes at Sara. "I always thought something was a little off. I even caught a faint scent of a curse during the Council meeting, but I wasn't certain." She approached Sara and laid her hands on the sides of her head. "Even knowing you are cursed, the spell is hard to detect. Makwa *is* a very powerful witch." She wrinkled her nose. "The spell is safeguarded and cannot be rebounded." Naomi closed her eyes and shook her head, as if swiping through a mental list of possibilities. "But . . . we may be able to break it." She snapped her eyes open and released Sara.

"Great, we need to do it now." Urgency laced her tone.

Ian stopped pacing. He grabbed the back of a chair, the wood groaning under his grip. "Hold on," he said. The authority in his voice startled Sara; even Bailey picked up her head and eyed him. "Why would Makwa curse you? And why, for that matter, would Dorcas then help you? Those two are thick as thieves."

"I don't know," she pleaded. "But I believe Dorcas. She said to seek Naomi to break the curse so my magic can be released and help save the forest."

Ian folded his arms again and arched a brow, unconvinced. "This isn't a fairy-tale game."

She rolled her eyes at him. "Ever since I came to Ware Woods, I've felt . . . off. It's hard to focus on anything magical—my thoughts slip around, and what little I can do gives me headaches, and I'm just so exhausted. I know something is wrong. It's like I'm trying to run but someone is holding my feet." She paused and inhaled, steadying herself to tell them more. "I feel like I've been held back all my life. Coming here, I finally found this big missing piece of myself, but something isn't right. I think my magic *is* being held back. If Naomi can break the curse, then maybe I can finally be myself." She looked back and forth between the two of them, anxious for their response.

Ian ran his hands through his hair again and glanced at the ceiling. "Fine." He sighed heavily. "But on two conditions: one, you do not leave the forest; two, we do not tell anyone about the curse. Makwa is respected as much as she is feared. No one has outright gone against her, much less tried to undo her work. And if the Sullivans and Walkers find out about the curse and that you even *try* to break it, they may have enough sway to convince Council majority to exile you—both of you—from the forest." Ian pointed at Sara and Naomi, his face grim and slightly pale.

"Understood," said Naomi with a tight nod. She turned to the open bulkhead, sprinted up the stairs, and called back to Sara, "Give me a head start to collect a few things from Helen, and meet me in the cemetery. And bring that bloody towel with you."

Ian stared after her and resumed drumming his fingers on his legs.

Sara broke the silence. "If this works, I may be able to heal Dad."

He stopped tapping and regarded her, terror and concern shining in his golden eyes. "I hope so," he breathed.

And in that moment, Sara read his fear of losing her and Charlie, of being abandoned again. Her heart broke for him—for all he had endured and the deep, invisible scars he bore. A warmth bubbled up inside her. *Oh, Ian.*

He held her gaze, as though he wanted her to know his secret pain. To know how much she meant to him. "Please be careful, and *promise* me you won't cross the wall. Samson is very powerful, and I'm still not sure why he's here. He may be after you." Ian's voice trembled. With a blink, he turned away and headed back toward his computer.

"I promise," said Sara, her vow hanging in the cool basement air. Not just a promise to stay within the wall, but a promise to heal their father—to be a family that never abandoned him again.

She ruffled Bailey's fur before leaving the basement, the stairs creaking under her weight. At the top step, just as she stooped to clear the bulkhead, Ian called out, "You owe me a new towel."

"I'm sure I can find a ripe replacement in the barn," she hollered back, tucking the bloody rag into her back pocket. A chuckle and the clacking of his keyboard drifted up the stairs.

At the end of the yard, the forest parted to reveal a new path. Assuming it was a shortcut to the cemetery, Sara ducked her head under a pine bough and followed. After a few twists and turns, she slowed her pace—partly to give Naomi time to gather whatever she needed, and partly to think about her precarious situation. Distracted by all sorts of terrors that Makwa and Kane could crush her with, she didn't notice the deer until she happened upon it, lying in the middle of the path, as if the forest had led her to it.

Eyes rolling and saliva foaming along its velvety muzzle, the doe twitched and bleated in pain. A hideous burn seared its hindquarter, leaving hide and muscle melted together and caked with a glistening crust of dried blood.

Sara fought the impulse to rush to its side, knowing it would stress the magnificent doe. Instead, she approached her cautiously and knelt, gently placing a hand on her rump. Up close, she could see the burn hadn't been caused by heat, but by cold. Ice crystals clung to exposed sinew. *Samson.*

"Easy now," she murmured, focusing her energy and that of the surrounding forest onto the wound. Warm white light flowed through her hands, healing the deer from the inside out, until even its hide appeared completely unmarked. The doe lifted her head and nudged Sara, innocence shining in her deep brown eyes. She rose from the path and took a few timid steps before flicking her ears and bounding off into the brush.

Skin tingling in awe of the deer, Sara ran her hands up and down her arms and stopped with a curious glance at her legs. The cuts from the brambles had vanished.

CHAPTER 32

S ARA EXITED THE forest path, stepped over the wrought iron fence, and wove among the headstones to where Naomi waited at the base of the cemetery tree.

She inspected Sara up and down. "Healed already. That's a good sign." She pointed at the ground near Ann's headstone. "Let's get to it. Bury your bloody cloth here."

Sara chuckled and dug a hole in the soft earth with her bare hands. "Ian is definitely not getting this back."

Naomi poked through the basket at her feet, picked out a sage stick, and lit it with a match. After letting the sage burn for a moment, she waved away the flames until only red embers clung to it, emitting a thick smoke. "Ideally, we should wait for the moon to be fully dark, but I don't mind a challenge now and then." She fanned the smoke with the back of her hand while Sara patted the earth firmly over the buried towel. "First step is a sage cleansing—also known as smudging—where the smoke draws out any bad energy and dissipates it."

"My mom used to sage the house every full moon," said Sara, squeezing her eyes shut, velvety smoke kissing and curling from her feet to the top of her head.

"I heard Eliza was an exceptional witch. Such power, combined with a mother's love . . . I can feel her presence with you."

Sara opened her eyes. The smoke was gone, and Naomi was now circling her while using a stick to draw symbols into the ground.

"These protection and manifestation symbols will further purify your energy and invoke clarity. Stay inside the circle while I cleanse you with incense and herbs." Sara stood still, shutting her eyes against a new round of smoke, until Naomi spoke again. "Done with the first stage. Now, go clean up in the lake." She handed Sara a pumice stone shaped like a star.

Sara palmed the rough pumice and cocked an eyebrow. "Is this part of the spell, or do I smell that bad?"

Naomi's chestnut-brown eyes twinkled. "Both. Here's some soap." She tossed her a handmade bar smelling of mint and lavender.

A smirk tugged at Sara's lips. "I'm terribly offended, but . . . this soap *does* smell good." She sprinted for the water's edge, stripping and running into the lake before Naomi could see the red stone at her chest.

Sara dove into the water and scrubbed with the soap and pumice, gratefully washing off almost two days' worth of dirt and sweat, until her skin was pink.

Rinsing soap from her hair, she glanced up and saw Naomi at the lake's edge, motioning for her to come out. She put a hand over the red stone and stayed, neck-deep, in the water. "I'll get out if you look away."

Naomi laughed so hard she almost collapsed onto the shoreline. "Since when did you become modest? I've seen you tackle an orderly in nothing but a thin gown."

Sara glared at her.

Naomi snorted. "Whatever. I'll be over here, *looking away*. But before you get out, fill this bowl with clay from the lake bottom." She flung a wooden bowl at Sara, narrowly missing her head.

Sara responded by throwing the soap and star-shaped pumice back at her. With catlike reflexes, Naomi caught them—one in each hand—and laughed again before busying herself at the other end of the clearing. Leaving the bowl to float at the surface, Sara dove to the bottom, grabbed a handful of muck, and resurfaced. "Gaa, this mud stinks worse than the pond."

"Good. Make sure you fill the bowl with it," Naomi called out with delighted amusement.

Sara scowled in her direction but filled the bowl and set it at the water's edge before running to the treehouse and changing into clean clothes. Fluffing her hair with a towel she'd nicked earlier in the week from the Main House, she descended the curved stairs and sat before Naomi at the base of the cemetery tree.

Naomi shifted to sit knee-to-knee with Sara and inhaled deep enough to make her chest swell. "This spell has cursed you with many negative things, but mostly doubt, fear, and . . . anger. You must capture all the harm this spell has caused you and write it down on this paper. This is no easy task. Take as much time as you need." Naomi handed her a small piece of paper and a red pencil before closing her eyes.

Staring at the paper, Sara could not imagine fitting all her self-doubt, fear, and anger—not to mention her pain, sorrow, and frustration—onto such a tiny scrap of parchment.

Naomi took another breath and, ever so softly, chanted in a strange, rhythmic language, her husky voice and foreign words soothing Sara.

With a heavy sigh, Sara shifted her gaze to her mother's head-stone and to the wildflowers swaying before her etched name. A longing tugged at the wound in her heart. Just the thought of having to remember all the challenges she had endured threat-ened to overwhelm her. She clenched her jaw and started at the beginning—as far back as she could remember—long before the sleepover incident. As if flipping through a scrapbook of night-mares, she slowly released every struggle and hardship, letting a whirlwind of emotions mix and boil down until just one thought clanged inside her. With a heavy hand that nearly pressed through the paper, she wrote one word.

Alone.

With Naomi's guidance, Sara held the paper away from her body, folded it three times, and then burned it over a black candle, letting the ash fall into the bowl of clay.

Naomi nodded her approval. "Mix the ash into the clay and form a flat disk. Then use your finger to carve this sigil into the clay." She pointed to the largest symbol she had drawn in the ground—a circle with what appeared to be three entwined broken hearts in the center. She continued chanting, observing Sara mold and carve the clay. "Put this in a safe spot to dry overnight in the light of the waning moon. In the morning, break it and bury the pieces." Naomi's face glowed in the warm light of the setting sun as she opened a small vial of oil from her basket. She anointed the cemetery tree and then used the oil to trace the sigil onto Sara's forehead.

Sara recognized the fresh scent of cedarwood, but another rich, woodsy fragrance she couldn't quite place floated in the background.

"I suspect this is a generational curse that has affected many in your family. It is a hard spell to break because the afflicted have suffered so long they take on the curse as their own—unable to believe they are capable of magic even when the bind is broken." Naomi packed up her basket and turned to Sara, meeting her gaze. "The greatest curse of all is the curse we give ourselves. Only you can break that."

Sara considered Naomi's advice as she sprinted upstairs and placed the clay form on her bedroom windowsill facing the lake. Patting the treehouse, she said, "I trust you'll keep this safe." The house gave a gentle shake, and the floorboards released a soft sigh. Sara chuckled. "We'll *smash* it to pieces in the morning," she called over her shoulder, and ran down the stairs, finding Naomi waiting near Winona's headstone.

When Naomi announced she was heading back to the Cahills, Sara eagerly joined her. She was anxious to see her father and, having barely eaten anything all day, she was starving for dinner. After a quiet moment along the forest path, Sara couldn't help but steal a glance at Naomi. Her familiar serene expression was comforting, and yet a contrasting tension often pulled back her shoulders. And just now, at Winona's grave, Sara had recognized the painful grief that had flashed in her eyes.

Naomi turned to her, a smile pronouncing the apples of her cheeks. "Yes?"

"I didn't say anything."

"You're not subtle, Sara. What's your question?"

Damn it. Sara tucked her chin and lowered her voice. "I was just wondering what happened at your site, the Hills?"

"Hmm," rumbled Naomi. Her face tightened, and Sara instantly regretted opening her mouth. "What Samson did—" She shook her head. "I still can't believe it. I can't believe everyone's dead. His brutality and the guilt I have for being the sole survivor is a nightmare—a spell I can't break."

Without thinking, Sara gave her a quick hug.

Naomi huffed a laugh, returning the awkward embrace before playfully pushing her aside. "What's gotten into you? Now you're modest *and* mushy?"

Sensing her need to change the subject, Sara gave her a smirk. "Don't tell anyone—it'll ruin my horrible reputation."

Naomi tipped back her head and laughed, brushing against a cluster of honeysuckle. The bushes quivered and filled the air with the sweet scent of their blossoms.

For the remainder of their walk, Sara kept her mouth shut and simply listened to the sounds of the evening forest—singing crickets, peeping frogs, and the wind rustling through the trees.

Helen greeted them at the Main House and, although dinner was over and most people had left for the evening, she filled their plates with a generous portion of leftovers and served them on the deck. Candles flickered on all the tables, and shouts of laughter rang out from groups of people playing in the dusky common.

Sara quickly scanned the open space and, before Helen could return to the kitchen, asked, "Have you seen Thomas today?"

Helen wiped her hands on the front of her overalls. "No, dear. I haven't seen him since yesterday morning. I'm sure he's busy patrolling the wall with his family and the Walkers." She grabbed an empty cup from the patio table and headed back inside.

A loud snort followed by a scream turned Sara's attention back to the common. Caleb ran past with one of his younger sisters on his shoulders. She giggled as he jostled her about, pretending to be a horse.

Naomi chuckled and pushed her dinner aside. "That boy cracks me up. At first, I thought someone must have dropped him on his head when he was a baby. Becca and I had a good laugh over that. If you'll excuse me, I'm gonna help her out with the kids." She left the table and joined Rebecca in watching a group of children play tag around the chestnut tree.

Sara observed them, noting the tension ease from Naomi's shoulders, while she finished scarfing down her food. After waving goodnight to Caleb, she returned her plate and Naomi's remaining dinner to the kitchen and then ran up the stairs two at a time to check on her father.

She pushed open the door and hesitated, letting her eyes adjust to the faint light streaming through the curtains. Her heart warmed at the sight of Ian dozing in the armchair, his long legs sprawled before him. Even in sleep, his face was tight with concern. On the bed, their father lay still as death, with no visible changes from when she'd left him that morning.

Careful not to disturb them, she crept inside and sat lightly on the bed. Taking her father's hand, she focused on the love she felt for him and imagined it as a bright light. When the stone at her chest warmed, she closed her eyes and pushed her energy outward.

Her power felt different this time, as though it ran deeper and stronger inside her. A flush of warmth surged through her, tickling her cheeks and the back of her neck. She snapped open her eyes and placed a hand on her father's chest.

But Charlie remained still as stone, his heartbeat barely perceptible.

"I won't give up," she whispered. "Not until you wake and walk again . . . and not until I kill Samson." She kissed his hand and rose from the bed, only to stop at the sight of Ian sleeping peacefully in the chair—a relaxed smile now spread across his face. His curly hair, golden-brown complexion, and full lips made him look like an angel. She smiled and planted a light kiss on his forehead before leaving the room.

She could have sworn she heard a faint *"Thanks"* in her head before clicking the door shut behind her.

By the time she crept down the stairs, the Main House was dark and empty. Even the kitchen had been picked up and scrubbed down for the night.

She slipped out the back door and paused in the clearing behind the house to inhale the sweet, humid air. A lightning bug landed on her arm, blinking on and off before drifting back into the forest, the insect's movement slow and dreamlike.

Her head felt oddly heavy.

With a roll of her shoulders, she tried to shake off the strange feeling when something light, almost feathery, swept across her shoulders. She tilted her head forward and raised a hand to the back of her neck.

What the—

Sara shoved both hands into her hair and yanked on thick, short locks at the back of her head—not a trace of baldness.

As she stood in disbelief, a playful breeze wrapped around her, ruffling her hair and obscuring her vision. She spluttered, wiping back errant strands, and abruptly halted when the wind died. Hundreds of lightning bugs floated around her, suspended like twinkling stars. Her mouth agape, she slowly spun around and hesitantly touched one. It glowed brighter. With a soft chuckle, she threw back her head and twirled among them, spinning faster and faster until they became a blur.

Lightheaded and with a tightness in her stomach, she stopped spinning—and gasped. Her feet were no longer on the ground. She floated in the night air, five feet above the grassy yard.

With a yelp, she willed herself back to the ground, instantly dropping. She landed hard enough to stumble before a breeze nudged her back upright. Taking a deep breath, she bent her knees and pushed off the ground, this time floating as high as the second-story windows of the Main House. Her whole body tingled with weightlessness, reminding her of floating in the lake. Holding her arms out to her sides, she rotated slowly and rose higher until she cleared the tree canopy.

Sara inhaled deeply, filling her lungs with the rich scents of the forest. Closing her eyes, she not only truly smelled the forest for the first time but felt it with her entire being. In her mind's eye, she could see the colorful aura of the entire sacred forest, including all its trees, animals, and gifted families—each with its own unique energy radiating a different hue. Every element was stunning by itself—but when composed together, it was beautiful beyond words: a living, breathing painting of light and color. The very sacred essence she and her family pledged to cherish and conserve, and to protect from darkness.

She shuddered at both the beauty and responsibility that now defined her.

When she glanced at the ground far below, her stomach lurched and the small of her back tingled. She willed herself lower, instantly descending a few feet. She willed herself higher and rushed back to the top of the tree canopy. Carefully edging a little higher still, she cleared the treetops, took a deep breath, tucked and flipped herself forward—somersaulting in the air. For a heart-pounding moment, the night sky was below and the earth above, and then the horizon returned to its usual appearance.

Taking another breath, she pushed up and back with her arms out and legs straight, somersaulting in a wide arc behind her, this time enjoying the sky's expanse below and above. Clenching her stomach muscles, she let herself drop to her side and barrel-roll, effortlessly turning just above the treetops. She held out her arms and stopped.

Laughing, she rushed up, down, and side to side until she was comfortable with her new ability—an amazing, glorious ability.

With tears stinging her eyes, Sara sank to the forest floor. She dug her heels into the soft earth and raised her hands to the night sky, like a tree connecting the Mother and Father. Tilting her head toward the stars, she remembered the blessing from the Council meeting:

Mother below and Father above,
I give my true self unto your love;
To feel the earth and touch the sky,
I choose to live before I die;
For I am you and you are me,
We are the light, so mote it be.

The forest shook and parted open before her. Sara glided more than walked along the new path, staring about in awe. Tree leaves no longer rustled dryly but rang brightly, like little bells. Sweet ferns curled and uncurled with the breath of the forest, evening dew sparkling along their tender leaves. Animals of the night took turns scurrying and swooping before her, their greetings echoing in her head.

Sara followed the path, expecting to end up at the cemetery, but instead she found herself in front of the forest wall. She laid her hands on the vibrating stones, wanting to hurdle over and seek Samson, but then grimaced at remembering her promise to Ian.

A sudden swooshing of air blew into her ears. Grasping the stone wall, she could feel it trembling, as though something were running along its spine. She turned toward the wind blowing from her right when a force flung her back, slamming her into a carpet of reindeer moss.

Sara sucked in a breath and choked, fighting to get air into her lungs. Silently thanking the moss for breaking her fall, she rolled over and sprang to her feet.

Thomas glared at her from atop the stone wall, his face pale in the thin moonlight. He heaved a breath, his chest straining against his fitted vest of knives.

"What were you thinking?" he growled.

"I don't know." She frowned and dropped her gaze, still confused by how she'd ended up at the wall and not at the cemetery. "But you didn't have to hit me so hard." Rubbing the back of her head, she looked up at him and expected to see his bright smile. But his jaw was clenched, and a fierceness glittered in his eyes. "Are you okay? You seem . . . different." She stepped toward him, reaching out with her palm up. His anger was so palpable she felt it nip her fingertips.

He put his hands behind his back and shifted along the wall, avoiding her touch. "You seem different too." He jerked his chin at her as a slight breeze blew her hair forward, revealing tufts of new growth.

Hoping to melt his anger, she gave him a wide grin. "I've got so much to tell you!" She tried to grab his leg and pull him toward her, but he shifted away again.

"I can't right now," he said curtly.

Hurt by his rebuff, she took a step back, brow furrowed.

His expression changed from angry to conflicted. "I'm busy tonight. Go back to the treehouse," he said, his tone slightly softer.

She blinked at him, internally reeling from his cold attitude, so opposite from the energy she knew burned between them. Indeed, the aura shimmering around him was tinged in black, like shadows clinging to him.

He cleared his throat. "Please." His brilliant blues flashed with both guilt and concern. "For me."

Shocked, she said nothing but took a step back, searching and questioning him with her eyes. What had Kane done to the Thomas she knew? The Thomas who had kissed her cheek just yesterday.

The muscle along his jaw twitched, and his eyes bored into her. She held his gaze a moment longer until forcing herself to turn away and disappear into the woods.

The chatter of night animals and gentle swaying of the trees did little to calm her this time. She walked absently to the cemetery, the elation from flying completely replaced by frustration and concern.

She chewed her lip, reviewing her plan. Just because she could now levitate didn't mean the curse was broken. She would have to wait until morning to know for sure if Naomi had been successful. Regardless of whether the curse still held, she would finish her task—even if she had to cut all the wood by hand to make Kane leave her and Thomas alone.

And then she would go after Samson.

CHAPTER 33

S HE FELL ASLEEP waiting, hoping Thomas would appear at her window. In her dream, the birch grove glistened under a thin layer of ice. Soft snow gathered and hung in the air until all she could see was white. Somewhere from the white void ripped a roar so unhinged with rage it made her hair stand on end. The roar grew into a terrible crash that rattled her bones and rang in her ears.

Sara jerked awake—her bed and the entire treehouse had lurched. Branches and leaves swayed in the aftershock, sending a flock of birds to the sky. Swearing she heard something break, she ran to the window opening and leaned over the sill. Scattered on the ground below were the smashed pieces of the clay disk. The tree groaned and moved again, swelling as if taking a breath—and exploded with growth. Branches creaked and stretched while leaves burst through bark and unfurled to face the morning sun.

As the tree erupted in height and width, the treehouse expanded with it, popping and cracking as it grew and adjusted. The bedroom stretched longer and wider, the windowsill under her hands quivering to keep up with the riotous growth. Sara clung to the sill, struggling to stay upright. Below her, the earth rippled and gravestones crept. Roots licked out, coiled around the clay remnants, and swallowed them deep into the earth.

Heart pounding and every nerve buzzing with energy, she dug her fingernails into the windowsill, afraid she would float away with the sensation of weightlessness spreading through her. Her headache and exhaustion evaporated, replaced by a newfound clarity that bloomed inside her, sharpening all her senses.

Tentatively releasing her grip, she patted the treehouse and grinned. "Well, now I see why you couldn't wait any longer to smash it."

Sara threw on some clothes and pulled herself up to sit on the windowsill. Gritting her teeth against the possibility of falling and breaking a leg, she leapt more than glided out the window—and levitated. Her breath hitched. Relief at not face-planting into a gravestone was quickly replaced by jaw-dropping awe.

The oak tree was massive, shading almost the entire cemetery, and the house was now a multitiered marvel. Various levels wrapped around the thick trunk and spread along the branches. Curved decks skirted large rooms and connected independent sections, while window openings and swirling turrets peeked through the foliage. Similar to the original structure, the interior wood remained a golden-brown, and the exterior walls mimicked the tree's furrowed bark. Having emerged from the tree itself, and being organically constructed in such an entwined fashion, the house was impossible to distinguish from the tree.

Hovering before the oak, she chuckled as it gave one final shake of its new growth and then settled back into the cemetery with a satisfied groan. She glanced down and almost choked on her own snicker.

"Shit!" Her stomach turned at the sight of the ground far below. Shaking her hands and inhaling deeply, she practiced a few flips and glided around the treehouse, crashing into branches as she searched every windowsill and open deck. Her heart grew heavy at not finding a single flower.

Levitating above the clearing, she settled her gaze on the two

Adirondack chairs by the lake edge and grimaced at her misshapen lump beside Caleb's perfect creation. *I wonder if my unbound magic is strong enough to fix that, or . . .* She turned her scowl into a determined grin. If she could whish objects like Thomas, she could easily finish her task, *and* she could use it against Samson.

Her grin deepened as she narrowed her eyes on the chairs. When they wobbled and floated above the ground, waiting for her direction, she nearly yelped. With a sweep of her hand, the chairs whished to the lower deck, landing with a heavy thud. She winced and muttered an apology to the treehouse, which shuddered in response.

Quite pleased with her new skills, Sara beamed and considered what else she could do.

She lowered into the clearing and bit her lip. If the curse was truly broken, maybe she could finally control her other power—the dangerous power hidden deep inside herself—and choose how to wield it. Rolling her shoulders, she inhaled for three counts and exhaled for three more.

For the first time, she let herself fully relax and believe.

A breeze blew across the clearing, and a surge of warm energy flowed from her core to her hands. White sparks danced in her palms—the flames crackled and tingled as they licked her skin and darted between her fingers. Cupping her hands together, the energy swirled and grew into a sphere, sizzling with power and emitting a faint metallic scent. Instead of directing the energy ball at a specific target, she released it high above the clearing. Like a firecracker, it exploded, sparks bursting in a beautiful display before winking out and dissipating into the forest air.

The surrounding trees swayed, and the lake rippled as forest energy pulsed through her, penetrating her very soul. She gasped and clutched the red stone beneath her shirt. Scanning the clearing, she glimpsed her mother's gravestone and levitated to the cemetery. "Mom," she whispered. The wildflowers on Eliza's grave bobbed their heads at her. "You were right."

Her attention drifted when a flock of birds swept over the clearing and flew northeast toward the Cahills. She followed in their wake, skimming the tops of the trees, her hair and skin damp from the misty morning.

From above, she easily spotted Ware Woods' five soul trees and protective stone wall. Outside the wall, trees crippled and sucked dry by blight scarred the outer forest in swaths of rusty brown.

Flying among shafts of sunlight cutting through the morning haze, Sara faltered and nearly fell from the sky when she spotted a tree inside the forest wall with rust-tinged leaves.

With astonishing speed, she flew to the Main House, tree leaves quaking in her wake, and landed hard enough to put a small crater in the central common. She flicked her hand to repair the grass, her work passable but not as flawless as Caleb's. She made a mental note to ask him for forgiveness.

Sprinting across the deck and bursting into the main room, her sudden disruption instantly grabbed the attention of the present Cahills and Atwells.

"The blight is inside the wall!" Her words ripped open the quiet morning, exposing everyone's darkest fear. Chairs scraped across the wood floor, many knocked down in haste as the Main House came alive like an army roaring to battle.

"Where?" bellowed Uncle Larry over the din of the room. A dozen people were already striding for the deck, awaiting her direction.

"On the far northwest side, an elm has been kissed. Its leaves are browning," she yelled, already turning to fly out the open door.

Caleb lunged at her, grabbing her wrist. "Go see your dad before meeting us at the tree." The slight smile on his face put her momentarily at ease. "And then you can tell me what happened to you." With a raised brow, he motioned to her thick, wind-tousled hair, then released her and thundered out the archway, snagging a pastry on his way.

Lily briefly caught Sara's gaze, her watery-grey eyes shining with fear as she dashed after Caleb.

Scanning the few remaining faces before they bolted for the forest, Sara heaved a sigh. No sign of Ian, and—unsurprisingly—no sign of any Sullivans or Walkers.

She raced up the stairs and pushed open her father's bedroom door. Ian, Ted, and Gran stopped mid-conversation and stared at her. Charlie still lay asleep, but his face now had a ruddy glow, and his cheeks were no longer sunken. His chest steadily rose and fell with a strong pulse.

"What's going on?" asked Ted, approaching her at the door.

"Blight is in the forest," she said, eyes on her father, hoping his lids would open.

"I'll stay with Charlie," said Gran immediately. "Now git!"

Sara hesitated, her eyes flicking from her dad to Gran's fierce expression.

"I'll get you as soon as he wakes up. But right now, you need to help the others," said Gran, pushing them out of the room.

Sara bit her lip, giving a quick nod before Ian took her arm and dragged her toward the staircase. As they followed Ted, barreling down the stairway, Ian glanced from her tangled hair to her feet that barely touched the stairs.

"Seems you and Naomi were successful."

"I've never felt so alive. All my senses are on fire," she gushed, jumping the last three steps. "I think I can stop the blight . . . and Samson too."

"Listen," he said in a serious tone, slowing his pace through the main room to maintain a distance between them and Ted. "Like it or not, you need to complete Kane's task and then work with him on stopping Samson." She started to protest, but he shut her down. "No buts—and don't forget your promise. No leaving the forest and not a word about the curse."

She rolled her eyes. "Fine," she huffed. Together, they leapt off the deck and fell into a steady jog. At the edge of the clearing was a new path, already trampled by the exodus to stop the blight. In the distance, Ted and a few Cahills disappeared around a bend. "Where is Naomi anyway? I need to tell her what happened."

Ian furrowed his brow. "I thought she spent the night with you to make sure the spell was broken. No one's seen her since dinner last night."

"That's odd." Sara frowned, a prickling sensation sweeping the back of her neck. She shrugged. "Since she knows so much about Samson, maybe she's helping the Sullivans and Walkers."

Before Ian could reply, the path emptied into a clearing where the Cahills and Atwells were gathered, assessing the large elm before them. Along the elm's trunk festered multiple sores, bubbling with rusty blisters as if the tree burned from the inside. The upper canopy leaves were completely dead. Crippled brown branches clawed the summer sky. The blight visibly crept down the trunk, sucking away life and leaving a burnt, papery husk behind.

The Cahills wasted no time. They peeled back a large section of the forest floor, exposing rich soil, while the Atwells called a rain cloud. Helen, Rebecca, and Jennie added potions—some a glowing green liquid, like Ian's medicine, and some dry powders of all colors—while Uncle Larry and Caleb mixed the mud. Once Helen approved the mixture, the Cahills slathered mud onto the lower trunk while the Atwells called small gusts of wind to painstakingly apply mud to the upper branches.

Taking a moment to observe the process, Sara approached Helen and Uncle Larry. "Can I try something? I think it'll be faster."

Uncle Larry hooked muddy thumbs into his overalls and scanned the clearing before turning to her. "Of course, darling. You and Ian can mud up that ash." He nodded at a nearby tree beginning to brown. "It's spreading like wildfire."

Sara spun around. Dozens more trees, from saplings to towering mature giants of all varieties, were browning, as though recoiling from an invisible fire.

An ominous blare shot through the forest, shaking the trees and scattering terrified wildlife. She froze and turned to Uncle Larry. He shook a thickly callused finger at her. "Walkers and Sullivans will take care of Samson. You and Ian focus on mudding that ash," he yelled at them over the blast.

Reluctantly accepting the order to stop the immediate threat, Sara turned to her brother. "Come on!" She grabbed his hand and sprinted to the newly infected section. "Let's hope this works." She released her grip on Ian and closed her eyes, finding the light within her and growing it until she felt it buzz around her. Energy crackled along her skin when she opened her eyes and fixed her gaze on the tree. Using kinetic powers aided by wind, she yanked one arm, summoning the treated mud, and then yanked her other arm to slather it onto the tree. Before the mud could slide off, she yanked both arms again, holding the mud in place by wrapping it with ferns and grass. She felt the tree sigh in relief as the salve stopped the spread of the burning blight. Pushing harder with her light, she tried to imagine the tree healing from within. But despite her repeated efforts, the tree did not regenerate. Frustrated, she moved on to the next tree and tried again. Although the mud stopped the spread, she could not reverse the blight's damage and heal the trees.

Pausing to swipe her forehead, she glanced up to find a small crowd, including Caleb, Ian, and Lily, staring at her. "I'm trying, but I can't heal them," she apologized.

"You're doing great, cousin," said Caleb, eyes wide. "Just focus on stopping it right now." With a gap-toothed grin, he turned back to the mud pit to make more salve.

Their efforts continued throughout the day, taking shifts for a quick lunch, until the sun hung low and the last tree was mudded. With the lull in activity, Ian turned to Sara, wiping his hands on his already filthy shirt. "Don't you have to meet with Kane today?"

A wave of dread hit her. "Oh shit," she breathed.

"Go on then. We've got this covered." Ian ran a muddy hand through his hair, smudging dirt along his temple. "Good luck," he called after her as she took off, grass and wildflowers waving in her wake.

CHAPTER 34

SARA BURST OUT of the maple tree, causing a pair of foxes to scatter from the adjacent Council stage, and rushed to the Walkers' barn. Cutting and stacking the remaining cords in mere minutes, she raced back to the Council tree and looped to the Lochton pine.

Sara paused a moment to catch her breath, viewing the brown house and garage from atop the hill. She waited for her heartbeat to slow before gathering the forest energy around her. Calling forth the surrounding tagged trees, she split them in mid-air with one large crack, launching a flock of sparrows, and stacked the wood neatly behind the brown garage. She wiped sweat from her brow and gulped a few breaths, exerted from using her powers at such a distance.

Time running out, the sky now a brilliant orange-and-fuchsia ombré, she flung herself into the pine and looped to the Sullivans' white ash. She popped out from the hollowed base—and almost crashed into Kane.

He stood before the soul tree, arms folded across his chest. His appearance startled her, partly because of the menacing grin on his face but mostly because he wasn't wearing his normal tailored office attire. Instead of a button-down shirt with cuff links, he wore a black polo shirt, sleeves tight over his muscles; and in place of pants and fine leather shoes, he wore jeans and heavy boots. Clothes she knew he wouldn't mind getting dirty.

"So nice of you to finally show up." He studied her, appearing every bit like a coiled snake about to strike and devour its meal. Behind him stood Violet, and farther away, near the barn, loomed Thomas. Sara tried to catch his eye, but he turned away to cough and clear his throat.

She pulled back her shoulders and squared off with Kane. "I just finished the Walker and Lochton cords." While she held his gaze, her hands anxiously brushed dried mud off the hem of her shorts.

"Really?" He raised his brow. "Even if that's true, you still have three cords left." He glanced at his heavy tactical watch and then stared at her, waiting. Before she could respond, they all turned at a rustle in the woods behind the garage. The same two foxes she'd startled at the Council tree came streaking across the yard. Violet remained still as the foxes approached her and phased into Matthew and Moira. The twins grinned at Sara, Matthew's expression somewhat encouraging, Moira's more of a delighted sneer.

Not caring for the audience, Sara shifted her stance to ignore the twins and turned back to Kane.

"Where do you want them?" She didn't try to keep the icy bite from her voice. He jerked his chin at the barn where Thomas stood beside the existing wood pile. Thomas coughed again and moved to the side, still avoiding her gaze.

Sara threw a bitter smile at Kane as she opened her arms and shot up into the air, hovering over the pasture. Satisfied with the shock on his face, she closed her eyes and focused on the energy of the forest, letting it gather and build around her, electricity fanning her hair. With a deep breath, she relaxed and summoned the remaining tagged trees. She then held them over the pasture like soldiers in formation and extended her hands, palms up, releasing a burst of energy that instantly split the wood. Opening her eyes and focusing on the barn, she waved her arms in a figure eight pattern. The wood glided and clacked as it merged and fell into three neat crisscross stacked cords.

Violet folded her arms and smiled while Matthew and Moira gaped at her. Sara didn't care about their reactions—only Thomas's. She focused on him, puzzled by his frozen expression and downcast eyes. Kane cocked his head and squinted at her, following her line of sight. He glided to Thomas and whispered to him. Thomas's jaw clenched, his face pale and his expression deadly. He levitated to the far side of the pasture and faced her, all the while keeping his gaze down.

Kane flicked his hand and whished pieces of wood on either side of his son. He then inclined his head at Sara and waited, the smug expression on his face pushing her too far.

She snarled at him, gritting her teeth before snapping her attention to the floating wood.

The logs exploded and burst into flames, releasing soft ash that floated around Thomas, save for one splinter, which shot directly at Kane, grazing his cheek.

Kane touched his face and eyed the blood on his fingertips. Sara tensed, expecting him to push back at her in a rage. But he calmly turned to Thomas and snapped his bloody fingers.

Instantly, she was hit with a force that flipped her over and slammed her into the ground. Gasping for breath, she brushed mud and blood off her legs, barely healing herself in time to push away from the ground before another burst shot at her, leaving a crater where she had been.

She launched high above the pasture and spun around, trying desperately to make eye contact with Thomas as he hurled another ball of force at her. Instinctively putting out her hands, she created an invisible shield, repelling the force. The energy flew back and struck him, pounding him into the barn. The entire building shook, and he slid to the ground.

Sara rushed to him and grabbed his arm to pull him up. Instead of feeling the familiar warm thrill of their touch, she felt an unyielding cold. He wrenched his arm from her, and she stumbled back. His face tensed with utter fury. He coughed up dark blood and wiped a muddy hand across his mouth.

"I don't need your help," he growled, and stood, brushing her touch from his arm.

Her heart shattered.

Kane glided to them, his pleased expression making her stomach twist, and said, "Finish the fight."

Sara stared at him, utterly appalled.

"Sullivans fight until someone is knocked out. If you won't fight him, then read his mind," he ordered, his voice low and guttural.

"No!" Fed up with his demands, she crouched, ready to rocket away, but Kane grabbed her arm and held her back.

His eyes bored into her. "You seem to be quite gifted. I want to know if you can read minds too. If you can't tell me what he's thinking, then *I'll* have to finish the fight for you. Consider yourself motivated," he said, eyes flashing.

Horrified by his intensity, she racked her brain for a way to protect Thomas.

"I'll know if you're lying," said Kane between clenched teeth, his hand squeezing her arm tighter.

She wanted to touch Thomas but couldn't bear it if he recoiled from her again. *"I'm so sorry,"* she thought, reaching out gently with her mind to him.

She expected to feel anger and frustration, but the toxic hate and fury lashing out from Thomas almost struck her to the ground—only Kane's hold kept her upright. A bitter taste flooded her mouth, gagging her as Thomas's thought slammed into her mind. Her vision clouded by his rage, she blindly lifted her face toward Kane. "He . . . he *wants* me to hit him?"

Kane released her and laughed. "Now that's the Thomas I know. Always looking for a fight."

She fell to her hands and knees, in shock, as her sight slowly returned.

Without even glancing at her, Thomas stormed off toward the garage, Matthew and Moira trailing behind him.

Sara looked up at Kane in disgust. "You're a monster," she breathed. Part of her wanted to destroy him, pummel him into the barn, and rip his throat out. But, remembering Thomas's words, a bigger part of her chose not to fight him, not to become like Dorcas and Makwa, full of hate and darkness. Though she despised Kane, he was still Thomas's father and part of her forest family.

Kane crouched to her level.

Scalding heat radiated from him, causing Sara to wince and turn her head away. When she averted her gaze, she spied the bottom half of a symbol branded into his bicep. The same brand Thomas wore on his forearm.

"I'm hard on him because I love him," he snarled. "Because we must be stronger than the darkness that hunts us. The real monster is Samson and all the dark magic out there. You best remember that." He rose, towering over her. "Since my efforts to put a break in the wall have stalled, we'll use you as bait to lure Samson to us."

Sara whipped her face to him.

"Don't act surprised. He seems *interested* in you, and I know you want vengeance. In fact, I bet you were already planning on using yourself as bait to draw him to you." A grim smile tugged the corners of his mouth. "But we can only fight him with our powers if he is directly on top of the wall. Your gifts combined with mine and Thomas's will be enough to kill him." He pivoted, boots grinding into the soil, and headed for the house. "Be ready. We attack Samson tomorrow night—with or without Council blessing."

She stared after him, speechless. Given Thomas's moody departure, Kane's words rang hollow in the gray evening. With a soft curse, she leaned back, sitting on her knees, and turned to the last person standing in the yard.

Violet dragged her gaze from the garage to Sara. She hesitated, her eyes wide and mouth partly open. But instead of commenting, she dropped her head and followed her father to the house.

Alrighty, then. Sara stood, her knees shaking, and wiped dirt from her hands. She faced the too-silent garage—not a light on. None of this had gone the way she wanted. She'd completed Kane's *chores,* but he still manipulated her and Thomas. Even her plan to attack Samson was now directed by him.

Staring at the garage, she shivered at remembering the chill from Thomas's skin. She had *felt* his rage, and yet . . . had it all been an act to appease Kane? Thomas indeed had wanted her to hit him, but something else she read from his mind lingered in her own. Something she needed to talk to him about.

But now wasn't the time. Not with Matthew and Moira hanging around, and not until he cooled off.

CHAPTER 35

LIGHTNING BUGS BLINKED about the open pasture, and crickets sang in the early night. It would have been a peaceful scene if not for the deep craters that marred the ground, reminders of her scuffle with Thomas. Sara forced herself to turn away from the Sullivan house and trudged for the woods, taking the closest path. She felt nervous and jittery, not because of Samson—she looked forward to killing the monster that took her mother—but because Thomas was not himself.

Despite the darkening sky, she wandered absently, thinking of him and of Kane's twisted expression of love. Deep in thought, it wasn't until a gust of wind grabbed her hair that she noticed how strangely quiet the forest had become. Her scalp tingled, and a wave of adrenaline washed through her, heightening her senses.

Something was following her. She froze, straining to hear anything in the dense forest.

"Thomas?" Her voice cracked at knowing it wasn't him. The stone at her chest pulsed.

"*Sara,*" said a familiar breathy voice in her head. "*Sara,*" her mother called again, this time louder, her tone clipped with urgency. "*The cemetery is a sanctuary she cannot enter. Go there now.*" A warm gust of wind blew back her hair and disappeared, taking her mother's voice with it.

The stone at her chest burned, and a rank odor like rotten entrails crept through the air. She gagged, her heart thundering with panic, as an image of Makwa flashed in her mind. Not taking chances along the forest floor, she pushed off to rise above the trees, only to be yanked back by a black bramble that grasped her ankle. She cried out as its icy grip seared her skin and pulled her toward the heavy shadows beneath a dead tree.

Sara shook her hands, but not a flicker of white flame came to her. Fear gripped her so tightly she could focus on nothing but fleeing.

She kicked, her entire body thrashing with the effort to free herself, but the brambles tightened. Desperate, she pulled out the knife her grandmother had given her and slashed at the dark vine. A high-pitched squeal pierced the night, and the vine oozed an oily black slime, momentarily releasing its hold.

She shot into the night sky, high above the canopy and emergent trees, and flew to the cemetery. An icy wind licked at her heels, howling in frustration as it failed to grasp her. Sara held out her hands, urging herself to go faster, her eyes stinging from the rushing wind. She spotted the cemetery tree and flung herself at it.

As though expecting her, the tree extended a branch. Afraid to slow down, Sara collided with it, the force of her impact causing a minor explosion of bark and leaves. She dug her nails into the tree and gasped for air, listening for the howling wind. But the night fell quiet once more. Besides her own panting, all she could hear was a faint lapping by the lakeshore.

"Sara!" Ian's voice rang in her head, his panic matching her own. *"What's going on? Where are you?"*

She cursed herself for dropping her mental shield and blasting her fear. Not only did his concern come through in his voice, but she felt it sweep into her mind and heart. To calm them both, she inhaled deeply and grounded herself with the tree before responding. *"I'm fine. Just a run-in with Makwa, but I'm safe in the cemetery now. She can't come after me here."* Anticipating her brother's reaction, she added, *"Don't come. I don't want you running into her too."*

She could have sworn he huffed at her.

"Are you bleeding?" he projected.

She chuckled at the suspicion in his tone. Technically, the welt on her ankle wasn't bleeding. *"No, big brother. I'm truly fine."*

Ian seemed to sigh as a slight breeze blew across her face. *"Makwa doesn't like daylight. Just stay in the treehouse until dawn, and then meet me at the Main House for breakfast. We need to tell Gran and Ted everything."* He paused. *"How'd it go with Kane?"*

She swayed with the tree branch, considering what she should share with him. *"I don't know. I completed the task, but something is wrong with Thomas."*

Ian chuckled. *"Let me guess: he's angry. Get some rest and tell me everything in the morning."* His genuine concern wrapped around her like a comforting blanket.

"'Kay. Good night, Ian," she sent before closing her mind to him.

Too exhausted to explore the tree's impressive new expansion, she simply gave the branch a grateful hug and glided into the bedroom. She barely kicked off her shoes before hitting the bed and instantly falling asleep.

The trill of a bird song woke her at dawn. Rubbing the sleep from her eyes, she stretched and jolted upright when something red on the window ledge caught her eye. It wasn't the flower she hoped for, but a robin fluffing its red belly. The bird trilled again and flitted off into the morning. She glanced at the other bare window ledges and sighed. If he was too stubborn to visit her, then she would go to him.

She needed to see Thomas, to know if he was intentionally playing Kane. And, perhaps more importantly, to get him to confess what she'd read in his mind.

Keeping a wary eye about her for any sign of Makwa, she tiptoed down the treehouse stairs and gingerly stepped past the cemetery's low fence.

Nothing. No snaking brambles or icy chill grabbed her.

She raced to the lake and jumped in. Gasping at the cool water, she quickly cleaned up and returned to the treehouse. Though she was tempted to roam the new expansion, she headed straight to her bedroom and changed. With a grimace, she whished her lake-scented towel to the windowsill and resolved to take a hot shower after breakfast. The leaves in the ceiling nodded as if in agreement, while the house sighed. Sara chuckled and raced down the stairs, her hand running along the tree trunk.

Instead of heading straight to the Main House to meet up with Ian, she took a detour to the Sullivans—impatiently tugged by her need to see Thomas. She wasn't expecting a conversation at this hour but perhaps just a glimpse of him to know he was alright and not seething with rage.

Popping out of the forest edge by the Sullivans' pasture, she instantly shot up to avoid the teeth and claws that lunged at her from the grass. A russet wolf with blazing amber eyes raked the air and let out a snarl as Sara hovered just out of reach.

"*Moira!* What the hell?"

Moira bared her fangs before turning into her human form and shaking a fist at her. "*What did you do to Thomas?*" she roared and changed into an eagle, swooping at Sara with razor-sharp talons.

Sara dodged her and carefully pushed out a protective shield, surprising herself with the care she took not to hurt Moira.

With a piercing cry, Moira returned to the ground and phased back into herself. "What did you do to him?" Her shout lost its heat, sounding more like a plea, and her face crumpled with anguish.

Behind her, a fox dashed across the cropped grass and phased into Matthew. He grabbed his twin before she collapsed to the ground. While clutching her, he looked up at Sara, his face tight with distress.

"Where's Thomas?" Sara asked, sinking to the pasture, her empty stomach twisting in knots.

"I don't know," said Matthew. "He's been gone a lot lately. I thought he was with you." A tinge of jealousy laced his voice, but his expression was soft, his amber gaze full of worry.

"Sara!" Ian's voice clanged inside her. She looked away from the twins and shook her head to clear her mind of the interruption.

"I'm in the middle of something. I'll be there soon."

"Our pine has blight! Hurry!" His desperation hit her with such force she fell to her knees.

"What is it? Is it Thomas?" asked Matthew. Moira whimpered and turned to Sara, her expression expectant and hopeful.

Sara shook her head again, rising from the grass. "There's blight on the pine," she breathed, the words poison on her tongue.

The twins yelped and shifted into falcons. They rose above the pasture and flew with lightning speed toward the Lochton pine. Sara rushed after them, silently screaming in unison with the biting wind in her ears.

CHAPTER 36

UPON REACHING THE Lochton pine, Sara halted in disbelief and felt her stomach clench at the sight of limp brown needles. At the base of the tree, Ian and Ted were frantically tearing up the ground with their bare hands. Matthew and Moira didn't even fully land before phasing into woodchucks and ripping into the soil, dirt flying in a continuous spray toward the pine. Ian jumped out of their way and searched about wildly before spotting Sara hovering above them.

"*Sara! Get the potions!*" His voice was a high, tight scream.

Needles rapidly browned and curled, as if the tree were burning under a giant magnifying glass. Even if she flew as fast as the twins, the blight was spreading too rapidly for her to fetch the potions. She stilled for a precious moment, ignoring Ian's cries, and listened to the forest. Closing her eyes, she tapped into the land's energy and envisioned the many bottles of potions resting on the counter in the Cahill barn.

In her mind, the bottles jumped and shook, twitching with energy like fish on a line. She tugged, and they shot through the forest so fast they seemed to manifest into the air before her. Raising her chin to the sky, she willed a heavy cloud to appear and rain upon the soil. As the ground turned to mud, she added the potions and mixed the earthy salve.

By now, the blight had consumed most of the tree, save for one main branch. Sweat streamed down her cheeks as she mudded the entire tree at once with a frenzied wave of her arms. Heaving to catch her breath, she landed and slumped to the ground, completely spent. She wanted to close her eyes and take a nap, but Moira pushed her into a sitting position and pressed a thermos to her lips.

"Drink it," she said, her husky voice soft and not a snarl for once.

Startled by Moira's gentleness, and slightly suspicious, Sara took a tentative sip. Liquid sunshine kissed her tongue and soothed her dry throat. The sweet taste of honey and flowers awakened her, and she gratefully drank the rest of the thermos. "Thanks," she rasped.

Moira shrugged. "It's Ted's," she said dryly, but without her typical bite of disgust.

Ted walked around the tree, assessing the damage. "Well done, Sara. You stopped the blight." He paused and smiled at her. "But there's no looping through this tree until we figure out how to heal it." He flicked a hand, and all the potion jars righted themselves and gathered at the base of the tree, clinking together softly.

Ted rubbed his face and heaved a loud sigh. "I'm sure Helen has plenty of your medicine on hand." He forced a smile at Ian, but the tremble in his voice betrayed his worry.

Ian stood still, mouth agape, a dirt-encrusted hand pressed to his chest, right above his heart. He stared at the tree, his eyes wide and glistening.

Matthew grabbed Moira and Sara and hoisted them up with ease, his strength surprising given his lean frame. He flicked his hair out of his eyes and fixed his gaze on Sara. "You look like you could use a bite to eat. Moira and I will keep searching for Thomas. We'll send him to the Main House when we find him." The twins phased into foxes and disappeared into the undergrowth.

Ted's gaze followed the twins, then turned to Sara. "What's up with Thomas?" He raised his brow. She recognized the gesture as one of Ian's familiar traits. For an awkward moment, she thought Ted saw right through her.

She blinked and cleared her throat while Ian picked dirt from his nails. "Um, we can't seem to find him this morning," she stammered.

Ted's raised brow did not move. "He probably ran patrol last night and is sleeping in. I'm sure the twins will ferret him out." He took the empty thermos from her and eyed her curiously, frowning at the pink welt encircling her ankle. "You do look a little peaked. Are you okay to walk or"—he twirled his hand in the air—"fly to the Main House?" He tilted his head toward a path that parted at the tree line.

"I can walk."

With a smile, he waited for her and Ian to join his side before heading along the path.

"Thanks for the tea," said Sara.

Ted playfully tossed the empty thermos into the air and caught it before whishing it to rest with the empty potion bottles under the tree. "I had a feeling I would need it today. Haven't had a strong intuition like that in a long time." His smiled faded, and his face turned serious again. "What you just did was something else. I'm telekinetic, and I can't call an object, let alone a trove of potion jars, from such a great distance." He fixed his blue-gray eyes on her.

She looked to the forest floor and let her hair fall forward, hiding part of her face. "Must have been luck and sheer panic on my part."

"I'm just glad you got here in time," said Ian. "I should have known this would happen. Something feels off. I hardly slept last night, and I feel different today." Pushing his hair back, he appeared about to add something when Ted interrupted.

"Something *is* definitely off. This blight should not be able to cross our wall or damage our soul trees." Ted flicked a hand, dispersing pinecones from the path, and tapped his temple. "I've told the Council about the pine and warned everyone to keep watch on the remaining soul trees until Makwa and Dorcas fix this. We just need to convince them to get off their asses and lend a hand. They're notoriously difficult to deal with and hate daylight, but this situation is definitely an exception."

Ian shot Sara an imploring look. *"Tell him."*

She rolled her eyes and sighed. "About that—" She hesitated.

Ted scanned Ian's face and then turned to her. "Oh?" he said, his expectant expression so much like her father's that her heart skipped a beat.

She swallowed. "Dorcas told me I was cursed by Makwa. It was a powerful spell, maybe even a generational curse, but Naomi seems to have broken it. I don't think Makwa is happy. She came after me last night."

Ted stopped and glared at them. "You're just *now* telling me this?" he said in a low whisper. The surrounding trees shivered, their branches clacking like they were scolding them.

Ian winced and rubbed his forehead.

"Mother Mary," Ted cursed, waving his hands and causing the trees to shake again. "Dorcas—" He stopped himself, mouth gaping open and closed, his arms falling to his sides. "Generational," he breathed, visibly paling in the shaded forest. He snapped his attention to Sara and Ian, his expression changing from shock to grim determination, a touch of fury bringing color back to his face. "We need to see your grandmother right now." He broke into a sprint for the Main House. "She always suspected Makwa interfered with our family, especially when Charlie and Eliza left. But if this is as bad as I fear it is . . ." Ted shook his head and turned to Ian, whose lanky strides had no trouble keeping pace with him. "We may need to call a Dragon," he said, his words and serious tone causing Sara to stumble.

The path took a sharp turn, and they burst into the Cahill common area. Ted slowed to a jog as they approached the deck steps. He jerked his chin at the outdoor dining area. "You two sit and eat. I'll be right back," he said, springing up the steps and disappearing into the Main House.

Sara picked a table piled with food and gratefully collapsed into a patio chair, helping herself to a blueberry hand pie dripping with icing.

Ian flopped into a chair opposite her, his leg bouncing nervously under the table. He stole a glance over his shoulder at the Cahills' chestnut tree and set two muffins before him. "So, what's really up with Thomas?" He threw back a glass of water before settling his golden-brown eyes on her.

When his gaze glinted with amusement, the thought of swiping his muffins crossed her mind. She gripped her own pastry, burying her thumb into the icing, and leaned in. "Something's not right. He seems furious, and he won't let me touch him."

Ian snorted, almost shooting water out of his nose. "Sorry," he apologized at her glare, wiping his face with the back of his hand. "He's usually angry—I did warn you—and I definitely don't want to know about any touching going on, especially when it involves my sister. Speaking of which—" He grinned, picking his timing just as she took a large bite. "You're doing a much better job of keeping your emotions to yourself." She kicked at him under the table, but he dodged her, his grin broadening.

She choked down her mouthful and grabbed a glass of juice. Instead of throwing it at him, she brought it to her lips and halted. "What did Ted mean 'call a dragon'? Like a *real* dragon?"

Ian straightened in his chair, his smile vanishing, and looked around at the nearly empty deck to be sure no one had heard her.

He put his elbows on the table and leaned forward, fixing her with a grave stare. "Dragons are partly human, but also partly something else entirely. I've never seen one, and I don't care to.

They regulate the natural balance between light and dark. If the balance becomes uneven, or if normals see our magic, a Dragon will correct the situation. But they are merciless, especially the ancient ones, and calling a Dragon either unintentionally or intentionally comes at a high price."

Her mouth had gone dry, despite drinking a full glass of juice. "How high?" she uttered, her question barely a whisper.

"They prefer wiping a slate clean by killing first and not asking questions later."

The blood drained from her face. *She brings death to the forest.* The prophecy rang in her head. "We can't call one," she blurted, panic rising in her voice.

"No, definitely not a good idea," Ian agreed. He sank back into his chair, his gaze growing distant. "Are you sure Makwa tried to attack you? Maybe she was just warning you about Samson."

Sara frowned while polishing an apple on her shirt. "Maybe. Especially if she enjoys scaring the shit out of me. 'Course, my encounter with Dorcas wasn't exactly pleasant either. But why curse me?"

He steepled his fingertips, considering. "She could know something we don't. Maybe it was for a good reason." Before either could comment further, he turned his attention to the common. Lily and her family emerged from the chestnut tree, crossed the yard, and ascended the deck stairs. When Lily came to their table and sat beside Ian, he used an index finger to push one of his muffins toward her.

"Good morning," she said cheerfully.

"Morning, Lily," said Sara, beaming at her before turning back to Ian. When she cocked an eyebrow at him, he immediately busied himself by biting into his own muffin. Holding in a snarky comment, she flicked her gaze to Ted and Gran striding onto the deck.

"It's not happening. Only a Magus can call one," Sara overheard Gran grumble.

Frowning, Ted approached the table and set a bottle of green swirling medicine in front of Ian. "Helen has a few weeks' worth, which should be plenty of time for us to figure something out." Ian grabbed the bottle and slipped it into his pocket.

"What's going on?" asked Lily, concern edging her tone. She put down her glass of juice and looked at Ian.

He shrugged. "The pine has blight, but we stopped it. Well, Sara stopped it." He took another bite of his muffin.

Lily's face paled, then flushed red. Her slim hand grasped Ian's forearm. "Blight on a soul tree?" Her voice was light as the wind. "Ted's right, we'll figure something out." She pursed her lips.

Ian's gaze flicked to her hand and then blankly focused on a knot in the wooden tabletop.

Sara was about to kick him under the table again when she felt a piercing pain rip down her spine. She arched her back and gasped. Seeing the surprised expression on Ian's face, she thought perhaps she felt his reaction to Lily's touch. But then another searing pain lanced through her entire body, and she jolted against the table, knocking over a pitcher of water and dropping her apple to the deck. She gulped a breath and stood, listening with her mind and body to a terrifying shift in the forest's energy.

Gran stiffened. "What is it?"

Unable to verbalize what she felt, Sara projected it into Ian's mind.

His eyes widened. "The tree!" He jumped up, flipping over his chair, and whipped around to the Cahills' chestnut in the center of the green.

Every leaf was trembling in the too-still air. Groaning loud enough to send shock waves rippling through the grassy common, the tree twisted violently, as though it was trying to pull itself out by its roots and flee the horror setting upon it. The tree's uppermost leaves appeared to melt into shriveled brown claws. Helen ran onto the deck and screamed. Her shrill cry echoed through the common and was immediately answered by Samson's deafening blare.

The Cahill clearing erupted into chaos. Birds and animals fled the area, seeking sanctuary elsewhere. Everyone clambered onto the deck and poured out onto the green, ripping up earth and calling forth rain as they rushed to the soul tree.

CHAPTER 37

Sara grabbed Helen's arms, shaking her to get her attention. "I used all the potions in the barn to treat the pine. Do you have any more?" She fought to hide her panic for Helen's sake.

For a moment, Helen froze in Sara's intense stare. "Y-yes," she finally stammered. "In the greenhouse." She gestured to the building beside the barn.

Sara released her and opened her arms toward the greenhouse, willing its glass windows and doors to open and release the potions. Somewhere on the green, Caleb bellowed, only to be drowned out by another blare that shook the forest. Startled, Sara prematurely yanked on the kinetic grip she imagined curling around the potions. Jars and bottles instantly flew through the air, shattering the greenhouse glass before exploding into the mud surrounding the tree.

Rushing to the chestnut, she stared in horror as the blight spread so quickly that the tree ignited. The incipient puff of fire blew back her hair and pierced her soul as the entire tree burst into flame.

The explosion sent her flying backward. She skidded through mud and broken glass while the tree became a living torch. A rumble, louder than the fire and families' screams combined, surged through earth and air, as if the tree and very forest itself roared.

Sara choked on her own screams. Thick smoke filled the common, turning the sky an eerie orange. A pair of hands hooked beneath her shoulders and hauled her off the ground. She grabbed at the hands, desperate to see Thomas and to somehow wake up from this nightmare.

"Sara!" Ian yelled, shaking her, his eyes wide and spilling tears against the smoky air. He hugged her and pulled her into a huddle with Ted and Gran. Ted's typical easygoing demeanor had been replaced by the serious countenance of a general. He put a protective arm around Gran while keeping his gaze fixed on the chaotic common.

"I told Kane and Bill to get Makwa and Dorcas. We all stay here until they report back to us. Cahills and Atwells can stop this with our—" He halted when the flames changed from red-orange to a sickening green.

"We can't stop this," said Gran, staring at the burning tree. She grabbed Ted's shoulder. "Summon Alice. Tell her it's time to leave the island." Her tone was deadly calm. Ted put a hand over hers, hesitating. She turned her fierce gaze to him and nodded. "Do it," she ordered, and strode away from the blaze, calling the children to gather around her.

Ted tilted his head and touched his temple, silently summoning Alice. As he lowered his hand, he glanced at the burning soul tree and then to Ian. They nodded at each other and ran to help the Cahills fight the flames.

Sara started after them but was tugged back by a slender hand. Lily emerged from the smoke, her pale skin and hair ghostly in the flickering green light. She linked hands with Sara and pulled her into a group of Atwells, collectively calling rain to douse the fire. Despite their efforts, the fire burned and roared louder, immune to water. Everyone in the clearing fell back as the flames grew larger and hotter. Rain-soaked and slipping in mud, they watched in horror while green flames leapt from the tree and onto the roof of the Main House.

Sara's stomach twisted, and a fresh wave of panic hit her. "Dad!" she screamed. The rain stole her voice, but the shriek from her soul reverberated through the forest.

"DAD!" she screamed again, this time in her head.

"Ted and I will get him," shouted Ian, his voice ringing through her mind. *"You work on stopping the fire!"*

Sara strained to see through the smoke and rain, glimpsing her brother and uncle as they jumped onto the deck and ran into the burning house. More screams filled the clearing. Her heart splintered at the terror-stricken cries of Gran and Helen. She frantically looked around but could not see them or the children they protected.

Choking on the ashy rain, she slipped her hand from Lily's grasp, breaking rank with the Atwells. This was no ordinary fire—it was dark magic, and no amount of rain could stop it. If water couldn't extinguish the flames, maybe the energy of the forest could smother it. Maybe this was what Ian meant when he told her to stop it.

She took a ragged breath and tried to focus on the rainbow-colored energy she knew shone throughout the forest, but fear coursed through her veins and weakened her. Images of her dad, Ian, and Ted flashed in her head, followed by visions of her mother and Thomas. Guilt slammed into her, and her heart stilled. *What if Samson had Thomas?*

Her spiraling thoughts were halted by a low groan so powerful, it seeped through the rain and shook the earth. Trembling with the vibrations, Sara turned to the chestnut tree, and it was as if time slowed. The groan rose to a terrible whine and ear-splitting crack. What remained of the soul tree splintered and crashed to the ground, rocking the entire clearing with the impact. She lost her footing and pitched into the mud.

Seething with frustration, Sara yelled at the storm of fire and rain and pushed off from the sodden ground. If she couldn't stop the fire, she had to get to the Main House and save her family. She lunged toward the burning building, but it gave in with a chilling moan. Its walls folded in on themselves, and the Main House collapsed into plumes of green embers and smoke. The only remaining upright portions were part of the stone fireplace and a few of the main supporting trees, which now burned like torches.

"*Ian!*" she shrieked in her head and into the ashy rain. "*Ian! Ted!*" she screamed again and again. Her heart seemed to turn to stone, crushing the air from her lungs at hearing nothing but the patter of rain and the crackling hiss of green flames.

She stared in disbelief at the leveled building, the thought of losing her dad and Ian and Ted so incomprehensible that her mind left her body. Hovering above the muddy clearing, she looked down at herself, at the collapsed building and fallen soul tree.

A blare thundered through the forest, and she snapped back into herself, the boom still reverberating as another blare resounded and shook her core.

Samson.

This was all his fault. She clenched her fists, anger swelling inside her.

Another blare sounded, as though mocking her. And she let herself explode.

CHAPTER 38

IN A BLIND rage, Sara screamed and pushed away from the muddy clearing, rising above the burning Main House and the smoldering soul tree. She shot upward through the thick ash and rain clouds until the summer sun shone on her face. Another blare echoed through the forest. Treetops rippled in the wake of the blast. She whipped her head to the north to see black smoke tendrils attacking the forest wall.

Sara flew over the forest canopy, aiming directly for the dark cloud creeping along the barrier. She didn't care what waited for her on the opposite side. She would make him pay for all he had done to her—all he had taken.

She rushed toward him at full speed, a mad smile tugging at her lips in anticipation of ending him.

The black smoke jerked back and hesitated. She surged across the forest boundary, feeling a slight tug on her skin and hair, like stepping through a spider web, and plunged into the black cloud. A guttural yell she did not recognize as her own filled the air when she finally released her monstrous power, completely letting herself go. A blinding, white-hot energy consumed her, indeed became her very being, as she sought to obliterate Samson and everything around her. Sara fed the energy everything she had and then dug deeper, drawing out years of anger and frustration.

Channeling all that power, she burned and twisted, her body and soul threatening to shatter. The effort of forcing out all her rage stole her breath. But she still gave more—for her mom, her dad, for Ian, for Ted, for Naomi and the Hills sacred site . . . and for Thomas.

Not caring about the consequences, she gave until she lost herself—until the white light burned out and blackness swallowed her.

She thought she was dead. She wanted to be dead, but a throaty laugh and familiar acrid stench pulled at her consciousness. Sara couldn't move, couldn't see. And this time, there was no pine-and-cinnamon scent, no whiff of ash and musk to save her. A cold and brutal darkness coiled around her and squeezed, crushing her lungs and very soul, like something beyond death had swallowed her whole.

Panic flushed through her, the instinct to breathe overwhelming all else. She needed air—needed it badly; the marrow of her bones ached for it. Thrashing about with her entire being, she wildly pushed and clawed at the pressing darkness until it loosened, and she spotted a faint glow of light impossibly far away. Struggling to move her leaden body, she mentally fought and willed herself away from the dark and closer to the brightness. Every piece of her straining with effort, she did not give up until she broke through the thin membrane separating dark and light. Tearing through the veil and gasping for breath, her entire body shook with exertion. The light surrounding her shimmered and faded until she found herself standing in a cage of twisted black brambles. Still heaving to catch her breath, she raised her gaze and blinked furiously.

Her vision took a painfully long moment to focus on the tall male figure standing before her cage. He wore all black, including a heavy military-style topcoat, which ordinarily would seem out of place in the summer, but a biting cold hung in the air. She shivered. Even his hands were dark, appearing stained as if they had been dipped into indigo dye that now collected in the cracks of his skin and along his jagged nails. Long, inky-black hair hung in irregular thick cords past his shoulders and down his back. His face was sallow and gaunt, possibly handsome at some point long ago, but little more than a skeleton now. On his head sat a top hat. He looked like the magician of death. But it was his eyes, obsidian black with a glint of red, that stole her breath.

Samson.

The living, breathing creature behind the wrathful black clouds. Behind her mother's death and the slaughter of the sacred Hills site.

Instinctively, she put a hand to her chest, remembering his icy touch from a lifetime ago in her bedroom.

He smiled, revealing bright white teeth, and waved his arms dramatically about. "That was a bit *excessive*, don't you think?" His sarcastic tone made her stomach turn more than the stench coming from the two dozen charred Taker bodies littering the outer forest floor. She grabbed the brambles to break free, succeeding only in slicing her hands and causing the vines to tighten around her.

Samson coughed, spitting up dark phlegm which he wiped away with a silky black scarf. "Tut, tut." He waved his hand at her, tendrils of smoke extending from his fingers. "Rookie mistake, really—coming at me all fired up," he said, his laugh a rasping, choking sound. He clasped his hands behind him and ambled around her cage. "You can't kill someone like me, not without knowing my true name." He stalked around and faced her, tilting his head, a vulture about to dive into carrion. "Here we are, one *monster* to another." He licked his lips.

Sara recoiled from his gaze and the words from his oily mouth. *Bastard.*

The way he'd stressed "*excessive*" and "*monster*"—the red glint in his sadistic eyes—he was taunting her. He had been watching her and Thomas, had heard every word of their conversations at the wall.

He leered, waiting.

Choosing not to take the bait, she remained silent, panting through her mouth. Her shallow breaths could not escape the stench in the air and succeeded only in making her lightheaded. She scanned the surrounding forest for any sign of Thomas before drawing her gaze back to Samson. He grinned, and the brambles tightened again, creaking and snapping. Her mind raced for possible escape options. But her reckless explosion of power had left her too drained to even heal the cuts on her hands.

"What have you done to Thomas?" She cast him her best death stare through the cage, her breath clouding in the chill air.

"Thomas?" He thoughtfully tapped his fingertips together, toying with her. "Ah, you mean the one who so graciously accepted my gift of blight."

She gasped, remembering the potion vial Thomas received from the Taker.

"You two are *pathetic* to watch, by the way. Makes me want to retch, which is really saying something." He grimaced.

"What did you do to him?" Sara ground out each word through clenched teeth.

Samson coughed into his scarf and pulled at the tight collar of his coat. "I didn't do anything to him. Makwa poisoned him to break you. And by the looks of it, she succeeded." He laughed thickly and spat at a Taker—his phlegm sizzling when it hit the burnt body. "Pity. I liked that one." He sighed and picked at his fingernails. "I'll just make more, which is all too easy nowadays. People are so hungry for any kind of magic, no matter how dark. It just takes a few drugs and hollow promises." He grinned at her, the sharp brightness of his teeth reminding her of knives.

Poison. Makwa had poisoned Thomas. Her mind reeled, fitting together pieces of an impossible puzzle. "You're working with Makwa?" she croaked, her throat still burning from the fire.

"Yes! Delightful isn't it?" He clapped his hands to applaud her deduction. "It was her idea, really. Makwa wants out of this forest prison, and I want a few things inside it. So, we teamed up to crack this egg." He waved his hands at the forest wall, and puffs of black smoke flared and dissipated around him. "Judging by the green flames, she seems to be wreaking havoc in your little bubble." He pulled at his collar again, tugging loose the top button and revealing multiple silver chains around his neck.

Sara flicked her gaze to the bodies littering the forest floor. Most of them wore a singular chain with a black stone pendant.

"Your warmth is nauseating." He grimaced again and flicked a hand, sending a gust of cold air at her.

As if a fist of ice had punched her face, her head jerked to the side, and she slipped on the greasy brambles. The cage creaked and tightened again.

He inclined his head and sniffed the air. Widening his eyes, he placed a hand dramatically on his chest. "*I* didn't kill your mother. The truck behind you did that."

Samson spat again and dabbed his mouth lightly with his scarf. "Your anger and need for vengeance made you blind to your real enemy." He sighed and rolled his eyes. "Another rookie mistake. I honestly don't know how you made it this far."

She glanced at the smoke and power billowing about him. "Take me and leave the forest alone," she blurted. It was the least she could do for Gran and everyone else. The cage of thorns was now so tight, she could no longer turn to watch him as he stalked behind her.

He laughed, his raspy snort turning into a deep, wet cough.

"So noble of you. Which, believe me, will get you nowhere." He prowled back into her view. "And you are not in any position to negotiate. Tut, tut. Especially with the likes of me." He flicked ice from his sleeve and wagged a stained finger at her. "The night you saw me outside your window, I came for Charlie, but I caught your scent—all your raw power—and *knew* I had to have you." He snickered. "And now, *bam!* You came to me—like a gift from the Mother. Ironic, isn't it?"

Sara glared at him. Maybe if she kept him talking long enough, her power would come back and she could free herself. "What do you want?" she growled as he disappeared behind her again.

"Foolish girl. I know your every thought. You can't break these vines," he drawled. The cage contracted again, razor-sharp thorns grazing her skin. "And it's not a *what* but a *who*." He cleared his throat. "Naomi, Charlie, and a boy . . ." Samson stopped in front of her, tapping his mouth with a blue-black finger. "I believe his name is Ian." At the mention of Ian's name, Samson grinned and appeared to grow larger, shadows and smoke gathering behind him.

The blood drained from her face, and she swallowed hard to keep from puking on herself. "Why?" she asked weakly, teeth chattering—her entire world turned upside down into a twisted nightmare.

"Well, let's see." He counted on his tainted fingers. "Naomi, because she is Winona's sister and the last gifted from the Hills sacred site." He paused, the wicked red glint returning to his eyes. "I've killed all the others," he confessed, obviously pleased with himself. "Charlie, because he took my Winona, and Ian, because he is the last piece of her." He paused and wiped indigo-black blood from his mouth. "I thought Ian died with Winona. Mother knows I set ice upon his tiny heart, and he should have died instantly. And then Charlie just disappeared. I had hoped he died of a broken heart. But it seems Ware Woods is just full of surprises. When I came sniffing around not too long ago, Makwa was kind enough to tell me they still lived."

"Wh—*Your* Winona?" Sara's face pinched, recalling the head-stone in the cemetery—the mother Ian never had the chance to know. Snowy crystals appeared in the air and stuck to the greasy bramble vine.

"Oh, yes. She was mine. She just didn't know it." His eyes flashed red as a cold gust blew over Sara's exposed arms and legs. "I was an outsider to the Hills and apparently not good enough for her. Their sap nearly killed me. In fact, they thought I had died— which, I suppose, a part of me did that day. With nothing left to lose, I invoked dark magic for my revenge." He sneered and put a hand on his slender chest. "You see, I'm just righting a wrong." He spat and paced in front of her, the acrid sulfur odor of his smoke making her eyes sting.

She choked and then laughed, partly at the absurdity of her situation but mostly to piss him off.

He stopped pacing and stared at her. Thick, smoky tendrils spread around him as a deep, humming shook the ground.

"You're too late," she said, narrowing her eyes at him. Her whole body trembled with cold, tears freezing to her cheeks. "Makwa killed them all."

Samson exploded into ebony smoke that billowed and swelled, blacking out the sky, as a deafening blare slammed into the quiet forest. Unable to cover her ears, Sara shut her eyes against the angry roar, her chest rattling as she choked on a blanket of ash. The blare rang until it was a dull buzz in her ears, the air gradually clearing until she could finally take a breath without violently coughing. Carefully opening her eyes to the eerie stillness, she was disappointed to see him still staring at her. Not a trace of smoke surrounded him. His calm demeanor and hungry expression caused her heart to skip a beat. He tilted his head, the sudden movement raptor-like, and licked his oily lips.

"I'll deal with that wicked witch later, but first I shall appease my blood thirst with a snack." He let the last word click loudly on his tongue.

Instantly, the brambles jerked Sara's arm from her side and

forcefully held it out, extending her hand to him. Blood welled and dripped where the vine grabbed her and cut into her skin. She tried to clench a fist and gather energy to throw him back, but she was still weak, and sickening terror had replaced her anger. He glided up beside her, his acrid stench making her dry heave as he bent over her hand. She screamed when something cold and wet ran across her knuckles. And then a searing pain stabbed her hand.

The brambles flexed, relaxing enough to allow her to pull her hand to her chest. Hot blood poured from her and soaked the front of her shirt as she desperately tried to staunch the flow.

Samson stepped back, casually chewing her small finger, his eyes glinting with satisfaction.

She stared at him in terror. Her vision spun and blurred, and she slumped in the cage, fighting back the threat of unconsciousness. Chest heaving with guttural sobs, she struggled to gulp down air. Squeezing her eyes shut against the pain, she expected darkness only to be jolted by a blinding white light accompanied by a tingling warmth spreading out from her chest.

I'm dying.

CHAPTER 39

Sara's first thought was of relief. To let go and be with her mother and father, and with the brother she loved despite hardly knowing him. But then images of the forest flashed through her mind. She remembered the elation of flying, her unmistakable connection to Thomas, and the blissful sense of finally belonging.

Something shifted deep inside her. Perhaps she wasn't quite ready to die. Perhaps she could do something more. Become something more.

Blood soaked through her shirt and dripped onto her shoes, the steady patter like the ticking of a clock. Clutching her hand tighter to her chest, she felt a hard knock against her breastbone.

She'd kept the red stone hidden so well she had forgotten it was there. As blood seeped and wrapped around it, the stone pulsed. Again and again, in time with her rapid heartbeat, the throb grew stronger, moving her hand with it. A warmth emanated from the stone and flowed through her until she no longer felt Samson's biting cold. The sound of dripping blood stopped, and her pain eased to where she felt comfortable. Safe, even.

And then she heard her name.

"Sara." The voice was deeper toned than her mother's and resonated with confidence.

Sara gripped the stone through her drenched shirt.

"Daughter, your blood on my stone awakens me. I am Mary, mother of Ann. My blood and magic flow strongly within you. I sense you are new to the forest, and yet you are not. Your presence has been expected."

Sara's vision changed from white light to images of the forest.

"As my descendent you will know Ware Woods is a sacred forest that hums with elemental powers. I lived here peacefully with other witches and families that instinctively felt the magical pull of the land. Over time, my love and protectiveness for the land and families grew strong, but the other witches turned dark with greed for more power. They did horrible things to the surrounding people until, at last, their ways could no longer be ignored.

"The villagers mistakenly condemned all witchcraft as evil and sought to destroy us all, but I fought to protect the sacred land and the families I had grown to love.

"After driving off the villagers, I summoned my power to heal the destruction and create a protective wall while the forest bonded its energy with the families, gifting them magical powers to protect themselves and the land. To ensure this magic, I fused my own energy with the forest so the wall and magical gifts would only grow stronger in times of need.

"I took pity on the two witches and, instead of stripping their power, I bound them to the forest. One was cursed to speak the truth, for her lies had brought too much pain. The other was stripped of her beauty, so she could no longer lure others to their demise.

"When I gave myself to the forest, I became the watchful tree overlooking the cemetery and all of Ware Woods. My roots grew deep and held tight while I waited, dormant until needed. But I slept too soundly and did not see the cursed witches falter and, in vengeance, cast a spell on my bloodline.

"Then you came—your power so strong it unraveled the spell. And now it is completely broken.

"You, Sara, are the High Witch of Ware Woods, and your magic transcends the sacred forest. Believe in yourself and rise, daughter. You have the power to free yourself and enlighten others who are pure of heart.

"Ware Woods needs you now. While one of the cursed witches may have seen the error of her ways, the other seeks to free herself by sacrificing the forest. Together, you and the families can stop her. You must weaken her, draw her close, and say her true name. Tituba."

Mary's voice and the forest images faded like morning mist. Sara remained still. Her ancestor's love and trust in her to be High Witch—to protect the forest and stop Makwa—was overwhelming. And yet she knew the radiant power shining in Mary's voice also flowed in her veins. It was never a monster she'd struggled to control. It was a fate she didn't understand. Until now.

A heavy quiet hung in the air. *Too quiet.* Sara opened her eyes and stared directly at the dark witch before her.

Shock flashed across Samson's face. He took a delicate step back, his shoulders tense and his onyx eyes fixed on her.

Sara shifted her gaze to her chest. Her hands were still fisted in her blood-drenched shirt, gripping the stone hidden beneath it. The stone pulsed, and a red light shone through layers of sticky, congealed blood. With a sickening wet rasp, she pulled her mangled right hand from the shirt and flexed her thumb and three remaining fingers. The wound, where her pinkie should have been, was neatly healed and pain-free. She wiggled her three fingers again, confirming the disfigured hand was indeed hers.

The stone's red glow spread warmth throughout her core, down her arms and legs, and into her hands and feet until she burned with energy. All cuts quickly healed, including the welt on her ankle. Heat radiated from her and hissed against the black vines. With half a thought, she shattered the thorny cage, the pieces igniting into wispy black ash that floated up and dissolved into the summer sky.

She turned her gaze to Samson.

His throat bobbed as he took another step back, eyes wide and shining with the reflected glow of the red stone. "I must admit, I did not see this coming. Let's meet for dinner another time, shall we?" he said with a mock bow and tip of his hat, never breaking eye contact with her.

She narrowed her gaze and pushed out with both hands, shoving a wave of white energy at him.

He instantly phased into a billowing dark cloud.

Energy and smoke collided in a shower of crackling white and red sparks. The explosive sound and blinding lights forced Sara to look away. After a whip of piercing snaps, she peered through squinted eyes. Floating embers winked out, and a haze of gray smoke hung in the outer forest.

No sign of Samson, not even a body or scorched earth. Wrinkling her nose, she summoned a gust of wind to disperse the smoke and bitter odor lingering in his wake.

When the air finally cleared, she glanced around at the dead Taker bodies and then smiled at the sight of the surrounding forest. Not one tree was broken, and the ground remained intact. With a flick of her hands, she buried the bodies in shallow graves so the forest could feast on their nutrients.

Hovering just above the ground, she turned to the stone wall and listened, completely focused on her next target. The true monster lurking inside Ware Woods. Makwa. *Tituba.*

Her skin prickled. The forest vibrated as something inside the wall twisted with dark magic.

"Stop!" The voice in her head was crystal clear, as if someone had shouted right beside her.

Her heart skipped a beat. *"Ian?"*

"Sara?" he answered softly, matching her incredulous tone.

"Ian! Where are you? Are Dad and Ted with you? I thought you all died in the fire."

"We're all fine. I'll explain later. You took off and I—" He paused. *"I couldn't reach you. We heard Samson and thought—"*

"Samson is gone," she said fiercely, interrupting her brother and setting his fears to rest. *"I need to find Makwa."* Sara levitated higher and glided over the stone wall. A slight elasticity pulled at her skin and hair when she crossed the invisible Ware Woods barrier. She put a hand to the soft, bubble-like tension and scanned the forest floor, hoping to glimpse Ian.

"She and Dorcas are usually found in the northern part of the wood. But I could really use your help right now to stop Thomas from killing Kane." Ian's voice sounded strained. *"I don't think I can hold him off much longer."*

Her burning need to destroy Makwa instantly quelled at the mention of Thomas. *"Don't hurt him! He's been poisoned. Where are you?"*

"I couldn't hurt him if I tried. He's too powerful." Ian grunted with exertion. *"Hurry! We're in the birch grove."*

CHAPTER 40

RISING ABOVE THE tree canopy, Sara spotted the Cahills' section of the forest, smoke lingering over the fallen soul tree and ruins of the Main House. Her hands clenched. *Makwa will pay for this. But first—Thomas.*

She veered away from the devastation and headed for the birches. From above, all she could see was a white haze obscuring the grove. Panicked at the thought of another fire, she soared past the grassy field where the nearly-full-moon party had been held and halted abruptly at the edge of the hazy cloud. Expecting to smell smoke, she frowned at the sharp scent of ice and sudden chill on her skin, then gaped at the sight before her.

A blizzard swirled within the grove.

Blue lightning flashed inside the squall, followed by an ear-splitting crack that whipped through the frigid air. Sara winced and crashed to the ground, overwhelmed by a surge of tension radiating from her brother. Picking herself up, she judged his location and trudged her way through the storm to the center of the grove. Blinded by snow and ice, she nearly smacked into the force field shielding Ian and Lily like an invisible dome.

"*Sara!*" He grabbed her hand and pulled her into the protected area.

Throwing her arms around him, she pressed her face into his shoulder and squeezed him in a tight embrace.

He returned her hug before pulling back, one hand extended with his palm out to maintain the surrounding shield, and scanned her up and down. His jaw slacked at her appearance. "Is that your blood? Mother—you're missing a *finger*!"

"Never mind me. What happened to *you*? I saw the house collapse. And when you didn't answer me . . ."

His shocked expression softened. "I'm fine. Charlie and Ted are too. They're helping everyone at the common." He shifted his gaze to the surrounding storm. "Once Alice came, Gran sent Lily and me here to the birch grove." He refocused his attention on the shield as a bolt of blue light slammed into it.

A gust of wind screamed at them, drowning out his next words until he projected them into her head. *"Can you heal Kane?"* His tone was anxious and edged with doubt. He jerked his chin behind them and then resumed his focus on maintaining the protective shield, a power Sara didn't know he had.

She tore her gaze from him to look back at Lily, her arms outstretched, trying to soothe the frenzied storm. For all her small stature, Lily was a force to be reckoned with, her gray eyes blazing with the swirling storm. She stood protectively over a broken body lying still as death on the snowy ground. Bright crimson blood stained his fine clothes and the white blanket of snow around them.

Forgetting her hate, Sara rushed to kneel beside Kane and assess his injuries. His gurgling breaths were shallow and thick with imminent death. Frozen trails of blood ran from his ears, mouth, and nose, while a large gash on his upper leg continued to bleed out. The warm liquid cut streams into the icy snow. She laid her hands on his twisted back and gasped at the intensity of his pain. Not only was his leg broken and a few ribs crushed, but he was rapidly drowning from internal bleeding.

Another bolt of lightning bombed the shield with such force

the forest floor shook. She crouched and held on to Kane's body as Lily summoned a gust of air to keep her and Ian from falling over.

When the tremors stopped, Sara took a deep breath and gathered her power. She concentrated on growing a healing energy, and as she exhaled, a comforting warmth prickled her scalp and flushed along her arms and into her hands. Light poured from her and into Kane—his entire body soon glowing. Sara kept her hands on him until his internal bleeding stopped, organs healed, and bones snapped back into place. Eyes still closed, he groaned, his chest now rising and falling with steady breaths.

Sara glanced up and found Lily staring at her.

"Y—you healed Kane. And—your hair," gasped Lily. She tossed a puff of warm air at Sara.

The gentle gust lifted Sara's hair, blowing it forward. She grabbed an unfamiliar lock, and her mouth dropped open. Not only was her hair longer and thicker, the color was now silvery-gray, peppered with a few darker strands. She pulled more hair forward, the short tufts now fully grown and cascading through her fingers and down her back.

Her wonder was interrupted by a blast of ice crystals that shattered like glass against the protective shield. Another blast followed, this time with a blinding blue energy that rattled their shelter. Ian slid back before digging in his heels and regaining his stance, while Lily focused on taming the icy wind.

Knees pressed into the bloody snow, Sara threw her head back and searched the swirling whiteout for Thomas when Kane grabbed her wrist. "Save him," he uttered hoarsely, his expression desperate before his eyes rolled and closed, his hand falling to his side.

"Always," she whispered and rose into the storm.

With one hand up, blocking the freezing wind from her face, she squinted into the white fury and called out, "*Thomas!*" As soon as she yelled his name, a blast of cold energy hit her, flipping her over before she caught herself from falling. But instead of fighting the frustration and rage whirling within the grove, she absorbed it, made peace with it. Channeled it.

The biting ice and wind stopped, leaving the air filled with clusters of fluffy snow. She glimpsed Thomas hovering on the far side of the grove, his black jeans and white T-shirt blending into the birches.

She sighed with relief at seeing him uninjured, but the energy stemming from him was something else entirely. She reached out and rushed toward him, this time speaking into his mind. *"Thomas."*

He flew at her, hands flaming with spheres of blue energy, the dark glint in his eyes almost reptilian. "Get out of my head," he snarled.

This time she expected his punch and pivoted aside, letting a bolt of energy scream past her. But he anticipated her move and pounded her with a blast from above. Her head snapped back as she careened out of the sky, splintering a cluster of young birch before striking the ground. She tried to pick herself up only to be hammered farther into the soil by a barrage of field stone and broken birch, her force field pressed tight against her by the onslaught.

"Enough!" she screamed and forced a bigger protective shield around herself. Pushing off the ground, she once again spotted Thomas hovering among the snowy birch.

With spheres of energy glowing and expanding in his hands, he reared back, poised to launch his power—not at her, but at the forest floor.

Sara tracked his aim to Ian's protective shield. Gritting her teeth, she rushed between him and Ian, and threw a round of white-hot energy at Thomas. Her heart clenched as he flipped back and slammed into the large birch tree with such force, a branch cracked and thumped to the ground, kicking up a cloud of snow.

With a roar, he hurled a bolt of lightning at her.

She lunged and rolled to the side, narrowly avoiding his throw which exploded the tree behind her. "Stop attacking me!" she shouted, and sped toward him. A startled look flashed across his pale face before his eyes hardened again and he pushed another cold force at her. She dodged it and rushed closer, ready to tackle him. If she could get close enough to touch him, maybe she could heal him from the poison.

"He deserves to be punished," he yelled just before she rammed into his protective shield and bounced back.

Her teeth vibrating with the impact, she flung out her arms to stop herself from falling and then pushed back toward him. The icy wind picked up, swirling around them like a hurricane, until all she could see was Thomas. She locked eyes with him, his usually brilliant blues now almost black with shadowy rage. Struggling against the wind and his protective shield, she held his gaze and saw through the poisonous, bitter hatred—to a glimmer of light still inside him. Their energies pushed and pulled at each other with such force that they began rotating with the hurricane winds.

"Just let me touch you," she pleaded, her hair churning in the wind and streaking across her face.

"No! Don't you get it?" He coughed and spat dark phlegm. "I planned this. I took the vial to Makwa and asked her to strengthen *my* power, to finally put him in his place for all he's done to me." Thomas roared and fired a ball of energy at Kane's shielded body. "For what he did to you," he added, whipping his gaze back at her. His face softened for a beat and then hardened with vicious rage.

"She didn't strengthen your powers. She poisoned you with hate and rage," Sara yelled over the whirlwind of ice and snow.

He held up a stained hand, glaring at the indigo-black that caked his nails, bled down his fingers, and lined his palm. He curled his lip in satisfaction and shot her a fierce look. Sara gasped, not at the darkness in his eyes but at an electric surge that jolted through her heart and along her skin, tugging her closer against his protective shield. Without intending to, she heard the thought in his head as clearly as if he had spoken it.

"Monster."

"Thomas," she breathed, her eyes tearing as her three-fingered hand dug into his force field. He swung his arms, gathering energy to fire at her when he glimpsed her mutilated hand—and faltered. A slight rip opened in his shield and she dove for it, punching her arm through and stretching until her fingertips touched the side of his face, his skin so cold it sent a shiver over her bones.

"You could never be a monster to me." She held his eyes, refusing to look away from his icy stare, and pushed her warmth—her very heart—into her fingertips until they glowed with energy.

The hate in his eyes softened. He dropped his hands, allowing his shield to dissipate until it was just a thin wall of energy. The magnetic power between them pulled Sara into his protected space. As they stared at each other, they continued rotating and rising above the birches, soft snowflakes floating in the air.

"This hate isn't you. It isn't *us,*" she said, reaching out and holding his face with both hands. Her touch sizzled on his skin as she drew out the poison and replaced it with her warmth.

He gasped. Inky blackness seeped from him and into her touch, the poison evaporating under the white flames dancing on her skin. The stains on his hands faded and disappeared, and his breathing was no longer wet with phlegm. His eyes brightened, returning to a brilliant blue.

Seeing the color return to his face and the familiar shimmer of his eyes, Sara exhaled a long sigh and ran her thumb across his cheek.

Thomas shuddered. He slid a hand under her long hair to cradle the back of her head and wrapped his other arm around her waist, pressing her close to his body. Their legs twined as they hovered, slowly spinning together. Any lingering scraps of coldness that clung to him melted under her burning heat.

His heartbeat throbbed against her chest, his rapid pulse matching hers and the stone hidden beneath her stiff, bloody shirt. Her entire body trembled. Thomas leaned forward, pressing his brow to hers, their deep breaths the only sound in their protected space.

Mother, help me. Her eyes fell on his slightly parted mouth, at a faint shadow of darkness on his lower lip. *Closer.*

Whether it was a need to heal him or a need from her heart, Sara didn't care. She gave in, tilting her chin until her lips grazed his. The bitter taste of poison was replaced at once by a sweet mix of honey and smoky ash as he hungrily returned the kiss.

Her mouth tingled, and a current surged through her. They both jolted, their connection now strengthened and snapping with electricity. A white-and-blue aura swirled around them. With a soft moan, Thomas deepened the kiss, his tongue finding hers, sharing her need to be closer. Her hands slid to the back of his head, gripping his hair. Closer felt dangerously good.

Afraid of possibly catching fire or floating off into the stars, she reluctantly broke their kiss and placed her forehead to his. Sharing heavy breaths, they stopped rotating, and the snowy clouds faded, letting the summer sun shine upon them.

By now, they were high above the birch grove.

CHAPTER 41

LIGHT GLINTED FROM the grove below. With a squint, Sara glanced down at the summer sun winking off wet snow, and caught Ian, Lily, and Bill Walker staring up at her. She instantly pulled her face away from Thomas's. But he moved with her and placed his lips to her neck—right behind her ear. Back arching, heat tinging her cheeks, Sara slid her hands to his shoulders and ever so gently pushed for his attention.

He leaned back, his brow slightly pinched as he ran his hand through her hair, watching it flow through his fingers. "Are you hiding any horns?" He grinned wickedly, reaching to grab another fistful of hair.

She fought the urge to smash her lips to his grin, remembering the important task she still had to attend to. "I'll let you search for horns later. Right now, I think we should check on your father." She tilted her head to the small crowd below.

At the mention of his father, Thomas stiffened and scanned the devastated forest floor below them. "Did I do that?" he said quietly. "Did I—" He returned his gaze to her, to her three-fingered hand in his, shock and fear in his blue eyes. "Did I hurt you?" His voice was so raw, she swore her heart fractured.

She withdrew her hand from his grasp, ashamed Samson had preyed upon her. "You didn't hurt me," she said softly and placed a light, reassuring kiss on his cheek. A tiny blue spark snapped. "But you sure gave your father a hard time." With a wry smile, she used her good hand to tug him toward the forest floor.

"Wait." He pulled her back. "I wanted to stop him, but . . . all that hate . . . I tried to kill him. I don't think he wants to see me." Thomas stared at his hands, at where the poison had stained his fingers and nails. He shook his head, guilt etched into his face.

"Thomas, he loves you." She rolled her eyes at his disbelieving expression. "I *felt* it in him. He asked me to save you." Still, he hesitated. "You were *poisoned*. Just admit you had a crappy plan, and let's move on."

Thomas snorted a laugh but didn't move.

"Please," she said while scanning the forest treetops for any signs of blight or fire. "Talk with him while I pay a visit to Makwa. All of this—Samson, the blight, the curse—this is all her fault."

"Curse?" His puzzled expression vanished as she tugged on his arm again. "Oh, no." He drew her back into him. "You're not seeing that poisonous witch without me. We settle this together." His firm grip, blazing blue gaze, and stubborn shift in his shoulders made her pause.

Her mouth twisted with half a smile at his stubbornness. "Fine. But first we need to handle this." She waved at the group below. He clenched his jaw, no doubt steeling himself for the consequences of his actions, and let her lead him back into the birch grove. The grove he'd destroyed.

They glided to the forest floor, to where Kane lay on the ground. Sara sighed with relief at the color in his face, his eyes open and tracking their approach.

Bill backed off a healthy distance, keeping a wary gaze on Sara.

With nods of encouragement, Lily and Ian stepped aside for Thomas. He knelt beside his father and leaned in, whispering. Kane reached up for him. Tears shimmered in Kane's eyes as he and Thomas embraced. She turned away to give them privacy only to face Lily and Ian who were staring wide-eyed at her.

Lily grinned while Ian looked liable to fall over. "I know I said to stop him, but that was . . ." He trailed off, mouth hanging open.

"Excessive?" Sara finished his sentence.

Ian huffed while Lily's bright laugh rang out like sunshine in the broken grove. Their moment of levity was interrupted when a pair of red foxes shot out of the undergrowth and phased into Matthew and Moira.

The twins immediately spoke with their father, their heads down in serious conversation before snapping their gaze toward Sara. Three sets of amber eyes assessed her and then approached.

Bill held a wide stance and cracked his neck, Matthew and Moira flanking his sides. "Thank you for healing him," Bill said gravely, nodding at Kane. He narrowed his eyes and pointedly glanced at her bloody shirt and missing finger. "And it seems Samson is gone. Is this true?"

"Yes. He's gone." She lifted her chin, shifting in the muddy snow and putting her hands behind her back.

Bill folded his arms across his chest, his eyes like liquid fire in the summer sun. "Someone else needs to be dealt with, and I think you know who."

"Yes, and I intend to stop her," said Sara, her voice deadly calm. She glanced behind her and caught Thomas's eye as he and Lily helped Kane sit on a fallen log.

"We're helping," said Moira with a flick of her hair.

Matthew stepped forward. "We found Naomi. Makwa has her. If she breaks her curse and returns to her human form, she will be too powerful to stop. She'll destroy Ware Woods and all of us. And then she'll unleash herself on the outside world."

Bill spat and rocked on his heels. "I never did care much for that witch." He thrust his chin toward the distant, lingering smoke of the Main House and soul tree. "Everyone else is still cleaning up the Cahill site, and I'll be damned if we need a Council meeting for this."

"No time for meetings. We go now," said Sara, the urgency of the situation fueled by Naomi's kidnapping.

"*Are you out of your minds?*" Ian shouted, waving his hands in the air and looking wildly between Sara and the Walkers.

"No, I—" began Sara, placing a hand to her chest, over the hidden stone. She stopped herself—now was not the time for questions and explanations. They did not need to know she was High Witch and wielded Makwa's true name. They only needed to believe in her.

She knew she couldn't stop the Walkers from helping any more than she could stop Thomas. But no matter how dangerous, she would protect them all. She pulled her hand away from the stone and clenched a fist. Inhaling deeply to ground herself, she regarded all of them. "I—*we* have the power to stop her. I know it."

"I believe her," said Thomas, coming to stand by her side. "Besides, we have little choice at the moment," he said with a slight smile, folding his arms across his broad chest.

She whipped her gaze at him. "That's not exactly encouraging," she said. His smile widened, taunting her. A spark cracked between them, and all three Walkers took a step back, their amber eyes narrowed.

Matthew cleared his throat. "Good to have you back, bro," he said with a head jerk at Thomas.

Thomas nodded and then dropped his grin. A muscle in his jaw quivered and his expression changed into the stony demeanor of a natural-born fighter, ready to kill.

Sara tore her eyes from him and turned to Ian. "Kane needs rest. Will you and Lily help him back to join the others?" She projected into his mind: *"Please."*

Ian frowned.

She loosened the tight hold on her mental shield and let him know she wore Mary's stone.

His pupils dilated and nostrils flared. "Yes," he breathed with an almost imperceptible tilt of his head. He stole a quick glance at Lily, who sat perched on the log, supporting Kane, and then turned back to Sara. *"Be careful. Do not underestimate Makwa,"* he said in her mind.

Sara held his gaze and they exchanged a silent heartfelt earnestness before she pushed off the muddy ground and rose above the trees, Thomas close behind her.

Moira called up to them: "Race you!" She phased into a russet wolf and tore off to the north. Bill and Matthew instantly phased and followed, mud flying in their wake.

CHAPTER 42

SOARING OVER TREETOPS with the wind whistling in her ears, Sara failed to ignore the flutter in her stomach, keenly aware of flying with Thomas for the first time. She stole a glance at him. The warm gleam in his eyes flickered when he caught her gaze.

"This won't be easy," he said, resuming his hardened face and studying her.

"I hope not. How else am I to learn my powers?" She wiggled her fingers at him.

"That's not exactly encouraging," he retorted with a huff and surged ahead, leading them to a marshy area at the north end of the forest.

Sara winced at the dark aura clinging like viscid oil in the marsh shadows. They slowed over a level area covered in thorny vines and wild parsnip whose deceptively alluring yellow-green flowers hummed with hornets. In the center slumped a small hut with a thatched roof, the old building partially sunken into the soft earth. Before it, a fire pit burned in a small clearing, wisps of smoke curling into the clear sky.

Thomas, hovering beside Sara, nudged her and angled his head to the edge of the clearing. She followed his gaze and noticed a dark shadow—precisely the size of a wolf. Her head jerked back, astonished not only at the Walkers' speed but their stealth in maneuvering through the dense brambles and poisonous weeds.

As if expecting them, the hut threw open its door and Makwa lumbered out into the clearing. Sara and Thomas dropped to the ground, landing hard enough to create a muddy crater before the fire pit. Makwa squinted at them, clearly annoyed by the daylight, and straightened, her bulk and height blocking Sara's view of the hut behind her.

"Hand over Naomi," commanded Thomas, arms loose at his sides and ready to throw power.

Makwa ignored him and grunted. "Two little birds escaped the bush to land at my doorstep," she said. Her voice was such a deep-throated rumble that she had to speak slowly, enunciating each word.

Sara's skin prickled at recognizing the voice. It was the same one that had broken into her mind at the Council meeting, telling her she didn't belong here and to run.

Makwa shook her mighty bear head, fur rippling along her neck. "You are a thorn in my side," she snarled at Sara. "And you—" She fixed her beady eyes on Thomas. "I didn't expect to see you again. I gave you enough rage to destroy the forest or die trying. You were to be a distraction while I focused on finally freeing myself." She heaved a giant breath, nearly extinguishing the fire between them. "And yet here you are." She gestured at him with her massive hands, more animal than human. Her thick, curved claws twitched and clicked.

"You Sullivans are typically so predictable, so power hungry." She cocked her head, the movement surprisingly humanlike, and looked from Thomas to Sara, flaring her black nostrils. "Never mind. I have a bloody backup." Her dark lips pulled back, revealing sharp canines and a yellow-toothed sneer. The brier behind her twisted and thrust forward, an unconscious body held tight in its grip. Violet's head lolled to the side, her face pale with black liquid seeping from her mouth and trailing down her chin.

"Violet!" Thomas yelled. He lifted his hands, kinetically trying to break her free from the vines. But his efforts only made the vine constrict, cutting into Violet's ashen skin.

Keeping her focus on Makwa's cruel smile, Sara pulled Thomas back. *"Don't. You're playing her game,"* she projected into his mind.

Thomas cursed and drew back his energy, coiling it and shaking with tension.

Makwa lifted her snout and snuffled the air. "Come out, Walkers," she rumbled.

A massive gray wolf crept from the edge of the clearing, head low, eyes fixed on her. Two russet wolves emerged from separate locations, followed by a large silver wolf, until all four wolves surrounded the witch. Sara glimpsed an irregular tuft of fur on Albert's flank, but otherwise the silver wolf appeared completely healed and ready to fight.

The bear witch seemed unfazed at being surrounded by a pack of wolves. "You know I only speak the truth, and I tell you she brings death."

The wolves snarled and held their ground.

Sara clenched her hands into fists, ready to punch the white-hot energy that flickered across her skin. "You do speak the truth, but it is *your* death I bring." She rose and hovered, looking down at the witch. "Release Violet."

Makwa glanced up.

Thomas took advantage of the distraction by angling closer to his sister.

The bear witch flared her nostrils again and swayed her head, thick fur shaking back and forth. "You smell like Mary, but you are *not* her. You may have broken my curse, but you are still *weak*, full of doubt and fear, and have *no* power over the likes of me." Makwa spat her words at Sara and then roared, the sound echoing around them. "Mary saved me after the witch trials, but she tricked me. She grew to care too much for this forest and you people," she growled at Thomas and the wolves surrounding her. "With powers such as ours, we should do as we please, but she didn't agree. She cursed me to no longer tell lies and to remain confined to these woods—this prison. I defied her once, and this is what happened." She shook her bear head and snarled, snapping her teeth like a savage animal.

Makwa grunted at Sara and loosed a heavy sigh. "That damn fool Samson should have killed you and freed me. But . . ." She glanced at Thomas, and a vine with razor-sharp thorns lashed out to grab him.

He jumped and flipped back, now farther from Violet's limp body.

Makwa growled at him and shuffled to the edge of the clearing, the wall of brambles writhing in her proximity as though awaiting her bidding. "After hundreds of years, I've learned you can't trust anyone. They'll just let you down—hurt you, curse you, kill you. All because they fear or covet your power. A High Witch must do everything on her own." She flicked a paw-like hand, and the vine shifted and snaked, bringing forth Naomi, her eyes wide with fear while the brier restrained her and gagged her mouth. Makwa sneered, her black lips pulling away from her wicked canines. "The blood of a spell breaker will finally set me free."

The wolves growled and snapped their jaws, inching closer. Thomas rose from the ground, arms out, ready to unleash the energy sizzling in his palms.

But Sara didn't move, keeping her face a calculated mask of fear. She'd anticipated Makwa using Naomi as a pawn. Counted on it.

Drawing strength from Mary's confidence in her, she mentally reached out to Thomas and the Walkers. *"Stand down until I say otherwise. Trust me."* She stared at the large gray wolf that was Bill until he nodded his approval, whining as if it hurt him to do so. Thomas pulled back, every muscle in his body stretched taut, and settled to the ground beside her.

The bear witch grunted and flicked her ears. "Now, it's time I finally get back to my true self." She waved a hand, and a hissing bowl of inky liquid rose from the firepit and whished toward her. She waved her other hand, and the brambles held out Naomi's arm.

Naomi bucked and thrashed, screaming into the vine that gagged her.

Makwa loomed over her and raised a clawed hand. When the witch brought down her claws and slashed into her arm, Naomi's eyes rolled into the back of her head. She passed out, her blood spurting and pouring into the bowl.

The wolves snarled and yelped for Sara's command. She flinched but said nothing, silently apologizing to Naomi, and took a step back, pulling Thomas with her.

Makwa seized the bowl with both hands and gulped the undulating liquid. With a swipe of her paw, she flung the bowl into the fire, flames instantly leaping and sparking. But instead of changing into a human form, the bear witch stumbled back from the fire and roared. She bared her teeth while slapping her giant hands to her head in pain, the potion visibly twisting inside her.

Sara let her mask of fear slip, a slight smile tugging at the corners of her mouth. She knew Mary had been a stronger witch than Makwa and any attempts to break the spell would surely backfire. Sara's smile grew wider. Her crafty ancestor had devised the spell to consider a bear to be Makwa's true self.

"NOW!" Sara shouted.

The wolves lunged forward, encircling the witch, while Thomas and Sara blasted her with enough blue and white energy to level a house.

Their blows hardly ruffled the fur on Makwa's head. She growled and shot back with a dark power so ancient it reeked of blood and stone and lifetimes of torment.

Thomas rushed in front of Sara, taking the brunt of the force as it flung them backward into a field of wild parsnip.

Poisonous pollen stung Sara's eyes and burned her skin while hornets swarmed around them, their ominous buzz deafening. Thomas tried to shield them from the frenzied insects, but he was too stunned from Makwa's blast. He moaned and collapsed on top of Sara, using his body instead of his magic to protect her.

Sara choked on the fiery pollen, her throat swelling shut. In her moment of weakness, the hornets pierced through her force field and lit upon them, each sting a burning stab. The stone at her chest pulsed. She shut her eyes and pursed her lips against the insects attacking her face and fought to calm herself.

Enough!

Blindly, she pushed up to rise above the field, pulling Thomas with her. Holding him tight, she called the wind and rain to disperse the hornets and wash off the pollen, then healed them both from the inside out.

Thomas coughed and grabbed her hand. She smiled at the familiar tingling warmth of his touch. "Ready for more?" she teased.

He clenched his jaw and nodded, his eyes shimmering. With a quick squeeze, he released her hand, and they rocketed back to the clearing.

By now, the small fire had erupted into a towering bonfire with Makwa writhing and screaming beside it. Her body swelled, fur bursting through flesh, as her ragged clothes split and crumpled to the ground. She fell to her hands and knees, and morphed into a hulking, savage bear.

Seizing his opportunity, Thomas rushed to Violet and Naomi, whose limp bodies still hung in the thorny brambles at the edge of the clearing. While he threw his energy into breaking the twisted brier, Sara focused on Makwa and the Walkers.

With Makwa weakened and frustrated, the wolves finally closed in and attacked. Bill leapt onto her shoulders, while the others pounced at her hindquarters. She roared and reared up—her massive paws swiping and flinging fire onto the vines near Naomi and Violet. Bracing her front legs, she slammed into the ground, the impact shaking the hut and entire clearing.

Albert and the twins yipped and fell back, but Bill still clung to her, scrabbling to keep his hold. The bear witch glared at Sara with a cruel, black-lipped grin. She shook her massive shoulders and flung Bill into the flames.

Sara dove for the bonfire.

Calling rain to douse the flames, she yanked Bill from the fire, healing his burns and broken ribs before laying his wolf form beside Thomas at the edge of the clearing.

A yelp pierced through the rain, and Sara turned just in time to see Makwa's paw connect with a sickening crack to the larger russet wolf. The force of the blow launched the lupine high above the clearing. Sara ceased the rain and called a gust of wind to catch the wolf and lay it beside Bill, who whined and licked the russet's face. "Protect them," she said to Thomas. But before she could push off the ground, he grabbed her arm, his eyes pleading.

"Do you trust me?" she said, sending him the image of them in the treehouse when he asked the same question. His eyes softened, and he nodded, releasing her.

Makwa stood on her hind legs and roared, completely unhinged and consumed by rage. She crashed down, shaking the ground, and swiped at the silver wolf biting her back leg. Sara reacted faster and pushed Albert away, safely into Thomas's shielded haven by the vines.

The remaining russet wolf leapt for the bear's throat, only to be tossed aside like a puppy. Sara softened its fall before it hit the ground with a snarl. Makwa raised her paw to crush the wolf, but Sara rushed between them, taking the full blow. She flew across the clearing and slammed into the brier. Struggling to get up, she dug her fingers into the soft earth and gasped for breath. Her arms and vision slipped, and she fell face-first into the mud. Everything turned a dreadful black.

Sara's body jerked, as if hit with a jolt of electricity, and she woke to a dull ringing in her ears. Pushing herself onto all fours, she gulped air. The ringing faded to Thomas's voice yelling her name over and over.

The ground trembled beneath her hands. She lifted her head to see Makwa barreling across the clearing for her, the russet wolf at her heels.

Thomas's yells were nearly hysterical until she flicked her eyes to where the vine ensnared him, arms restrained behind his back. She met his gaze and winked, chuckling at his shocked expression. Closing her eyes and rolling onto her back, she gathered her energy . . . and let the bear come to her.

She lay still as death, wagering her life on her hard-earned knowledge that most bullies played with their victim before finishing them.

Makwa slammed to a halt in front of Sara, the impact flaring her hair and bouncing her head against the ground. The bear lumbered over her and snorted hot, putrid breath on her face. Sara winced and turned to the side, slitting her eyes open to gaze directly at the russet wolf. But before she could make eye contact, Makwa thrust a paw into her side, cracking her ribs and piercing a lung. Sara cried out and heard Thomas bellow in response. Panting with the effort to heal herself, she looked again to the wolf, catching sight of it flick its ears and snarl.

She silently called, *"Moira?"* The wolf nodded. Sara gazed into her blazing amber eyes and grinned. She shot her an image of the first time they'd met, when Moira was a fisher cat.

Moira bared her teeth in a menacing lupine smile.

Makwa roared into Sara's face, spit flying, and rose on hind legs, preparing to crush her. As she swayed, towering over Sara, a black shadow dove from the sky and clawed at her face. Glancing up with an irritated shake of her head, Makwa raised her massive paws and swatted the sky.

Trouble squawked and dove again while Moira flashed into a fisher cat, darted up the bear's back, and tore a hole in her throat. Thick blood instantly poured from Makwa's neck.

Moira leapt from her back and streaked to the far edge of the clearing, joining the others as Makwa released a gurgling shriek and pawed at her throat.

This was the moment Sara had been waiting for. Done playing the victim, she shot up from the ground and grabbed Makwa's head. She stared into her eyes, into her dark soul, while the stone at her chest burned hot and glowed. The bear shifted its gaze to Sara's chest and froze at the red light shining through her bloody shirt.

Sara pulled her closer. "Go to hell—Tituba!" And as she shouted the name, a surge of energy burst from the stone and pierced the bear's heart.

Shock filled the bear's face as the witch succumbed to the deadly blow. Her eyes glazed over, and Sara let her fall.

A venomous hiss filled the air when Makwa struck the ground. Green flames erupted from the muddy grass, consuming her body in a hot flash that forced Sara back. Another hiss, and the fire died out as quickly as it started. What remained of Makwa crackled into black ash and dissolved into the forest floor.

CHAPTER 43

A SNAPPING AND cracking resounded throughout the clearing. All around them, the briers splintered and broke into jagged pieces. Thomas stumbled forward with his sudden release from the binding vines and serrated thorns. Blood streaming from his arms, he turned and lunged to catch Violet and Naomi. With a tight-lipped wince, he gently set them down and scanned the clearing. Sara locked eyes with him. But a loud splinter had her swinging her gaze to the receding thicket—to a third person who had been trapped deep within. She cursed as Dorcas fell to the ground with a soft thud, eyes closed and unmoving.

The entire clearing was a horrific scene of blood, ash, and mud. Sara wanted to rush to Thomas, but a glance at Violet, Naomi, and the battered wolves beside him sobered her into tending the wounded first. Wiping bear spit and blood from her face and hands, she started to glide across the clearing but froze when Moira let out a mournful howl. The hair on Sara's neck stood up.

Moira phased back into herself, tears running down her cheeks, and slumped over her twin's broken body. "Matty!" she screamed.

Bill phased back and held Matthew's wolf form in his arms, his face pale and stiff as he rocked back and forth with his son.

"No, no, no!" screamed Moira, her voice pinched with hysteria.

Sara rushed to the Walkers and lunged, digging her hands into

Matthew's fur just in time to catch his last breath and pull it back into his body. Using her energy, she massaged his heart and cleared his lungs, then concentrated on pulling bone fragments from his swollen brain and healing his skull. She trembled when his heart fluttered and began beating on its own.

With a faint moan, Matthew flicked his ears and opened his eyes to Moira and Bill crying and burying their faces into his thick fur.

Sara leaned back, a bead of sweat trickling down the side of her face. Leaving Matthew in the care of his father and sister, she stumbled to her feet, her vision faltering. Thomas caught her, his hands tight around her waist. Steadying herself, she gasped at the vicious cuts marking his struggle to free himself and help her. A soft groan escaped his lips when she gingerly laid her hands on his bloody forearms, the wounds closing and healing under her touch. After giving him a tender squeeze, she shifted her attention to Violet and Naomi, waiting patiently behind him.

Though sitting in the sun, Thomas's sister shivered and wrapped her arms around her chest. Beside her sat Naomi, one arm around Violet's shoulders and her other arm resting in her lap, still bleeding from Makwa's brutal gouge.

"Seems you two could use some help," said Sara, her voice sounding like someone else's. She stepped away from Thomas and knelt before them. Clasping Violet's stained hands, Sara closed her eyes and pushed out a warm light to wash away the poison. Violet shivered again and returned her grip so fiercely that Sara felt her knuckles crack. As healing energy flowed through her, Violet heaved a wet sigh and spat dark mucus until her lungs and hands were free of stain. Sucking in a breath, Violet finally let go of Sara's hands. "Thank you," she rasped, and took another gulp of air.

Sara turned to Naomi, who laughed her wonderful laugh, reminding Sara of roses and cherries. "You've come a long way since our first meeting. Your mom would be proud," she said. Her chestnut-brown eyes twinkled, and a wide grin spread across her face, pronouncing the apples of her cheeks.

Sara smiled and nodded at a small wildflower in the wet grass beside them. "She is always with me."

Naomi put a comforting hand on Sara, then gasped. Eyes wide in awe, Naomi watched the cut on her arm close and heal until only a pink scratch remained.

As Naomi ran her fingers over her smooth skin, Sara reached for Thomas and let him help her up. She attempted a step on her own but faltered. He clasped her three-fingered hand and looped his other arm around her waist, drawing her close to him. "You're very pale. I think you should rest," he said softly, concern etched on his face.

She looked into his shimmering blue eyes and wanted to kiss away the worry on his pouty lips.

He smirked. "You're also covered in bear spit, blood, and Mother knows what else," he said, playfully tightening his hold on her.

She grimaced but knew he was right. It took all her effort to stand before him, to not dry heave and crumple to the ground, her bones aching with exhaustion. Gripping his hand, she glanced around the clearing. "Where's Albert?"

"He went to the Cahills to tell Alice and Gran what happened."

Sara nodded and gave him a tight smile before turning to the decimated thicket. "Dorcas needs us," she said. She took a deep breath and, leaning on Thomas, shuffled through the broken brier to where the witch lay. "Dorcas," Sara called gently.

The witch opened her eyes, stunning Sara with their clear beauty. In shock, Sara fell to her knees and took Dorcas's hand. She was no longer bald but had thick shaggy blonde hair—even her skin was noticeably clearer. Dorcas laughed, the sound light and innocent.

"It seems I finally made the right choice," she said. Her voice was the same tinkling of bells Sara had heard in her mind when Dorcas told her about the curse. She dropped Sara's helping hand and pushed herself up. "I'm fine. Takes a lot more than a cranky bear and brimstone briers to hurt me," she said. She narrowed her eyes at the blackened thicket, the precarious slant of the hut, the group of gifted in the little clearing, and the site of Tituba's ashes.

Delight and then malevolence flashed across Dorcas's face before she assumed a placid expression.

"You best be getting back to your families," Dorcas said sweetly, gesturing to the battered group in the clearing. "I'll clean up this mess and make a new home for myself. 'Tis something I've wanted to do for a long time."

Sara stared at her smile, at the bright white teeth she now had. "We're your family too."

"Aye," said Dorcas and nodded thoughtfully.

Sara rose from the muddy ground only to have the weight of the day, the toll of all her healing, crash into her. And she collapsed into Thomas's arms.

CHAPTER 44

THE SWEET SONG of a hermit thrush tickled her consciousness. Its melody began with a sharp whistle and finished with soft echoing notes, pulling her from a deep sleep. Sara woke to cool bedsheets and the scent of honeysuckle—so heady she could nearly taste it. Smiling at the familiar creak of the treehouse, she opened her eyes to find Thomas dozing in a chair beside her. The chair pressed close enough to the bed that she could have reached out and touched him.

She studied the rise and fall of his chest, the angular set of his clean-shaven jaw, and the sweep of his dark hair and eyelashes. Her heart fluttered when her gaze settled on his mouth—on the soft lips she remembered kissing in the birch grove.

As if hearing her thoughts, he grinned and opened his eyes. Her heart pounded in response. The intensity of his brilliant blue gaze never failed to send a shock through her.

She shifted her legs under the snug sheets, trying to remember why she was in bed and why he was sitting beside her in the treehouse. Her last memory was of healing Naomi and seeing Dorcas's clear eyes.

What happened? Why am I— She meant to speak out loud but found her tongue stuck, her mouth too dry.

"Ted said to give you this when you woke up." Thomas handed her a stainless-steel thermos.

She furrowed her brow, opened the thermos, and used both hands to take a shaky sip. Liquid sunshine rolled across her tongue, the taste heavenly in her parched mouth. Realizing how thirsty she was, she began gulping it down.

"Whoa, easy there," he said, pulling the thermos back.

The tea trickled through her chest and splashed into her empty stomach. *When was the last time I ate?* She ran her tongue across her teeth, now surprisingly slick and clean from the fresh drink.

"Better?" he asked, concern softening his deep voice. He leaned forward in the chair, one hand resting on the bed and the other overlapping hers on the thermos. The air stirred with his scent.

With an impatient flick of her hand, she levitated the thermos aside and grabbed his shirt. Pulling him to her until their faces were just inches apart, she peered into his glimmering blues. He stared back, eyes wide, and she saw it—flashes of hunger and vulnerability—the same swirling mix of want and need that coursed through her. Her heart soared.

She tightened her grip, tugging him closer, and gently kissed him. Her lips tingled at the contact. Before she could pull back, Thomas returned the kiss, his lips eagerly parting hers and deepening their connection until her entire mouth burned with him.

He took her face in his hands and groaned, the sound melting her insides. Stroking her cheeks with his thumbs, he reluctantly broke the kiss and pressed his forehead against hers. "Mother below, you had me worried." He sighed, his shoulders visibly relaxing.

"I did?" she whispered, her voice paper thin.

He slumped back into the chair, keeping a firm grip on her arm as if she might slip away. "You've been asleep for almost three weeks." He blew out another breath and rubbed the back of this head.

"I have?" She looked down at the thick, silvery-gray hair cascading over her shoulders, and at her clean clothes. *How is that possible?* She touched her strange new locks and faded dysprosium T-shirt, trying to remember when she had changed.

Thomas shifted in the chair. "I've been waiting. Watching over you the *entire* time."

Her cheeks instantly burned. He smiled wickedly, holding her gaze for a heart-pounding moment.

"Well, Lily and Gran came a few times and shooed me away." He nodded at her clean shirt.

A wave of relief washed over her, and he chuckled. Remembering the stone, she put a hand to her chest to feel its presence hidden beneath her shirt.

His brow pinched slightly, and he tilted his head, studying her.

To cool his curiosity and the heat in her cheeks, she shifted her gaze around the room, its expansiveness and surrounding tree growth reminding her of the broken curse. Clusters of fresh honeysuckle covered the windowsills, spilling over the edges and calling bees to their sweet nectar. Beside Thomas stood a small table with empty cups and birch beer bottles arranged neatly on top. Guessing it was early afternoon by the sun's angle over the lake, she plucked the thermos from the air and finished the tea.

"Gran said you overdid it and needed to rest. She called it a magical stasis. We didn't know how long you would be asleep." He ran a hand over his face. "Actually, your father knew. He came at noon and is waiting downstairs for you."

Her eyes widened. She pushed back the sheets and nearly fell out of bed, her legs buckling. Thomas put an arm around her and helped her to the window.

"You're like a newborn fawn. Take it easy." He tucked her hair behind her ear, brushing her cheek with his fingers before pointing below.

Expecting to see the clearing between the cemetery and lake, Sara was stunned at the scene before her. There was her dad, alive and well, sitting beneath the graceful branches of a mature apple tree, a table full of food before him. Around the tree spread a stone patio stretching from the cemetery entry to a new cottage. The cozy building was made of the same stone as the patio and had a chimney and window boxes spilling with colorful flowers.

"Three weeks?" She gawked in disbelief. Her father seemed so healthy, and the patio and stone cottage were already kissed with moss, as if they had grown from the ground decades ago.

Thomas huffed a laugh. "A lot has happened. You'll see." He pulled her to him and kissed her, making her legs buckle again. "I hope this means you forgive me for trying to kill you."

She pushed his shoulders back to read his face.

Under his tight smile, the muscle along his jawline pulsed. "Poison or no poison, you should know I make a lot of mistakes, and sometimes"—he paused with a quick purse of his lips—"I can't stop myself from making bad choices."

With his arms around her, she felt the torturous guilt shredding his insides, along with a sharp fear of being pushed away. But she would never deny him. Her desire for him was beyond words, beyond expression, beyond even all the stars in the sky. She touched his temple and ran a hand through his hair. "Of course I forgive you. Now and forever." As his tension eased, she leaned in, grazing his ear with her lips, and whispered, "I'm sure I can find a way for you to make it up to me."

He groaned again and placed a lingering kiss on her neck in response. "I like forever, especially when you're so pushy." He breathed across his wet kiss, causing her to shiver, then leaned back. "As much as I'd enjoy making it up to you right now"—a devious look spread across his face—"I know Charlie is anxious to see his beautiful daughter."

She rolled her eyes.

"You are beautiful, even though you've gone gray before me. And sometimes you drool in your sleep." He chuckled when she pinched his back. "Besides, I know you're just as eager to see him. You both have a lot to talk about."

Thomas tried to pull away, but she held tight, remembering poison and black witches, afraid to let him go. His arms slid back around her as he softly kissed the top of her head. "I'm fine. And you're fine. Makwa and Samson are gone."

Sara stiffened. She saw Makwa die, but Samson . . . It had been too easy to get rid of him.

Thomas squeezed her. "Relax. Take your time and then come over to my place. It's Saturday and everyone is home. My father wants to see you too." He laughed when she rolled her eyes again. "He's a changed man, thanks to you." And with another grin, he released her and whished out the window.

She rubbed her lips and sighed, trying to settle the fluttering inside her. Her body stiff and weak, she took her time pulling on her shoes and lightly descended the roomier treehouse, focusing on each step to wake up her muscles. Though she wanted to fly to her father, she chose to walk—to show him she was still the same girl. Changed, but still his daughter.

She touched her mother's gravestone as she passed it and continued picking her way through the calm cemetery. "Dad?" she called out.

He turned and rose from the table. His smile trembled as he waited for her to come to him.

Once she passed the cemetery fence, she gave in and launched herself into his open arms. He squeezed her in a tight hug. Shaking, he said her name over and over.

"Oh, Sara, I'm so sorry for everything. Sorry we took you away and didn't tell you. Sorry for believing a false prophecy, for keeping you and Ian apart, for losing Mom." His voice wavered. "And I'm sorry I wasn't there for you after the accident." His chest swelled with a deep breath and he regained his composure. "Your mother and I thought leaving Ware Woods was the only way to keep everyone safe. We tried, but we failed you and Ian. I'm so sorry." His hug tightened, crushing her face into his shoulder.

"Can't . . . breathe . . ."

He chuckled and loosened his hold.

She kept her face pressed against his shirt and inhaled deeply, his pine scent so similar to Ian's and Ted's. "It's okay. I know you both did everything out of love for us." She pulled back, wiping tears from her face, and eyed him up and down.

Gone was the shadow of a man on his deathbed. Before her stood the father she knew—vibrant and youthful, with an easygoing and charismatic demeanor. "I thought you'd never wake up or walk again. No matter how hard I tried, I couldn't heal you. And then—" She paused, reliving the horrible fire. "I thought you and Ian and Ted died in the house."

Charlie wiped a tear from her face. "We almost did. But something extraordinary happened. I think you *did* heal me, and when you broke the curse, Ian gained new powers. It's the only explanation I can think of. I woke to the smell of smoke with Ian and Ted beside me. When the house began to collapse, Ian manifested a protective shield and helped us get out safely."

He shifted his legs. "Thanks to you, I'm walking again and"—he tapped the side of his face—"I don't need my glasses anymore." Laughing, he pulled her back into a hug, kissing her forehead. "My little firecracker. I should have known all along."

She blew out a breath and steeled herself to ask the question burning her heart. "Can you forgive me?" she said, her voice a mere whisper.

He leaned back and studied her tear-stained face. "For what?"

"I'm sorry I couldn't save Mom," she said, staring at her feet.

Charlie tightened his hug, crushing her face into his shoulder again. "It was never your fault. You are *not* at fault for anything—not Mom, not your powers, and certainly not for the man who died years ago. I know you hold on to that guilt, but he died from a heart attack. You are not at fault for anything."

But I *was the heart attack.* Sara had been at a sleepover at Isabell's—the sweet girl who later turned on her and became the vicious pack queen. The very moment Sara had seen Isabell's uncle, his sweaty face and shifty eyes, she knew what he did to her friend and what he intended to do to her too. And she'd lost it. She had used her power to squeeze his dark heart until he dropped dead.

Sara shook her head to stop her downward spiral, denying the memory an opportunity to overtake her with guilt and ruin this moment.

Charlie pushed back her hair, giving a curious smile at the silvery-gray locks, and put a hand to the side of her face. "Wow. You're feeling so much at once I can't keep up. Just know your mother and I love you fiercely. Her spirit is still with us—always watching and loving us."

"Always watching," Sara breathed. She glanced over his shoulder at her mother's grave, remembering Kingsley's words: "*You're being watched.*"

They embraced for a long, quiet moment. Her stomach grumbled, and Charlie laughed again, releasing her. "I know you're hungry. Sit and eat. Your grandmother, Ted, and Ian are about to join us."

Her mouth watering, Sara gratefully filled a plate with meat pie, cheese, fruit, and pastries while Charlie turned to the path at the rear of the cemetery. As expected, Ted, Ian, and Gran popped out of the understory and approached the table, giving a round of tight hugs before everyone sat.

Gran settled into her chair and cast a sly smile at Sara. "I'm sure Thomas was relieved to see you wake up," she said. Loudly. Sara almost dropped her fork.

"Ah, yes, Thomas," said Charlie, clearing his throat. "He seems to be quite the caring young man." He scrutinized Sara, though she avoided meeting his eyes by taking a bite of melon and glancing at the lake. "The last time I saw him, he was a toddler. So much has changed." Charlie sighed and patted Ian on the shoulder.

Ian gave a genuine smile and bit into a pastry.

Anxious to change the subject, Sara swallowed a mouthful of melon, nearly choking. "How're the pine and chestnut trees?" she said a bit too eagerly.

"The pine is healing, and the chestnut has already sprouted fresh growth," said Gran, spooning sugar into her iced tea. "With Samson and Makwa gone, the blight completely stopped throughout the inner and outer forests. Fortunately, it only affected the trees above ground. With no root damage, all the trees are growing back. The Cahills have been working overtime to coax new growth and rebuild the Main House." She tapped off her spoon while gesturing to the patio and cottage. "Jennie helped me put this together for you. Since you've bonded with Mary's tree, I figured you could use a small kitchen of your own and a bathroom." She winked at Sara. "You can't bathe in the lake when it's frozen over in winter."

"Thanks, Gran." Sara beamed at her before turning to her dad. "You can move in with me," she said with a smug smile, making the point she intended to stay in Ware Woods.

Charlie didn't blink. He scanned her face, and she felt his awareness—his power—wash over her, gently probing as if confirming her mood. His shoulders relaxed, and he set down his tea. "About that. I've made arrangements to move all our belongs from the old house. Ian and I closed the florist website." He gave her arm a quick squeeze. "And the university is allowing me to teach and continue my research remotely." He picked up a blueberry muffin from the basket in front of him. "Anyway, thanks for the offer, but I'm already settled into the house with Ted and Ian. We have a lot of catching up to do. Besides, I think you may enjoy a place to yourself." He bit into the muffin, hardly concealing his smile as he avoided her gaze.

Sara's mouth went dry. *Crap. Does he know my feelings for Thomas?* The tips of her ears tingled.

"At least enjoy a bath first," said Ian between mouthfuls. "I love you, but you stink like lake mud."

Ted choked on a biscuit, shooting Ian a dirty look as Sara sniffed her hair.

She stuck out her tongue at her brother. "Love you too," she said out loud, and mentally added, *"Shithead."*

Charlie snorted, almost spurting iced tea through his nose.

"He started it," protested Sara. Her father, uncle, and brother all had the same infernal wide grin on their faces.

"It's true, you do smell," said Gran unapologetically. "Come on, I'll show you the new bath while I answer the unspoken question you have for me."

The red stone warmed and pulsed against Sara's skin. She stopped chewing, her fork clattering onto the plate. *Hells. I have more than* one *question.*

Gran ignored Sara's pointed stare and rose from the table, pulling a handkerchief from her bosom. "It's so good to finally have all my boys together." She sniffed and dabbed at her eyes. "Damn allergies."

"Love you too, Mom," said Ted, his eyes twinkling with laughter as she turned away from the table.

Sara pushed back her chair to follow when her dad grasped her hand, rubbing the spot where her finger had been. "Whenever you're ready, talk to me about what happened—about everything," he said softly.

Sara glanced at her misshapen hand; it seemed like a nightmare from long ago. "I will." She hugged him. "Love you, Dad."

He responded immediately in her mind. *"Love you too, firecracker."*

She smiled, his voice echoing inside her.

CHAPTER 45

SARA FOLLOWED GRAN into the cottage and hesitated, taking in the bright interior. Before her was an open sitting area with a floor-to-ceiling stone fireplace occupying the left wall. Tucked to the right gleamed a kitchen with a small island. On the far side of the room were two doors, one of which swung open of its own accord, revealing a brightly lit and spacious bathroom.

Gran stood by the sitting area's couch and swept her arm through the air. "The building is fed by a well, though it's up to you to run the water and use your energy for heat and power. It might take a few tries, but you'll get the hang of it."

Sara frowned, unsure if she could do such things. Dizzy from all the change within and around her, she leaned against a chair, her fingers gripping a white pillow. She inhaled for the count of three, gathering courage to ask her questions about the stone she wore and, more importantly, to ask for help. "Gran, I—"

With an impatient flick of her hand, Gran interrupted. "You did something great. Getting rid of Makwa was something that needed to be done for a long time. You've changed so much, and I don't mean your hair." She gestured to Sara's long silvery-gray locks. "You changed not from who you were but *into* who you truly are. You were meant to wear the bloodstone."

"Bloodstone?" A painful memory flashed in Sara's mind of her bleeding and clutching the red stone through her soaked shirt.

"When some witches die, their last drop of blood forms a stone. It doesn't happen often. A witch must have considerable power and skill to concentrate their magic and bind it into a bloodstone. And even then, many refuse to do so because a bloodstone can be used for good or bad magic. A dangerous weapon if in the wrong hands." Gran settled heavily onto the couch.

Sara dipped a hand under her shirt collar and pulled out the stone, cupping it before her. Flames winked from its center. Without taking her eyes off the stone, she edged around the chair and sank into it. "How is this a weapon?" Another memory flashed in her mind, this one a red spear of light driving into Makwa's heart.

"It's an amplifier—it magnifies the powers of whoever wears it. But only a High Witch or equally powerful witch can touch a bloodstone. Anyone else will die—the power is so great it burns them alive."

Sara dropped the stone, letting it fall outside her shirt. "*What?*" Gran shrugged.

"You—*you* gave this to me? Not just deadly sap, but this too! You could have *smoked* me. Literally." Sara nudged the innocent stone. *This couldn't possibly burn someone alive. Maybe Gran wants to scare me so I won't lose it. Definitely devious.* She narrowed her eyes at her grandmother.

"I wasn't trying to kill you."

"Pfft!"

"I believed in you," said Gran. She chuckled when Sara rolled her eyes. "Ted had no idea I slipped it into your stuffed dog. Of course, only Alice and I knew you had the stone. We couldn't risk Makwa finding out until you were strong enough to face her."

Sara leaned forward, staring at her grandmother. "Why me?" She was asking not just about the bloodstone, but about everything.

"There's the question." Gran's expression softened, and she

patted Sara's knee. "When my mother, Ann, died, she gave me Mary's bloodstone and made her own for Alice. But the moment she passed and formed her stone, Alice and I lost our magic. We knew Makwa and Dorcas had done something to us, yet without our powers and no spell breakers in Ware Woods, we could do nothing. When they demanded we hand over the bloodstones, Alice and I hid them and lied. We told Makwa and Dorcas our mother had destroyed Mary's stone and didn't leave one of her own.

"Makwa was furious. She said the Lochton family was no longer capable of leading Ware Woods. And without our powers, we couldn't challenge her when she declared herself as High Witch. So Alice and I bided our time, waiting for you."

Sara frowned again, shaking her head. "Me? I still don't understand."

"My mother instructed me to give Mary's bloodstone to my one granddaughter in her moment of need. For a long time, I questioned her request and kept a close eye on Makwa. I was prepared to give the stone to Charlie or Ted or Ian, hoping they were strong enough to handle it, if Makwa so much as sneered at them. Thankfully, she left all the boys alone." Gran shifted on the couch. "Now I know it's because the generational curse she placed on me and Alice also weakened their magic, and they didn't pose a threat to her. But you did. A child from Mary's bloodline *and* one of the five families not only could challenge her as High Witch but could kill her.

"When Eliza was pregnant with you, Makwa bent the truth and created a false prophecy to keep you away from Ware Woods. Alice and I never spoke up about the prophecy because we feared Makwa would kill you and seek retribution on the rest of us. Like your parents, we thought the only way to keep everyone safe was for you to stay away from the forest. Then all Hells broke loose when Samson hunted you. And I knew it was time for you to come home."

Her jaw slack, Sara gaped until her brain caught up. "Seriously? Why didn't you tell me any of this when I got here?" Wanting to scream, she instead gripped the chair arms so fiercely, her palms singed the wood.

Though Gran flared her nostrils as the burnt odor wafted through the room, she held her calm demeanor. "Because you were already going through enough, and I wasn't sure how long it would take for you to fully develop your magic. I thought your struggles were caused by emotional distress. I didn't realize Makwa had boosted her curse, specifically targeting you. But you refused to be held back. Not only is your magic powerful, so is your will. You are the true High Witch of Ware Woods—our Magus. Your powers extend beyond this forest, as they always have. Everyone will defer to you now."

Eyes wide at the sudden responsibility, Sara released her hold on the chair, worry replacing her frustration. She clutched the stone, which pulsed in time with her heartbeat.

"Gaa," said Gran waving a hand at her. "Don't let it go to your head. We all have our roles here. Speaking of which, Alice and I have our full powers back—including my premonitions." She arched an eyebrow, her steel blue eyes sparkling. "Some think one of us is High Witch, though Lily and Ian already know it is you. I understand if you need a few days to process, but the families need a formal announcement soon."

"I don't think a lifetime would be enough to process," mumbled Sara.

Gran rose and stepped toward the door. "I left clean clothes for you in the bathroom. And Sara—" She hesitated, a serious expression on her face. "It won't be easy. As High Witch, you will face many challenges, both outside and inside the wall. Dorcas pretends to be your ally, but never trust her."

"Thanks, Gran." She sighed and rolled her eyes. "I can always count on you not to sugarcoat things."

"*Pfft*. You're certainly not made of glass. You're Mary's blood-line, Lochton steel, and Cahill cleverness. Never forget you are surrounded by an entire forest of family and a lot of *love*." She held on to her last word and then left, but not before Sara spied a sly smile on her lips.

Crap. Does everyone have to know my feelings for Thomas?

Sara approached the bathroom and gave the free-standing, marbled-wood tub a dubious look. *Alrighty, then.* She turned on the water valves and used magic to coax the well water until it flowed freely, its roar echoing in the stone-tiled room. Dipping a finger into the clear water, she flinched at the cold before letting her hand burn with energy. The water steamed, scalding hot. She cursed and let some drain, then refilled the tub with cool well water to get just the right temperature. *I can't even draw a bath. Why would anyone defer to me?*

After scrubbing her hair clean with a few rounds of shampoo, she dried off and grabbed her familiar camisole, blue tee, and denim shorts. Grooming complete, she heaved a sigh. She was in no hurry to meet with Kane. Even though Thomas had said he'd changed, she would have to see it to believe it.

And even then, she wasn't sure she could ever forgive him.

CHAPTER 46

INSTEAD OF LOOPING or flying to the Sullivans, Sara wandered along a forest path—stalling. The Kane she knew would yell at her and assign punitive chores for going after Samson on her own, and, she feared, for liking Thomas. Maybe she should put Kane in his place and tell him she was High Witch.

She bit her lip, staring at the forest floor. *What if he laughs at me? What if everyone does?* After all, she was still learning her magic and knew practically nothing about Ware Woods, not to mention other sacred sites and the Global Council.

A grunt and snuffle froze her mid-step. Recalling the trauma of cracked ribs and hot blood spraying her face, Sara winced and slowly lifted her head.

A black bear loomed along the side of the path, a few hornets buzzing around its massive head.

Her breath hitched. *"Braxton?"* she called out with her mind.

The bear swung his head to her, snorted, and then returned to gorging himself on blueberries.

With a soft chuckle, she rushed past him, rounded a bend in the path, and skidded to a halt at the edge of the Sullivans' pasture. Across the field, Thomas and a familiar young boy sparred under the giant ash tree. Both wore T-shirts and shorts and black boxing gloves. Their back-and-forth assault was so controlled it seemed choreographed until Thomas swept the boy's leg, sending him tumbling. When he got back to his feet, Thomas adjusted the boy's stance and tapped gloves with him. The moment Sara stepped into the pasture, Thomas tousled the kid's hair and gestured toward the house with one gloved hand. The boy playfully punched him in the side before tearing off for the back porch.

As she picked her way through the field, Thomas turned to her. His smile hit her with a wave of warm energy, and her legs weakened. Afraid she would trip and fall, she levitated the remaining distance to him. "Was that your brother?" She sounded much too breathless.

"Yeah, Connor. His hand-to-hand is getting good." He pulled off his gloves and tugged her down, kissing her forehead. "You smell nice. Apples and oak and . . . fire." His voice was low, roguish.

The heat in his eyes matched the flames burning her core. She leaned back ever so slightly, afraid she wouldn't be able to stop herself from devouring him if his lips touched hers, and swallowed hard. "You can thank Ian. He told me I stank like the lake." Averting her gaze from his mouth, she finger-combed her still-damp hair.

Thomas huffed a laugh, tucked his gloves under his arm, and unwound the cotton wrap from his hands. "I'll be sure to thank him." He looked up from his bindings, a playful glimmer in his eyes. "My turn to clean up while you head to the house. My dad's expecting you." Motioning to the slate-tiled house, he gave a curt bow, then headed toward the two-story garage.

"Wait. You live . . . in the garage?" She took a tentative step, following him.

Laughter exploded from him, and he rushed back to her. "It only looks like a garage on the outside." He leaned in, inhaling deeply as he pushed back her hair. "And yes, I live there. It's my studio. You can check it out another time. Right now, you're stalling." His words tickled her neck, teasing her. "My dad promised not to bite, and Vi's out front, waiting for you. I'll be there soon.

Right after I take a *cold* shower." He turned away and flew to the second-story balcony at the back of the apparently not-a-garage building.

Seriously.

Sara hesitated, not wanting to see Kane by herself—afraid she might say or do something she would regret. If she mentioned anything about being High Witch, Kane would tell Thomas. And she couldn't endure the thought of jeopardizing whatever was going on between them. Before she could tell him she was High Witch, she needed Thomas to say what she had read in his mind.

With a sigh, she faced the house and trudged across the yard. The clink of pots and pans and the flow of water being turned on and off drifted through an open window. Kane's familiar deep voice followed. "She has so much to learn. We don't even know all her powers yet. Father of Night, she has no idea . . ." His voice trailed off. Sara intentionally veered away from the open window, not wanting to be accused of eavesdropping. And yet she strained to hear the delicate female voice that answered him.

"For once, Thomas is happy. Let them be." Her words were a soft yet firm command.

Sara grinned, deciding she liked Thomas's mother already.

Skirting the side of the house and passing the front porch, she heard Violet before she saw her. Sitting on the low stone wall, Violet flicked knives with deadly accuracy into wooden targets on the opposite side of the street. Sara marched through the front yard and sat beside her.

"Hey, Vi." Sara jerked her chin at Violet, noting how much healthier she looked than the last time she saw her. Though no longer on the verge of poisonous death, Violet was definitely angry, which seemed to be a typical Sullivan trait.

She tossed back her dark braid, mumbled a hello, and continued her throwing.

They sat for a long while, with nothing breaking the silence but the consistent thwack of knives hitting the soft pine targets. Sara didn't have to read her mind to know what she was thinking.

When Violet ran out of knives, Sara turned to her. "It's okay to be angry, just don't let it consume you. Don't let a dead witch have power over you."

Violet ignored her, hopped off the wall, and walked across the old road to retrieve her knives. When she came back, she faced Sara. "I don't like being a victim." Her voice was quiet and cold.

Sara raised her hand and smiled, wiggling three fingers at her. "Neither do I. So choose not to be." She folded her two outside fingers and made a foul gesture, causing Violet's fierce expression to melt into a grin.

Their moment was interrupted by a screen door screeching open and bouncing shut.

Sara yanked her hand down and whipped her gaze to see Kane and his wife standing on the front porch. *Shit.* With a raised brow at a sniggering Violet, she rose from the wall and approached Thomas's parents.

Kane gestured to the woman beside him. "Sara, this is my wife, Abigail."

Sara recognized the slender woman from the Council meeting. Her hair was pulled back in a braid, similar to Violet's, which accentuated her high cheekbones and kind eyes. She surprised Sara with a firm grip on her shoulders and a light kiss to her cheek. "So nice to finally meet you. Thank you for all you've done." Her smile radiated from her like the summer sun.

Pain pinched Sara's heart as she fought the urge to hug her, to hold on to her as if she was Sara's own mother. She blinked and returned the smile. "It's nice to meet you too, Mrs. Sullivan."

"Please, call me Abby," she said with a wave of her hand. She lowered herself onto a patio chair, sinking into the cushions.

Kane eased into a chair beside her, his leg visibly stiff, and motioned for Sara to sit in front of him. Following her line of sight to his leg, he straightened and cleared his throat. "I'm fine. Just need to strengthen some muscles."

His slight smile shocked Sara. It was the first one he had ever given her, and it reminded her of Thomas.

"I owe you an apology." Kane inhaled and exhaled loudly. A muscle twitched along his jawline, and Sara saw Thomas again in his face. "I'm sorry I was hard on you. I take my role as protector of the forest and the families very seriously." His gaze shifted toward Violet, the dull thunk of her hits rising to the porch. Abby took his hand. "You see, we've already lost a few children, and we refuse to lose any more." He paused and clenched his jaw. "It's why I train them so hard and expect perfection—because we cannot bear the thought of losing another."

Stunned by the raw emotion in his voice, Sara stared at her hands and rubbed at the missing finger. Unsure what to say, she sat in awkward silence and almost jumped out of her skin when Connor threw open the screen door and froze at the sight of them.

"Uh, hello," he said with a polite wave.

Grateful for the interruption, she gave him a big grin and waved back. "Hi. You're Connor, right?"

His face instantly lit up with an infectious grin. "Yep!"

Abby stood and steered Connor back into the house, shutting the screen door behind them with an approving smile at Sara.

"Why is her hair gray?" Connor's whisper floated through the screen as their footsteps faded into the house.

"Because she is brave," drifted Abby's response.

Kane cleared his throat. "Some of my past actions have been inexcusable. I've asked my family for their forgiveness and patience while I try to . . . be better." He caught her eye before continuing. "I hope you will also be forgiving."

Sara ground her teeth, nostrils flaring. *Inexcusable, indeed.*

"Hmph. I admit I deserve your *reluctance*, but there is something else you need to know." He leaned forward and lowered his voice. "There are only two explanations for you to have powers outside the wall. One is dark magic. The other is that you are High Witch of Ware Woods."

She shifted under his piercing stare.

"You defeated Samson and Makwa. I know who you are now. And I am"—he cleared his throat again—"grateful and honored to fight with you to protect our forest."

Sara leaned back, struggling to keep her face a calm mask while her mind reeled. The part of her that wanted to punish him had thawed at seeing his emotional side—at hearing the loss in his voice. A loss she understood all too well and knew could make you do things you normally wouldn't do. But she did not forgive easily. And now he knew she was High Witch.

Fear kissed her like frost at the edge of a window. Not at his knowing, but at what he expected.

At what they all expected.

Kane inclined his head and sat back, his chair groaning. "I haven't told anyone, as I assume you will make an announcement soon. With Makwa and Samson gone, we may be safe for a while. However, a lot of dark magic exists out there, and it always wants to take what we have. It's a continuous battle."

Before she could respond, Thomas rounded the side of the house, his hair wet. He approached the porch steps and paused, sweeping a wary gaze from his father to Sara. "Everything okay?" he asked her.

Eager to end her conversation with Kane, she nodded and stood. "Yes, everything is fine. I was just about to leave." She cast a stony expression at Kane. "I'm sure we'll talk again soon."

He raised an eyebrow. "Undoubtedly. Have fun tonight," he said, waving them off.

Thomas took Sara's hand as she descended the porch steps, a flash of light-blue energy popping at their touch. From behind came a gasp. She glanced over her shoulder to see Kane rise, chair scraping. Staring wide-eyed at them, he grabbed the porch railing and chuckled.

Sara narrowed her eyes. "Is he *laughing* at us?" she said from the corner of her mouth. *Maybe his brain still needs to be healed.*

Thomas hesitated. "I wasn't expecting that reaction either. Let's hurry before his mood changes." He strode for the side of the house, tugging Sara along, and called over his shoulder, "Come on, Vi."

Violet hastily packed her knives and jogged over to them, whishing her tactical bag to the porch.

"Where are we going?" asked Sara, drawing closer to Thomas as they walked toward the path behind the pasture. She wanted to be alone with him yet was curious at Violet's excited demeanor.

"Well, sleeping beauty," he said with a wink, "tonight is Vi's nearly-full-moon party. She pledges at tomorrow's Council meeting."

Shocked that a month had passed since her first horrific Council meeting, Sara slowed her pace and tightened her grip on his hand. A burst of electricity pulsed from her palm and through her body, kicking up leaves before dissipating into the soil.

Thomas jolted and tugged her back into step with him. Instead of acknowledging her burst of energy, he avoided her gaze, staring at the shaggy bark of a nearby hickory tree.

Sara glanced at their hands and shrugged. Maybe she had been asleep too long and needed to release some energy. "So, your mom seems nice," she said, attempting to fill the quiet. Abby did seem nice, perhaps too nice for Kane.

"Oh, she is. Her charm is sincere and her will is just as fierce. Fiercer than my dad's," said Thomas. His statement caused Sara's pace to slow again. He shot her a broad smile. "What? You weren't expecting that were you? Don't worry, she's eased up on us too."

"But not on Dad," chimed in Violet. "She wipes the floor with him every time they spar." Violet barked a laugh. But before Sara could ask for a front row seat to their sparring, Violet, now levitating more than walking, surged ahead and said, "I hope Lily made a cake." When she said "*cake,*" she rose higher above the ground.

Sara laughed at the thought of Abby trouncing Kane, and at Violet's eagerness. She playfully swung Thomas's hand in hers. "Knowing how thoughtful Lily is, I bet she did. Just be sure you get some before the boys eat it all."

Thomas gave her an affectionate bump with his shoulder, sending another electric shock through her.

"Why are you walking?" Violet groaned.

"Because Sara needs to stretch her legs. Besides, you know it's important to stay grounded. You can't be floating with your head in the clouds all the time." Thomas kinetically pulled her down from hovering, grunting slightly at her resistance.

Violet sighed and scrunched her face at him. "I've been *grounded* for sixteen years. I can't wait for Dad to let me run patrol after tomorrow night. I've killed seven Takers, and now I finally get my chance for more."

Though her bloodthirst stunned Sara, she remembered Kane's words and understood it was simply how they lived—under constant threat of attack. Again, Violet levitated and rushed ahead of them. Thomas shook his head, letting her go.

The setting sun shone through the tree canopy, dusting them in golden light. Sara dragged her steps, increasing their distance from Violet, and tugged Thomas closer. "What happened to your siblings?" she asked quietly.

A slight pinch formed in his brow. "Did my dad mention them? Is that why things were strange on the porch?"

She held his gaze, waiting. A breeze stirred the trees, dappling the light along the path as his face rippled with emotion. "I had two older brothers who were killed by Takers."

"I'm sorry," she said squeezing his hand.

Thomas stared ahead, looking lost in thought. They walked in silence, their footsteps soft beats on the pine needle-covered path.

"Every day, I think of them," he said breaking his reverie. He jerked their hands, lifting his forearm and showing her the branded welt on his skin. The mark appeared harsh in the fading light of the day.

Sara twisted their hands to peer at the figure eight shape.

"It's called a still circle. It symbolizes the eternal bond between life and death. The balance between light and dark. Many gifted choose to wear this symbol after we've lost someone," he explained.

Sara chewed her lip. Her father had said his tattoo was a combination of the infinity and yin-yang symbols. At the time, she assumed it related to his metaphysical research. Now she knew it was for someone he'd loved and lost. She thought of Winona's headstone and remembered the Sullivan gravestones in the cemetery. She tilted her face up at Thomas. "When did they die?"

"When I was twelve."

She stopped walking, her fingernails digging into his skin.

"Relax," he whispered, his mouth grazing her ear. A soft chuckle escaped him when she arched her back and loosened her grip. "My father didn't do this. In fact, he was livid I branded myself."

Her breath hitched. He had branded *himself*. She took her other hand and lightly traced the welt, her fingertip glowing with a white flame.

Thomas gasped. The muscles in his arm tensed and his grip on her hand tightened, blue flames flickering across his skin. She glanced up through her eyelashes. His jaw was clenched, his eyes blazing.

The forest fell silent.

Sara froze. "I'm sorry. I just wanted to touch it. Did I hurt you?" she whispered, afraid to move.

He squeezed his eyes closed. "No. Quite the opposite," he gritted out and shifted his weight.

She smirked and reached for the branded still circle again when he snapped open his eyes and returned the curl of her lips. "You wicked little monst—" He cut himself off when Violet rushed back.

Sara dropped his arm, her cheeks and ears burning as Violet hovered before them.

She gave them a curious look, like she was deciding whether to tease or scold them. "Hurry up," she chided, before proceeding to glide ahead into the Cahill clearing.

Thomas hissed out a long breath and strode after her.

Standing at the edge of the clearing, Sara took in his broad shoulders before gazing past him. The clearing reflected none of the burnt and muddy devastation she recalled. In fact, had she not been there and witnessed the fall of the chestnut tree and the Main House, she would never have believed it from the scene before her now. A small noise of astonishment bubbled up from her.

CHAPTER 47

Hoping she wasn't dreaming, Sara stepped out of the thick forest and into the Cahill clearing. Although the large chestnut tree was indeed gone, in its place grew a cluster of trees sprouting from the old roots. The new growth—easily thirty feet high—was covered in light green leaves that fluttered merrily in the soft summer breeze. Where the old Main House once stood, a new multilevel building, featuring a dozen giant trees, sprawled along the edge of the common. It reminded Sara of a tiered treehouse village.

"It's beautiful," she whispered, scanning the entire clearing, which included a new volleyball court and wooden play set full of Cahill kids under a young oak tree.

Thomas was already halfway across the common when he paused and turned back for her. She hurried to catch up to him as Caleb came out of the barn carrying two steel buckets.

With a whoop, he dropped the buckets, spilling ice, and ran to Sara. He crushed her into a hug, picking her up and swinging her around like one of his younger siblings. "Look at you!" he crowed, setting her down. "Nice hair." He gave it a playful yank and laughed when she batted his hand away. "Gran and Helen said not to worry, but it sure is good to see you up and about. And just in time for the party." With a grin, he jogged back to the buckets while gesturing toward the new wrap-around deck. "Check out the house and grab the food from my mom. I'll meet you both at the table." He hefted the buckets with ease, forearms rippling with muscles, and whistled an upbeat tune as he headed off toward the field.

Thomas took her hand, sending another electric jolt through her. Though his shoulders twitched, he said nothing, so she shrugged it off again and turned her attention to the Main House.

The fresh scent of wood mixed with pine needles and green leaves filled the air, intensifying as they stepped onto the deck. Although the flowing deck and wide-open interior appeared similar to the original Main House, it was easily three times the size.

Sara stared at the expansiveness until Thomas nudged her and pointed at the kitchen near the back of the main room. Weaving through clusters of wooden furniture, they made their way to Violet and Rebecca talking over the stone countertop of a U-shaped island. Sara's mouth dropped at the full commercial-sized kitchen behind Caleb's mother.

Rebecca glanced up and waved them over. "Impressive, isn't it?" She beamed. "Gran said we should make the Main House bigger to accommodate more people."

"Did she?" said Sara, more to herself than Rebecca. She glanced around, wondering if this had anything to do with Gran's premonitions. "It's wonderful. I'm sure the whole house is amazing." The smell of food hit Sara, making her mouth water and stomach grumble. When she leaned against the kitchen island to hunt for the source of the scent, Rebecca reached over and put a hand to the side of her face.

"It's so good to see you, love." She patted Sara's face before reaching below the countertop to pull out six large bags filled with steaming containers. "Okay, I may have made too much food, but I figure more is better than not enough, especially if Caleb is at the table. This time, the menu is Vi's favorite—hamburgers." She winked at Violet. "There's plenty for both carnivores and vegetarians. Now go on and have fun." She stood with her hands on her hips, her face lit in a beaming smile.

"Thank you," shouted Violet, whishing two bags and rushing from the kitchen.

Thomas and Sara thanked Rebecca, physically grabbed two bags each, and followed Violet to the field. The scent of burgers and fries made Sara's mouth water again. "I'm so hungry I might actually eat more than Caleb."

Thomas snorted. "You'd have to be asleep for a year before that could happen. And even then, I might put my money on Caleb." As they approached the wide clearing, he whished their bags to the table. The setting sun filled the sky with a soft rosy glow.

"You'd bet against me?" Sara punched his shoulder, setting off a flash of white light.

He grinned and lifted a hand toward her, but his eyes flicked to the table, and he redirected his hand to the back of his head, giving it a rub.

Following his gaze, she faltered.

Everyone was seated and staring at them.

Sara took a step away from him, hoping no one had seen the flash of light. Whatever was happening to her, either her connection to Thomas or being High Witch, she didn't want to talk about it. Not yet. Not when she didn't fully understand it herself. Swallowing hard, she gave a short wave and quick smile.

Lily popped up from the table and gave her a hug. "It's about time you woke up."

"I can't believe how much has changed," said Sara, giving her a tight squeeze. Lily's hug was equally crushing as Caleb's, her strength defying her delicate appearance. Sara subtly turned her back to Thomas and lowered her voice. "Thanks for helping take care of me. And for . . . keeping things between us for now."

A knowing smile parted Lily's heart-shaped lips. "Sure thing. Though you shouldn't hold back anymore." She gave Sara another tight hug before returning to sit with Ian and Violet at the far end of the table, a large white cake with candles between them.

"Sit already. I'm hungry," said Caleb. He stood at the center of the table, handing food to Matthew and Moira, who sat opposite each other. The twins took their plates and slid over, making room at the end of the table.

Sara eased onto the bench beside Moira and nodded at Matthew. "You look a lot better than the last time I saw you."

Before he could reply, Thomas bumped into him as he sat down, causing a loud snap of electricity to flash between them.

Matthew flinched and rubbed his shoulder. "Bloody hell, bro—what was that?"

Thomas tucked his chin, shifting closer to the end of the table, and silently accepted a plate of food from Caleb.

Matthew's nostrils flared, his eyes darting between Thomas and Sara, a slow feline grin spreading across his face.

Avoiding his sharp gaze, Sara tilted her head, letting her hair fall forward, and grabbed one of the birch beers Thomas whished to their end of the table.

"Sara, you want meat or veggie?" asked Caleb, holding up two plates.

"Both," she said, eagerly reaching in front of Moira to grab them.

Moira jerked back, as if she had been pushed. "Mother below, why are you buzzing with energy?" She grimaced and waved her hand around like she was flicking away flies.

"I am?" Sara set the plates down and glanced at her arms.

Matthew swallowed and pointed with his burger at Thomas and then Sara. "Yeah, you're both snapping with little bolts of energy." He grinned and took another bite.

"Must be the weather or something," muttered Thomas, keeping his eyes on his plate. His leg bounced under the table when Lily frowned at the sky. He cleared his throat and turned to Matthew. "So, I hear you and Moira are making vacation plans."

Since Matthew's mouth was full again, Moira spoke for her twin. "With no Takers bothering us at the moment, we figure now is a good time to get out for a bit."

"I was thinking the same thing!" Lily added excitedly. "Let's go to the ocean like we planned at the beginning of the summer."

"I'm in," said Ian, before taking a swig of beer.

"Road trip!" shouted Caleb. He slammed his bottle onto the table, and the cake jumped. "Let's leave before the next moon so we're back before harvest starts. You're coming too, Vi." From her end of the table, Violet grinned at him and flashed a smug look at Thomas.

Putting down her second burger and grabbing another beer, Sara faced Moira. "Well, that escalated quickly."

"Sure did," said Moira with a hint of a smile. "Just don't get in my way," she growled, shooting a warning glare at Caleb, who mocked a surprised expression.

"Moira's on the hunt for an alpha male," said Matthew, his eyes like fire in the setting sun. Sara choked on a fry as Moira flung a fork at him. He easily caught it and flicked it back at her.

Ian stood up, giving them a reproving frown before they could start throwing food. "Anyone have matches for the candles?" he asked.

Everyone shook their heads except Lily. "Sara can do it," she said matter-of-factly and began clearing the table for cake. Sara froze. If she had been sitting near Lily, she would have kicked her under the table.

"I don't know about that," said Ian. "Alice hasn't taught her how to control witch fire yet." He shot Sara an apologetic look. *"Sorry. I told Lily your status is still a secret and not to push you, but she's being feisty about it."*

"Status? Feisty?" Sara snorted. "He's right, I might blow up the

cake," she said, though the expression on Violet's face made her reconsider. "Okay, fine. I'll try—but no promises." She carefully levitated one candle up and away from the cake. Squinting, she focused on creating a tiny spark until the wick flickered with a white flame.

"Thanks," said Lily with a triumphant tilt to her chin. She plucked the candle from the air and used it to light the remaining candles, their glimmer bright against the evening sky.

Thomas leaned back, his lips twitching into a curious smile, and narrowed his eyes at Sara.

She ignored him by leaning down to retie a shoelace. She had every intention of being ready to run—and tackle him in the grassy field.

After they'd sung to Violet and had their fill of cake, Moira announced it was time to start the game. "I'm it," she said, stepping away from the table and flicking back her hair.

"I'm taking my head start this time," stated Caleb, rising from the table. The field parted for him, and he drove into it at a run, grass weaving together like a wall behind him.

Moira waited patiently. "Vi, you're next," she said sweetly, gesturing with a mock bow.

Violet threw her a devilish grin and disappeared. She was soon followed by Lily and Ian who left together—hand in hand—and then Matthew, who slipped between the blades of grass as quietly as a shadow.

Once her twin vanished, Moira turned to Thomas and Sara. "Do us all a favor and put out the lightning bolts before someone gets hurt." She raised a perfectly shaped eyebrow and flaunted a sultry smile before phasing into a fisher cat and leaping into the grass, lightning bugs blinking after her.

Sara huffed and took a step toward the grass, but Thomas grabbed her and pulled her to him. The sides of her arms tingled with energy, pleasantly burning under his touch. He tightened his hold on her and leaned in, his lips grazing her neck. "I was hoping we could play our own game tonight," he said in a low voice, his chest pressing against her.

Sara gasped at a wave of energy washing over her. He lightly kissed her neck again, sending a tingle up her spine and nearly making her moan. The entire field swayed innocently as she struggled to catch her breath.

Her swoon shattered when a guttural scream ripped through the still air. Sara instinctively pivoted toward the cry and tried to levitate, but Thomas held her back.

"Moira! Are you kidding me?" Caleb shouted from the grass. "At least let me make it to the birches!"

Thomas rumbled a laugh and turned Sara into him. "They're fine. Besides, Moira basically ordered us to leave." His eyes shimmered, and he pressed into her again.

Another surge of power slammed into her, and she jerked back.

Thomas instantly released her. "Of course, only if you want to. I-it's totally okay if you don't," he stuttered, face full of concern and confusion. He rubbed the back of his head and fixed her with his burning blue eyes.

She lifted her chin to him, the early moonlight illuminating his intense gaze. "Well," she drawled with a smirk, taking her time. "I do like a good chase." She stepped back, stopping just out of his reach, and slowly eyed him up and down.

A silky grin spread across his face, and he widened his stance, shoulders tensing as if ready to pounce. His eyes narrowed with a competitive gleam.

The night fell quiet, every leaf and blade of grass ceasing to murmur. She licked her lips, fighting back a smile at having his full attention focused on her mouth. Twisting her foot into the soft soil, she shifted her weight to the balls of her feet and braced herself. "Let's see if you can catch me before I make it to the treehouse."

CHAPTER 48

SARA ANTICIPATED THOMAS'S lunge and dodged it before launching up and away from him. Tearing across the sky, she glanced back to find him close behind her, amusement on his face. He reached for her and missed as she dove under a large elm tree, laughter trailing behind her. Quickly approaching the lake, she stayed low to the forest floor and popped out from the tree line to skim the glassy surface of the water. With Thomas still close behind, she put a hand in the lake to spray him, but he rose above her and sped up to cut her off. She rushed to him and barrel-rolled to the side, barely dodging another one of his charges.

"I'm not going too fast for you, am I?" She laughed again and flew faster, only to be surprised when he matched her speed and rushed beside her.

"I can keep up." He grinned and grabbed for her waist, but she let herself drop, plummeting like a stone until barely stopping at the treehouse deck. She hovered near the edge—hesitating—then yelped when Thomas whished her around to face him as he crashed into her.

He seized her, pinning her arms to her sides while his momentum sent them both sailing over the deck. In mid-air, he pivoted, placing himself between her and the floor. Their eyes locked as he took the fall and they slid into the main room. With their bodies pressed together, he fisted her hair, close to the scalp, and smashed his lips into hers, claiming her with an unrestrained kiss that ignited a fire inside her.

A bright burst of white and blue energy erupted between them. They both jolted and pushed away, hovering on opposite sides of the vast room.

"What was that?" he panted.

Sara glanced at the sparkles on her skin and at the same shimmer on his. "I don't know—and I don't care," she said, whishing them both together in the middle of the room.

Thomas grunted as they collided. "So aggressive," he rumbled and grasped her shoulders, sending a zip of energy through her. "I caught you." His words tickled her ear, his hands running down her sides.

She wiggled from his grasp to run her hands down his arms. "I let you," she breathed.

He tilted his head back and laughed, shaking them both. The treehouse swayed and creaked in response. Taking her hands in his, he interlaced their fingers and leaned in, resting his cheek against hers. "Well, now that I have you, I don't intend to ever let go," he said, his voice a husky promise.

She pulled back, his faint stubble scraping against her face, and saw a sincere fierceness in his eyes. The fire inside her blazed, threatening to consume them both as her heart responded with the same vow, and her energy twined with his. White and blue lights swirled around them, and they levitated, slowly rotating in the air. She put a hand to his chest, over his rapidly beating heart. "Promise," she said, a statement rather than a question.

"Promise," he replied, and kissed her brow. "I can do without us trying to kill each other, and please don't ever lie down in front of a bear again—"

"Stop talking," she said, and pressed her face into the curve of his neck, savoring his musk-and-ash scent.

He gently cupped her chin and lifted her face to his. She kissed him coyly at first before parting her lips to him, wanting more. Thomas groaned and deepened the kiss, his tongue sweeping across hers, matching her hunger while he buried his hands in her hair again.

Sara grabbed the back of his neck and slid her hands down the taut muscles in his shoulders and back. Gripping his leather belt, she pulled his hips into her and felt her insides melt as he moaned again. *Closer.* She wanted him closer. Sara clawed his lower back, untucking his tight shirt.

Another burst of energy flashed between them. This time, instead of letting go, they held tighter. Locked in an embrace, their energy pushing and pulling them, she stumbled backward up the stairs, tugging him along and into her room. Thomas paused, chest heaving. The tree groaned and rustled its leaves.

"Are you sure? I may have cheated and whished you to me." His voice was raw, hands trembling at his sides.

"Just accept the fact that I let you win," she said between ragged breaths. The skeptical expression on his face instantly vanished when she whished off his shirt. A slight gasp escaped her lips at the sight of his bare, sculpted chest—at the hard plane of his stomach muscles dipping below the waist of his jeans. He smirked when she touched him. Tiny blue and white flames fluttered, trailing her hands across his smooth skin.

He placed one arm around her waist and slid his other under her knees, lifting her up and kissing her as he gently set her on the edge of the bed.

She broke their kiss to pull off her own shirt, shivering not from cold but from need.

Thomas choked an odd sound. And instead of embracing her, he reared back and slammed into the wall behind him, shaking the tree with his force. His gaze was fixed on her chest.

"What? What's wrong?" she panted, self-consciously crossing her arms in front of her thin camisole.

Thomas pressed against the wall, transfixed by the bloodstone pulsing and glowing against her skin.

Heartbeat thundering in her ears, she clasped the amulet, as if by hiding it she could reverse the sudden change in Thomas. Her mind stumbled. "I—I'm sorry I didn't tell you. I couldn't, and then . . . I was afraid to." She slid off the bed and approached him, terrified he would rush out the window.

He stiffened, banging his head against the wall when she placed her hands on his chest, flames dancing around her touch.

"Please don't be mad," she said, her eyes stinging with the threat of tears.

He kept his hands on the wall behind him and stared at her, his expression conflicted. "If that's what I think it is and you're High Witch, I'm not mad. *Surprised* is an understatement, but not mad." Keeping his eyes on her, he shifted away from her touch and sat heavily on the bed. "Mother below, this changes things." He dropped his head, silent for a moment. "I think I should go," he said quietly, levitating.

She tackled him back onto the bed and climbed on top of him. His eyes turned wild, a spark igniting where she touched his chest. "You're not going anywhere. Tell me what's going on—why this changes anything." She leaned over him, the stone dangling between them.

He clenched his jaw and turned away from her—from the stone.

"Thomas . . ." she pleaded, touching the sides of his face to feel what he refused to say. "Seriously?" She turned his face to her. "You don't think you're good enough for me? Because of this?" Her voice cracked with disbelief. She grabbed his hand and pulled it to her chest, placing it over the stone—over her heart.

His entire face went white with panic as he struggled to get up and pull his hand away.

"Stop fighting me! I love you too, damn it." She choked out the words and fell on top of him.

He stopped struggling and lay still beneath her, one hand on the stone pressed between them. With a soft sigh, he reached out with his other arm and held her tight, stroking her back until she stopped sobbing.

"How long have you known?" he said quietly.

She shifted her hips, slowly sliding off him while keeping his hand to her chest, and turned her face to him.

"Which part? Me or you?"

Thomas pushed back her hair and smiled. "Both."

"For you, the night your dad made me read your mind. And for me . . . I think it was the first time I saw you." She whispered the last part, placing her other hand on his chest. A faint glow ignited from her touch.

He took her hand and tenderly kissed the palm. "I *know* it was the first time I saw you. When I kissed your hand and *felt* you—it nearly undid me. It was all I could do to behave myself." He purred his last few words. Turning into her, Thomas kissed one corner of her mouth and then the other, and softly bit her lower lip.

Sara's fluttering heart melted, her insides completely liquid. Digging her fingers into his chest, she opened her mouth to him with the same claiming passion he gave her when they crashed into the treehouse. In a frenzy of kissing and grabbing that rocked the bed hard enough to sway the entire tree, they tugged and whished off the rest of their clothes.

Thomas pulled back and flicked his gaze over her, his wicked grin almost predatory. "Well, now you have *completely* undone me," he growled, eyes blazing. He brushed his thumbs across her cheeks and then slowly trailed his hands down her body, nipping and kissing every inch of her along the way.

Sara writhed and moaned as his touch stroked and swept her until she burst with energy. "Thomas," she breathed, shuddering under him.

He chuckled and gave her a very satisfied male grin.

"My turn," she said, and pushed him back. Thrilled bliss lit his face. He tried to grab her, but she used her power to pin him down.

"Not fair," he protested with a mock scowl.

She narrowed her eyes at him. "Hold still," she whispered. He stopped struggling, a bit of a smirk on his face. She leaned over him and traced her fingertips up and down his collarbone. "I've been wanting to do this for a while."

"You didn't have to pin me down to do that."

"I do for this." She licked his neck, feeling his chest shudder under her hands, and slowly kissed her way down the front of him. His stomach muscles twitched as he sucked in a sharp breath and then groaned—and cursed. Sara chuckled low in her throat, sending him over his own edge with a burst of hot energy.

Thomas panted, his chest heaving under her. "Sara," he pleaded, his voice guttural. "Let me go. I want to . . . hold you." He groaned again. "Hells, I *need* you."

She put a finger to his flushed lips. "Not yet. There's something else I've been wanting to do."

He cursed again. "You wicked little monster," he said in a low whisper when she took her finger from his mouth and traced white flames along the still circle branded into his forearm. He jolted, almost bucking her off the bed, as she kissed every bit of the welt. Sniggering, she peered up through her lashes to find his eyes shut and both hands clenched, blue energy gathering around his fists. With pleasure, she laid another wet kiss in the center of the still circle.

He roared, his power launching them both into the air. Just as they were about to crash into the ceiling, he flipped her under him and lowered them back to the bed.

Sara held his gaze while he cradled her in his arms and gently brushed back her hair. Their energies merged into a white-blue light, pulling them closer. She shut her eyes and sighed, letting go of everything except Thomas—completely giving in to her need for him until he filled her body and soul.

She felt as though she were floating, weightless in a warm sea that caressed every inch of her. Wave after wave of empyrean energy crashed into her and through her as she clung to him. Her heart filled until she couldn't take anymore, and still she reached for him again and again, letting his blue light consume her.

CHAPTER 49

T HE FAINT SOUND of fluttering woke her from a heavy, blissful sleep. Sara thought it was the sound of her heart until a soft wing brushed across her arm. She opened her eyes to a cardinal hopping about the bed before perching on the windowsill and calling to its mate.

The scent of musk and ash drifted from her skin. She could feel Thomas's heartbeat as he lay beside her—spooning her—his arm tucking her close to his sleeping body. Kissing his hand, she carefully lifted his arm and wiggled out of bed. He sighed and continued the steady breathing of a deep sleep.

After silently rummaging through her duffel bag, she pulled on clean clothes and then hesitated. Studying his face and the content smile on his lips, she wanted to kiss him—to consume him—but decided it best to let him sleep while she stretched her sore legs.

Her bare feet quiet on the wood floors, she set off to finally explore the expanded treehouse. All the original rooms were larger, including the staircase and decks, and all the new rooms and levels seamlessly blended into the original floor plan, as if the tree had thoughtfully planned the addition since the beginning.

Recalling the Cahill Main House expansion, Sara placed her hands on the tree trunk, feeling the soft beat of its heartwood, and wondered what the forest knew about the future. *Gran must know something. Maybe she'll tell me her premonitions if I ply her with mints or a new knife . . .* Her thought trailed off when she returned to the bedroom and almost tripped over Thomas's heavy black boots—lying exactly where she'd whished them the night before.

Assured by his steady breathing, she left the treehouse, padding down the spiral staircase, and sat beside her mother's grave. A garland of sunflowers and daisies, no doubt left by her father, adorned the carved stone. She ran a hand over the flowers. "I know you're with me, but I wish I could hug you—tell you how much I love you and miss you. And tell you I'm where I was always meant to be." The wildflowers around her grave swayed in response. With a sigh, she levitated from the cemetery and headed toward the new cottage beside the lake.

She squinted against the mid-morning sun and her stomach grumbled, eager at the prospect of finding something to eat in the little kitchen. Clearly expecting her need, someone had left a large basket of food, the drinks still cold, on the patio table under the apple tree. At the bottom of the basket, hidden beneath fruits and pastries, Sara spotted a star mint. She laughed and popped it in her mouth. Psychic grandmother, indeed.

After taking a quick bath, she grabbed the basket and headed back to the treehouse. Halfway up the stairs, she paused with a hand on the tree trunk, listening. *Should I be worried about how quiet it is? No chores, no blaring attacks, no razor-sharp vines of death . . .*

The tree shook its branches from side to side.

Good, because there's a handsome wickedness I'm still attending to. She raced to the bedroom, sat in the chair beside the bed, and pulled a thermos from the basket. After a few sips of iced tea, she cleared her throat. Loudly.

Thomas's arm stirred and swept the empty space where she had been sleeping. He turned over and fixed his gaze on her, his bright blue eyes making her stomach flutter.

"I wore you out. You've been asleep for weeks. And I've been watching you. The. Entire. Time." She bit her lip, fighting to keep a straight face.

He snorted a laugh and pushed himself up. "You're a *terrible* liar. You always chew your lip and glance to the left." Thomas ignored her huff of indignation and whished the thermos out of her hand. Snatching it from the air, he took a long drink and then levitated it to the small table. "Besides, you haven't worn me out." He smirked. "Yet."

She yelped when he whished her to him. With blue flames dancing in his palms and flickering along his skin, he brushed his thumbs over her cheeks and kissed her. She moaned, deepening the kiss, as he slowly drew his hands from her face and down her body, gathering her closer until every bit of him pressed against her. Only then did he stop their kiss to bury his face into her neck, at the tender spot just below her ear. "I love you," he murmured.

Her heart so full she thought she would explode, Sara kissed the silky soft skin at his temple, tasting a touch of salt and honey. "I love you too. Now and forever."

Another flash of white and blue lights emanated from them.

She melted into him, slipping back into their blissfully undulating sea of need and want.

Sara twitched awake at the low growl from her stomach. Before her dozed Thomas, his limbs entwined with hers. She tore her eyes from him and gazed at the now-empty basket of food and late afternoon sun glinting off the lake, its bright light an irritating reminder they needed to leave and attend the Council meeting.

At the thought of Council, a vague premonition swept over her. It felt like lace being dragged through her mind, except instead of an enlightening caress, it snagged and left a dull headache at the base of her skull. Something unpleasant was about to rear its head tonight. She swallowed the thought, refusing to let it cool her flushed skin.

"Thomas," she whispered. He snuggled into her and responded with an indulgent nip to her earlobe. The small of her back instantly tingled. "Stop," she groaned, playfully pushing him away and sitting up. "We need to get ready for the Council meeting."

He sat up beside her and ran a hand down his face. With a lazy smile, he reached over and held the bloodstone in his palm. "Its heartbeat matches yours," he said softly. "I had my suspicions—your powers outside the wall, how quickly you picked up your magic, how powerful you are—Mother below, you lit Violet's candle like it was nothing." He narrowed his eyes at her. "Gran and Lily know, don't they? Anyone else?"

"Ian does. And your dad figured it out after finally realizing I wasn't an evil inbred," she huffed.

"Ah, there's the real reason for the death stare you gave him on the porch." He chuckled and let go of the stone.

"I just . . . I don't want to tell everyone yet. I didn't know myself until recently. And I'm still trying to figure out what it all means . . ." *And what my responsibilities are.*

"It means Ware Woods is no longer misled and isolated. With you as High Witch, we can join the Global Council and connect with other gifted. It's a good thing, and we'll all help you if you let us."

She relaxed a breath. "Good, because I need all the help I can get."

"This is true." Thomas chuckled again, deftly catching her fist before she could jab him. "I love it when you're aggressive," he teased, kissing her knuckles. "But please stop trying to kill me."

"What—" She tried to pull back her hand, but he tightened his grip, muscles flexing.

He tilted his head toward her chest, eyes brazenly wandering before settling on the red amulet. "Only a powerful witch can touch a bloodstone. Anyone else will die. Supposedly in a burst of flames."

"I thought Gran was joking!" she blurted, eyes wide. She grabbed the stone with her other hand. "And—well, I . . . forgot."

Thomas arched a brow. "You *forgot* you're wearing a deadly weapon?"

"You—um, your *chest* distracted me," she spluttered.

He snorted a laugh. "I'm not sure if I should be terrified or delighted by my powers of distraction."

"Apparently delighted. Your gift is so powerful you can touch a bloodstone without so much as a scratch." She lifted her chin and gave him a smug smile.

"Not true. Unless they've already healed, I pleasantly suffered multiple scratches." His eyes smoldered as he licked her knuckles. The surrounding air crackled with electricity. "I'm strong, but my powers are just kinetic. I think this stone allows me to touch it because you want me to." His thumb gently stroked the edge of her palm—where Samson took her finger. A sudden severity flickered across his face.

He dropped his gaze to their clasped hands. "I'm sorry I wasn't there for you," he said, his voice rough with emotion. "I promise it won't happen again." He kissed the spot, his mouth lingering.

"No, it won't happen again," she said, her tone fiercer than she intended, and pulled back her hand. His brow knitted together, and she kissed it to ease his worry, then glanced out the window opening. The sun hung low near the horizon, casting rays across the lake's smooth surface. "Though I could stay here forever with you, we need to go." She pulled on her clothes. "You should probably clean up and change," she said, eyeing him with a sly smile.

He ran his hands through his rumpled hair. "Fine, but only if you agree to check out my place after the meeting." He flashed her a grin before whishing over his discarded clothes.

"I would love to." She ran a finger along his collarbone and sauntered from the room, grateful to have something to look forward to after a possibly unpleasant meeting.

CHAPTER 50

I NSTEAD OF FLYING, Sara took her time and walked through the woods toward the Council tree, her heart so full it ached. Itching to play with her magic, she released a ball of energy and called forth a gust of wind, swirling the white sparks into a still circle before letting them dissipate into the forest. Just as she was about to release another burst of energy, the forest path opened to the Council tree clearing.

She held back her power and scanned the gathering before her. Almost every seat was taken. All five families were eating and laughing, conversing jovially with one another. She stood at the edge of the clearing, her mind racing. *Do I sit at the Lochton table or with Thomas? Should I take the stage and tell everyone I'm High Witch?* Her slight headache throbbed, a reminder of her vague premonition. *I see nothing even remotely unpleasant or dangerous.*

Her gaze swept the crowd again and stopped on Gran, who stood and motioned her to the Lochton table. Sara hesitated, inhaling to the count of three, before striding into the clearing and approaching her. "Thanks for the basket," she said in a low voice. Gran waved off the acknowledgment and returned to her seat beside Charlie, a smile tugging at the corners of her mouth.

From the opposite side of the table, Ian's golden-brown eyes shone with amusement. He set down his fork like he was about to say something but cleared his throat and downed his medicine instead.

As Sara watched him, the bloodstone pulsed hot against her chest. Fighting the urge to put a hand over the stone, she gave him a tight smile, her gaze lingering on the medicine bottle. Goosebumps rippled across her skin. With a slight shudder, she turned her head to the rear of the clearing. A cluster of young pine shook, and another late arrival emerged from the woods.

"Hey, firecracker," said Charlie, bringing her attention back to the table. "Get some food and come sit." He nodded to the empty chair beside Ian.

Distracted by the late arrival, she paused before leaning over and hugging him. "Thanks, Dad, but I think I'll sit farther back tonight." Savoring his pine scent and tight embrace, she added, "Let's meet for breakfast tomorrow and spend the day together."

He kissed her forehead. "I'd like that. Just come to the house as soon as you're up." After a tight squeeze, he released her and turned back to his dinner.

"Did you ask Ted to put you on the agenda?" sounded Gran's voice in her head.

Sara tottered back a step. *"Gaa, I didn't know you could—"*

"Everyone descended from Mary can speak telepathically. So, did you?" Gran took a swig of beer, her eyes twinkling, and gave Sara an expectant look.

"No, I have some unpleasantness *to attend to at the back of the clearing. Besides, tonight is about celebrating Violet's pledge."* Sara met her steel blue gaze.

Gran narrowed her eyes. *"Hmm, as you wish, clever granddaughter. But I sense your night will not be completely unpleasant. Shall I deliver another basket of food tomorrow morning?"* She chuckled.

"All Hells!" Sara turned on her heel, face burning. After a few steps, her mortification changed to boldness. *"Yes, please, sweet*

Grandmother." Her cheeky smile grew ear-to-ear as Gran's laughter burst out behind her.

Picking her way through the crowded clearing, Sara still held her smug smile when she noticed Bill Walker stalking her.

"Good to see you've recovered," he said, closing the gap between them with a few strides. His voice was so deep it rattled Sara's chest. "You made some gutsy moves in the fight against Makwa. I don't know how you did it, but I'm grateful. My family is indebted to you for saving Matthew." He tilted his head, his amber eyes boring into her.

Sara shifted her weight, uncomfortable with the praise. "You don't owe me anything. We're family."

"We are," he said with a toothy grin, stepping back as Matthew and Moira pushed past him.

Sara nearly stumbled when Moira launched forward and hugged her. "Since you're not sparking with pent-up energy, I can give you a proper thank-you for saving Matty," she purred.

Matthew flicked his hair and gave her a fist bump. "Thanks, Sara." He glanced over her shoulder and jerked his chin. "Here comes your other half."

Thomas snuck up behind her, jolting her with energy when he placed one hand on the small of her back and fist-bumped Matthew with his other.

The twins grinned, identical sets of gleaming white teeth. "That was quite the light show last night," taunted Moira, her amber eyes smoldering.

"All night and most of today," added Matthew, shooting an approving look at Thomas.

Sara's eyes flew to Thomas, her cheeks burning. *Mother below!*

"Um, yeah," muttered Thomas, one hand rubbing the back of his head, the other gently steering Sara away. The twins howled with laughter as they walked off.

Sara kept her head down, face still on fire, and let Thomas lead them to the edge of the clearing. When she stopped and studied his chiseled face, a different heat replaced her embarrassment. It melted her insides. With a soft sputter, tiny white flames erupted and danced along her arms. Thomas stepped closer and blue flames from his arms leapt and blended with hers.

"Is this normal?" she whispered, brushing them off.

"I don't know." His voice was a low rumble. "I honestly thought it would stop after . . . last night." That wicked grin spread across his face.

She smirked and stole a wary glance at the crowded tables. "I don't think we should sit together." Every eye seemed to be on them.

"Good idea," agreed Thomas. He winked at her before abruptly turning and walking off toward his family.

Sara loosed a long sigh, strolled to the buffet tables, and grabbed two plates of food. With a nod at Lily and Kingsley, who waved at her over the desserts, she navigated through the family tables until she stood before Dorcas at the rear of the clearing. Eyeing the witch's new pale-blue dress and the enormous cat at her feet, she handed her a plate and asked, "Mind if I sit with you?"

"Please do," answered Dorcas, her voice light and pleasant. She shook back her long, wavy blonde hair and gestured to the empty chair where the bear witch had sat during the last meeting. "Thanks for the food. I appreciate it," she said, setting the plate on her lap.

Not caring to sit in Makwa's seat, Sara whished over a different chair and sat on the other side of Dorcas. After a long silence, Sara turned to her. "Why did you tell me about the curse?"

A sadness flashed across the witch's now-youthful complexion. She plucked a piece of meat from her plate and fed it to the cat. "Long ago, Mary saved me from prison. Tituba too. I told you about the curse as my salvation."

Sara stared, waiting for more. When the witch remained silent, Sara cleared her throat. "Care to elaborate?"

"Not at this time."

Alrighty, then. You're not the only one with a secret around here.

Sara feigned a casual shrug. Though all her senses were heightened, searching for any hint of dark magic, she detected nothing but a shimmering purple-black aura, which clung to Dorcas like a cloak. Keeping her own thoughts and emotions close to herself, she focused on her meal and listened as Ted officiated the meeting. When Uncle Larry announced that both the blight and Samson were gone, Sara slumped in her chair, content to stay in the shadows.

No one mentioned the bear witch.

The meeting concluded when Violet pledged herself to the forest and drank the soul tree sap. When everyone cheered and rushed toward the stage to congratulate her, Sara remained in her seat, placing her half-eaten dinner on the ground and clapping. If Dorcas hadn't been there, she would have released a burst of indigo stars, their precise color matching Violet's eyes, to shower the clearing. But it didn't seem prudent to reveal any of her powers to Dorcas, especially when she had no idea what the other witch was capable of.

Dorcas whished their plates, licked clean by the cat, to a nearby vacant table and rose from her chair. She stood beneath the pine tree and turned to Sara. "I'm here for you when you need me." Her tone sounded sincere.

Sara tensed. *Why would she say that?* "Um, thank you," said Sara, hoping her voice sounded equally sincere, and shifted in her chair to face Dorcas.

A gust of wind shook the tree, causing shadows and early moonlight to spin around them. Before Dorcas disappeared into the woods, light swept across her face. A peculiar glint in her eyes sent a chill down Sara's spine. Something slippery hid behind her mask of perfection.

The stone at her chest burned, and she gasped. *What if Makwa had left a bloodstone?* Bile coated the back of her throat. *What if Dorcas now had that stone?* The blood drained from her face.

She bit her lip, scanning the forest behind her. While Dorcas could be an unpleasant threat, the witch would have to wait. Sara had a much bigger problem on her hands—Samson.

Getting rid of him had been too easy. If she needed Makwa's true name to vanquish her, it followed that she would need Samson's name to be truly rid of him too. When she had seen Ian take his medicine, she knew for sure Samson was still alive.

She scowled. The smoky bastard was probably laughing at her while picking his teeth with a bone from her finger.

I'll find you and I'll kill you.

A breeze smelling of pine and sun-ripened berries blew across her face, reminding her she was safe in the forest. Sara unclenched her fists and jaw, then inhaled for the count of three and exhaled. She turned her attention back to the clearing, to the celebrating families. They were all her family now. Her heart ached with a fullness she never thought possible—a passionate mix of love and belonging and purpose. She would do anything to protect them and Ware Woods.

The crowd shifted as a few people strayed away from the stage. Sara rose from her chair, scanning the clearing for Thomas, when she spied Kane walking stiffly toward her. *Here we go.* She shoved her hands into her pockets, hiding the faint shimmer lining her palms.

A teasing expression lit his face when he joined her side and looked toward the stage. "I told Thomas to give us a few minutes. Let's see how long he can wait." Kane snorted a short laugh and shook his head.

Sara arched a brow at him, her mouth a firm line.

"I saw the *actual* sparks between you." He flicked a glance at her and froze his grin. "Father of Night—you have no idea, do you?"

"Whatever it is you have to say—spit it out." She glared at him.

Her stomach was still tied in knots over Dorcas and Samson. The last thing she needed was any more unpleasant surprises.

Kane tucked his chin and softened his voice. "It means you two have a rare bond. So rare, it seems Thomas doesn't know either. Otherwise, he would have told you."

Sara snorted this time.

"This isn't to be taken lightly. I know how fierce and stubborn Thomas is." Kane rubbed his leg. "But you certainly seem to be his equal. Mother help us." He sighed.

Sara rolled her eyes at him.

He dropped his smile. "The bond can be complicated. You must have noticed your mother and father's bond. Though I don't think it was remotely as strong as the pull between you and Thomas." He tilted his head toward the Lochton table. "Ask your father about it."

Sara nodded and gazed at the festive clearing, waiting. The tension in Kane's shoulders suggested he still had more to tell her.

He matched her posture, casually slipping his hands into his pockets, and sighed again, concern creasing his face. "You didn't announce yourself as High Witch. You're not the type to be scared or back down from a challenge. There's something else causing you to hold your tongue." Kane studied her for a moment before fixing his attention on Violet near the front of the stage. "Regardless of your reason, I hope you enjoy this time of peace, Sara. You have certainly earned it."

Her breath hitched, and for a moment she debated telling him about Dorcas and Samson. As tempting as it was to share her anxiety, she heeded his advice and let them all enjoy this time—however brief it might be.

He cleared his throat. "But we need to be ready when dark magic threatens us again. Because it will. I need to know you are prepared to step up, lead when needed, face challenges, and make sacrifices. It's a big responsibility, and one I can help you with." He turned to her, his kind, fatherly expression startling her. "Are you ready . . . High Witch?"

She held his gaze for a moment before turning to the rising moon, hoping its light would settle her mind and emotions before answering him.

He shifted as Thomas rushed up to them.

Thomas nodded in greeting at his father and held out his hand to Sara. "Ready?" he asked, eyes blazing.

She clasped his hand, a light-blue spark igniting from their touch, and stared directly at Kane.

"Yes. I am."

LEAVE A REVIEW

If you enjoyed Witch of Ware Woods, I would be extremely grateful if you could leave a brief review at your online retailer of choice. And heck yeah, you can leave the same review at multiple locations and then bask in the good karma! ~ Sonja

Review links can be found at:
www.sonjafblanco.com/w3review

Reviews are crucial to an author's success and to spread the word so other readers may enjoy this story. Sharing your review on social media, around the water cooler, and shouting it from the rooftops is also encouraged.

DISCOVER MORE

Get your FREE copy of Witch of Ware Woods – Flood & Fire, the series prequel where magic, love, destruction, and sacrifice combine in the spellbinding creation of Ware Woods.

Free download at www.sonjafblanco.com/f2

Witch of Ware Woods – Book 2 . . . coming soon!

Get sneak peaks, giveaways, and insider info
by subscribing to Sonja's newsletter at:
www.sonjafblanco.com

ACKNOWLEDGEMENTS

This book has swirled around in my head for many years and would never be in your hands without the help and support of so many people. But before I carry on, I want to thank YOU—the reader. Thanks for taking a chance on a debut author and opening yourself up to a new fantasy world that is a part of me, and now, I hope, a part of you too.

To my dear husband, David—Thanks for always remaining calm despite my freak-outs, for offering tech assistance since I repel technology, for being my design consultant, for being the chief dishwasher, and for supporting me in SO many more ways. You are my rock and I mean that in the best way. Fork 'em Devils!

To my children, Mia and Jason—Thanks for keeping it real, and for not running the blender and chainsaw at the same time while I was working. Just kidding; we don't own a chainsaw and you did run the blender. I love you and (cue the sappy music) you can do anything you set your mind to.

To my parents, Don and Donna—This book exists because of your support, encouragement, and love. Thanks for raising me to be an independent, relentless bugger (I've been called many other things, but we'll leave it at this), for always letting me pick out everything I wanted from the Scholastic flyer, and for providing a forest in our backyard.

To my brother, Chris—Your endeavor at starting your own book planted the seed for me to write my own. I'll always look up to you, big bro. Thanks for inspiring, supporting me, and shipping me Ware Woods birch beer. You're the best!

To my frister, Tami—We did it! You know me so well and have been with me through all the cursing, tears, and laughs, that this accomplishment most certainly belongs to both of us. Our friendship means the world to me, and I thank my lucky stars for you, every single day.

To my friends—How blessed am I that there isn't enough space to list you all? (that and I'm terrified of forgetting anyone). For those of you who have known me since grade school, or high school, or college, or my previous life in landscape architecture and development, or from our kiddos school yard—thank you for embracing my quirks and sometimes laughing at my horrible puns, and for supporting my writing.

To my cousin, High Priestess Lady Jesamyn Angelica—I am beyond thrilled to have shared this story specifically with you. Not only does magic run in your veins but you know the original Gran and Ware Woods. Many thanks for your multi-faceted expertise, verifying the accuracy of my spells, and for providing my first swoon-worthy review.

To my beta readers, Maya, Tamra, Sarah (with an h!), Jesa, Izzy, Regan—Thank you for saying 'yes' and jumping on board to read my first manuscript, and for nicely giving me the good, the bad, and the ugly. I am profoundly grateful.

To my editor, Katrina—I swear the planets were aligned when I found you. Thank you for (buckle up): holding my hand on this awesome-sauce writing journey, patiently answering all my questions, showing me how to improve my writing, steering me in the right direction, laughing with me, supporting me in so many ways, and (bwahaha) becoming a kindred-soul friend.

To my editor, Hannah—I am truly blessed to have you on my

team. Not only does your editing prowess amaze me but you are a beautiful soul and an absolute delight to work with (yay to emojis and exclamation marks!). You are worth your weight in gold and Melona Bars.

To my proofreader, Kelly—Thank you for being my proverbial fine tooth comb and using your magic eyes to see the forest through the trees.

To my design team, Stef, Maria, Kolarp, and David—Thanks for listening (okay, humoring) my ideas, and knowing when to push back with your genius creativity and knock my socks off.

To Joanna Ruth Meyer—Thanks for meeting with me so many moons ago in B&N, introducing me to the snowflake method, and for being such an inspiring author. Special shout-out to Michelle for the introduction and for tempting us with tasty treats!

To Barbara Hinske—Your advice and encouragement at the cusp of my writing career meant more than you will ever know. I'll never forget when you looked me in the eye and, without hesitation, told me I could do this. Many thanks to Leslie for introducing us!

To the towns in and around the Quabbin, especially the Town of Ware, MA—I hope this story brings a positive awareness to your history and beautiful forest. Special thanks to Lynn, Stephen, Heidi, and Polli for connecting with me and sharing your expertise. Much appreciated!

To my writer friends and organizations, Mark Dawson and the SPF-Genius-Mastery groups, Alexa Bigwarfe and Write-Publish-Sell, David Gaughran, Bryan Cohen, Dave Chesson, ALLI, Indie Author Support, Ann and everyone at ALWAYS, and my awesome accountability partner Diana, —Thank you for the advice. You all are rock stars.

To my social media peeps—WOW, just wow for all your support. Writers and readers are an utterly amazing positive group and I'm so thankful to be a part of this growing community. Some of you have been with me since the bumpy beginning, and so many more of you are with me now. I am grateful and humbled. Thank you!

To all you fellow writers, musicians, and artists—Thank you for inspiring me with your humor and poetic prose, kick-ass music, and vibrant colors. Keep it coming.

And finally, thank you Universe for the magic.

ABOUT THE AUTHOR

Sonja F. Blanco grew up in New England where she ran barefoot through the woods, chased lightning bugs, tapped maple trees for syrup, and built towering snow castles.

Having an ancestor that was hung as a witch, Sonja is naturally drawn to all things magical and fantastical—trees and cemeteries in particular.

At 5'2" she is often caught climbing tables, chairs, and small children to reach the upper shelves. She likes coffee and tea equally, both of which most certainly contributed to her diminutive stature.

Witty comics easily amuse her, as do heavily jowled Hell Hounds that talk in their sleep.

She writes fantasy as if it were real, because believing makes it so.

Get sneak peaks, giveaways, and insider info
by subscribing to Sonja's newsletter at:
www.sonjafblanco.com

Follow and connect with Sonja at:
Goodreads: goodreads.com/sonjafblanco
Instagram: @sonjafblanco
Facebook: @sonjafblanco
TikTok: @sonjafblanco
Twitter: @sonja_blanco